PENGUIN BOOKS

MOONCRANKER'S GIFT

Barry Unsworth was born in 1930 in a mining village in Durham, and he attended Stockton-on-Tees Grammar School and Manchester University. He has spent a number of years in the eastern Mediterranean area and has taught English in Athens and Istanbul. He now lives in Italy. His first novel, *The Partnership*, was published in 1966. This was followed by *The Greeks Have a Word for It* (1967); *The Hide* (1970); *Mooncranker's Gift*, which received the Heinemann Award for 1973; *Pascali's Island*, which was shortlisted for the Booker Prize in 1980 and has been filmed; *Stone Virgin* (1985); *Sugar and Rum* (1990); *The Rage of the Vulture* (1991); *Sacred Hunger*, which was joint winner of the 1992 Booker Prize; *Morality Play*, which was shortlisted for the 1995 Booker Prize; *After Hannibal* (1996); and *Losing Nelson* (1999). Many of his books are published by Penguin.

Barry Unsworth received an Honorary Doctorate of Letters from the University of Manchester in 1998, and recently taught at the Iowa Writers' Workshop. He is currently visiting Professor at John Moore University, Liverpool. Barry Unsworth is a Fellow of the Royal Society of Literature.

BARRY UNSWORTH

MOONCRANKER'S GIFT

PENGUIN BOOKS

PENGUIN BOOKS

Published by the Penguin Group
Penguin Books Ltd, 27 Wrights Lane, London W8 5TZ, England
Penguin Books USA Inc., 375 Hudson Street, New York, New York 10014, USA
Penguin Books Australia Ltd, Ringwood, Victoria, Australia
Penguin Books Canada Ltd, 10 Alcorn Avenue, Toronto, Ontario, Canada M4V 3B2
Penguin Books (NZ) Ltd, 182–190 Wairau Road, Auckland 10, New Zealand

Penguin Books Ltd, Registered Offices: Harmondsworth, Middlesex, England

First published by Allen Lane 1973
Published in Penguin Books 1977
5

Printed in England by Clays Ltd, St Ives plc
Set in Linotype Times

For Valerie, and for
Madeleine, Tania and Thomasina,
who were dragged along.
With love.

Part One

1

The street that led to the hotel was crowded, the narrow pavement cluttered with stalls and people striving to sell things; small articles of daily use. In his delicately clumsy, wavering fashion Farnaby very nearly trod on a fellow human at one point, a legless man softly soliciting alms at the kerb. Too many people too close nearly always caused a feeling of tension in his throat, impaired his coordination, making him step short sometimes as if about to embark on a leap. Though taller than most he didn't see the beggar until the last minute because the man was truncated and therefore well below eye-level.

'*Affedersiniz*,' Farnaby said, but the beggar was busy with his plaint and seemed not to hear. The naked livid stumps of his thighs were displayed for casual pity. Farnaby stepped round the murmurous, diminutive form, unable to see the face because of a cap.

The incident, his own ineptness, agitated him, increased in some way his worry at the prospect of meeting Mooncranker again. He walked thereafter on the inside of the pavement, acquainting himself with the photographs that flanked many of the doorways, photographs of wrestlers and strippers mainly: the wrestlers bullet-headed, oleaginous, impressively bulging as to genitals; the strippers plump and shameless, nothing but a scattering of spangles or sequins, something of that sort, over their key convexities. Body hair non-existent he noted, not a hint of fuzz or floss, razed to pristine smoothness. Or is razored the *mot juste* there? Of course, it is enjoined upon Moslem women, whether public performers or no, he reminded himself with an attempt at dispassion: Farnaby the travelled man, making a Mental Note. His mouth had filled slowly with saliva. A public performance. Promising opening for a eunuch barber. Had Mooncranker, in gaining his hotel, scanned these pictures? He would have arrived by taxi. It was a strange region in which to be encountering Mooncranker again after all these years. But any region would have seemed so, probably. Perhaps a foreign city like this was in fact best, a place alien to both of them. There was no congruity in the meeting anyway, except possibly in the mind of Uncle George, who had brought it about, whose letter reposed at present in his inside pocket. *Nephew of my old schoolfellow and team mate. Whom you will remember well from the 'Oaklands' days.*

Farther down the street two girls at a first floor balcony sat close together, gesturing in a way that seemed rehearsed, almost ritualistic. They leaned towards each other, faces intent, pale hands languidly, studiously gesturing; both with long black hair, both half turned away from the street, presenting to each other faces which at this distance and in profile were so alike that they might have been emblematic: Graces or Hours or the loves of a god.

Perhaps they are whores. I wish I could bring Mooncranker's face to mind. He was the umpire. He was dressed in white. Trying to visualize that face is like getting a picture just out of focus, before he can be brought into clear view, he starts leaking away, every time the same thing. The white leaks over the outlines, Mooncranker dissolves himself. *Always a brilliant scholar and of late years a celebrity too. A name to conjure with.* Only Uncle George used phrases like that. Farnaby could picture his relish, penning the letter, getting everything just right. *How fortunate that you should be there in Istanbul and in a position to.*

But I am not in a position to. He slowed his steps, anxiety in his throat increasing, stepping affrightedly amidst the crowd, addressing a mental remonstrance to Uncle George, all those miles away in Surrey. I am not in a position to at all, not at all, I only remember him as an umpire, dressed in white and the other time when he handed me the little figure. Quite faceless, yes. I was only thirteen at the time. During the summer that my parents got divorced and I came to stay at 'Oaklands', a large house with a rambling garden and two hard tennis-courts behind. Undeniable that he was a frequent visitor, but not to me. He only sought me out that once...

8

The wrestlers continued to alternate with the strippers, festooning the portals on his right. *Formerly the homes of Venetian merchants whose ships rode at anchor in the Golden Horn below.* The wrestlers all frontal, faces set on a victory; the girls on the other hand variously posed, appearing to be inviting penetration from every angle. They knelt, reclined, straddled, squared plump shoulders at the camera, dimpled their bottoms cunningly at Farnaby, displayed capacious, intricately whorled navels, beautiful globular breasts, nipples dead centre like bullseyes. *Turkish breasts, that is the breasts of Turkish women, have a configuration somewhat different from those of their European counterparts, being rounder, fuller, lower slung.* Is that really true? Strive now for purposes of comparison to visualize a pair, but whose, whose? *He used to umpire for you in your tennis tournaments. How fortunate that.* Strange, how much of the letter he remembered.

Now that he was getting nearer he did not think they were whores at all, those gestures were not for delicate reference to erotic zones, they were talking about clothes he suddenly realized, fitting and cut and so on, that was the reason for such intimate yet hieratic behaviour. He had not identified with certainty any whores in Istanbul except for one monstrously fat woman who had wobbled up to him one evening in the street and petrified him with a throaty *chéri.*

It had been strong though, the sense of ritual they had conveyed, and it persisted in him as he drew nearer to the hotel, blending somehow with his anxiety, now that the meeting was imminent. He did me an injury, he reminded himself. Mooncranker did me an injury in those Oaklands days. He clung to this as a reason for being there, for walking down this street where maimed people begged, girls gestured overhead, crowds jostled, various persons strove to interest him in combs, leather belts, packets of almonds. Mooncranker is of that tiny number who have modified me. Strange that I cannot recollect his face. Not even at the moment when he handed over the little white figure on the cross, not even at that moment surely quintessential, Mooncranker smiling, inclining himself forward a little as one does when making gifts, especially to someone shorter in stature, handing over the little swaddled figure. Some words he must have uttered surely, some formula. But nothing remained.

Nothing but a sort of effigy. In a straw hat tilted forward over his eyes he had umpired with a certain effect of querulousness, sometimes jerking his shoulders forward as an accompaniment to announcing the score. What was the face like, under the straw hat? What did he look like, when he was standing, walking? No context existed but that stooping smiling moment; and then the tennis games, with Mooncranker a foreshortened, occasionally jerking figure in the canvas chair, crying out in a voice whose tone and pitch had also vanished beyond recall, the scores, loves and deuces and double faults.

Farnaby paused on the pavement, waiting to cross. He was not sorry to be quitting the photographs: those inviting postures, interspersed with the virile wrestlers, had been making him feel inadequate. *Put them all in together and buy a ringside seat.*

His nervousness increased as he entered the hotel and stood at the reception desk, waiting for the attention of the clerk. He was aware of the high-ceilinged lobby, columns of veined marble ringed at intervals with thin bands of gilt, little bamboo tables and large-leaved glossy plants in pots. Would Mooncranker at all remember *him*? He had been polite but noncommittal on the telephone when Farnaby had called him some two hours previously. Mooncranker was to give a lecture that evening at the British Council and Farnaby had thought he might need some assistance, of a practical sort. If I can be of any assistance, he had said, and heard the deep, totally unfamiliar voice repeating his name with an effect if not an intention of irony, Farnaby, *Farnaby*?

'Mooncranker,' he said to the clerk. 'Mooncranker.'

'*Effendim*,' the clerk said. He had started to scan a list, but not it seemed in a spirit of optimism.

'He is an Englishman,' Farnaby said. He looked past the bamboo and ferns through open doors into a dining-room which had chandeliers and enormous baroque mirrors and a ceiling painted with mythological ravishments. '*Ingiliz dir.*'

'Ah,' said the clerk, brightening. 'It is room sixty-eight. I will telephone to him?'

10

'No, thank you. He is expecting me.'

He straightened his tie in the antiquated lift, regarded for some moments his long, rather equine face. The frame of the glass was ornate and gilded, fat *putti* swam or flew at the corners as though struggling to reach some haven beyond the frame. Farnaby had positively to struggle against a suspension of identity, stepping softly out of the lift on to faded plum-coloured carpeting.

He had to ring three times, a delicate tingling silence between each ring, before the door was opened and a person stood there wearing a smile that rapidly faded. Mooncranker in the flesh. Or so he was obliged to assume. A high-shouldered elderly man in a black velvet jacket. He held the door open, looking at Farnaby in bemused inquiry.

'Good evening,' Farnaby said, with nervous briskness. 'I am James Farnaby.' He thought he recognized now the high-shouldered stance, the prominent beak of a nose. Ash-grey hair long at the sides and swept back in a fashion Farnaby was accustomed to call statesmanlike. Gentle blue blinking eyes. Anticipating an immediate invitation to enter, Farnaby took a step forward and then stopped, not knowing what further to do or say. He looked with smiling shyness at Mooncranker and then beyond him, into the room.

'Ah, *Farnaby*,' Mooncranker said in deep tones, giving way at last. He backed a little, holding the door open wider. Farnaby caught a whiff of some strangely familiar petrolly odour as he entered. He came to a halt in the middle of the room with a confused sense of limited space, ornate clutter disposed on low tables around him. Directly overhead was a heavy chandelier, the lower crystals of which, not more than a foot or two above him, had commenced a faint tinkling, in response no doubt to the draught from the door. It was very hot in the room. 'Well, well, well,' he heard the slow voice behind him, and he turned in the direction of the sound, smiling.

Two days of almost continuous gin drinking, Turkish gin at that, had clouded Mooncranker's mind and impaired his vision, so that during this early phase of the visit it seemed to him that the young man had a sort of radiance about him, he seemed to gather and reflect all the available light, which made it difficult to survey him steadily. The rest of the room by contrast was obscure and impenetrable. His friendly repetition of the other's name had been merely a social reflex, a sort of host response. He had no idea who his visitor was, but thought he might have come to collect something.

'Would you mind waiting a moment?' he said, trying to gather himself together. He blinked at the dark corners of the room, and a suspicion grew in him that this might be an employee of the hotel, come to badger him about tickets. 'Is it about the tickets?' he said. 'Because I've told you I don't want them.'

'No, no,' Farnaby said. 'I phoned you earlier, if you remember –'

'I've told them repeatedly, I don't want any tickets, I was merely inquiring.'

He could actually see the light streaming down from the crystals on to the young man's smooth fair hair and white shirt-collar and the front of his fawn linen jacket, increasing his effulgence in a frightening way. 'We have met before, haven't we?' he said, doubtfully, and Farnaby answered at once, 'Yes, at Oaklands.'

Oaklands. Mooncranker closed his eyes briefly on the word. Behind the lids he still felt threatened. There was an association of strenuous effort about this young man, as if he might at any moment start leaping about, destroying things, blasting them with light. He must be kept still, until he provided some clue to his business. Above all, don't let him see you are frightened. Like dogs, they are like dogs.

'Well, well, well,' he said. *Oaklands.* If only I had not gone to the door. But I thought it might be Miranda, coming back to me. Three times the bell rang. Only someone who felt sure I was there would have rung three times. Miranda would of course, she would have rung as many times as were necessary, anticipating delay on my part. I did not dare not to go in case it was she. But this person, how could he have known? Such persistence indicated special knowledge, and then this dangerous brightness...

'I phoned earlier,' Farnaby said again. 'About your lecture

12

this evening.' Things were not proceeding at all as he had imagined. Mooncranker seemed strangely at a loss. It was true that he looked distinguished, with his high-shouldered stance and statesmanlike hair, but his manner was unexpectedly muffled and inert, and he was repeatedly looking away into corners of the room, or closing his eyes for several seconds at a time, a sort of prolonged blink. It did not inspire confidence. Surely he must be quite different when conducting his interviews and posing questions to his panels on radio and television.

'I thought I might be of assistance to you in some way,' he said.

Mooncranker glanced round the room again. 'Now where did I put them,' he said. He ran a long-fingered white hand over the top of his head. 'If you wouldn't mind waiting a moment,' he said.

'Of course not.' Farnaby was conscious of that faint ache of the facial muscles that results from excessive falsity of smiling.

'So long as it's not about that,' Mooncranker said.

'About what, sir?'

'The tickets.' Suddenly a solution came to Mooncranker, a perfectly reasonable social solution: he would get this dangerous youth trapped in a chair. 'Won't you have a seat,' he said, or perhaps did not actually utter the words, merely enjoyed the clarity of the idea, because after several seconds his visitor still had not moved. A wave of nausea caused Mooncranker to lower his face and study the carpet for some moments.

'No, nothing to do with the tickets,' Farnaby said clearly. Hardly one's idea of a distinguished elderly person greeting the nephew of an old friend. Nor did he seem credible as the smiler in white who had handed over the little white Christ on the Cross, with the forward inclination of one freely giving, that distant summer amidst smells of cow-parsley and creosote. And what is this strange, unexpected, yet not unfamiliar odour that lurks in your room?

'I don't suppose you remember me at all, sir,' he said. 'It is quite ten years now since the Oaklands days.'

'Oaklands days,' Mooncranker repeated, with sudden alertness. *'Oaklands days?'* His mouth, Farnaby noticed, had a habit of suddenly twitching up at the corners, a curious involuntary movement that he suddenly felt he remembered. A slight, civilized grimace.

'Those were great days, sir,' he said, insincerely.

'Oaklands,' repeated Mooncranker. The name was one he had heard before, as was the name of his visitor. It sounded like a private sanatorium. Perhaps this was the clue. They had both been on a cure together, writhed on neighbouring beds, suffered sedation in company. But this creature of light ten years ago would have been a mere child, too young surely for such excesses.

'Ah, the delights of convalescence,' he said, playing for time. 'Strange they are so little celebrated in our literature. Can any of you recall a single instance? Farnaby?'

'There is a story of Chekhov's, I remember,' Farnaby said, feeling it rather odd that Mooncranker should address him as one of a group.

'So there is, so there is,' Mooncranker said. He thought of the final phase, identity recovered, strength returning, gentle rambles, sunlit lawns and woods. Oaklands ... Feelings of nostalgia invaded him, a film of moisture slid over his eyes. 'How you have grown,' he said. 'Quite amazing.' This was what one said to young people after an absence of years. Juvenile alcoholics were not unknown after all. Ten years ago. Where was I ten years ago. Was that the year I was visiting village colleges in Cambridgeshire lecturing on the relevance of the classics? Did I have a bout in that year? But his mind staggered, all bouts were the same bout.

'And have you succumbed since?' he said.

'I beg your pardon, sir?'

'Have you managed to keep off it since?'

'I'm afraid I don't ...' Farnaby smiled helplessly. The only possibly deleterious habit of his at that time had been intermittent self-abuse. Surely Mooncranker could not be referring to that?

'Never mind, never mind. A painful subject no doubt. Still you have certainly grown. A very commendable growth. I congratulate you on it.'

'Thank you,' Farnaby said, automatically responding to the

words of praise. He was bewildered by these questions, but lacked the assurance needed to follow them up. He noticed with dismay gleams of moisture, either from tears or some sort of condensation, on the sides of the professor's nose. 'You used to umpire for us,' he said. He smiled at Mooncranker who now advanced a little towards him.

'Won't you have a seat,' Mooncranker said. 'That one is very comfortable.' He pointed to a deep armchair angled in a corner of the room.

'Oh thank you.' Farnaby thought of adding, 'And a jolly good umpire you were,' but the words died on his lips. Such an utterance would have been ridiculously inappropriate to Mooncranker's present limpness and vagueness. Besides it was not the way he felt about that summer. It was the sort of remark Uncle George would have approved of, suggesting that all was hearty fun, no ill feelings; not corresponding in the least to his private sense of it which, he recognized now in this totally different setting and perhaps for the first time with complete assent, had the pulsing numbness, the involuntary recoil of nightmare. Beginning with the sudden break, the snap in his parents' torsion of unhappiness which had spun him off to Oaklands and Uncle George and Aunt Jane while his father and mother, wearied with the rancorous years, made final plans for separation. Beginning there, nightmare permeated every aspect of that summer, radiating from its own still centres: stiff hot leaves, the rustling fevers of the shrubbery; the hushed limits of the courts; Mooncranker jerking in his canvas chair or imperishably smiling, handing over the gift; talking to someone just out of sight; stirrings in the white folds of bandage that Jesus was wrapped in. He smiled at Mooncranker, saying nothing.

Mooncranker, who had not himself sat down, returned the smile, but with what seemed a private sense of significance. 'Umpired,' he said, and then repeated the word with his habit of apparently ironical stress. *Umpired?* He placed thin hands rather gropingly on the back of a chair. His nausea returned as he struggled to reconcile the spent but optimistic feelings of convalescence with the more strenuous associations of umpiring. Distrust of his visitor came creeping back. 'You say you telephoned,' he said. 'Your name is an evocative one, suggesting to my mind military manoeuvres and daffodils.'

'Oh, really?' Farnaby said, from the depths of his armchair. He was resolved not to betray by his manner any sense that the interview was going oddly. It was as though by entering Mooncranker's room he had stirred up some sort of muddy deposit or sediment in the other's mind. The only thing to do was wait for it to settle, affecting in the meantime to notice nothing. This was difficult, however, not only because of Mooncranker's failure to utter any even faintly appropriate sentiments, but because he felt himself dislocated somehow by having acknowledged the true ghastliness of that summer, by his inability to keep up a sporting tone when referring to it. A determined jollity about the past had always been Uncle George's essential idiom, almost his distinguishing feature. And if Mooncranker had taken this tone, Farnaby would have adapted himself with his usual alacrity to it. But he did not know what was expected of him now. He had never really known, but had always striven to muffle his impact on other people until they gave him the needed clues; an innate deference expressed also in his appearance, with which he took considerable trouble: hair long rather than short but not too long; jacket and trousers of traditional design. His aim was to be appropriate rather than elegant.

Mooncranker however furnished no clues; and Farnaby was drifting now, relaxing the alert, respectful manner he had deemed suitable for an old friend of Uncle George, a notable radio and television interviewer and chairman, adopting to some extent the dreamy deliberateness of Mooncranker himself. He leaned back in his armchair, shaping in his mind questions. Why these sudden changes of tone, Mooncranker. Why are you treating me with such reserve. Do you know me now for the boy you gave the Christ to. Thirty seconds it probably took, that whole transaction, wouldn't you agree, handing it over, and then a few words. Thirty seconds the extent of our real acquaintance before this evening, or would you say less. But what was the reason. Why did you make me such a gift, a Christ whose body you must have known would rot, fashioned as it was in sausage meat. And why did you

16

involve her in it, the girl, what did she have to do with it, what seas, what shores? A thirteen-year-old boy. And what is this smell, occasionally emitted to me from your person or perhaps some other quarter of the room. A resinous gluey odour, not petrolly as I formerly thought. Certainly not the smell of Christ's decay. Reminding me of privacy, solitude...

'No,' Mooncranker said. 'I merely inquired, you see, about the possibility of getting tickets. I did not, repeat not, ask the hotel to obtain them for me. So it is no good at all your coming to me now and producing tickets and so forth, least of all now, when my secretary has left me. I was intending to take her to the theatre, *Rhinoceros* in Turkish, very stimulating, yes, but would you say it was relevant? Farnaby? She has left me, my secretary, Miss Bolsover, has left me in the lurch.'

His sensation of nausea increased. He wanted a drink very badly indeed, but the long habit of secrecy prevented him from drinking before his visitor. Besides he did not believe in Farnaby, felt that the other was waiting to pounce. Impossible to tell, though, what he would regard as a false move. Better to risk nothing. Moreover, his vision had again been affected and he seemed to catch glimpses of other visitors sitting about the room in the shadowy corners just beyond his range of vision: officials of some sort, formally dressed, with a sort of sharply angled structure about the neck suggesting old-fashioned wing collars, they were listening carefully to the conversation, leaning forward stiffly from the waist. He knew that these figures were illusory, but they troubled and distracted him. He felt convinced now too that Oaklands was not a sanatorium at all, but something much more sinister. The shape of the gin bottle was present to his mind and its blue label. Nausea and thirst slaked together...

'It is a name,' he said with no alteration of manner, 'that links Hampshire to the North Riding. As for this talk of umpiring,' he added, 'I should have thought they could provide you with a better story than that.'

This was such an extraordinary thing to say that Farnaby did not register it at first, replying merely that his name was quite a common one. Then he said quickly, 'What do you mean?'

But Mooncranker had lowered his face again and was looking at the carpet. His hair, trained back in two sweeps over his ears, seemed in some inexplicable way to have become disarrayed since Farnaby's arrival, and this, combined with the high-shouldered posture of the body, gave him the look of some slightly dishevelled or perhaps sick or injured bird. He stood thus for some time in silence, resting his hands on the back of the chair, among the other objects in the room, oval mirrors in gilt frames, a worn silk screen patterned with peacocks all facing the same way, a mahogany cabinet with massive paws, numbers of low square tables, on the wall a copy of Bellini's portrait of Fatih Mehmet, conqueror of Byzantium. Beyond Mooncranker a half-open door led into what appeared to be a smallish bedroom. The chandelier from time to time shivered and tinkled, so perhaps a draught was coming from there. He could not feel a draught himself, but seemed to sense a displacement of air in the room, heavy air stirring as though at the action of a fan. I know what the smell reminds me of, model aeroplanes, a bench in the garden shed, home-made fan churning on hot evenings after school, windows permanently jammed and cobwebbed and the swathes of air, heavy and spirituous with odours of newly cut balsa wood and glue and silver paint, and the Spitfires and Messerschmitts dangling on threads from the ceiling; smell of safety, parents safe and quiet too in the house, not quarrelling then; calls of children from the street the only sound; and brief outcries of blackbirds in the garden. Nothing however to connect Mooncranker with all this. Not on the face of it.

'Let me give you a word of advice, Farnaby,' Mooncranker said, but a sudden wave of nausea prevented him from going on. He looked down again at the carpet. Through the mists that assailed him a piercing recollection came, white figures curling and uncurling in a shaft of light, the tennis games, and this was the nephew of Jane and George Wilson and Oaklands was not a sunny convalescent home at all. He had vaguely known this all along, but kept the knowledge at bay out of wilfulness, and a fear of too much radiance, too much play of light on the past.

'My mother lived near by at one time,' he said, raising his

head. 'I have not been back to that town since she died.' How did George Wilson know I was coming here? There has been no communication between us for years. From the papers perhaps. He was always the sort of man that followed things up. 'Fine man, George Wilson,' he said. 'Salt of the earth.' George Wilson's face flickered at him before he could resist it, the blue-eyed fullness of regard, almost brutal in its assurance; bald, freckled temples. 'Yes indeed,' he said. 'So you are George Wilson's nephew.' He noticed that his visitor was leaning forward attentively, but could not think why. His back had started aching again. He swivelled his eyes sideways in an attempt to catch the seated officials napping, but they drew back offended. 'I don't think there is any advice I can give you,' he said after a pause. 'I'm terribly sorry.'

'That's quite all right, sir,' Farnaby said.

'How is he?'

'Well I haven't seen him for some years. Not since Aunt Jane died.'

'Quite so,' Mooncranker said instantly, as if Aunt Jane's death had made her husband difficult to get at. 'Sad business, that,' he added. What he had been in a way fearing was happening now, consecutive memories like rings or hoops settling over him, the white gate with the name on it in metal letters, *Oaklands,* a drive flanked with thick-bladed leaves, the squarish red-brick front of the house with its single clumsy gable. Lawn and shrubbery. Tennis-courts at the back, white figures leaping and flexing in a permanent pool of light. Miranda. I offered my services as umpire in order to watch fifteen-year-old Miranda in her pleated white tennis dress. Partnered by this Farnaby whose terrible cunning on the courts I remember, she kissed him when they won. His shy smile, long-fingered scratched hand, taking it from me, that gift. Perhaps that is why you alarmed me so, standing under the lamp, charged with brightness from moment to moment, bright with vengeance. Even though no lights had been switched on. I was associating you with the violent and unpredictable motions often required in tennis.

'Can I help you at all with your lecture?' Farnaby asked.

Mooncranker looked blankly at him a moment. His desire

for gin could no longer be denied. 'Perhaps,' he said, 'perhaps you would like to go out on to the balcony. You get an excellent view from there.'

Farnaby rose obediently and following Mooncranker's instructions passed through thick brown curtaining material on to a long narrow balcony. He gripped the railing and looked out, momentarily confused after the confinement of the room by the broad spaces before him, the clear air. Unwilling for the moment to cope with all this he looked down at his hands. Hands now clinging to the rail were hands in that remote absorption shaping fuselage and wing section, shifting a sweaty grip from forehand to backhand, eliciting with considerable ingenuity pangs of fearful pleasure from my, ah, principal appendage. The things these hands have done.

Mooncranker did not follow him, as he had been half expecting. However, he went on talking and Farnaby could tell from the direction of his voice that he had moved to another part of the room. He had the impression that Mooncranker was busying himself with something.

'One of my most cherished memories,' he heard the slow voice say through the curtain, 'of those early days. A distinguished philosopher whom it fell to my lot to interview, on the occasion of his seventieth birthday. I won't mention his name.'

Farnaby realized after a moment that what he was hearing was an excerpt from Mooncranker's forthcoming lecture, 'My Life in Radio and Television', which Uncle George had told him about in the letter.

'No names no packdrill,' Mooncranker said. He had taken the tumbler full of gin at a draught and immediately felt better. The pain in his back was gone and his vision was clear, except for some few hallucinatory shreds and whisks. However, when he heard Farnaby's voice through the curtain commenting on the view, he began to feel somehow threatened again, doubts as to the young man's *bona fides* again invaded him. He knew it was Farnaby yet doubted it. Could it be some stranger posing for purposes of his own as nephew, tennis-player, provoker of the wickedness of that distant gift? 'A marvellous man,' he said, quietly pouring out another tumbler. 'Bolt upright in his chair, mind like a trap. Lucid, articulate, the soul of courtesy. The only trouble was, he had a bladder ailment. Every few minutes he would have to excuse himself, right in the middle of some marvellously lucid and articulate –' He strove while he was speaking to recall that summer at Oaklands more exactly. It was like looking down a funnel-shaped perspective at a group of distant yet bright and distinct figures separated from him by years and by a sort of abyss. Memory was like a lens, with adjustments it might sharpen detail but could not make these creatures more comprehensible. Dressed in gleaming white in the crashing silence of his memory they expanded and contracted themselves, made darting movements within white squares. And among them, somehow seeing them from close at hand, my own mind moves, my own eyes and mind are there down the funnel recording the results of those contortions from moment to moment with a sort of compulsive fidelity. He drank a little. 'The voice of the Farnaby is heard in our land,' he said. More like a gun-sight now than a funnel. Distance not time that makes those figures small. A touch on the trigger, the gentlest of pressures stills all that activity for ever. Stand aside Miranda. My obedient darling stands on the side lines, holding her racquet, fair hair contained by clean white headband, limbs flushed and roseate from her exertions. She watches with some anguish, which I shall shortly soothe, her companions being mowed down. 'I hope you don't mind my taking your name in vain like this,' he called through the curtain. 'Not at all,' Farnaby answered politely. All the same he felt slightly shocked by this levity or rather by the continuing failure of Mooncranker to come up to expectation. Had he, Farnaby, come to offer his services, run errands, bear the brunt of nervous irascibility if necessary, at the behest of Uncle George and therefore on a mission hallowed as it were in advance, and with the virtuous certainty of this reinforced by his own stores of respect for authority and academic distinction and so on, which were considerable – he was one of nature's acolytes after all, and knew it – only to hear snatches of a lecture and his name used in biblical contexts by a wandering voice through brown curtaining material? What on earth could Mooncranker be doing all this time?

He looked over the huddle of mean buildings immediately below him, towards Galata and the gleaming water of the Golden Horn and beyond this to the marvellous skyline of the old city, the great mosques along the summit, Valide Hanim just beyond the bridge, then Suleyman, Beyazit, Yavuz Selim, the shapes black and definite against the paling sky as if some advance wave of darkness had entered them and was for the moment contained.

'They certainly knew where to build, these, er, Osmanli builders,' Farnaby said, speaking in clear tones so as to carry through the curtain. 'Don't you think so, sir?'

'Farnaby, I do.' Mooncranker emerged at last on to the balcony. He took up a position at the rail three or four yards away from Farnaby. He seemed altogether more self-possessed. However he said nothing for the moment.

Together they watched the sky softening and hazing towards dusk. A sluice of darkness was already filling the streets. Across the glimmering water, domes and minarets were still firm-edged against the sky, but below this everything had dissolved in the deepening haze so that the mosques appeared now to be rising from some territory between land and sky.

'This is what one likes about Istanbul,' Farnaby said. 'This massiveness made almost insubstantial by the light. You never quite know where you are, do you?' He was worried by Mooncranker's continuing failure to make any sort of preparation for his lecture – due in less than an hour's time at the other side of the city. A number of people, perhaps two or three hundred, the intellectual *élite* of the capital, at this very moment in various districts would be preparing to go and listen to this lecture. Wives would be asking husbands to zip them up and so on, husbands looking for cuff-links. Farnaby found the thought of all this activity, in conjunction with Mooncranker's inertia, his *intensifying* inertia if such a thing were possible, very disturbing. He had a deep respect for programmed events, all scheduled activity. This lecture had been publicized and promulgated. Surely Mooncranker could not be proposing simply not to turn up?

'Your lecture is at eight-fifteen, sir, isn't it,' he said.

Immediately upon these words Mooncranker began moving

in an immensely leisurely manner along the balcony rail towards him, as though drawing nearer to impart some confidence. The expression on his face, however, was cautious and rather sly as it had been when the reference to umpiring had been made. 'The dome and minaret,' he said, 'comprise bebetween them in my opinion everything that can be expressed architecturally or is worth expressing.' He had experienced, on hearing Farnaby's reference to the lecture, some return of that malevolence which had caused him to squeeze the trigger and immobilize the leaping tennis players. At the same time the desire to speak to someone about runaway Miranda was becoming imperative. 'The soaring spire, vulnerable aspiration and on the other hand the shape of containment, the hump, the delectable . . .' His vision was clouded again, the figure of the young man had grown indistinct. 'Do you really think so?' he said, under the momentary impression that it was Farnaby who had spoken thus about domes and minarets.

'What?' Farnaby said.

Mooncranker laid a hand on the young man's arm. 'Listen Farnaby,' he said. 'My secretary has left me.' At once, with the words, tears of desolation came to his eyes. 'She has gone away and left me,' he said. Farnaby's face had blurred, mingled with the first stars of night. 'I am sorry to hear that,' Mooncranker added, with a vague sense of anticipating Farnaby's reaction. 'She left two days ago.'

'I am sorry to hear that,' Farnaby said. Now that Mooncranker was so close the smell of model aeroplanes had intensified. Only of course it was not model aeroplanes. How can I have been so obtuse? The old boy has been having a drink or two. Alcohol, ingested some time previously, processed with other fluents in Mooncranker's system, now exhaled or exuded in a form reminiscent of my industrious boyhood. He looked away in some embarrassment. It occurred to him now to wonder whether or not Mooncranker was married. It was a question of congruity rather than a deductive process. Could any part of that summer's territory have belonged to a Mrs Mooncranker? Looking out across the darkening city he tried to introduce such a person, physically place her among the grey courts and green nets and fresh white lines, the hush and menace of the adjoining shrubbery. Perhaps she had crouched there, watching the rapidly curling and uncurling figures on the courts, reading the signals they made with their racquets against that sky of burning blue. Or a matronly figure dispensing tea and cakes in the intervals between sets. But no, there had been no intervals, his memory of that summer admitted no intervals, no Mrs Mooncranker. The only female of mature years had been Aunt Jane. She might have been at home, of course. Or dead. Was there any aura of grief, any odour of bereavement about the umpire? Not that I can remember.

'She is very young,' Mooncranker said, turning towards Farnaby once more, and there was no mistaking it now, Mooncranker was a bit squiffy.

'Yes, it is true that she is young,' he repeated in his slow and curiously patient tones.

Night was advancing rapidly. The mosques had surrendered at last their firmness of outline, presenting now a diffused or charred aspect, like charred wood, as though darkness were leaking from them into the sky. *Darkness comes to the city of Istanbul*, Farnaby observed to himself, *with the effect of a flooding from within*.

His pleasure at this insight was soon lost in the continuing uneasiness about Mooncranker's condition, and the lecture in particular. He felt distinctly unwilling to act as confidant in this matter of the runaway secretary, mainly because he sensed in it the prospect of unpalatable revelations, admissions that might oblige him to revise his whole attitude to Mooncranker, and this was the last thing he wanted. It was wrong for people not to be predictable, especially elderly persons like Mooncranker. He himself always tried to do what was expected, when he could discover it. More particularly, however, he felt that he had been granted by Uncle George's letter the sort of second chance that comes rarely in life, and these vagaries of Mooncranker's were impeding him in seizing it, which was unfair and unjust. It had reached him so unerringly, the letter, with its precise information as to Mooncranker's whereabouts, like a message from a higher power which he had been chosen specially to receive and act upon. By patience and cunning he might discover why Mooncranker had sought him out that summer day, had come walking towards him through the shrubbery, paused before him smiling, handed him a small effigy of Christ on the Cross, done up in folds of white bandage. Mysteries that I never thought to penetrate until this letter from Uncle George, this meeting far from home.

He knew too, in another part of his mind, with a sense half-despairing, half-resigned, that there might be nothing really to explain, no case to answer. It had been a random, a gratuitous act, possibly, a mere pimple of evil as it were, squeezed out, forgotten long ago by everyone but himself. Certainly, Mooncranker could not have known, no one could have known, the effect of it on him, the violent clash between pleasure at the gift and subsequent horror at the putrefaction and his feelings of betrayal, utter abandonment, and *guilt*, not resentment, he had never felt that. Mooncranker it was who by accident or design had set all this in motion, so much was beyond doubt. And he sensed that his chance of learning more depended on preserving the trappings of the past, preserving Mooncranker in his role of stable adult, radio and television personality, visiting lecturer, friend of Uncle George; not a person dishevelled, deserted by his secretary, smelling of drink, disinclined apparently to fulfil his engagements. Mooncranker had to be kept in his place. Though he had not anticipated having to struggle so to keep him in it. And it was to occur to him not much later that the particularly fatiguing nature of this interview, the sense of strain he was already conscious of feeling, came from precisely that unremitting effort to bear Mooncranker up.

'While I was in the bath,' Mooncranker was saying, 'while I was actually having a bath. She packed a suitcase and departed. She did not leave any note. The day before yesterday, in the morning, about nine o'clock, was the last time I heard her voice. She left me at a time when I could ill afford to spare her.'

'Where would she go, what would she do, in Istanbul?' Farnaby said.

Mooncranker turned his head slowly towards him. 'Oh no, you don't,' he said with sudden distinctness. 'You don't catch me like that.'

'What do you mean?' Farnaby was bewildered.

Mooncranker edged away from him along the balcony. All his doubts about his visitor had returned. 'I know where she is,' he said. 'Tomorrow, when I am feeling better, or possibly the day after, I will go and get her back.' He regretted now having spoken of Miranda to this young man, who was obviously a spy of some kind. After a moment he said, 'Shall we go inside now? It's getting chilly isn't it?'

The room was in semi-darkness but Mooncranker made no move to switch on any lamps. 'Time is getting on,' Farnaby said, nervous in the dimness. He peered at Mooncranker who was standing still in the middle of the room. The peacocks on the screen had merged into abstract patterns. On the wall, light still dwelt on Fatih Mehmet's lean and crafty jaw and on the collar of his kaftan.

'George Wilson,' Mooncranker said sorrowfully. 'The salt of the earth. You could always depend on George Wilson. I may be old fashioned, but I believe in that public-school code. You know where you are with men like that.'

'Yes,' Farnaby said. 'But do *they* know where *they* are?'

'In family life, in professional life – ' Mooncranker began, then tailed off into inaudibility.

'It will soon be time for your lecture,' Farnaby said valiantly.

Mooncranker made a sudden movement, as if startled. 'Dear boy,' he said, 'I wonder if you would be good enough to slip down and get me a packet of cigarettes? I would ask one of the staff, but they might think I was referring to the tickets again.'

'Of course,' Farnaby said. He saw now that Mooncranker had no intention of delivering the lecture, and this realization marked the sudden collapse of his efforts to keep the relation between them fixed. 'What kind?' he said, peering confusedly through the dimness. If there was to be no lecture what were they both doing there?

'Yeni Harman, please. Not the filters, the ordinary ones. They are in orange-coloured packets.'

Farnaby made his way rather blunderingly to the door and opening it admitted a shaft of brilliant light from the corridor, which fell in a long stripe across the carpet. Mooncranker stood just beyond this. Farnaby was possessed by an odd sense that there was something which could now be said, something of transfiguring importance that would put them both in the track of the light as it were, change the whole nature of their meeting and conversation, but he could not bring anything to the surface of his mind and turned away wordlessly, stepping out softly into the corridor. He began to close the door quietly behind him, then at the last moment inserted his hand and removed the key from the inside.

Mooncranker stood still, in the wake of this silence, enforcing stillness upon himself; cautiously, voluptuously controlling his impulse to make straight for the bottle, connoisseur even now in his own pain and suspicion. No sound of steps receding along the corridor. Carpet would muffle these of course. Care of the essence, however, care of the absolute essence. He may not have gone yet. He may well be pausing, waiting, just outside in the blinding corridor, waiting for the right moment to slip back in again with some seemingly innocent request. Now perhaps. Yes, time enough now. Light enough for this familiar sequence of actions.

He looked up for a moment, blinking at the dim ceiling, destroying in his mind all the lights and lives above him in that hotel until nothing intervened between him and the night, the soft buoyant darkness above the roof, which did not press upon him, but sought rather to gather, to assume. His upper lip slid over the rim. He tilted the glass but did not drink yet, delaying for the integral pang of self-outrage, not unclamping the lip from its soft adhesion, tilting till the lip itself was immersed. The gin stung his lip.

Far off from the Marmara the hooting of a steamer, sudden maniacal whoop, again silence. He lifted his lip delicately from the rim, and the liquid slid between glass and lip, welled like corrosive saliva, over barriers of teeth, collected to a quantity swallowable, and he swallowed. And swallowed. And he refilled his glass.

2

Getting the cigarettes took longer than might have been expected. There was no kiosk in the immediate vicinity of the hotel, so it was not until some twenty minutes later that Farnaby was emerging from the lift again and making his way down the corridor. He made use of his key to enter, noticing as he did so that the room was now lit by a crimson-shaded table-lamp in the far corner of the room. Mooncranker himself was not immediately visible. However, as he advanced into the room he became aware of hasty activity on his far right, and his mind took in Mooncranker's movements vaguely yet at the same time with a definiteness of impression, in sharp blinking shots like a rapid series of stills. Mooncranker to begin with flat on his back, but this position was antecedent to my entering the room, surely he must already have been in motion at the first sound, assuming a sitting position, swinging his legs sideways, setting them down on the floor, bending a furtive torso, attempting to don shoes, or at any rate this was what he seemed to be doing – the only way on the evidence available to account for the sudden flurry of activity in the region of Mooncranker's feet, which were, however, still invisible . . .

Having succeeded in hiding his glass under the divan, Mooncranker looked smilingly at the young man. 'So there you are,' he said. His body leaned forward slowly, then slowly righted itself. 'I was beginning to think you had got lost.' His voice was unrecognizable, so thick and slurred had it become.

'Yes, here I am.' Farnaby had experienced an immediate horror at this change in the other's voice. It seemed like a sort of bemonstering, the beginning of some grotesque metamorphosis, as though Mooncranker's face too and his whole form would shortly begin writhing. The old boy has been having a quick one, he said to himself, seeking reassurance in traditional levity.

'Don't put any more lights on,' Mooncranker said, though Farnaby had made no move to do so. With something of an effort Farnaby looked squarely at the former umpire. The statesmanlike wings of hair had fallen over his ears and he was regarding the source of light, the red-shaded table-lamp against the far wall, with a face that seemed still to be bemusedly smiling, though this too might well have been an illusion – Mooncranker's real expression might have been quite different; the soft pink light was deceiving. The attempt to get his shoes on, if that was what Mooncranker had been doing, had obviously failed, since he was still in his stocking feet, grey woollen socks, and this, together with the dishevelled hair and the impress of his body on the divan, were details that seemed suddenly to Farnaby too intimate, too revealing of Mooncranker's private existence. 'Here are your cigarettes,' he said, taking some steps towards the divan, holding out the packet.

'No need to bring them here. Put them on the table, dear boy.'

Obediently he turned towards the table. He had been close enough however to see the sudden gleams of moisture on the other's face, as if keeping him off, preventing him from getting too close, had been a prodigious effort; and at this sight concern invaded him, contended with his reluctance to admit that there was anything wrong or strange about the conversation so far.

'Perhaps,' he said, after a momentary hesitation, 'I'd better ring them up and tell them you are ill.'

Mooncranker nodded, seriously and judiciously, 'It might, at that, be a good idea, young Farnaby,' he said, as though conceding a point in argument. And while Farnaby, with a despairing sense of having lost his bearings, was searching out the number in the directory, he was aware all the time of Mooncranker's voice, hesitant and slurred, expressing some views about tobacco, the virtues of Turkish tobacco, perhaps led to this by thoughts of the cigarettes Farnaby had brought.

'It is dried out by natural processes,' he said. 'It is cured in the sun, you see, young Farnaby.' At this point he stopped short, his thoughts led off helplessly to rows of persons recently emerged from drink and delirium, sitting in their dressing-gowns on the sheltered terraces of sanatoriums, raising convalescent faces to the life-giving orb. He raised his own face blindly. Cured in the sun. Myself one of the row. Miranda

29

tucking me in. Ah, why did you leave me? Why did you give me no sign? A rush of grief pricked his closed eyes and pained his extended throat. He opened his eyes slightly, saw through a haze of tears Farnaby still puzzling over the directory. Insensitive lout. His feelings changed to cautious anger and malevolence towards this interloper.

'That telephone directory is *private*,' he said, in low tones. The lout did not look up. And now Mooncranker saw that there was another person in the room, a shadowy figure sitting just beyond Farnaby, in a judge's wig, with a writing pad on his knee.

'It is surprising,' he said, trying to enunciate clearly for the benefit of this newcomer, who was obviously taking notes, 'how conditions of our life today nourish superstition. We abandon the old ones with reluctance and eagerly devise new as the areas of our ignorance extend. And they are extending all the time. The frontiers of ignorance extend with every increase in knowledge. Make a note of that.' He attempted to peer round Farnaby, but the note-taker had vanished.

'Ah, here it is,' Farnaby said.

'Set against this,' Mooncranker continued, after some moments of uncertainty, is the great, grand, simple concept of the sun, which we regard as a germ-killing fire.'

'I'll phone then, shall I?' Farnaby said, a faint hope still remaining that Mooncranker might have changed his mind.

At this Mooncranker stopped speaking. The words continued to form however in his mind with a curious sort of laborious persistence, like slow drops of some muddy precipitation, and he was under the impression of uttering them, or at least of their being uttered. Germ-killing fire. Though one might, taking another view, regard the sun as a maggot-breeding agency. So much depends on the point of view. And what is yours, Farnaby? What – is – your – point – of – view? Delicate wrist, supporting the telephone. Small-boned despite your tallness. I see your thin form of the years ago, thin arms sun-freckled emerging from short sleeves. A suggestion about you of haplessness, imperfect coordination. Your face I did not look at, but I saw your long-fingered, scratched hand, taking the Christ from me. And now you have come to take something more. Or possibly repay. Thou out of heaven's benediction comest to the warm sun...

'Hello,' Farnaby said earnestly into the telephone. 'Is that the British Council? Can I speak to the person responsible for arranging lectures and so on?'

'Strings and strings of tobacco leaves on these long poles,' Mooncranker said aloud, observing the respectful manner in which Farnaby addressed the instrument.

'Confined to his hotel,' Farnaby said. 'No, quite impossible, I'm afraid.'

Little clumps of them, green leaves about the size of a single lobe of a chestnut leaf, a well-developed specimen of that last, *bien entendu*, and offered to the sun, which in the course of time shrivels them of all injurious juices. Miranda was always a little slow in the mornings. Her juices took some time to get flowing. She trailed after her still the odours of the night. Sweetly clogged eyes. It took her a long time to wake up. She did not move briskly at that time of day. Yet in the space of half an hour she had packed and gone.

'He is suffering from nervous exhaustion,' Farnaby said gravely, as if to a relative of the patient. He listened, agreed, apologized; replacing the receiver finally as gently as restoring an egg to the nest. 'There are quite a lot of people there already,' he said, somewhat exhilarated.

'That argues planning, Farnaby. It was not done on the spur of the moment.' Mooncranker got up from the divan and moved along the wall towards the adjoining room. Some injurious juice I have left though not I suppose a great deal when measured in cubic centimetres. The sun has shrivelled me at scalp and scrotum. Though it is a process not yet complete.

'He was awfully fed up when I told him,' Farnaby said, keeping the other warily in view.

'Whereas I cannot help feeling,' Mooncranker said, 'that factory processes do not expel these carcinomatic substances but keep them trapped in the veins of the leaf. I cannot rid myself of this feeling, Farnaby, struggle as I may. Excuse me one moment.'

He padded across the remaining three yards of carpet with a

surprising burst of speed, and disappeared into the next room, not quite succeeding in closing the door behind him. Farnaby, still standing beside the telephone, heard after some moments the unmistakable choke and gurgle of a person vomiting, followed soon after by the flushing of the lavatory. Mooncranker reappeared, white and smiling, more collected in manner and speech.

'There is something that has been exercising my mind,' he said. 'Ever since I arrived at this hotel. It is in the next room.'

Farnaby looked with simple curiosity at Mooncranker, possessed by the strangeness of knowing that only minutes before that body had been convulsing itself, poised above the lavatory-pan for the next choking spasm; and was now in only precarious control, upright, surmounted by a face that had not forgotten the need for smiling, albeit in ghastly bedewed fashion. 'In the next room,' he repeated, with a sense that anything at all could be revealed. He suddenly felt terribly tired. How long had he been there? Certainly not two hours yet. In that time he had struggled to keep Mooncranker in his place, the Mooncranker of memory and tradition, with direct authority from Uncle George, empowered to divide up time that might otherwise have been as undifferentiated as that in Eden, with his loves and deuces, vans in and out. He had seemed in his white clothes to be the perpetual arbiter. Time and the application of rule will settle everything, he had seemed to say. Time and rule will bring all sets to a conclusion, there will be winners and losers. Time will expose your illusions, rot your dreams. Rot your Christ on his pathetic crucifix of lathe. When he handed it over he smiled, because he knew this. His head turned through an angle of possibly ninety degrees, as if scanning to either side.

Yes, high-priest of time and rule during that summer. But now too human and complex, dazed with drink, rambling in speech. Your status of umpire is gone for ever.

'Come and see,' Mooncranker said, and Farnaby followed him into the adjoining room and over to the head of the bed where, set into the wall a little to one side were three bell-pushes one below the other in a faded, red-plush panel.

'It concerns the nature of the persons summoned by these bells,' Mooncranker said.

Stooping, Farnaby read the word *Service* in dim sepia copperplate against the top bell, with *Bonne* below it and finally *Groom*.

'It is the last one that interests me,' Mooncranker said, and his speech was quite clear now. 'What meaning can the word *groom* have for us, Farnaby?'

It was at this point that Farnaby departed from a life-long habit of caution, and acted in a completely unauthorized way. He had always done what was expected of him, more or less. His sense of propriety was highly developed. Passing at night for example he would not have peered into lighted interiors. He always shut gates after him in case the cows got out. But talking to Mooncranker had been a strain; just keeping them both more or less decorously there and not yielding to some force he felt threatening to sweep them into limbo had involved him in a series of expedients, like trying to hold down a table-cloth with all the tea things on it in the midst of a picnic disrupted by sudden inexplicable gales. In these circumstances the limits of the permissible are extended. A reckless impulse rose in Farnaby. He looked tensely at Mooncranker, then he said, 'We can jolly soon find out, sir,' and pushed his thumb against the bell.

'Don't ring it, you're not ringing it are you?' Mooncranker said and made a jerky sort of gesture as if to restrain him. He looked rather frightened. 'Don't ring it,' he said again, but by this time of course it was too late. Farnaby removed his thumb. They stood there beside the bed, regarding each other.

'No immediate effect,' Mooncranker said, after a moment. 'No immediate effect, Farnaby.' His high-shouldered frame relaxed a little, drooped. He moved some steps away. 'Probably disconnected years ago,' he said. 'What earthly use could there be for a *groom*?'

Once more in the sitting-room, Mooncranker sat in the armchair he had first offered to his visitor. He smiled kindly across at Farnaby. 'Tell me something about yourself,' he said. 'What have you been doing over the years?'

His voice was clear and slow, his manner collected. With a

feeling almost of disbelief Farnaby realized that he and Mooncranker were about to have a chat. For the first time in his visit their mutual attitudes were going to be more or less in accordance with his sense of fitness. Perhaps something could be salvaged after all. He began to tell Mooncranker about the latter years. Filling in the picture, Uncle George would have called it. It was a placid tale. Farnaby was conscious himself that his life had been lacking in dramatic incident. There were no peaks in it much. Nor could it be described as a plain really, but rather as a sort of flattened-out trough. He had always done what was expected of him. Ever since that summer. That summer had marked the end of several things, though he did not explain this to Mooncranker at present. The end of his religious phase certainly – the thought of Christ's person filled him with horror even now; the end of his acquaintance with Miranda and with Mooncranker too; the end of tennis; the end of his expectation of similar summers. Yes, quite a lot of ends. Each of them contained a beginning too, but the beginnings were not so easy to discern. He did not speak of this to Mooncranker, of course.

After school, where his faulty coordination, the slightly maimed grace of his movements, were the despair of games masters, he went on to university, where he read modern history. A creditable, by no means brilliant degree. Some months of idleness and indecision. Taking Stock, Uncle George would have called it. A loafing, dandruffy period.

'I thought I'd better have a look round first, you know,' he said, aware from experience that this sentiment was unimpeachable.

'Absolutely right, dear boy.' Mooncranker had placed the tips of his fingers together and his chalk-white face looked benignantly over the cage thus formed. 'Absolutely essential when it comes to choosing a career. A choice which after all, let's face it, is a choice which . . . I mean, absolutely crucial.'

'Then I applied for a research scholarship from my university.'

' "Making a recce", we called it, in my army days.' Mooncranker continued in brisker tones. 'Fired upon, flat on your face, make a recce.'

Rather surprisingly, he had succeeded in obtaining the scholarship, and was now committed to producing a thesis on Ottoman Fiscal Policy in regard to the Foreign Millyets. Precisely what aspect of this, however, after three months in Istanbul he had still not determined. The field was so vast. His mind groped among mounds of facts randomly yet patiently assembled. The suspicion had been growing in him lately that he was not really cut out for academic work. In the meantime, however, it was activity of a sort, and it gave him a certain sense of purpose, albeit intermittent. Mornings in the library; solitary walks about the city after lunch, making Mental Notes; haphazard reading in the evenings. He knew almost no one in the city.

All this he was trying now, as tactfully as possible in view of Mooncranker's well-known interests and abilities, to explain and Mooncranker was sitting back in his chair and nodding to denote continued attentiveness, having grasped his role at last, as it seemed to Farnaby, which was not that of a dishevelled vomiter in bathrooms, but courteous subserver of a distant evil, mature now in years and experience, interviewer of the celebrated for the benefit of a listening nation – himself listening now with a kindly irony in reserve to a promising young protégé – when there was a sudden loud and most disconcerting scraping sound at the door as though some dog or cat were scratching at it, but higher up than dogs or cats would normally be expected to scratch.

Farnaby's voice tailed off into silence. The smile of kindly interest disappeared without trace from Mooncranker's face. He looked for a moment slightly anxious, as if he were striving to hear distant music. Then Farnaby saw his mouth slacken and fall open a little. 'Go and see who it is, will you?' he said. There was a sound now from the door as of someone attempting to insert a key but in a very fumbling fashion as though the person beyond was encumbered or handicapped in some way. 'No, wait a minute,' Mooncranker said, in a curiously hurried and indistinct voice as if he had some obstruction in the throat. 'Don't open it, put the catch on. Hurry up for God's sake, before it gets in.'

Farnaby went to the door. After a momentary hesitation he

35

opened it, and at the same time almost without thinking pressed down a switch at the side of the door. Light from the chandelier flooded the room with a dazzling brilliance. Farnaby felt for a moment as if he were at the soundless flaring centre of an explosion. He heard Mooncranker speaking indistinctly behind him, and he was aware of enormous responsibility in shedding this bright light on Mooncranker's person. He held the door open and looked out. A strangely accoutred, veiled creature was fumbling on the threshold. It staggered a little, having apparently been leaning lightly against the door in its efforts to gain an entry, hampered in this by black leather gauntlets and by a sort of cylindrical weapon terminating in a nozzle, which it had been holding high up against black mackintoshed chest during the struggle with the lock. It must have been this that made the initial scraping sounds, Farnaby thought, regarding speechlessly this horrific, fumbling visitant whose features were entirely concealed beneath a thick black veil attached to the brim of a sort of helmet, like a large solar topee, also black, enclosing the whole face and head in a box-like, cage-like structure to some extent reminiscent of the apparatus worn by beekeepers but altogether sturdier and more impenetrable. Tall rubber wading-boots completed the picture and muffled syllables issued from behind the mask as the figure, having now regained its balance, confronted Farnaby. Eyepieces, in the form of glasses or goggles, gleamed disconcertingly from behind the veil. Farnaby heard a high-pitched voice, barely recognizable as Mooncranker's shout, 'It's the *groom*!' and a moment later a door slammed. The figure commenced to back towards the opposite wall but before reaching it turned away from Farnaby. It held the cylindrical instrument in both hands now. Raising its legs high off the ground with each step it began to walk away down the corridor.

Farnaby closed the door again carefully, retaining as he turned back into the room a very vivid image of that high-stepping black figure retreating down the brightly lit, empty corridor. 'He's gone now,' he called loudly towards the bedroom door, surmising that Mooncranker must have taken refuge in there. After a moment or two he repeated the call. The door opened a few inches and Mooncranker peered out. Seeing only Farnaby he opened it wider, straightened himself, and stood in the doorway, blinking rapidly and smoothing the hair back over his ears.

'Please put off that light, dear boy,' he said.

Farnaby obeyed, but even when the room was restored once more to its roseate dimness, Mooncranker did not move from his position in the doorway.

'There must be some perfectly good explanation,' Farnaby said.

'*You* rang for the groom,' Mooncranker said, and for a moment his expression appeared vindictive.

Farnaby said, 'I intend to follow the matter up.' He felt this utterance to be irreproachable, but it elicited no immediate response from Mooncranker who had lowered his head and seemed to be pondering. 'I shall phone down to the management,' Farnaby said.

At this Mooncranker looked up. 'No,' he said, 'Go down in person. It's the only way. I myself have always been noted for the intellectual rigour with which I have pursued everything and interred it, so to speak, *enshrouded* in its conclusion. Phoning is no good, you will only get at cross-purposes. Slip down and inquire.'

'Very well,' Farnaby said.

Mooncranker said, 'Excuse me one moment,' and closed the bedroom door in Farnaby's face, almost. Farnaby heard sounds of vomiting. Then complete silence. He left without attempting further speech with Mooncranker.

His face seemed the same in the lift mirror: long, large-jawed, equable. The clerk watched his approach with what might have been an intensification of sadness, resting immaculate hands flat on the reception desk. Farnaby knew that his Turkish was nowhere near adequate to the situation. 'You don't speak English, do you?' he said. 'Oh, *français*. Well, *s'il vous plaît, qui est l'homme masqué, avec les grands gants, qui a essayé d'entrer il y a quelques minutes la chambre numéro soixante-huit?*'

37

'*Masqué?*' the clerk said, frowning slightly.

'*Oui, masqué, je veux dire qu'il portait un chapeau avec une voile épaisse ...*'

'*On vous a volé?*' the clerk said.

'No, no. Not *vol, voile.*' Farnaby and the clerk regarded each other for several moments in silence. A sense of being inextricably entangled in Mooncranker's life as in a web, a sense of enmeshment and imprisonment possessed Farnaby. The present toils were linguistic only, but they were symptomatic he felt of an entrapment that had begun in the first seconds of his visit to Mooncranker. 'Yes,' he said dully, '*et il portait aussi des grandes bottes de pêcheur ...*'

'Excuse me,' a voice behind him said. 'Can I be of service to you?' The English was good except for an excessive sibilance. Turning he saw a slender, elegant middle-aged man with hair parted in the middle and luxuriant eyelashes. Slowly and carefully he described the visitation of the groom, then waited with a set and expressionless face while the matter was explained in Turkish to the clerk.

'It seems that a mistake was made,' his interpreter said, infusing these words with a courteous regret.

'Oh yes?'

'It was thought that your room was unoccupied.'

'Yes,' said Farnaby, 'but who actually *was* this person?'

'It is of no importance,' the other said, with a rather winning smile. 'Permit me to introduce myself. I am Papazian. Here is my card.'

'Thank you,' Farnaby said. 'James Farnaby. Look here, I should very much like to get to the bottom of this business.'

'I am a dealer in antiques,' Mr Papazian said. 'You are welcome any time at my shop, for business or just to take a coffee.'

'Thanks very much. Would you ask him again who the man was?'

'It is no use to ask these people anything,' Mr Papazian said. Nevertheless he turned again to the clerk and resumed his questioning. Farnaby assumed a look of conscious patience. He felt suddenly that he was living through the end of an era: nothing could ever be the same. Papazian was speaking to him again now, in his precise English. Farnaby listened gravely, head slightly inclined.

'Yes,' he said at last. 'Yes, I see.' He looked up at this moment, to see Mooncranker in a long black overcoat, hair standing up wildly, go rapidly across the lobby, looking neither to right nor left, and pass through the swing-doors at the entrance.

'Beetles you call them, I think,' Mr Papazian said.

'No, not beetles.' Farnaby made as if to withdraw. 'Thank you for your help,' he said. In his mind he had retained a vivid image of Mooncranker's wild, distraught pattern of movement against the rococo ornamentation of the lobby.

'Not beetles? How do you call them, these little creatures that infest the cracks?'

'I think they must be bugs, or termites perhaps. I shall have to be going I think.'

'Bugs, termites,' Papazian said to the clerk, reproachfully, as if he should have known that much English at least. 'Are you interested at all in antique coins?' he asked Farnaby.

'Not at the moment, thank you.'

'Icons?'

'No.'

'I offer competitive prices,' Mr Papazian said. 'My telephone number is on the card.'

'I will keep it in mind,' Farnaby said, and they shook hands. Mr Papazian's was small and hot and dry.

3

Outside on the pavement he looked up and down the street but there was no sign of Mooncranker. He did not know which way to go. He berated himself for his weakness in politely lingering there with the Armenian when he should have rushed in immediate pursuit. There was a peculiar desolation in having lost Mooncranker, particularly as he felt certain now that he had been sent to inquire about the groom so that Mooncranker could effect this escape.

After some hesitation he began walking back along the street the way he had come. The balconies were in darkness now. The night air was cold, too cold for sitting out of doors. He wondered whether the two girls were continuing their conversation elsewhere. There was a dankness in the atmosphere, no doubt emanating from the near-by waters of the Golden Horn; the street-lamps, old-fashioned and ornate in this part of the city, were faintly aureoled; they diffused their light. The fancy came to Farnaby that the lamps were *bandaged* with some gauzy material that muffled their light, and immediately he thought again of the figure on the cross that Mooncranker had handed him, which had actually been swathed in white bandage. Fashioned in sausage-meat and afterwards bound in white bandage. He could remember how *pure* the bandage had seemed to him. With a sort of familiar, almost cherished horror, as when some sequence in an evil dream or in delirium is recalled to mind, he remembered the clearing, the secret place at the far edge of the shrubbery, the seamed, grey trunk of the birch where he had pinned up the Christ. He had felt inviolable in that place because no one in the world knew of it. And yet it had been so close to the tennis-courts that he could hear the umpire's voice from there and the sharp, implosive sound of racquet meeting ball ... The cobbles of the street appeared to be exuding moisture. Ancient cities have their own secretions – processes analogous to the glandular. Looking down the street he could make out pockets of brighter light at the thresholds of the nightclubs whose festooned portals he had passed earlier, but it was still too early for any great concourse there. The sky above the street was black, scattered with pale stars. A feeling of alienation swept over Farnaby, a sense of being far from the source of any kindness. He thought of Mooncranker wandering distraught through the night in his long overcoat.

Unwilling to pass once again the long gallery of nude artistes, Farnaby turned off suddenly to his right down a narrow street, little more than an alley, with high blank walls on either side. His steps put cats to flight. The street declined steeply for the first hundred yards or so then levelled off to a junction with a rather broader one at right angles, and Farnaby again turned to the right with the vague idea of remaining in the neighbourhood of Mooncranker's hotel. After a minute or two the pavement widened into a semi-circular area with a small fountain set in the middle of it, enclosed on three sides by a railing. Farnaby paused at the fountain and conscientiously, by the light of the single street lamp, examined the panelling and sculpting of the two marble basins and the green and gilt Arabic characters above them informing the passer-by who built this fountain and in whose reign. From below him came the sudden, insanely brief whoop of a ferry boat. *In unfrequented by-ways of the old City, the visitor will stumble upon antique fountains whose excellent state of preservation bears witness to Turkish Piety and Love of Water.* Suddenly and quite unmistakably, from the darkness beyond the fountain, there came to Farnaby's ears the strangled, inhuman sounds of a person vomiting. He started forward round the fountain railing, arousing as he did so, however, a series of muttered plaints from a person he now saw for the first time, who had been sitting, perhaps sleeping, with his back to the railing. 'For the love of Allah,' he heard this seated person say. A beggar obviously, but he took no notice for the moment, peering into the gloom beyond, where hunched against the wall he could make out a tall figure. He advanced some paces towards this. 'Is that you, sir?' he said. The figure at once straightened itself, moved away from the wall and stood upright and motionless for a moment or two, looking towards him. He saw at once, from the high-shouldered stance and slightly vulturous dishevelment, that it was Mooncranker. But when he attempted to draw nearer, the other made a violent movement with his left arm, as if fending him off, then began to move rapidly away round the fountain railing. He circled the fountain on the opposite side from Farnaby, evoking in his passage fresh supplications and references to Allah from the seated figure. Then he made off at a rapid shambling walk down the alley the way Farnaby had come. Farnaby began to follow, but this meant passing the beggar again and he now saw that this man had no legs. He was lopped off at the upper thigh, terminating in a mass of rags. The cap was familiar and the voice. It was the man he had almost trodden on earlier. At

41

this moment the man raised his face and Farnaby saw that he had no nose either. His face was almost completely flat. What other features were missing or decayed he did not attempt to determine, keeping his own face averted while he fished in his pockets for *kurus*, then looking only at the outstretched palm into which he dropped the coins. The voice of the beggar did not change; the plaints continued behind Farnaby as he proceeded down the alley, reminding him now in some strange way of Mooncranker's voice, the same patient, gentle quality, as though speech were a sustained despairing signalling, not an attempt to converse.

His delay with the beggar had lost him some ground. When he emerged on the main street he thought he had lost Mooncranker again, then saw him on the other side, still walking rapidly and surprisingly steadily in a direction away from the hotel. He followed circumspectly. He had no plan, no idea of what to do or say when he came up to Mooncranker again. But he felt it to be terribly important to keep the other in sight. With something like fifty yards between them they traversed a number of streets unfamiliar to Farnaby, finally emerging at Tunel, the terminus of the underground train. He thought for a moment that Mooncranker intended to enter and get a ticket but he turned left up Istiklal Caddesi. The pavements here were crowded. Bars, cinemas and restaurants were brightly lit. Mooncranker was halted at a junction, waiting for a gap in traffic that would allow him to cross. Farnaby saw him turn and say something to two young men standing waiting beside him, saw one of them shake his head in perplexity, saw Mooncranker courteously smiling. He put on speed and came up to them. 'Can I help you, sir?' he offered.

'Oh, you speak English?' Mooncranker said. 'I wonder if you could tell me the address of a doctor in the vicinity? You see, I am looking for a doctor. I am a stranger in this city. Though I have been here before. I was here before the war, you know, several times. And again in 1956.'

'I know of one near the British Embassy,' Farnaby said, 'not very far from here. I'll go with you if you like.' He was not sure whether Mooncranker genuinely did not recognize him or was merely affecting not to do so.

'That is really extraordinarily kind of you.'

'We can go down this way,' Farnaby said. They turned into a narrow, less frequented street. Walking side by side with Mooncranker meant a series of small collisions of shoulders and arms, since he was swaying very slightly as he walked.

'It is pleasant,' Mooncranker said, 'to meet with a fellow countryman in a foreign city. To tell you the truth, what I need is vitamin B.'

'Vitamin B?'

'I must have some.'

'But why?' Farnaby was bewildered. It was as if Mooncranker had suddenly asked for some bauble or delicacy.

'I fear I am becoming dehydrated,' Mooncranker said shyly. 'I have not been able to keep anything down for some days. That is a regrettable phrase. If I don't get some vitamin B quickly, I'm afraid I shall be gravely ill, gravely ill.' He said this in an almost facetious way, as if he too felt that it was an absurd thing to be suddenly asking for.

'But how are we going to get vitamin B?' Farnaby said. 'We could not get any without a prescription.' He felt offended with Mooncranker for this assumption that one can just walk up and get things without going through the proper procedure.

'Is that the doctor's house?' Mooncranker said, stopping and peering upwards. 'There is a plate on the wall.'

'No,' said Farnaby, after a moment's scrutiny. 'That is a circumciser, not a doctor.'

'He wouldn't have any vitamin B, I suppose?'

'Highly unlikely,' Farnaby said. 'No, it's farther down. How do you propose to get some?'

'I thought we might simply ask for some, dear boy.'

'He would insist on examining you.'

'Not necessarily.' Mooncranker felt himself beginning to tremble and strove to conceal this by hunching up his shoulders and thrusting his hands into the pockets of his overcoat. 'Not necessarily,' he repeated. 'Some time ago, in Athens, a person was able to obtain some for me. My secretary as a matter of fact. She is not available at the moment, unfortunately. Well, I will be frank with you, she has decamped. Ask for it in tablet form.'

'She must have a way with her,' Farnaby said. He was impressed by this resourcefulness of the secretary's. It had haphappened before then, similar binges, culminating in vitamin B deficiencies. It was not now too fanciful to think that in those Oaklands days, that long white summer of his umpiring, there had been times when a similar charge of nourishment had been needed . . .

'I have a wife too,' Mooncranker said. 'But we are estranged.'

'This is the doctor's,' Farnaby said.

They stood together at the foot of the steps and Farnaby noticed that Mooncranker's whole body was shaking. He brought the events of the evening together in rapid review, remembered Mooncranker's abrupt changes of manner and mood, his vomiting, the way his drunkenness had seemed to fluctuate. He sensed too that the other, though striving to keep up a certain suavity, was really quite badly frightened at the prospect of dehydration. 'We can but try, I suppose,' he said, and experienced, as he turned to mount the steps, an appalling insight into Mooncranker's real condition. This person was capable of self-destruction, was one of that select and terrifying band capable of this, not by snapping the thread in some violent gesture of despair, but by a prolonged course of self-outrage, weakening himself, hurting himself repeatedly to the point of death. The first exponent of this uniquely human art that he had met.

He got to the top of the steps, selected the doctor's bell, and pushed it. He had not been waiting long, however, when he realized something was wrong. Mooncranker had not followed him up the steps. He felt himself to be alone, standing there. He turned and looked behind him, but Mooncranker was nowhere to be seen. The pavement at the foot of the steps was empty. He looked rapidly up the street towards the thoroughfare they had left: no time for him to have got that far. He must have taken the other way, farther down the dim street. Farnaby had heard nothing; but then, he had been concentrating on the manner to adopt when the door was opened, he had not been alert for sounds behind him. He began to descend the steps. At this point, however, the door was opened by a stout woman in a white overall and he lost some moments trying to explain things to this person who stood motionless above him irradiated by light from within the house. She made no reply to his stammered apologies, merely stared at him silently. He made an awkward gesture of farewell and set off along the pavement at a brisk pace. There was no sign of Mooncranker in front of him.

Perhaps he crossed over and went down this side street. Yes that was it, he must have crossed immediately or I should have been bound to see him. Moreover it was the sort of thing he would do, having lost his nerve at the last minute, he would seek, like any creature in extremity, darkness and a narrow space.

Entering the sidestreet, Farnaby acknowledged himself unambiguously now the hunter, felt the other as a quarry, already wounded, he was stalking through the streets of the city, but whether to heal or destroy he was not sure. He thought of the beggar at the fountain. Vitamins for Mooncranker: for that noseless, legless creature a handful of coppers. Palliatives both. A pity there is no absolute remedy for all the misery sitting or lying or walking about in the dark. But of course there is one...

Nobody passed him in this narrow street. Far away, in the night beyond the city, a ship's siren sounded. He heard from time to time the rattle of trams from the busy street that ran parallel to this one. It occurred to him suddenly that there existed, after all, hospitals – with rooms kept lighted all through the night – waiting to receive people like Mooncranker. Perhaps he could persuade Mooncranker to become a patient at such a place. He had no doubt that he would find Mooncranker again...

The street curved, joined at a very acute angle another wider one, with a small mosque at the junction, the courtyard of which abutted on the pavement. An alley ran along the side of the mosque, which meant that there were three ways Mooncranker could have gone. Farnaby paused at the corner, not knowing which way to take. Opposite him, light and a low babble of voices came from beyond a narrow door with an upper part of frosted glass. He walked slowly across the street, opened the door and looked in. As usual with city bars of the cheaper sort, the long narrow room was almost unfurnished, brightly lit by the harsh white light from the fluorescent strips overhead. A handful of men stood at the bar, among whom he saw Mooncranker immediately, at the far end with his back to the white wall. He entered the room and went up to Mooncranker, who at once drained his glass, as if Farnaby's purpose in approaching him had been to appropriate it.

'Ah,' Mooncranker said. 'So this is one of your haunts. This is where you get to. This is Farnaby,' he said, leaning over the counter and addressing the barman, a thickset man with small ears who reminded Farnaby very strongly of the wrestlers he had seen earlier. 'This is Farnaby,' Mooncranker repeated. 'I was just telling you about him. My friend from the Oaklands days.' The barman, several of whose teeth were missing, grinned and nodded. He seemed to find Mooncranker in some way comical.

'*Raki güzel*, eh?' he said.

Mooncranker raised his glass, which the barman had refilled.

'They don't stock gin,' he said to Farnaby. 'Will you have a drink?'

'No, thanks.' Farnaby said.

'He has given up the habit,' Mooncranker said to the barman. 'He has conquered it.' His eyes were bright and he seemed steadier, more in control of his movements. There was no way of knowing whether he associated Farnaby at all with the person who had accompanied him on the abortive visit to the doctor's.

'Happy days,' Mooncranker said, raising his glass. He did not mind drinking in front of Farnaby here. This was a bar.

'Oaklands for ever!' he said.

'I don't know if you remember,' Farnaby said, drawing nearer to Mooncranker and speaking in low tones. 'But once you gave me a present. I don't know if you remember. A small figure of the Crucifixion.'

'No, my secretary must have taken it with her,' Mooncranker said instantly. 'She will be back shortly. My secretary has left me in the lurch,' he said to the barman.

'No, I'm talking about that summer holiday,' Farnaby said. Relief at finding Mooncranker again had emboldened him. 'I saw you, you know. Go and get it I mean. And I saw you talk to somebody just before. Yes. I was in the garden. Why did you give me such a thing?' He looked closely into Mooncranker's face as he spoke. The eyes seemed to be looking beyond him. 'Don't you remember?' he said. Suddenly Mooncranker's mouth twitched upwards in that brief grimace which was so familiar.

'He used to umpire for us in our tennis matches,' Mooncranker said, turning his gaze slowly towards the barman. His eyes were now completely unfocused. 'George Wilson had two sons, Henry and Frederick,' he said. 'Budding gynaecologists. He is the salt of the earth.' His voice had slurred again.

'*Baska?*' the barman said.

'No,' Farnaby said. 'Don't have another one. Let's go back to the hotel.'

'Very well, dear boy.'

This compliance surprised Farnaby, gave him his first taste of that half unwilling sense of power which was later to colour so strongly his relations with Mooncranker. It was Mooncranker who led the way now, walking upright and steady out of the bar and some yards along the pavement outside. Suddenly, however, and without warning, he doubled up, clinging helplessly to Farnaby's arm. Completely inert like this he was a dead weight, and Farnaby had to exert himself considerably to hold him up, prevent him from collapsing on to the pavement. In this way the two of them shuffled along together fifty yards or so, like a single crippled animal with two labouring heads. Then Mooncranker relinquished Farnaby's arm and clutched at a lamp-post, refusing to go farther. Standing above him, heart thumping, Farnaby could see in the lamplight the pathetic paucity of hair at the crown, streaks of pale scalp shining through, the affrighted curling wisps low on the neck. That side of Mooncranker's face which was visible was damp and livid, slightly contorted.

'It's my back,' he muttered, holding on to the lamp-post with both hands.

Farnaby looked up and down the street. He did not want to

attract attention in case it ended up as a police matter. He bent down and spoke solicitously into Mooncranker's ear. 'You wait here for a minute or two while I go and get hold of a taxi.'

There was no response from Mooncranker who remained in a hunched position holding on to the lamp-post. Farnaby set off down the street. He had been hoping to emerge once more on Istiklal Caddesi, but the twistings and turnings of Mooncranker had ended by destroying his own sense of direction and he did not find again the mosque on the corner, which he had been keeping in his mind as a landmark. Instead he came after some minutes to a small square with a kiosk in the centre, a tea-house and a few shuttered shops. There was a tram-station here but nobody was waiting. However, a number of men were sitting gravely in the tea-house and Farnaby was about to go in and ask about taxis when a *dolmus* entered the square and began to go slowly round it. It stopped at his signal. He got in and pointed out to the completely silent driver the way he wanted to go. They found the street again without any difficulty, but Mooncranker was not there. The lamp-post stood solitary in its pool of light. The street was empty. After a moment of consternation, since he had been quite sure Mooncranker was too ill to move, Farnaby instructed the driver to turn right at the next junction. They negotiated several one-way streets and found themselves back outside the bar again. The driver turned his head and looked inquiringly at Farnaby. *'Simdi nerede?'*

In near despair Farnaby gestured to the left, another lucky guess – indeed it was to occur to him subsequently how often that evening he had got on to Mooncranker's track in this accidental way – because immediately on turning the corner he saw Mooncranker half-way down the street, walking in the same direction with his head down, and staggering slightly.

'Arkadasim,' Farnaby said eagerly to the driver, pointing at Mooncranker. 'He is ill.'

They drew up alongside and Farnaby got out. 'Here's the taxi,' he said, not making any reference to Mooncranker's defection from the lamp-post. The other made no demur about getting in. He seemed now to be beyond protesting or indeed reacting at all to anything. Farnaby gave the name of the hotel.

No one spoke on the way back. Farnaby paid off the driver, tipping him extravagantly, concerned before all else not to let his charge escape again. He supported Mooncranker through the lobby, under the gaze of the reception clerk, into the lift and up to room sixty-eight. Mooncranker made immediately for the bathroom where he remained for the following fifteen minutes or so.

He wandered back finally, high-shouldered and chalky of face, dressed now in a green dressing-gown with a tasselled cord round the middle. His back did not seem to be troubling him so much, but he appeared to have forgotten again who Farnaby was. He sat on the edge of the divan, plucking at his tassels, talking in a slow patient voice about the extensive use made by the Ottoman Sultans in the *belle époque* of aphrodisiacs. At one point he wept a little; the tears flowed easily, without checking his discourse. Farnaby found two salami sandwiches – remnant of some former meal – and ate one. Mooncranker was persuaded to have some of the other, but after a couple of mouthfuls he went purposefully off to the bathroom again and the closed door did not completely shut out the sounds he made there. This cannot go on, Farnaby told himself as Mooncranker reappeared and stood groggily before him. But the terrible thing dawning on him was that it could: there seemed no foreseeable end to the suffering Mooncranker could absorb, the metamorphoses he could undergo. Indeed, in the different faces he put on his sickness and pain, the transitions he managed to effect between incompatible moods, the varying control he achieved over his own body and movements, there was something slippery and repugnant to Farnaby; something protean, indecent, even frightening, almost as if it were a physical property of Mooncranker's to squirm and change. It occurred to him suddenly how strange it was that Mooncranker should not have referred in any way to the strangely accoutred figure who had scratched on their door.

'That groom, you know,' he said. 'It was a fumigator really.'

Mooncranker appeared not to hear this. 'Let's face it,' he said with a rather ghastly attempt at urbanity. 'That is a horrid phrase, don't you think?'

'Yes, it is, isn't it?'

'Employed exclusively by those aspiring to managerial status.' His mouth was too slack now for that civilized twitch. 'You will no doubt recall that phrase about the collarless herd who eat blancmange and never say anything witty? They wear collars now, and they eat frozen scampi, and they say "Let's face it". I have never heard such nonsense in my life.'

'I think "Pardon my French" is an absolutely detestable expression, don't you?' Farnaby said.

'Nonsense, quite a different kettle of fish, that is a phrase I employ constantly. Without euphemism our civilization would collapse. Some of you may think that the life of a radio and television personality is all beer and skittles but I am going to tell you something now. It is a harsh, keen struggle, it is a fiercely competitive world. There are highlights of course. Moments stand out like ... er ... radiant peaks. I remember once interviewing a famous philosopher, just as an illustration of what I mean, he had a bladder ailment, yes. Marvellously lucid and articulate, he looked like a remote goat. The snag was that he had to be getting up every few minutes. That was quite some editing job as I daresay you can well imagine. Er ... Farnaby.'

'Yes.'

'That *is* your name, isn't it? Farnaby of Oaklands?'

'Yes.'

'I must have some vitamin B.'

'Vitamin B?'

'I need vitamin B, Farnaby, as a restorative.'

'I doubt if you'll get any without a prescription.'

'On similar occasions, my secretary –'

'Yes, I know she managed it, but I haven't got her powers of persuasion, probably. I don't think there's much point in wandering about looking for vitamin B, actually, besides we've already tried it once, haven't we? No, the only thing I can think of is the hospital.'

Mooncranker remained silent at this, looking at Farnaby blankly.

'The French hospital at Harbiye,' Farnaby said firmly. 'They will have facilities there ... I'll go with you, if you like.' He looked at Mooncranker who was plucking at his tassels again fussily. Suddenly and with a sensation of pure amazement, he perceived that he had arrived at a position of power over Mooncranker. It had never occurred to him as possible that power could flow that way.

Mooncranker raised his head. His lips were bloodless. 'Very well,' he said. 'Perhaps it would be wise.'

'No time like the present,' Farnaby said, infusing this with a sort of cheerful briskness he was far from feeling.

'If I am entering the portals of a hospital,' Mooncranker said, 'I suppose I'd better have a shower.'

'By all means.' Farnaby spoke as one granting permission.

After a short time, Mooncranker reappeared, dressed now in a dark grey suit. He looked dispirited, meek and sick, damp hair combed back over his ears, shoulders high and disconsolate.

'It was impossible,' he said, 'to obtain any hot water.'

Farnaby smiled sympathetically, trying not to think of Mooncranker having a cold shower, the fine spray playing over Mooncranker's long, thin shrinking whiteness, veined nerveless arms clutching suffering torso, wretched genitals purpling and pimpling at the onset of the chill. It was the sort of vision, the sort of knowledge of Mooncranker he had been resisting ever since his arrival: the apprehension of the other as forked animal, idiosyncratic and frail, stripped of his insignia of straw hats, flannels, vestments of authority, mantle of Uncle George's approval; simply the creature, naked and fearful, writhing beneath the cold mist of the shower, behaving unstoically. This was not the person who had handed him the gift that distant summer day. That person was dressed in white, in command of himself. He leaned forward, courteously, his face under the straw hat smiling. A civilized twitch at the corners of the mouth.

'Let's go, shall we,' Farnaby said.

Part Two

1

Tall iron gates set open; a locked and deserted lodge at the
side; the great white building before them faintly incandescent,
with an irregular pattern of lighted windows; hushed forecourt. They were required to wait for some time in a corner of
the marble-appointed entrance-hall, dimly lit in this quiet time
of evening by small lamps bracketed against the white walls.
The floor was covered with squares of some rubbery material,
beige in colour. Farnaby remained standing while Mooncranker, who looked completely exhausted, sat on the marble
bench that ran along the whole length of the wall and, after a
moment or two, closed his eyes. A very faint humming sound,
like the sound of distant bees, emerged from his closed lips.
Farnaby glanced at his watch: not quite eleven. Four hours
ago Mooncranker and I were distinct and separate persons.
Now, though he is sitting and I am standing, try as I may to
resist, I am implicated in the chill that will be striking from the
cold marble through the thin cloth on to those meagre, flat-
tened buttocks.

This entrance-hall had an extraordinary acoustical reson-
ance, perhaps due to the marble, the absence of furniture in it.
That quiet humming seemed to fill the whole space from floor
to ceiling. From time to time steps sounded along the corridors
beyond the hall, and on two occasions pairs of nursing sisters
in white robes and stiff white head-dresses passed through the
hall; each of them, as though especially sensitive by nature
or training to distress, looking only at the seated man. A
slow deliberate movement of the head-dress. A long regard.
A slither of steps on the floor, a rustle of skirts, they were
gone.

A doctor appeared at last; a slender, youngish man with an
alert carriage of the head. He approached them soundlessly on

white plimsolls. His white coat was somewhat too large – it descended towards his ankles and had been rolled up neatly at the sleeves. Farnaby explained the situation in low tones.

'There are withdrawal symptoms?' the doctor said, in careful English.

'Not that I know of,' Farnaby said. Calm brown eyes surveyed him lingeringly. 'I have not noticed anything of that kind,' he said again, defensively, as if some negligence were being imputed.

Mooncranker had stopped humming as soon as he heard voices, but his eyes were still closed.

'When did he stop drinking?' the doctor asked.

'About two hours ago.'

'I have a colleague here on duty who has specialized in such disorders.' The doctor gave Mooncranker a swift, impersonal regard. 'She has studied in America,' he added. 'I am going now to inform her.'

This time the wait was briefer. The lady doctor walked quickly across the hall towards them. Her open white coat billowed out somehow expectantly behind her. She was young, about thirty, with long, very dark hair and lustrous quick-glancing eyes and a square-shouldered, stocky figure. The unbuttoned coat showed mohair beneath, a bosom of impressive proportions rigorously confined.

'Is this the man?' she said, and Mooncranker hearing no doubt the note of authority in the question, opened his eyes and got to his feet. He assumed a dejected penitent air. In the grip now of clinicians, he essayed no extravagances of speech or manner.

'You are an alcoholic,' the doctor said, in the tone of a statement.

'Yes,' Mooncranker said, looking fixedly at her.

'Whisky, gin, *raki*?'

'Yes.'

'No, which? I mean which?'

'Yes.' Mooncranker said. He swallowed painfully. He looked extremely ill. 'Gin,' he said.

'Ah,' said the doctor. She looked significantly at Farnaby, as if to make sure that the import of these questions was not escaping him. 'You stopped when? The last drink, how many hours ago?'

'About two hours ago.'

The doctor's manner seemed to become more intense, more portentous. 'How much did you drink in the last twenty-four hours?'

'I don't know, actually,' Mooncranker said.

'Two bottles, three?'

'Yes.'

'*Large* bottles,' the doctor said to Farnaby, with a kind of triumph. She nodded her head at him, narrowed her brilliant eyes, in some private appraisal. Farnaby had an uneasy sense that he was being somehow mingled with Mooncranker in the doctor's mind, involved medically, as if he were one of Mooncranker's more easily recognizable symptoms. 'I thought I'd better bring him along,' he said.

'How do you feel now?' the doctor said, and her question fell between them.

'Not very well.' It was Mooncranker who answered, in his slow, deep-toned voice. 'I have been vomiting frequently since mid-morning, I cannot eat anything without vomiting almost immediately afterwards. To be quite frank with you, I am afraid of becoming dehydrated.'

'Dehydrated,' the doctor echoed, in the tone of one whole-heartedly concurring. It seemed to Farnaby that her bosom heaved. She held up pale, short-fingered hands, palms outward. 'Put your finger tips against my palms,' she said, and Mooncranker obeyed. While this contact endured she looked shrewdly at Farnaby.

'Yes,' she said finally. 'Yes, yes. You have got the shakes, haven't you?' And indeed contact with Mooncranker had caused her two hands visibly to vibrate as at the communication of some dynamic force or current. She looked into Mooncranker's face as if seeking to elicit some vivid personal statement or demonstration in keeping with her own sense of the seriousness of his condition; but Mooncranker maintained the same dejected air he had worn ever since being obliged to take a cold shower. He stood there shaking, meeting her brilliant, highly charged, almost beseeching regard with a white blank

54

face. She switched her gaze suddenly to Farnaby, who had been allowing his thoughts to dwell with too great a particularity on her full-breasted, thick-waisted, possibly slightly deformed body, and who was consequently rather disconcerted by the sudden transference of her attention to him.

She said, 'He cannot be admitted for treatment – and he needs treatment badly, at once, he is very ill – unless there are with him two strong boys.'

'Two strong boys?'

'Yourself say, and a friend, remaining with him throughout the night.'

'Surely that isn't necessary,' Farnaby said in gentle tones – pleased to be thought of by the doctor as a strong boy.

'Absolutely essential you do not leave his side throughout the night.'

'No, I mean about needing two. My friend is very calm, as you can see.'

'Ah, yes, perhaps so, to the outside appearance. But when the withdrawal pains are on him, it is a different story. In that madness two strong boys will find it difficult, even two of you, to nail him down. He will struggle.' A shade of doubt, however, appeared to cross her face as she looked again at Mooncranker's features and bearing, of such a conspicuous mildness and dejection were they. 'We could not manage it without two strong boys,' she said.

Mooncranker endured this scrutiny dumbly. He had broken out in a sweat again.

'They shout loudly,' the doctor said. 'They writhe, and enter into convulsions.' Something, however, some element of confidence, had disappeared from her manner.

'Look here, I need vitamin B,' Mooncranker said, or perhaps again it was merely felt, not actually uttered, because neither of the two persons with him looked in his direction. He had not been able to follow their conversation, largely because he was concentrating so hard on maintaining his upright posture. He did not know how this was being achieved, having lost all sense of the weight of his body and its centres of balance, but he knew that there was a certain distance between his head and the floor and that this distance must be kept more or less constant. I need infusions of minerals and vital salts. I need my plasma restoring. The doctor's white coat hurt his eyes. He saw without being able to believe it completely a person in a white wimple crossing the hall, a pink expressionless face framed in this white head-dress looked full at him, turned away, glided past. I need the ministrations of nurses.

The lady doctor said, 'One man once, a Turk – it was during my first year here – a man with a similar complaint, escaped from the sisters who were trying to restrain him and threw himself in delirium from an upper window. He was dashed to pieces below.'

'My goodness,' Farnaby said. They both turned to regard Mooncranker again, as if hoping for some frantic symptoms.

'Their strength is greatly enhanced,' the doctor said.

'Well actually,' Farnaby said, 'I don't think he's that sort at all. I don't think he wants to drink any more. I think he's frightened and he wants to be cured.' He had taken this line because of the difficulty of finding another strong boy, but as soon as he began speaking he knew it to be absolutely true. Mooncranker has had interviews of this sort before, he thought. These thoughts and sensations he has had before, in bars, in streets, in lonely rooms. Changing his socks. Examining his tongue. He is interested in the doctor only as representative of a Healing System, an organization within which he seeks self-repair. She is the drip-feed, the vitamin injection.

He said, 'I think I could manage on my own. If I promised to stay with him the whole time ...'

The doctor paused, considering. Then, 'Very well,' she said sharply, as if with an access of impatience or frustration.

'But it will be your responsibility. You must not leave his side during the night. Wait here please.' To Mooncranker she said, 'This way please, would you follow me.' He walked after her in the wake of her billowing coat without another glance at Farnaby.

Farnaby waited there till almost midnight. An old man and a pregnant woman entered the hall during this time and were respectively met and led away by nursing-sisters. Once he thought he heard a distant outcry of voices; twice there was a rattle like the wheels of a trolley from some near-by corridor. Otherwise the place was silent, with a silence that seemed fraught and threatened, like that in a very lonely, enclosed place or a deep forest. Along the white wall, some feet above the bench, were smudges where weary heads had rested. Creatures had waited here, just as he was waiting, till a regard should fall on them. The weight of sickness and succour that he felt in the hospital was oppressive to him. 'This Christian Enclave in the heart of' – his mental note collapsed before it could be properly framed. There was a stiff and undistinguished oil-painting of the Holy Family on the opposite wall. He stared at it for some minutes, closed his eyes finally on the dimpled infant, the gravely attentive mother. Many believe that the Mother of God took ship for Asia Minor after her son's death, and ended her days at Ephesus. I myself have no views about this. Where she died to me is immaterial...

'Bon soir, monsieur.'

He opened his eyes on a nakedly benign face framed by a white head-dress.

'Bon soir, ma soeur.'

'If you will have the goodness to follow me.'

Down brightly lit corridors where smells of ether and disinfectant contended. Two turns to the right, one to the left, through another, narrower hall, left again ... He ceased to take note of the way they were taking.

'Your friend is in here,' the nun said and gave him a bright conspiratorial smile, at the same time holding open the door. He saw Mooncranker's profile against a pillow, turned to thank his guide, but the door was already closing behind him. There were two beds in the room and Mooncranker lay in one of them, bathed in light from a standard lamp near the head of it. He was lying on his back staring calmly up at the ceiling. A white coverlet was drawn up to his neck. His left arm lay outside the coverlet – the institutional white pyjama jacket had been rolled up and something, some attachment, was bound round the forearm. A bottle containing clear liquid was suspended above him and attached to him by thin tubing. He did not turn his head at Farnaby's entrance. There was absolutely no sound in the room. For a moment Farnaby stood there, gazing. The protean Mooncranker had undergone yet another metamorphosis. He was himself now swaddled, swathed in white. This was so startling that Farnaby found himself for the moment unable to move. He had expected to see Mooncranker in the guise of patient. But to find him resembling that corruptible Christ, to experience this sudden confusion between the giver and the gift, was more than he was for the moment prepared for.

'So there you are,' Mooncranker said, in his customary deep-toned voice.

'Yes. Is there anything I can do for you, sir?'

'Nothing. I would be well enough on my own here.'

'I am obliged to stay with you.'

'Yes, I know.' Mooncranker continued to look up at the ceiling, which undulated or heaved, like an oily sea, but very, very slightly. The injection they had given him was taking full effect now. His limbs were leaden and his own voice sounded remote in his ears. 'They expect me to start frothing and screeching shortly,' he said. 'But I am afraid I must disappoint them. I have never gone in for that kind of thing. Many of us don't, you know. It is only the exhibitionists. Where is the other strong boy?'

'I couldn't find one.' Farnaby sat on the edge of the other bed.

'A pity. The pair of you might have put on a show. Weight-lifting or something of that sort.'

'Ha, ha, yes,' Farnaby said. He bent down, unlaced his shoes and slipped them off. His jacket too he took off and laid at the foot of the bed. Then he lay down full length, not getting inside the sheets however.

'Reverting to regrettable phrases,' Mooncranker said, 'things that are better not uttered, there are people who actually say: "Hello there!" and others, or perhaps they are the same, who say: "Good-bye now!"' Drowsiness was overcoming him – he resisted it in the blissful knowledge of ultimate defeat. 'Show business people,' he added, in a voice that had slurred again.

'What does dehydration actually involve?' Farnaby asked, regarding his own section of ceiling earnestly.

'You have a thirst for knowledge, I see. Three quarters of

the body is water. That is the first fact you have to get into focus, young Farnaby, we are composed very largely of water.' He paused.

It was becoming difficult now to understand him because of the way his words ran together. After a few moments he went on, very slowly:

'There is a plasma in the blood, to put the matter simply, to put it at its very simplest, and this plasma in the blood, if this plasma is diminished ...'

After waiting a little while for the sentence to be finished, Farnaby looked across and saw that Mooncranker was apparently sleeping. He watched in some fascination the colourless fluid in the bottle suspended above Mooncranker. The level was steady; but from moment to moment a globule was dispatched down the tube on its vital mission of redressing the plasma deficit in Mooncranker's veins. Farnaby could trace the run of the bubble all the way down the tube. The bloodless profile had a certain nobility in it, Farnaby thought, a sort of beaky austerity. It brought him in mind of death-masks. Impossible too, seeing the other's features in such wax-like detail, to go on confusing him with the little effigy bound in bandage, which had had no features at all, merely the shape of a head ... It was, however, possible, he reminded himself, by studying the accidental folds of the bandage, to attribute features to that little figure, eyes, a nose and mouth. I thought of him, in a way, as *helmeted*, perhaps solely because of this lack of forehead or hair. Besides, features were not necessary; they were not necessary to a sense of his humanity, hanging on the cross. Cross of lathe roughly sawn to the right proportion of crosspiece and stake, roughly nailed together. The figure tied, not pinned, to it. How did Mooncranker know that I would venerate the gift? From the previous October my thoughts had been filled with that sacrifice, with the beauty of Christ's holiness. That October I was thirteen. Just a month before they gave me a New Testament for twenty-five consecutive attendances. A blue cover and gold lettering, the new paper smelled of purity and loneliness. *I am the way the truth and the light, no man cometh unto the father but through me*. And that winter I prayed among the others, for the first time, all of us

59

kneeling, a silence, and then my voice speaking confidentially
to God. 'I did not realize this,' the Leader said, 'I did not fully
understand that you had made this decision until I heard your
voice raised in prayer.' The Leader had a luxuriant fair
moustache, red lips. He was an accountant and a pacifist. 'I
have often been troubled by impure thoughts,' he once told us.
He told the assembled class about his struggles against the
temptations of the flesh. 'Now I thank God you have made
this decision,' he said to me. 'You must bear witness, of course,
but do not feel that you have to tell your parents at once.'
Leading the chorus with his joyous baritone, I will make you
Fishers of Men if you follow me. For a year of my life I
thought that I would be a Fisher of Men, netting the sinners,
reeling them in from pools of sloth and sin, hauled naked and
spasming from the depths, to have their gills adapted. Breathe
on me breath of God. I suppose I believed in this mission till
that summer afternoon when Christ's putrefaction was conveyed to my nostrils. Believed in it even though I knew I was
sinning all the time, and making him my accomplice in it. No
doubt that Christ became my accomplice ...

The drip goes down the tube like a flexing of light into
Mooncranker's sleeping arm. No dreams appear to be troubling
him. How did he know I was vulnerable to Christ? I was on
holiday after all, a sort of holiday, no, you cannot call it by
this name when your parents are getting divorced, and find it
more convenient not to have you at home. No, but at any rate
a stranger there, I had told no one of my obsessions. Let me
try to remember. Somewhere, in some mind or place or piece
of behaviour there must be the essential clue to it. Let me try
to remember ...

I see him come round the side of the house. Where am I
standing? He comes round the side of the house, dressed in
white, wearing a straw hat with a black band. I am in the
shrubbery of course, but how does he know I am here? Is that
why he stops on the way, to find out where I am? He does
stop, that is certain. Someone must have told him. Who is he
talking to there? Someone hidden from me, someone I never
saw. Or perhaps he has seen me from an upper window. The
gift is there, in somebody's room up there perhaps. Some-

where. Ready to be bestowed on me. The sausage-meat has been bought, at the butcher's in the high street, conveyed home, moulded while still moist and malleable into shape, bound in clean white folds of bandage, tied (not pinned) to its cross of lathe. Giver and gift in readiness, recipient located. The work of a moment to take it up, walk through the shrubbery preparing his smile. The stop on the way, is that premeditated? There is something in his posture, while he stands there conversing, some quality of deliberate elegance, that I have noted in him before. I do not know, however, if this is an impression stemming from that moment or something I thought later. Impossible now to be sure.

It could not have been Henry or Frederick, the two sons of Uncle George, aspiring gynaecologists, they were playing tennis. Standing at the baseline driving at the ball with all their strength. Playing a good hard game, they would doubtless have called it, no quarter given or asked. No subtlety. Daily delving now perhaps into afflicted females. Gropian in the fallopian. On the bonny banks of Clyde. Uncle George's job is vague in my mind. He was in some way responsible for sanitation, over a wide area. He went off every day in a green Rover. He was a rugger blue. All that family argued about facts all the time, in loud hectoring voices. Things that could have been verified. Which is the longest river in the world? What was the date of issue of the very first postage-stamp? Uncle George, however, the ultimate acknowledged authority in all questions relating to names, dates, maps, time-tables, things actually taking place in the external world. *Un homme pour qui le monde visible existe*. The latest A.A. touring book was always on his shelves; he referred to the maps at the back with clean fingers. He moved among works of reference with confidence. No possibility, ever, of his failing to find an answer. Authority in every lineament. Even in the act of urinating, Uncle George maintained complete control. When was it? Very distant morning, cold and pearly, thin white ice in furrows. A party for a morning walk. As so often before and since I was separated from the brisk, loud-voiced group, in among the bushes, the bramble and bryony leaves gushing in bare hedges, thrushes' nests forlornly full of snow and crouching among all this and there was Uncle George, overcoat unbuttoned, feet planted apart, strange sharp-looking instrument spraying a precise arc. His urine glittered palely. Face severe, abstracted. He shook it up and down, before buttoning up. Strange, fearsome, this tapering white root of Uncle George's being. But he handled it, he managed the whole manoeuvre, with the confidence, the surety, with which he would have flicked through an index, a distance chart. Such casual adult efficiency. I do not think I should have been surprised to see him dismantle his member piece by piece, unscrewing first the sharp nozzle, what a contrast to my own absorbed, half terrified fumblings, stirrings, swellings, pulsations . . .

Aunt Jane perhaps provoked such reactions in him, though that is difficult to believe. Aunt Jane died. That was years later. She had a seizure while pruning the roses at the front of the house, and had to be carried indoors. That was years later. She met me at the station, that summer I came to stay, that summer I played with Miranda as my partner in the tennis-tournament, and Mooncranker gave me the gift. She met me at the station.

2

Aunt Jane met him at the station. She picked him out from all the other emerging passengers with a 'there you are' and a kiss and he was surprised in a way that she didn't need to hesitate more over it. He would have had to. He remembered her of course, the thinness, grey hair, eyes still as blue as when she was a young girl, as he had heard his mother say. Lines of control about the mouth, as if Aunt Jane were combating convulsions all the time.

'My, how you've grown,' she said.

'You haven't changed at all, Aunt Jane,' he said, smiling at her but not too beamingly. A broad smile would not have been seemly in one like himself with the smack of bereavement about him. No one had died, but his parents were going through a bad patch, as he had heard it described. They had decided to separate for a bit and see how that worked out.

'Well, come on,' she said. 'I expect you're ready for something to eat, aren't you?'

He refused to let her carry his case. They walked across to the station car-park where Aunt Jane had left her car, a grey Morris Minor. She drove with visible nervousness at first, sitting bolt upright, narrowing her eyes over the steering-wheel. When they had left the city-centre, however, and got into the suburbs where traffic was thinner, she grew more confident and began pointing out to him some of the changes that had taken place – new houses, a big green roundabout. But his last visit had been five years previously, when he was only eight; such changes of detail were lost on him, everything was unfamiliar. It was new territory to him, and the fact that Aunt Jane didn't see this made him realize that in the stress of driving and talking at the same time she was forgetting who he was.

Uncle George must have heard them coming down the drive, because he appeared at the door as they were getting out of the car. Booming, presumably welcoming sounds issued from him, in which however at this distance no words could be distinguished. The boy walked over to the front steps and stood there, in his neat grey flannel suit, strapped suitcase on the ground beside him, stood smiling upward with squared shoulders, speechless, smiling unwaveringly, but still taking care not to seem culpably unconscious of his situation. He had always found Uncle George a fearsome being, bulky, noisy, unpredictable. Now his awe was increased by finding his uncle dressed in a maroon track-suit instead of ordinary clothes.

'You got him then,' Uncle George said in a soft blurting roar from the top of the steps, exactly as if the boy were something Aunt Jane had gone out in pursuit of. 'Jolly good,' he said. 'Come in, come in.' The three white steps leading up made it seem as if Uncle George were on a pedestal. Still smiling, the boy commenced the ascent. The maroon shape above him gave way a little, retreated down the passage. He paused again at the threshold. Aunt Jane took his arm. 'Come along in,' she said.

'How are you keeping, young man?' Uncle George said. The boy looked up steadily at the square, big-nosed, straight browed face. 'I am very well, thank you,' he said. 'How are you, Uncle George?'

'I keep going,' Uncle George said, dropping his voice suddenly.

'Have you been running, dear?' Aunt Jane said. She moved from the boy's side and went farther down the passage.

'Limbering up, you know,' Uncle George said. 'Limbering up.'

'He thinks nothing,' Aunt Jane said, 'of running fifty times round the back lawn, and that is quite a big area. I don't know if you remember the garden behind the house?'

'Not very well.'

'Keeps me in trim,' Uncle George said.

'How many times did you go round today, dear?' Aunt Jane was now standing beside Uncle George about half-way down the passage.

'Just the statutory fifty,' Uncle George said loudly. '*Mens sana in corpore sano*,' he said, looking at his nephew.

Aunt Jane too was looking at him. They stood together in the middle of the passage, regarding him, Uncle George standing slightly sideways so as not to seem to be blocking the way, Aunt Jane at his side, a little beyond him, coming barely up to his shoulder.

He had expected to be scrutinized. But there was in this conjunction of their faces something that seemed formally composed and after a moment he realized that they were like Joseph and Mary in one of the coloured pictures in his New Testament, standing together on the dusty road to Bethlehem. The similarity was not of course in their garments or general appearance, but simply the two faces at their different levels, and perhaps because of the artist's incompetence, something strained in their benignity as if they were nervous at becoming the parents of Jesus, daunted at the prospect and drawing together for mutual support. This impression was fleeting, but it distressed him. He was fully prepared to do what was expected of him, as far as he could perceive this, and obviously a manly fortitude was what Uncle George would have found laudable, but the two of them together, mutely looking, drawn up in welcoming order, made him uncertain of his part. Pain tautened his throat, a sense of how pitiable he might seem in their eyes, a sort of evacuee from the danger zone of warring parents.

'I expect you're ready for something to eat,' Aunt Jane said, moving with a sudden bustle farther down the passage, away from them.

Uncle George said, 'Hungry as a hunter I expect,' with a blurt of relief at having found a formula, looking at the boy's tall, shrinking thinness with unintentional derogation. He swung his body farther round against the wall and the boy with a sort of wary decorousness stepped past him down the passage after Aunt Jane. Uncle George made noises of approval behind but did not follow.

In the kitchen he was given tea and buns. The buns had thick white icing on them and he felt sure they had been bought specially for him. He never had such things at home. Their sweetness, dissolving in his mouth, confirmed his alien status. Aunt Jane talked to him, bustling about the kitchen. She had taken off her coat and in her green woollen dress looked amazingly thin and tense. He noticed something about her movements now that he did not remember: a curious rigidity about her upper half as if the legs carried her body along under protest, hasting legs and active hands seemed in their movements to belie and contradict the real tendency of her body, which was to recoil from things, in some sort of abhorrence which he couldn't understand. And this, in his tranced consuming of the sweet buns, this haplessness and reluctance of Aunt Jane's upper half, mingled in his mind with visions of Uncle George pounding and panting round and round in his maroon track suit.

She did not, out of tact, ask him anything about home or his parents. She told him instead how Uncle George had dealt with an impertinent baker's delivery man. 'He did not raise his voice above its normal speaking tone,' she said. She compressed pale lips. The boy tried to imagine Uncle George's normal speaking tone. 'We never had any repetition of it,' Aunt Jane said. She told him about the garden and the desultory attitude towards work of Matthews the gardener, whom the boy vaguely remembered. 'He's getting old, of course,' Aunt Jane said. He wondered how old a gardener could be who seemed old to someone as old as Aunt Jane. 'Your Uncle has to give him a dressing down from time to time,' she said. She told him that Frederick and Henry would be home soon for the summer holidays. Those fierce twins, whom Aunt Jane had given birth to in her forty-second year. He knew this because he had heard his mother telling someone, in that tone she used for reprehensible actions. He had thought it greedy of Aunt Jane to have twins, so late in life. Yes, after all those years they had almost given up hope. She went and had twin boys. One after the other their damp little heads. She had a bad time but she was conscious when they were born. Even when you are expecting it, it is a shock, Jane said, to see two. It sapped her strength, she was always frail.

This account of the birth of Henry and Frederick had impressed him vividly, especially the dampness, these two ruthless damp-haired babies bursting forth from Aunt Jane and commencing to sap her. He had regarded them ever since as demonic; one of the few things he remembered from his last visit was the black hair that grew plentifully on the backs of Henry and Frederick's hands. It had seemed to him the very sprouting of their destructive energy.

'They will be home on holiday soon,' Aunt Jane said. 'You will see them,' she promised him. 'They will be able to take you around.' They were both in the sixth form at Dover College, having gone through the school together, evinced a bent for science together and latterly declared an intention of taking up medicine together: a mutuality which the boy found additionally disquieting.

After tea he was taken up to his room, which was on the third floor, just below the roof; an attic room in fact, though it didn't have a sloping ceiling. The room was roughly square in shape and had pale green walls.

'You will be wanting a rest, I expect,' Aunt Jane said. She remained a minute or two, touching various things in the room with a sort of vague haste. 'If there is anything you need,' she said, 'don't be shy about asking. I want you – your uncle and I want – you – to be happy here.'

When she had gone he began his unpacking. He handled his

garments with deliberation, as if the coolness and loneliness of the room conferred a sort of ritual significance on them. Most of his things were being sent on by rail; he had only brought with him what he would be needing immediately. It seemed unsatisfactory, however, to fill only the two drawers of the chest and leave the others quite empty, two drawers were not enough to qualify him for occupancy. By a process of judicious distribution he contrived to make it impossible to open any of the drawers without finding at least one article belonging to him. Then, from the pockets at each side of the suitcase, he took out the few personal possessions he had chosen to bring with him: magnifying glass, electric torch, swallowtail butterfly in transparent plastic case, and his New Testament, recently awarded him for twenty-five consecutive attendances at the Crusader Class. He stood at the window, looking out, holding the book in his hands. His room overlooked the front garden with its neat terraced lawns, yew hedges, rose-garden and line of silver-birch trees screening off the road beyond. The Morris Minor and a dark green Rover were parked on the circular gravelled area at the front of the house, just below him. He heard no sound from the house or the garden. He looked down at the New Testament, at the dark red morocco and gilt lettering of the cover. He began to leaf through it, pausing briefly at texts which he had underlined in red: 'Let your light so shine before men, that they may see your good works, and glorify your Father which is in heaven.' 'I must work the works of him that sent me, while it is day: the night cometh when no man can work.'

The pages were thin and crisp and smelt of newness, and this unusedness, the pristine unsullied quality of the pages reinforced in his mind the purity of heart they enjoined. Towards the end of the gospel according to St Matthew, there was a picture in colour of Christ on the Cross. Christ's eyes were closed and his head had declined slightly on to his breast. It had been clear to the boy from the moment of seeing this picture and had constituted its main fascination, that though Christ had not actually died yet, he was *in extremis*. The artist had avoided giving him a Nordic look. His face was sharp-jawed, shaven and semitic, with a sort of dusky, creamy pallor.

The hair was dark and parted in the middle to fall in two smooth sweeps about his ears and the nape of his neck. There was no dewy anguish of torture about him, but a spent, languid quality as if he had been through storms which had exhausted him. He was naked except for the scantiest of loincloths and the whole of his body had the same yellowish pallor as his face.

The boy scrutinized this picture intently for some moments. Then he closed the book, still remaining however at the window. He thought of the ceremony at which he had been presented with the New Testament by the Leader. Afterwards the class had sung, 'I will make you Fishers of Men' all together, and he had been in the midst of the singing, borne up by it, full of happiness and pride. He looked out at the garden again: its quietness seemed inviting now. He thought that if he could make his way to the garden behind the house he was not likely to be noticed. His first instinct was to put the New Testament away in the drawer with his clean handkerchiefs; but he remembered what the Leader had said, that one must bear witness. He did not find it easy to confess Christ directly, but he thought if he left the New Testament on top of the chest of drawers where it could hardly fail to be noticed by anyone entering the room, it could serve as mute witness, and if it were remarked upon, it would give him a natural occasion. So he did this, and afterwards went quietly downstairs and out into the garden behind the house.

It was a warm afternoon, rather sultry, with banks of cloud, pale-slate coloured, low in the sky, and a sort of pewterish, soft, polished effect of sunshine striking through. The square lawn behind the house needed cutting, there were puffs of flowering clover in it. Matthews again, he thought. It had rained not much earlier and his footsteps cut dark swathes in the grass and stirred the scent of the clover. There were wet webs in the flower borders, slung to delphiniums and lupins. The garden was oddly shaped, quite narrow at first, easily kept whole in the mind between its hawthorn hedges, but afterwards much broader, thicker in vegetation so that one soon lost a sense of physical limit or confine. This process of enlargement was unexpected, unremembered from his previous visit – the

garden had seemed formless to his eight-year-old eyes, formless, immense, embrasive as the sea, immersing him in sensation – and it was in this way he had thought of it ever since.
Now, with the added perspective of the last five years, he was
able to note where the lawn and borders ended, the exact extent of the shrubbery beyond, with its paved walks amid
rhododendrons, azaleas, dwarf magnolia trees. Once through
this, however, and something of those former feelings began to
return; the sense of bearings slipping away, safe confines receding, the sense almost that a swimmer might have, who can
disport himself with a freedom unimaginable on land yet is in
continual danger of engulfment.

He began to negotiate this area, which he sensed to be
roughly rectangular, making his way circumspectly through a
clump of birch trees, skirting the triangular pool with lily-pads
floating on it and a half-submerged raft of planks. Beyond this,
he knew, there was a small orchard of apple trees, with the two
tennis-courts adjoining. He did not go this way, however, but
moved outwards into the central parts of the garden. Here it
was completely untended, an area of gigantic bramble bushes,
cow-parsley and willow-herb, interspersed with japonica and
laurel and various of those glossy-leaved bushes that never
seem to flower; everything growing apparently quite un-
checked. His passage disturbed and sent up on wavering flight
clouds of little brown thick-bodied butterflies that had been
feeding on the bramble flowers. Dingy Skippers he informed
himself, faintly contemptuous of them for being so easily
identifiable. A few faint, softly metallic gleams of sunshine fell
across the garden, silvering the leaves of the birch trees. The
house was not visible from here, nor was there any sound of
other people. Blackbirds, perhaps with young near, detected his
presence and set up a minatory fluting. He stood among the
bushes and felt the throb of life in the garden, like a sort of
pulse that had leapt with alarm at his approach, now slowly
settle round him. Enveloped thus, screened and secret, he muttered rhetorically to himself the opening of what was currently
his favourite poem. 'At the mid hour of night, when stars are
weeping, I fly to the lone vale we loved when life shone warm
in thine eyes.' The lack of congruity between the night-time

feel of the lines and his own immediate surroundings did not bother him, nor did the fact that there was no person he could have spoken to like that. The melancholy of it was absolutely right and appropriate. The sense of bereavement and abandonment that lay more or less constantly below the surface of his consciousness mingled now with unlocalized feelings of sweetness and excitement: he felt as he had felt several times of late that some revelation was imminent, something that it was intolerable for him not to know. This ebbed slowly and he looked up in bewilderment at a darkening sky.

The sunshine had gone now and the leaves around him rustled in a sudden breeze. Moved by an impulse of haste, almost of alarm, he made his way quickly out of the shrubbery; but he was obliged by the thickness of the bushes to make a detour which at first took him farther from the house into a more open area of sprawling blackcurrant bushes bordered by a tall hawthorn hedge. This hedge he took to be the farthest limit of the garden. He moved along it with the intention of returning to the house by a circular route, passed once more through the birch trees and found himself amid the reedy fringes of the pond. Green scum sidled on the surface as if something had very recently taken a header in there. He had a sense of tenacious cannibal life in the depths. A bright-emerald dragon-fly darted across the surface, hovered, settled on the stem of a kingcup. At rest it lost iridescence immediately as if it had drained its colour into the vegetation. The hush of the place seemed to him curiously temporary like a sort of lull – prelude to some violent resumption.

He skirted the pond, feeling the soft ground give a little under his feet, and reached the small orchard of apple trees with a sense of release. The ground here was still scattered with dried, curled petals. He was about to turn back towards the paved walks and clipped yew of the central area and the glimpsed house beyond, when he caught sight through the maimed branches of a figure on the nearer tennis-court, a person in shirt-sleeves bending low to the ground. Immediately, there came to him the conviction that this person, though apparently absorbed in some task, knew everything that was happening in the garden, had been aware all the time of his aimless movements about it. He advanced through the trees, across the cleared space adjoining them. The figure straightened, bent again, not seeming to have heard his approach. He stood at the edge of the court, looking through the tall wire-mesh fence that surrounded it at an old rheumatic man with bushy ginger sideburns and a bald tanned head. He was renewing with fresh white paint the boundaries of the court. For some moments the boy said nothing, watching the careful charging of the brush, the meticulous application of it, the laborious, stertorous shifts in position this activity involved. Then he said, in what he hoped was a conversational tone, 'That's quite a job you've got, isn't it?' This must be Matthews, he thought.

The man straightened and turned, presenting an old round face with a whitish stubble along the jaws and a mumbling habit of the mouth as if he did a good deal of self-communing.

'Once a year it needs doing,' he said. He stood with head stretched forward in a tentative reptilian way, and the boy observed the seamed lines of his neck, and thought that they might have been caused by innumerable alarmed retractions. Like a tortoise. 'And who might you be?' the old man said.

'I'm staying here.'

'*They'll* be here soon, clumping about.'

'Who do you mean?'

'Clumping about the place. I keep out of their way, I do.'

'You are Mr Matthews aren't you?'

'That's right. I seen service in three wars.'

'Have you really. Do you mean Henry and Frederick clumping about?'

'Then there's him. Puffing and panting round, ah, I keep out of his way as well. He'll have a seizure. Round and round he goes, grunting and groaning. He slipped yesterday and fell flat on his face. Flat – on – his – face. He'll have a seizure, one of these days. She's the only one I talk to.'

'Aunt Jane?'

But Matthews had turned away now and laboriously bent once more over his task. The clean white paint glistened. He only had the baseline to do on this court. The boy stood some moments longer, wondering whether Matthews, by resuming work like this, had meant to indicate that the conversation was at an end. But while he was trying to decide about this, large drops of rain began to fall, speckling the court. At the first touch of wet, Matthews took up brush and paint-pot and began to move slowly off across the court. He did not look back at the boy. The rain increased. The boy after some hesitation made his way back to the house.

3

That was the last rain for two whole months. Next day began cloudy, but in the middle of the afternoon the wind changed direction; the clouds dispersed. The sky showed through, soft blue, a milky haze in it at first, as if the clouds retreating had left a stain, but deepening in the days that followed to a burning cobalt that pained the eyes when you glanced up, not just in that part where the sun was, but throughout the whole extent of it as if the sun were diffused; the whole sky charged with brilliance, meshed with brilliance. It was meshes that you saw if after looking up you closed your eyes; a myriad overlapping meshes of light. The boy did this frequently; closed dazzled eyes on this depthless burning blue; confronted behind his lids this quivering latticework of light, a fairly rigid armature at first, by degrees dissolving into milky haze ...

No, it wasn't either of them, Henry and Frederick, the damp-haired twins, they were still on the tennis-court. Mooncranker spoke to someone else, before coming to me in the garden and handing me the little bandaged effigy of Christ on the Cross. I was pleased with the gift. I hung it up on the birch tree in the secret place that only I knew about. Even Miranda didn't know about it. Miranda liked me, though she was two years older. She was my partner in the doubles and we won, we had just won against Henry and Frederick, and she kissed me when we won. Henry and Frederick said I played a sneaking game because I tipped the ball just over, bringing them rushing up to the net, then Miranda would lob over their labouring backs, just inside the line, time after time. Mr Mooncranker called the score.

They got angry and wild, driving at us with all their strength; once Frederick drove straight at Miranda and the ball hit her upper arm, she was wearing a sleeveless tennis-dress with pleated skirts. He looked pleased when it happened; he only remembered afterwards to look concerned. Her arm was red where the ball had hit. She smiled at me. She had her hair tied back with a piece of white string; auburn hair. I knew then that we would win. I will always remember her face, broad-browed, widely spaced eyes, a mouth always near to smiling. She had a depth, a sort of flushed duskiness of complexion not usual in English girls. How beautiful I thought her. When we won she kissed me, right there on the court. 'They are getting rattled,' she said. 'Keep it up.' She was a marvellous player for her age, everybody said so. I was not strong enough in the wrists, but I had a good eye and I was quick on my feet – my faulty coordination didn't start till later. To make up for my weak wrists I had developed some very cunning sliced shots that dropped just over and bounced short ... How they hated being beaten. They began by jeering – a girl and a thirteen-year-old boy opposing them. Good-natured chaff, Uncle George would have called it. She put her arms on my shoulders and kissed me on the cheek.

We had just won our game. I had gone for some reason into the house, for a drink perhaps. Henry and Frederick had started a furious singles game and Miranda was looking on. I must have been intending to return to the court, but went first out into the garden, into the shrubbery. From there I saw Mooncranker in colloquy with someone at the back of the house, someone dressed in white. Then he came towards me and he had the Christ in his hand – he knew exactly where to find me. He bowed a little and smiled. I remember the civilized upward twitch at the corners of his mouth and I remember that he uttered some words – although most of my attention was on the thing in his hands that he was offering to me – the blunt-headed, or perhaps helmeted figure, in the ancient posture of suffering, wrapped in folds of clean white bandage. Something he said at the time, something I feel now to have been surprising or unexpected; but I was full of triumph at our victory and wonder at the kiss and then at this effigy and courteous Mooncranker. On this heady occasion something essential was overlooked by me, something I may never find now. Why he did it is probably what I shall never know, how I provoked that malignity. To give me an object calculated to arouse reverence at first, knowing as he did my feelings about Christ (and he could only have known this from Miranda); and afterwards to destroy reverence in disgust. The whole process calculated, buying the meat, moulding it, encasing it, attaching it to the cross, handing it over like a time-bomb, its inevitable putrefaction the fuse within . . .

Possessed by this mystery, he turned his head on the pillow to regard once more Mooncranker's sleeping profile. You were gone, I do not remember you as being around, when that gift of yours began to stink badly enough to be identified as the source of stink, when it began to sift through its containing bands. And a peculiar shame held me from taxing any person with the trick that had been played on me. I felt too, I suppose, that everything in some way had been due to my fault, my peculiar sins . . .

This is what nobody could have known, the use I would make of the gift. Surely nobody could have known. Even Mooncranker in his heyday, fully vitamined and hydrated, could not have had such evil prescience, could not have known how Christ had become my accomplice, before even that gift was made. Not that I knew this at the time myself, not fully. The sallow, sleek-loined, dying Christ in my New Testament, whom I pained by my repeated sin, I wanted to solace him, with a force equal at least to that of my repentance, wanted to change the nature of his sorrow by provoking commotions similar to mine beneath his loin cloth. Failing this, I prayed to him. My voice muttered promises, promises. My eyelids pressed tight shut. Achieving a sort of purity necessary for the full pang of my sin.

There was a place in the grounds that no one knew of but me. The shrubbery that covered a large area at the side of the house was quite untended, had been so for years. Large parts of it were trackless. In the summer-time the bushes were interspersed with great clumps of white daisies and goldenrod and enormous hollyhocks; flowers that bravely went on seeding themselves in that wilderness and only by a lunging, straggling disorderliness of the stems, a certain craziness of growth, denoted neglect. Matthews never went near them. A murmuring remote man with a laboriously deliberate habit of body. He never bothered with anything but the herbaceous borders and lawns and the tennis-courts. If you went in under the bushes at one point, there were twenty yards to crawl and you could stand again in a sort of bower roofed by the low branches of three silver-birch trees, walled by a tangle of hawthorn and privet and the summer foliage of a lime-tree, thick around the lower trunk. The shed nearby had been creosoted; the smell of it was sharp when I crouched in my hiding-place. And everything around me in that place was in flower, white flower, the privet and the hawthorn and the briar roses in the hawthorn and the cow-parsley that grew among neglected blackcurrant canes near by. Sunlight came down in straight shafts through the birch branches, on a still day. Lay in blocks and tablets of light on the trunks. I pinned the Christ on to the trunk of the birch tree about six feet, seven feet, the limit of my reach. Where the sunlight, shafting down in precise rays, dwelt on the figure, caused its mummy bands to gleam, cast a radiance about the blind, helmeted head.

Did he know what I would do with it? In that case others knew of my secret place in the garden, knew of its existence at least. Miranda again? Perhaps Henry and Frederick followed me one day, stalked me through the bushes. Betrayal in any case. The summer is redolent of betrayal and the private anguish of being betrayed, coexistent with life itself. I am tricked and betrayed again each time I think of it; the flowers smell of it; Christ oozes with it. I could ask Mooncranker now, but he is sleeping.

Henry and Frederick would not have bothered to stalk me, would not have cared where I went or what I did. No, Mooncranker was the stalker. Or he had an informant. For all I know he followed me around all the summer. I was always meeting him in places just a little unexpected, where he had no real business to be. One of the memories of that time I have carried away, always seeming to be finding Mooncranker athwart my path, the slight, inevitably disagreeable shock of recognizing that figure ... At what stage did I meet him? It must have been quite early, quite soon after my arrival, because the whole of the summer is permeated with him. Impossible now, however, to determine when. Uncle George introduced us, in some suitably jovial form of words no doubt. What would he have said? Our young friend from the north. Something in that vein. Not in his tracksuit that day, or was he? Nephew of an old friend of mine. Mr Mooncranker, or is it doctor? No, no, no academic pretensions whatever, quite the opposite in fact. A lounging, high-shouldered figure, thin face, pale eyes. I see him smiling down at me with a sort of fastidious interest, a weedy dandyism. This high-shouldered, rather ceremonious posture what I chiefly remember now, and the narrow courteous face below the hat-brim. A courtesy delicately denigratory ... This was on the terrace at the front of the house. I think about a week after my arrival. At any rate before Henry and Frederick came home for the summer holidays.

Those first days were spent placidly, watching butterflies in the garden, reading my New Testament, holding further conversations with Matthews. Uncle George went off every morning in his green Rover and I did not see him again till the evening. The three of us had supper together during which meal the conversation was desultory. At night I remember, if I did not close my curtains, I would see white moths hanging motionless on the outside of the pane, as if by stillness they entreated admission. Once during that week I went with Aunt Jane on a green bus into the town. Aunt Jane bought a burgundy-coloured twin-set at a shop called 'dorothy's' – the name was written above the window in flowing script and with a small *d*. We went to a tea-shop and had tea and cakes.

Then at the weekend Henry and Frederick arrived from Dover College, changing everything by their arrival, as if by some massive injection of energy and noise. They filled the house with footsteps and slamming doors and loud plans. They shouted from one end of it to the other. Even in the coolness and sanctity of my room I heard distant tremors, the whole place seemed to throb with them. When Uncle George came home in the evening there was more hubbub, his blurred booming tones mingling with their lighter, more strident ones; and supper was a livelier meal than usual with both Henry and Frederick recounting some of the exploits of the term. They were almost exactly alike in appearance as in pitch of voice; both tall and strongly built, with black hair and serious straight black brows and narrow inflexible mouths.

'So I told him just what I thought of him. He had been playing well, I grant you, but that is not the point, is it, father? It is teamwork that counts. Individual brilliance is all very well in its place, of course –'

'Quite right my boy.' Uncle George lays down his knife and fork and looks round the table. Prominent, naked-seeming blue eyes. Same code on the sports-field as it is in life, the lessons you learn on the sports-field are invaluable in later life. Strong similarity between father and sons. Only the eyes different; in Uncle George pale and prominent and staring, in them deeper set, serious and dark. They ignored me, for the most part.

I was glad enough, most of the time, to be left alone. I think I had already realized then, that I would not be returning home. Not, at any rate, to the home I had known. Home was like a territory that had suddenly become inaccessible, as if by obliteration of every possible path and landmark. I was haunted all the summer by this sense of no return, a feeling of broken continuity, which conferred a sort of precariousness, a provisional quality, even on the present, on my immediate surroundings. Having no retreat denies substance to what is immediate, though one would not think so. That is a lesson I learned then, I think, during that summer. There was nevertheless, paradoxically perhaps, a vivid particularity about everything around me, all the events and impressions of my stay there. The sense of loss heightened my awareness, as love is said to do. My senses clenched things, the grain and feel and detail of things with a tenacity like that of one who fears drowning, or falling off. A butterfly in the garden, the fresh lines on the tennis-courts, the loud voices of Henry and Frederick and Uncle George swooping down on a name or date. The attention I paid to everything was the measure I suppose of my desolation, my loneliness. At the beginning anyway ... Later I think it was because of meeting Miranda.

Mooncranker did not join in their arguments. He nodded and smiled in a non-committal way. High-shouldered, thin hands bunched in jacket pockets. There was a sort of jauntiness about him, a sort of indifference. He used to come in the afternoons mostly, when Uncle George was at work. I would see him in different parts of the garden, on his own usually. Sometimes I saw him talking to Miranda. She laughed a lot when he talked to her. I didn't like his manner at those times, he lounged and leaned forward. He spoke quietly to her, in a low voice, leaning down towards her. She looked away from him and laughed. I never liked seeing them together. Whenever he was anywhere near she was different, not herself. He was standing there, waiting for us, when we came crawling out of the bushes, standing there, one hip thrust slightly out as if about to turn away, but no, he had been intently waiting there, for how long? In white, a white suit, and his narrow-brimmed straw hat, beyond him the burning blue sky, when we looked up. I saw her face change, when she saw him there, her eyes seemed to darken...

All that summer it hardly seemed to rain at all. Week after week. Matthews had to water the garden quite frequently. He had his own way of doing this, taking the water straight from the cistern behind the house and distributing it about the garden by a complex system of shallow channels. The earth in among the shrubbery was baked hard, cinnamon coloured. The tennis-nets stiff and motionless. Miranda and I played at tracking. Her idea, it was her idea, to go crawling into the bushes. You could hear quite clearly from the shrubbery voices and sounds from the courts. The curious sound of racquet on ball, soft and ringing at the same time, like a bursting from within. The hasty voices of Henry or Frederick or one of their friends, calling out 'Hard luck' or something of that kind, insincerely. Mooncranker announcing the scores with a voice of considerable carrying power. Perhaps even then, in that summer, through those months of drought and whiteness you were debilitating yourself secretly, sir, dehydrating yourself in the privacy of your own apartments. Somewhat analogous to my own private activities at that time ... There is a plasma in the blood and this plasma, if this plasma ... Though judging by your fidelity to the scores, the fluctuating fortunes of the game, you were not in that era hitting the bottle. That day, in any case, the day I am thinking of, you were not umpiring, you couldn't have been, because you were waiting for us when we emerged from the bushes ...

The air in the shubbery was so still, the leaves so motionless, it seemed that one heard minute things, the track of an insect, a butterfly bending a stamen, the contractions of the earth. In the intervals of tennis, we played a game of tracking sometimes, pretending to be hunters, freezing into immobility from time to time. A harmless game really. Be your age, Uncle George would have said. Though that is what we were being, really, myself thirteen, she fifteen, at once mocking the game and taking it seriously; acknowledging dimly that such a physical convention, involving agreed responses to the other's body, was necessary to our knowledge of each other ...

Straight from the tennis-courts, in our white clothes. *Rhino!* I arrest my body suddenly in a dramatic pose and she follows suit, her sun-flushed face simulating wariness. Then move slowly forward to get up-wind of it, treading on the baked dusty earth as if there might be twigs to snap underfoot, animals ready to startle. Legs pale gold, slender white-socked ankles, rounded calves flexing slightly with her steps as each took briefly the main weight of the wary trunk. Her idea.

One of the few bits of tracking she actually set under way: a grizzly in the heart of the bushes, in the depths of the cave formed by their ancient ramifications. A lurking, vindictive bear. Their bodies in the passage through the glossy dusty leaves thunderous in the absence of all other sound. Their breathing was loud when they finally reached the heart of the bush, in the cave formed by the outward arch of branches. Here they were able to kneel, regard each other with a laughter trembling into solemnity at this isolation from the world at large which they had contrived for themselves. She was flushed with exertion and the sense of occasion, brown hair sunbleached falling forward round her face. Her tennis-dress had no sleeves in it. Close-fitting across the breast and at the waist. Having got there, having attained the lair, this created a precedent, established the ease with which whenever they wished

79

they could cut themselves off from the rest of the world; and with this established they would almost certainly have crawled out again immediately, regained the path, but they were prevented by Matthews the gardener who came round the side of the house carrying a spade, and took up a position not a dozen yards away. The presence of someone outside, near by, someone bound to see them if they emerged, imposed a sort of guilt on them, a feeling of constraint. They watched Matthews through the leaves, watering the garden.

It was not his practice to wander about the extensive garden holding hose-pipe or watering can, administering to each part its share. Early that summer, with a prescience of drought that bordered on the magical, he had dug irrigation canals in a system of his own devising, all over the garden. It was necessary only to open the cistern, to send the water gushing down the main channel and then stand by with a spade, clearing or damming certain key points – it was to this end that Matthews had stationed himself there, obliging them to remain concealed, since it seemed evident to both that they could not come crawling out of the bush in his full view...

Farnaby stirred and sighed. No sounds of any sort reached them in this room. Mooncranker was motionless, his eyes shut. The globules flexed like light down through the tube. Farnaby wondered if he should switch off the lamp near Mooncranker's bed, but it seemed pointless now to do that. He was conscious of the faint beginnings of a desire to urinate.

'The reluctance to be spotted by Matthews argues some guilty intention on our part.' For some reason he had whispered this aloud, watching Mooncranker's face, and he was distinctly startled, even rather frightened, to see the professor's eyes open suddenly. He held his breath, wondering if Mooncranker would answer him. But after a few moments of bemused staring at the ceiling, Mooncranker muttered some indistinguishable words, seemingly on a note of interrogation, and closed his eyes again. Odd that he has refrained so far from asking me anything about the groom. He must be curious to know the outcome. Odd, blurred creature that he is, improbable now as the prime mover of evil, which was for years what I thought him. Eyes closed, motionless profile, he can sleep and feed at once. Strange if he were thinking of that summer too, recreating behind closed lids and in his own darkness some of those scenes and conversations, that time he stopped me for example, that time, stopped me on my way to play tennis, there on the edge of the shrubbery, he was alone there and he stopped me and said, I believe you are interested in religious matters and I said nothing, but smiled in embarrassment. That was a time that the Leader would probably have thought suitable for bearing witness, but all I did was smile, feeling his eyes on me, pale lingering eyes. His tie was tightly knotted, a bright tie in a very small tight knot, and his shirt broad-collared and floppy, so there was a contrast, somehow elegant, somehow characteristic of him ... Well, well, well, he said. I think now the idea was already in his mind, then, at that very moment, the intention fully formed, *mature*, of giving me the sausage-meat Christ ...

Farnaby lay on his back staring up at the white ceiling. After a few moments he looked cautiously towards the other bed, but Mooncranker's eyes were still closed and he made no movement. There was no sound in the room. He glanced at his watch: two o'clock. Once again, deliberately, he set himself to remember ...

4

We were walking down the high street which had cobbled verges on either side, very wide ones, there were people who claimed that high street to be the widest in England. I had fallen behind to look at kittens in a pet-shop window. I saw Henry and Frederick stop and talk to two girls. One of them smiled at me as I came up. White teeth, long lashes. She was as tall as I was. This is our cousin. We shook hands and I heard the name Miranda pronounced by one or other of the twins. Miranda Bolsover. Her hand was warm. There was something in her smile that made us allies ...

Later that day, that same day, after meeting Miranda, I prayed in my room. In the coolness of my room I confided in God, but Miranda's smile of complicity kept returning to me. I said the Lord's Prayer with eyes tight-closed. I looked at the picture in my New Testament. Christ's arms, outstretched thus, tautened the skin of his chest, brought into prominence rib-cage and breast-bone. His abdomen and pelvis passed sleekly, vertiginously down into the shelter of the white loin-cloth, the legs below were slender, shapely, quite hairless. When I looked at this picture, Christ's desperate situation, poised thus *in extremis,* made him in some awful reverential way an *object,* which could be thought about in ways not possible for a completely living and human person. I could look at Christ's body with complete immunity, but as I looked a sudden sense of wrong and sin took me by the throat, I convicted myself of baseness, and I was bewildered because I did not know the source of this welling of guilt.

Afterwards, on this same day, it is the afternoon of the day I met Miranda in the high street, immediately after my scrutiny of Christ, and infected by this unworthiness, I went to the dressing-table and stood before it to look at myself, and almost at once another feeling, excitement and a kind of pain arose in me and I went quickly and turned the key in the door. Once more in front of the glass I undressed myself, and stood naked there, hands at my sides in a position of attention. I surveyed my form, long-bodied, sallow-skinned, thin. My fairish pubic bush. My exposure excited me in the cool room. Slowly, as I stood there, my penis erected itself, reared up a swollen cowled head. It was the only part of my skin that was not white. I touched myself but I was frightened by the sickness almost, the giddiness of excitement that assailed me. I took my hand from it as from a fire. I dressed again, quickly, carelessly, and hastily left the house.

No, it was not on that occasion that I began doing it, it was not until a week later, I began the day we went along the river. This day, the day I am thinking of now, I dressed quickly and went out into the garden.

Day after day without a hint of rain. Each day identical with the one before: clear cloudless skies, a hot sun, windless mostly, except for sporadic breezes springing up sometimes towards the end of the afternoon. People constantly remarking on the weather, how difficult to recall such a long succession of perfect summer days. In the fields around the house, grain ripening. The garden itself humming, throbbing, germinating. Order and decorum in the areas attended by Matthews, in the rose-garden, the shrubbery, the flower-beds round the lawn – where gladioli full-fleshed consorted with hollyhock and lupin, a regular riot of colour as Uncle George no doubt would have it, conceding that Matthews knew his job all right, though an insolent fellow. Yes, all in order there; but regions existed beyond his scope, there were places he never penetrated, over on the other side, beyond the little lake and straggling orchard, an area roughly square-shaped, perhaps a hundred yards across, a midsummer wilderness now, dense with nettle and dock and tall grasses with silky bluish seed-cases, cow-parsley with flowers bigger than human faces growing among neglected currant-bushes, and great clumps of white elder-flower – all the flowers in that part of the garden, all that I can remember, are white.

I make my way here, today, as on numerous other occasions; it is my favourite part of the garden. I am not thinking now of the day I rushed out from my room, but of a day later on in the summer, when everything was more advanced. Mooncranker had already given me the Christ then, it was fixed to the tree in the secret place that only I knew about. This was after Miranda and I had won the tennis tournament.

I walk through this part, sometimes bending to move aside the thick clumps of elder which grow so close to the ground. Beyond are the hawthorn hedges bounding the garden, they are in white flower too; with wild roses and honeysuckle growing amongst them, also white – everything that emerges, flowers out from the green mass of leafage, is white in colour and characterized by a thickness of odour, a certain rank sweetness. Things originally delicate in scent, like the wild roses, get drawn in, overpowered, add their thin tributary stream to the confluence. At times it is like wading, half-submerged, in a green sea, flecked along its soft crests with the flowers and odours; I feel the whole expanse heave around me as if I am indeed among waves, the whirr and hiss of insects like the sibilance of ocean; the multiple scents too an accompaniment to the sway, as if the very heaving and exertions of the ground released the odours of its existence in degrees of intensity quite unpredictable; alternate clamour and hush through which I wade, bearing my own need, the taut excitement of my intention, because I know what I am making for and what I shall do when I get there, I have done it often before that summer and in that place.

Excitement fills me, indistinguishable from a sort of panic, as if I might be engulfed before I can reach my sanctuary, but I always do reach it and stand within the enclosure of thickly leaved branches, bounded on all sides, the hedge beyond rising to a height of perhaps ten feet and quite impenetrable, an inviolate area into which the frantic life of the garden does not penetrate. Grass beneath my feet, kept low and green by the perpetual shade. Before me, against the seamed silver trunk, the effigy of Christ shines luminously, sunlight falls through the upper branches on to it; on to the lateral folds of bandage, the blind, helmeted head, around which, in this zone of sunlight, I see the gauze and glint of insects' wings and hear a faint liturgical humming, as I unbutton myself to free the rigid pulsating creature or sometimes undress partially and standing or kneeling in my refuge enact the ritual I have come for in suffocating silence, in full view of the figure on the tree whom I make thus, guilt contending with pleasure, my accomplice, yes, he became my accomplice that summer, the server of my corrupted imagination and the outrage I did to him deepened my final spasms – which I had learned by now to protract ... It was not far from the house really, in a material sense at least. Sometimes, in the pensive aftermath of my indulgence, I would hear sounds from there, or from the tennis-courts, if there was a game in progress, you could hear voices, the sharp resonant impact of tennis racquet and ball ...

But that was much later in the summer. I was practised then in Solitary Vice. That was what the Leader called it. 'I am speaking now,' he said, 'to each and every one of you, your body is the temple of God.' He looked at us one by one. Deighton went red. 'I too have had to struggle with impurity,' the Leader said. 'Pray for strength.'

The first time was not when I undressed that day in my room, though it nearly was. The first time was after we went for the walk along the river. There was a river that ran through the fields in a wide valley not very far from the house. After lunch one day we set off for a walk along it and that was only the second time in my life I spoke to Miranda. There were about ten of us altogether I think, all friends of Henry and Frederick, all older than me – I was always the youngest. I don't remember them all. The asthmatic boy was there and his sister and Alan. Miranda of course, and two other girls. The girls walked all together at first, in front. Henry had a Webley air pistol. The girls walked together, talking quietly but occasionally breaking into quite loud laughter which made them cling together. Alan's girl, who I had found out was called Mary, was wearing slacks, but the others were wearing dresses. I watched Miranda walking, the slight rounding of her calves as she set her feet down. I thought she walked beautifully. She was several inches taller than the other girls and she walked very upright. Even when they stopped for their clinging mirth it seemed that she did it on sufferance only, indulging the others. The river wound in slow curves through meadows knee high in grass and clover and buttercups. After the rainless days the water was down, the banks of dried reddish clay sloped on our side to flat verges of shingle.

The boys were constantly balancing on the edge of the bank, crumbling the clay down into the pale brown water. It fell with a soft, sifting, sighing sound. They laughed and shouted, digging their heels into the dry overhanging banks, falling picturesquely, arms outstretched, down the sloping bankside, their feet sliding in the rubble of the bank, to stop at the shingled verge of the water.

The sun was hot. Young corn in the fields around, still tender green in the shoots. We passed through a field of beans in flower, the whole field scented. Moorhens scattered away from us up river. An occasional plop as frog or vole took a header at our approach. The path got narrower and more overgrown and this slowed people down, brought the party more or less together. Mary dropped back to walk with Alan, but Miranda was still in front. A vole, slower than the others, jumped from the bankside almost at my feet, scuttled across the shingle and dived into the water, the water was shallow there. It did not attempt to get under the surface but struck out strongly across the river. When it was half way across Henry shot it in the back with his air pistol. I knew he had hit it because it dipped in the water. We stood there on the bank watching, streamlined body cutting through the water, outline beaded with tiny bubbles, nose and back one cleaving shape, smooth as flowing stone across the bright water, thin swirl following behind, so effortless. Then Henry raised his arm, the pistol must have been loaded all the time, pointed his arm full length and fired and the smoothly swimming back ducked or dipped in the water as if at some sudden weight and I knew Henry had put a pellet into the vole's back. It swam on with the same smooth motion, and disappeared into the density of vegetation on the opposite bank. What chiefly lives in my memory is that resumption of its smooth swimming. It was involuntary of course but seemed a sort of dignity all the same.

Henry said something in thoughtful derogation, something about there not being much power in the pistol after all. Frederick said the vole was as good as dead, the pistol was one of the most powerful currently manufactured. Father told me. Then Henry got tenser, remarking that the vole had gone on swimming with undiminished energy or was Frederick asking him to disbelieve his own eyes and Frederick said it was mere survival instinct that drove the vole thus and in the middle of this altercation Miranda's voice, suddenly vibrant with feeling: 'Do you realize that you are talking here and you have condemned that animal to a lingering death?' Probably there was only me to look at her closely, see how upset she was, with bright eyes and a voice lower pitched than usual in the effort of control. 'Just wantonly,' she said, 'and now you are talking about stupid things. You ought to be ashamed.' Frederick said he wasn't ashamed, but his face was red. 'You don't understand sport,' he said, and then I spoke too, surprising myself by my own temerity, 'I don't call that sport.' It was all for Miranda, not wanting her to be hurt or humiliated because I knew already from experience and would have known anyway by instinct that people in distress only get more hurt when confronted by such obstinately unmoved and fact-treasuring people as Henry and Frederick and that this ever more will be so. But the remark drew their combined contempt on me, what do you know about it, you can't even throw or jump, remarks of that nature were heaped on me and the other boys laughed but I don't think Alan did. Anyway I didn't care. Then Frederick suggested building a dam.

The river was narrow there and shallow. A few large stones, set irregularly across the stream, rounded, and sleek with wet moss. The stream gushed through the gaps they made, over and down in miniature rapids. Frederick's idea was to reinforce this line with smaller stones prised up from the river bed, and clay and pebbles. Henry and Frederick both wanted to direct operations. They ordered the others about. The girls giggling, wading, sleeves rolled up, the hems of their skirts dark with wet. That boy with the noisy breathing earnestly responsive to orders, perfect labourer, his trousers rolled up over the fleshy knees. Alan got bored I think, went off somewhere, probably with Mary, I don't remember seeing them any more that afternoon. 'Why are you standing about up there?' they asked us, and Miranda said, 'I'm not going to have anything to do with your dam, not after what you did to that vole.' I dumb and awkward up there on the bank beside her, heart however swelling at my own secret courage in thus withstanding their contempt, for her sake. Brown water flecked with white, stayed in its course by their constantly crumbling dam, eddied, sidled, crept up the shingle, the froth on it dirty looking as if fouled already by this delay.

We walked away together along the bank, farther along the river, walking in file at first, then, as the path widened, side by side. We didn't speak much to begin with, I felt an excitement and constraint almost unbearable at being alone with Miranda, two years younger, walking along with her, a sense of terrible responsibility, for the outcome of this walk. This wore off but it was very strong and almost choking at first, so much so that for a time I did not notice my surroundings. Then the scene fell into place as it falls now, around me, the long gleaming curve of the river, the quiet banks, gently rising fields on either side, the skyline on our side wooded.

She said she couldn't bear them any longer. Henry and Frederick. Imagine the mentality, arguing like that after what they had just done. Always concentrating on facts and disregarding feelings is a symptom of the fascist mentality. Mr Mooncranker said that. He is very much against all forms of authoritarianism. The father of course is quite dreadful, that's your uncle isn't it, I hope you don't mind? I mean always going on about physical development to the exclusion of culture. Mr Mooncranker calls him the salt of the earth but concedes that he is an elderly barbarian.

You seem to know a lot about Mr Mooncranker's views and attitudes.

Summer afternoon waning, paling. We met no one on the way. Rings of ripples denote the rising trout. Her face was vivid, flushed with the day's sunshine and the vehement talking. A strong face. I watched her clear profile, the beautiful, faintly hollowed plane at the temple. 'They have all got sexual hangups,' she said, and this too turned out to be one of Mr Mooncranker's dicta. 'Yes, well, he talks to me quite often. He came to our school once, to give a talk about the importance of television and the need for standards. So when I saw him at your uncle's house, I knew him at once.'

'You won't stop coming, will you? Because of Henry and Frederick?'

I don't think I actually said that, only thought it, experienced the anxiety of the thought, while she went on talking about Mooncranker who was the only one without sexual hangups. Separated from his wife because it wasn't a perfect relationship. That is him all over, it is typical. Break down these outmoded conventions, break free. He is to the left in politics of course, but basically he doesn't trust institutions at all.

I tried to tell her something about my life. I remember describing my parents. Our purposes are seldom clear to us at the time and I think now that I was trying, with the inadequate resources at my command, to convey to her the feelings of one like myself, obliged before he is ready to consider his parents as mortal beings, seekers after a happiness to which he was not integral; knowledge that weakened precociously my own sense of permanence, and made me observant, as if the world were scattered with clues. This is what I probably intended to say to

Miranda but whether she gathered it from my words I have no means of knowing, words mainly devoted to my mother's tendency to wear large hats and get flustered on the telephone, my father's fastidiousness and swearing. I think now that I was trying to make myself interesting to her and I think that in this I succeeded. I told her I had prayed for a reconciliation between my parents and for more amity and tolerance among the peoples of the world generally, but as they were going on with the divorce proceedings it must be God's will. I told her about my twenty-five consecutive attendances and my New Testament. She said I was a funny boy. She said in reference to my parents that she did not think people had the right simply to consult their own happiness. She had a way, while she talked, in moments of eagerness or enthusiasm, a way of brushing aside the thick fringe of hair that fell over her forehead, dividing it at the centre of the brow with two light quick nervous gestures of one finger, left and right, very like the lateral part of the gesture of crossing oneself.

We came to a place where the river formed a roughly circular pool with a little shingled shore at our side, and Miranda, I think it was Miranda, suggested wading. Laughter, and her hand in mine, down the bank. We left our shoes on the shingle. The water was very cold. Feel of stones underfoot. The current flowed past us, swirled at our ankles first, then higher as we waded in, and the minnows scooting off at our approach. Deeper than it looks, in the middle. Miranda had to gather her skirt, light cotton skirt of a summer dress, patterned in small blue flowers, lift it over her knees, up round her thighs at one point, and I saw the slender, firmly rounded fronts of her thighs, pale gold in colour, taut against the chill of the water and shifting stones underfoot, and this tentative taut posture of her body, the laughing face as she looked into the water before her, the modesty and necessity of the gathered skirt, all fused into an image of beauty that I was destined never to forget; my mind was still lost in it when she stumbled, seemed about to fall, I moved to her quickly put my arm round her waist and she stayed a moment like this against me and the glittering swirl of water, the stirring silver undersides of leaves above the banks, the blank sky, all reeled together ...

89

It was impossible to get out at the far side. The clay bank was deep and crumbling. The water had undermined it, scooped it out from below, carried the subsidences of clay downstream. There were sandmartins' nests amid debris, some with eggs inside still intact, victims of this undermining and collapse. We had to wade back again. She let me dry her feet and legs with my handkerchief. Then the way back and it was evening now, we had walked farther than we thought. We came to Henry and Frederick's dam and Miranda asked me to go in and break it up, which I did gladly. The water, brimming at the barrier, poured away through the first breach. I demolished their dam stone by stone. The river gleaming now, an evening river. Sun and moon were in the sky together. Cows in the riverside fields, breathing, tearing and munching, raise their heads to watch us go by. I have forgotten what we talked about on the way home. I remember that she said, thank you for the walk, with a sort of smiling, teasing formality. She didn't take me altogether seriously because I was younger.

My late return had not gone unnoticed. At supper that night it was mentioned. 'You had a good walk out then, this afternoon,' Uncle George said, having first laid down his knife and fork.

'Yes,' I said. Henry and Frederick were looking at me.

'Along the river you went, did you?' Uncle George said.

He looked at me with complete seriousness and a sort of curiosity too, as if I were a species somewhat outside his ken. They were all looking at me and there was a silence. Again I felt their involuntary, almost helpless, collective contempt. In their minds it was accounted odd and unmanly, even perhaps degenerate, to have gone wandering off along the river with a girl. I knew that Uncle George was setting me down as a weedy specimen.

'Nothing like a good hike,' Uncle George said. 'Blows the cobwebs away, good for the liver. Who was that philosopher who walked his thousand paces a day? *Mens sana in corpore sano*, eh? Who was it again?'

Nobody knew, though both Henry and Frederick frowned and looked away into corners as though the name were bobbing about just below the level of consciousness.

'Alcibiades was it?' Henry said at last.

'One of those fellows,' Uncle George said. 'Someone with his head screwed on the right way.'

'No,' I said, I found the defiance to say, stimulated probably by their scorn, 'no, we just sauntered along, really. I don't like strenuous exercise,' I said to Uncle George, and to Henry and Frederick I said 'sorry but I destroyed your dam on the way back, I just couldn't resist it.'

None of them made any reply at all.

The day after that. I am walking in the garden, moving towards my secret place but with customary trepidation, as if some inadvertent movement of my own might start things up around me, and there is another feeling less familiar, a tension in the region of throat and breast, rigid like a spring yet tremulous too. White flowers, suffocating; swathes of heavy scent. Hum of insects, like the vibration of the garden. Sound of tennis from the courts. Voices of players and resonant sound of racquet on ball. People putting in some practice for the tournament. My agitation and excitement mount as I draw near the place, bend low to get under the branches. Once here it is as though isolation is the element that was needed, the precipitating factor. I touch my body and that image of Miranda which had been piercing and beautiful, the picture of her wading in the river, which had seemed only yesterday charged with, guarded by, this very beauty, I now imagine it as wanton, the revealing of the thighs, done to tease and entice, I begin to think of the parts of Miranda I was not able to see and the tumescence immediately consequent on these thoughts demands to be freed from the confinement of clothes, the swollen pulsing monster thus revealed I hoist and jerk about in my hands in a frenzy, handling myself roughly in my ignorant excitement until all this violent activity is stilled by a sort of distant threat, the terrifying intimations of the first orgasm of my life; and the thick greyish fluid that emerges in irregular spurts from between my helpless horrified fingers, tangible signs of that dissolution sinners are warned of. My semen. Sign of maturing powers, advancing manhood. Taken by me then to be the very discharge of disease.

I stand there stained with my seed, in terror at what has

happened, my hands sticky with my own corruption, while the sounds of the tennis game continue to reach me, signals from a world I have lost. I remember pamphlets glanced at without comprehension, picked up from the table at the entrance to the Sunday class, and the words of the Leader: 'your body is the temple of God'. I know now, beyond doubt, that the interior of my temple is in a state of deliquescence. There is no Christ yet on the tree to pray to. But I slip to my knees and pray up through the branches, in murmurs. I am aware of the infinite distance my words have to travel. The fear and self-disgust abate however, by slow degrees, to be replaced as I come once more to my feet and prepare to leave the place by a feeling of sadness, a sense of irreparable loss. I feel singled out and apart from everybody, an outcast because of the enormity of my actions, and chiefly because I have perverted the memory of Miranda wading in the river which I had thought so beautiful. Where has it come from, this skill in perverting things?

As I emerge I am aware of a sort of hush over everything, a silence in which the sounds of my moving body, my tainted body with its cargo of disease, seemed disproportionately loud. The sounds from the court had stopped I think. The game must have been over by then. Yes, Mooncranker had been umpiring, it was his voice I had heard, high, carrying, petulant-seeming voice, announcing the scores. The game must have been over because I met him there just beyond the shrubbery. I wonder if he was waiting for me. He was standing there, tall and thin, white hat, fawn-coloured jacket. His face bird-like, narrow, big-nosed, and patient somehow like a watchful bird. Patient, high-shouldered, slightly foppish. How do you find things here? You needn't pretend with me dear boy. You are out of your element. Barbarians, shooting things, yes. Well it's not your scene is it? George Wilson was at school with my father. They were great friends I believe. I keep up the connection. Salt of the earth, oh absolutely, in his own way, but limited, limited, and then those two sons of his. I believe you are religious. What do you think of Miranda? You had a rather long walk and talk together didn't you, yes. She has a great capacity for freedom. Boundless, yes. And the energy. She and I have long talks. You must come and see me at my house. I live not very far away. It is my mother's house. My father is dead you know, he died in the war. I will give you the address. He touches his hat in a gesture of courtesy perhaps ironic, and saunters away. I watch his thin erect back recede among the bushes, disappear finally from sight.

I never went to his house. The next time I talked to him was when he gave me the Christ. I do not remember anything of what he said to me. How did he know those things about me? Miranda must have told him, there is no other explanation. At the time, elementary and obvious as it seems now, at the time I do not think I came to this conclusion, that Miranda was his informant, rather, because of the potency of the gift, I attributed a sort of evil prescience to Mooncranker.

That night an even worse thing happened. I had thought it might have been an isolated instance, a sort of warning, the over-mastering excitement, violence done to myself, the unexpected and terrifying issue of corruption. By prayer, by averting the mind, repurifying the images, perhaps I could recover health, be like other people. Or perhaps it had been a single stroke of punishment, not to be repeated. But that night in my sleep I dreamed of an elderly woman, with her hair in curlers, who underwent disgusting changes of feature, was at one time Aunt Jane, another the cleaning woman who used to come to our house, finally a stranger. I was undressing her in my dream and though she was willing, even avid, there were inexplicable delays while I wrestled with the various voluminous articles of her clothing. I tugged at the elastic of her navy blue bloomers while she in my dream suddenly toothless, bared pale gums and fondled me. Before I could uncover her the awful spasms rose and assailed me and I woke in the midst of protracted shudderings, to find pyjamas and sheets wet with the same sticky substance ... For a long time I lay sleepless in my clammy sin, possessed by fear and the certainty of my dissolution.

I think now, however, that this experience, coming on me in the helplessness of sleep and so soon after the first, proving prayers and vows unavailing, after the first terror had been endured, hardened me, rendered me obdurate. I knew that I was lost, but this made me merely more circumspect, more deliberate in my pleasures. Not that I abandoned prayer. Indeed, as I became more convinced of my damnation, and more skilled too at extracting pleasure from my body, so I grew more adept at prayer and it sometimes seemed to me that all these things went together, were mutually reinforcing, dependent on each other for their peculiar nature, and there was a sweetness in their intermingling. I looked at the body of the Christ in my New Testament in a different way, with a different sort of scrutiny. His languor had become more ambiguous now. I looked at the declivities below the pelvic bones, the sleek convergence of the lines towards the groin, and I thought of what lay under the loincloth and wondered if he did it too. I knew such thoughts offended him, or at least I was ninety per cent sure they did, and in my prayers I expressed contrition. But in a certain way Christ became my accomplice...

Water seeps steadily across that side of the garden, flowing along channels that can be dammed with soil and diverted. The water is muddy brown, swirling. Light breaks through the leaves in slabs and is reflected in thick dollops on the muddy brown water. The water eddies and hesitates, finding a way, there is soiled froth on the surface. Matthews turns the soil with a sharp spade. We are there, in among the bushes, watching him. Tracking. The only piece of tracking she initiated. 'Rhino,' she said, making her body go tense, creeping forward into the bushes, and I followed. We tracked rhino and we tracked each other, trying to surprise each other, get a sort of vantage point. Difficult in the thick dry bushes, the crackling grass, difficult to steal up on another person without being heard. That was late in the summer. After a long succession of rainless days. We ended up together in the heart of the bushes, suppressing our laughter in case Matthews heard us. We had planned to come out at that point, emerge, but Matthews was there before us and we didn't feel like crawling out in his full view, so we sat close together, no she was kneeling, sleeveless tennis-dress, her slender but vigorous sun-tanned arms, delicate hairs on the forearms daintly burnished in the light and her vivid laughing face turned towards me in the shadow of the slithery laurel leaves, putting on an expression of mock alarm, sitting back on her heels, and I was aware in one fleeting

94

second but for ever of the life in her, the vibrant stalk of her body, the long arch of her neck and the small breasts under her white tennis-dress. She had taken off her white headband and her hair fell forward over her brows. This is what is called a compromising situation, she said, with the usual teasing smile, and I didn't know what to say to her. I have challenged Henry and Frederick to a game of tennis, she said. We two against them. Will you be my partner? My look must have told her that I would do anything for her, be anything she asked, my face must have said this, for she laughed, but differently, and I think more shyly, and she looked away, back through the bushes to where Matthews turned the soil with his spade. The wet spade gleamed, soil and small stones briefly glittered in falling. The water slowly sidled round, flowed heavily into light. The garden between Matthews and us, the flower-beds beyond the lawn were awash, light flexible and thick on the water. Drops from the spade flung glittering across the sunlight...

Let's get back, we'd better get back this way. Don't want old Matthews to see us, do we? He'd jump to the wrong conclusions right away, old Matthews would. We crawled through the bushes again, going now laterally across the garden. Dusty and dishevelled with the dust and pollen of summer in nostrils and throats, relaxed with so much laughter, we crawled out into the open and I looked up and saw Mooncranker in his white clothes standing elegant above us, and Miranda's face darkened, caution came into it when she looked up and saw him, standing there silent and smiling, as a person might stand at a foxhole patiently waiting for the animal to emerge.

I think he saw us go in and stood waiting there. I can remember no speech from anyone on that occasion, only my sense of being somehow detected in a wrong act or at least somehow caught out. We stood there guilty before Mooncranker. That was *after* he gave me the little effigy of Christ swathed in white bandage and tied to a cross of lathe: a piece of deduction on my part, because I have no sure way of relating those events, but I remember the guilt I experienced, standing there rubbing dusty hands on grey flannel trousers, the guilt comes off the memory like a wave, a hot wave of guilt mingled with the smell of hot leaves and the sweeter smell of summer dust we bore on our persons from in among the bushes. I could measure the summer through my accessibility to guilt. At the commencement I see myself as free from it, quite whole, then as the summer progresses I fall prey to creeping guilt, symptom of my festering interior condition. So this guilt was immediate, unerring. But there was more to it than that, I fancy. I should not have felt so discomfited, if Mooncranker had not already given me the Christ; established between us that sort of intimacy, donor and recipient. No, he had already given it to me then, not much before, obviously, just a few days probably, as it had not yet started to rot, not yet drawn my attention to it by any obvious decomposition. No, it was still a wonder to me, evidence, if anything, of Mooncranker's interest in me, desire for my spiritual welfare. It was there, in my secret bower, hanging above eye level on the trunk of the silver birch tree. Did Mooncranker know of this place? Did he count on my hanging up the Christ there? Certainly in the house someone else might easily have noticed it before me, exclaimed in horror, taken it and thrown it away perhaps, so Mooncranker's intention, and there must have been an intention, some motive, I mean he wanted to inflict something on me for reasons of his own, I must believe that, what is the alternative? Mooncranker's intention was that I should hang it up in my secret place. In a house the whole thing might have misfired.

Was it she that he spoke to just before he came across the lawn towards me carrying the gift? Someone who came down the stairs quickly, the interval between the glimpse at the landing and the sound of Mooncranker's voice very small. Someone dressed in white, as from tennis ...

How marvellously she played. There was a natural grace and concentration in her movements. She had shown talent two years before, had been coached by a professional, had already been selected to play in the junior county team. There was a sweep and rhythm in her play that I had not seen before in anybody and when she was on court she was absolutely ruthless, absolutely set on winning. I had already watched her in action against Alan, who was a stylish but desultory player with a very hard service. I see the mica in the surface of the courts shine and twinkle, the white lines gleam, Miranda's body, arms and legs in a flurry of controlled motion. That was the day he gave me it, the very afternoon of the day when we beat Henry and Frederick, our triumph. On the lawn she announced it, in the middle of the morning, we were having tea – they drank tea in that house, morning and afternoon, almost never coffee. I think Uncle George had some theory about coffee being a debilitating drink, anyway it was almost never served and this morning it was tea as usual, Aunt Jane made it. I see her in pale pink with a tray, her long face benign and humourless. Uncle George was there too, it must have been Saturday. He said, 'Miranda wants you to be her partner for doubles,' looking at me in the curious way he had, quite affable but suspicious too, as if everything he found out about me confirmed him in the belief that I was an odd and discreditable person. They all looked at me and I think Henry or perhaps it was Frederick laughed, and I heard Miranda's voice saying, 'We'll take Henry and Frederick on,' and afterwards jokes and exclamations, but Aunt Jane's face never changed.

It was that afternoon that he came up to me, Mooncranker, quite out of the blue, sauntering up with the white gift in his hands. He spoke to someone on the way, he stopped just near the house to speak to someone, then he came over to me. Smiling. He inclined his body forward courteously and said some words, like, please accept this gift, or, I'd very much like you to have this small token. I was very touched that Mooncranker should have studied my tastes, found out about my interests. It struck me at the time as almost incredible that he should have bothered to do so. I went and hung it up on the tree in my secret place. Just above eye level, just at adoration level, where the broken sunlight came through in strips and blocks and patterned the gauzy figure. At times a radiant light played around the helmeted head.

The evidence of my guilty dreams must have been noted in due course – perhaps by Aunt Jane though I don't know if she would have recognized such signs, too delicate a clue for her detective powers, noted anyway by someone and reported to Uncle George, because one day he stopped me and said, 'Don't abuse your body, laddie, never do that. Your body,' he said, 'in its natural state, that is a state of health, is a marvellous instrument but it can be misused just like anything else and quite frankly, between you and me, you seem in a fair way to doing just that.'

I didn't at first and for quite a long time know quite what he was getting at. The almost frantic guilt and evasiveness which his single glance filled me with was more than I could bear almost, and I thought, is he talking about my walk with Miranda, my sentimental objection to shooting voles, my unmanly recourse to dictionaries, my sneaky slicing shots at tennis? Any or all of these might be implicit in his pale-eyed regard. Where did this take place? I have a vague recollection of standing in a room somewhere, while Uncle George spoke to me thus. He always spoke to me indoors, and Mooncranker always spoke to me out. Between them, as it seems to me now, they covered every eventuality. Yes, we were indoors, possibly he had cornered me in the kitchen and the more I think of it the more I think it probably was the kitchen, because there was a bluebottle buzzing and a steamy, resonant buzzing it was, yes the kitchen, with Uncle George and I standing not too close together, possibly divided by the kitchen table.

'Yes,' he said, 'I fear you will be an also-ran if you don't watch it. Since your parents are having this spot of bother and you are far from home I consider myself in *loco parentis*, I have two of my own after all, I know what boys are. Now listen, don't weaken yourself. You have got a vital flame inside you, but that flame will flicker and it may go out altogether, if you tamper with your body. Leaving you drained and debilitated. If you feel in danger of being overwhelmed, there is one thing you can do, I told this to my own boys and you can see that they aren't stunted weaklings. If you – let's be frank, we're men of the world, if you feel yourself stiffening, it is while you have the stiffness that you feel the urge to waste yourself, just you imagine a great anvil lowering down from the sky, a blacksmith's anvil slowly being lowered on to your crotch, you just imagine this massive weight pressing down on your equipment and you will start shrinking and the danger will be past. You just concentrate on the anvil my boy and you will find it therapeutic, yes I venture to say that you will find it makes a big difference. So I want you to promise me that next time you are in that position you will just try visualizing the anvil.'

I promised, I suppose. I found it difficult to look Uncle George in the face, once I had caught his drift. Shifty little beggar he probably thought me. But whether I promised or not I don't think I tried out the anvil that summer. Not because I was not visited by remorse and fear: I was. But now they were mingled with pleasurable excitement, the remorse had become an integral pang. So it was not the season for anvils. At first, when I was assailed with awful fear of dissolution, then might have been the time for anvils...

I walk through the garden. Again I am in danger of drowning or suffocation as I penetrate the denser vegetation. I am on my way to the shrine. Matthews has creosoted the toolshed and the smell of the creosote fresh and pungent lies over the whole area, like some rough and liberally applied disinfectant, like something daubed on a wound, and this smell of creosote mingles with the sweet smells of summer, and always afterwards I am to associate certain conjunctions of odours, the smell of tar and rank late summer flowers, with stealth and urgency.

One hasty glance upward at Christ in his bandage, at the white arms held from embracing by their bonds, the blind helmeted head on which the sun gleams. I catch the gauzy glints of flies' wings around him, and a muted buzzing, before sinking to my knees and unbuttoning myself while the slow swarm of accustomed images settles round me and my penis stiffens in my hot hands and I begin my curiously patient hieratic pattern of caresses, persevering in this until I am brimming and a touch injudicious brings me to the brink, forbearing becomes too impossibly difficult and I make the one decisive move which brings me off in shuddering spasms, grimacing face skyward pointing. I open my eyes on silence and the white figure on the tree. In the desolation that ensues I note more coldly the flies and the glintings and murmurings, there are too many flies and so I pull myself to my feet and cover my limp contrite offender and walk nearer the tree and look up. Which sense first is violated how can I now remember?

There is an intensity of purpose in these hoverers – some have settled. I see a blue fly run along the rim of a bandage fold, duck under and disappear, reappear farther on. The smell I notice now, detachable at last from the complex odours of the garden, particular, local, deadly, the smell of animal decomposition, and now, probably a second or two later there is revealed to my more discerning, more horrified scrutiny, a movement, a frill or gentle lift along the line of the bandage, not caused by any fly, but the movement of Christ's body inside the folds of bandage, they are white too, which is perhaps why further scrutiny is needed before I discern the greyish, wax-coloured maggots seething within the containing bandage and realize with a rising dizziness that his body is rotting, a dark pink mess of substance, seen in seams between the folds, and in this moment of nausea and insight I perceive that this body is minced-up meat, he has been fashioned in meat. By Mooncranker. With this knowledge my identity departs from me. There is a roaring which threatens to come nearer and a sort of sponginess in my vision. I succeed in walking several steps and I am there at the exit point, gulping in the heavy air, facing out across the garden, about to escape, when Uncle George, in his red track suit, comes bursting through the shrubbery, head up and mouth wide open, arms working like pistons. He bursts through the bushes and comes running past me, looking neither to right nor left, knees raised, one two, one two, disappears briefly beyond the orchard, but before I can move he is round again on the other side and even at this distance I can hear his harsh tormented breath. He is doing his twenty times round the garden. I can see his labouring face blindly raised, his open noisy mouth and suddenly he is a part of the awful thing happening to Christ behind me in the shade, and it is happening to me too because of my Solitary Vice and Uncle George is fleeing from it round and round the garden. The sponginess gets flecked with red, the roaring engulfs me. All the different persons I have been merge into an awful perception of what I am. I fall backwards, flat on my back, in a dead faint . . .

5

He was now experiencing a definite desire to visit the lavatory. Sensing some slight activity on the neighbouring bed he looked across. Mooncranker's head on the pillow was turning from side to side, very slowly, as if striving to avoid leisurely blows or memories. Perhaps he was in the throes of a dream. Farnaby sat up and swung his legs down to the ground.

'This plasma,' Mooncranker said suddenly and clearly. His eyes had opened again. He said, 'You are a strong boy Farnaby.'

Farnaby stood up. 'I'm just going to find the loo,' he said.

'This plasma,' Mooncranker said, 'contains indispensable materials. If it is diminished beyond a certain point, the vital salts suffer a weakening of function. Exhaustion and death ensue.'

Farnaby moved slowly towards the door, nodding his head, to show that he was following these words.

'Treatment is by infusion into the veins of water, chloride solutions, sugar. Stay a minute Farnaby, don't rush away, dear boy. I want you to go and get her for me.'

'Go and get her?' Farnaby repeated, looking at Mooncranker with a face of surprise.

'I know exactly where she has gone.'

It took Farnaby some moments longer fully to realize that Mooncranker was talking about the secretary again. 'Oh I don't think I could do that,' he said.

'There is a pool in Western Anatolia,' Mooncranker said, looking up steadily at the ceiling. 'Near a town called Denizli. A thermal pool with a sort of hotel built round it. People go there for their health, you know. And for other reasons too, of course. The water is believed to contain medicinal properties. It is on the site of a very ancient city, which attracts the historically minded. An interesting place. I have my reasons for thinking she has gone there. I want you to go and bring her back.'

'But she may not be there at all.'

'She's there all right. I should pay all expenses of course, for a reasonable period, say three or four days. It may take you that long to persuade her.'

'I must go to the lavatory,' Farnaby said. The unexpectedness of Mooncranker's request seemed to have intensified his need. 'We'll discuss it when I get back,' he said. He glanced back once as he stepped outside, but Mooncranker's profile was grave, composed. It was not very likely, in the few minutes that he was going to be out of the room, that Mooncranker would start behaving indecorously.

Outside, however, in the brightly lit, completely empty corridor, he did not know which way to go. The room he had just left was about two-thirds of the way along, so he decided to turn right and go down the shorter part of the corridor, with a vague idea of not straying too far from Mooncranker and his stricken blood plasma. White globes, set at exact intervals in the ceiling, shed along the corridor a shadowless, absolutely unvarying light, visual equivalent of protracted monotone shriek or howl, extending to the glass double doors at the end. Underfoot, rubbery beige floor-covering partially deadened the sound of his steps. Appalled by the vista of glazed light, he glanced at the white doors which succeeded one another on either side. Some had numbers on them, some not. Surmising that the numbered rooms might be wards or private rooms for patients, he tried an unnumbered door and found himself staring into a long narrow room, with an overhead strip-light, piles of white linen stacked in shelves up the walls. He retreated hastily from this, feeling more agitated than before. Now he was nearing the end of the corridor.

After a brief hesitation he turned right, thinking that if he kept turning right he would eventually find himself near Mooncranker's room again. Or, failing that, he could retrace his steps by turning left whenever presented with a choice. However, he was now faced with a double swing-door, and passing through that found himself in a small square hall, with the corridor continuing beyond it. Sitting on a chair against the wall was a sandy-haired man in an overcoat. His head had declined on to his breast and he did not look up as Farnaby entered. Thinking him asleep, Farnaby began cautiously to cross the hall, but the man looked up suddenly and nodded.

'*Uz numera?*' Farnaby said, in low tones, but the other made no reply, merely gazed blankly for a moment, then again lowered his head. Farnaby hesitated, wondering if he should ask about lavatories in some other language, but he decided against it. He proceeded across the hall and into the corridor again.

Some way down, he opened another unnumbered door, and looked appalled into a small shining kitchen. There must have been an inner room or recess invisible from the door, because immediately on his opening it and looking in, a clear female voice called out, '*Kimse?*'

Without pausing to think, Farnaby closed the door softly and walked hastily away down the corridor. Possessed by the fear that the woman he had disturbed might come to the door to look out, he took a turning to the right, another, shorter corridor with a glazed glass door at the far end. He felt a fugitive, a person being hunted through these corridors. The increasing urgency of his need to urinate became confused in his mind with guilt, with the need to escape detection. His heart was beating quickly. He thought he heard somewhere ahead of him a door closing. Dread of some unavoidable confrontation possessed him, of some person in white suddenly appearing before him in this pitiless corridor. A sense of all the persons, robed and veiled and masked, working in this labyrinth, appalled him; he was an interloper, a person without function here; moreover, he was lost and the lost are prey to those who know their bearings. He looked at his watch: five minutes past three in the morning. He thought briefly and sacrilegiously of pissing against the white wall. Then, when he felt he could bear no longer to go on down the corridor, he came to a narrow passage terminating in a dark door, not a white internal one, a door obviously communicating with the outside world. It was bolted at top and bottom, with heavy bolts which he eased back quietly, working with beating heart and tormented bladder, to effect a means of egress into the night.

He succeeded finally, stepping out into a sort of interior courtyard enclosed on all sides by hospital buildings. He took some paces forward and then proceeded to void his bladder, close up against the wall for secrecy and silence, a scaldingly blissful operation. Buttoning himself he looked up at the tall buildings rising on all sides. Most of the rooms were in darkness but here and there were lighted windows. He found it odd to think that in one of these rooms Mooncranker was lying being intravenously fed. If these rooms, all these hundreds of rooms, were regarded as cells, then each was infected with disease, impaired by some disability; yet the organism as a whole functioned well ... Time to be getting back to Mooncranker, he thought. It had not occurred to him yet, except as a sort of vague foreboding, that he had no exact idea where Mooncranker's room was.

In returning to the door he heard a scuffling and a faint clatter from the darkness to one side. He stopped, peering into the darkness, and saw after a moment a double row of metal bins standing against a low wall. He had startled a cat from its scavenging and in its flight it had set one of the lids clattering against the bin next to it. He saw in the faint light thrown from a second-floor window the contents of this uncovered bin, which could not have been of much interest to a cat, being composed in its top layers at least of wads of cotton wool with dark discoloured patches that he did not examine or think about too closely. The waste products of the healing process.

As quickly as possible he retraced his steps, passed through the door again, bolted it behind him. The hush of the hospital settled round him. He stood there in the passage for some moments, breathing deeply. Then he cautiously emerged on to the corridor. He knew he had to turn left to begin with and then at the next junction right but after this he found himself at a loss. He walked down a corridor that seemed longer than any he had met on the way. From somewhere near he thought he heard the rattling of trolley wheels. His former apprehension began to return to him. Moreover he now realized that he had omitted to make a mental note of Mooncranker's room-number. It was about two thirds of the way down. But from which end will I now be approaching it? The numbers of the rooms along Mooncranker's corridor were in two figures. Seventies and eighties. Or perhaps thirties and forties. Why did

I not take care? I didn't expect of course to be wandering so far afield. That mistake over the linen closet first confused me. And then the voice from the kitchen, inquiring into my identity. I should have said strong boy. *Kouvetli oglan.*

He had not, as far as he could remember, gone up or down any stairs in his wanderings. So he must be still on the same floor as Mooncranker. He reached the end of the long corridor, passed again through double swing-doors, which made a faint susurration. Here there was a narrow hall with a number of doors set fairly close together. They had no numbers, but several had metal plates with names on them. Consulting rooms or offices of the staff, presumably. Beyond them, as a sort of narrower continuation, another corridor began. He set off along this corridor, noticing now that his fear of encounters had made him sweat – the shirt stuck to his back. These shiny white walls, along which the light from overhead strips seemed to melt and spread, this glazed beige rubberized substance beneath his feet, the smells of sweet suffocation that seemed part of the emission of light itself, these things had been accompaniments of his life always. He was made for upright progress through these labyrinthine arteries as if he were himself some dazed enzyme or protein, some humble mineral agent in the veins of the hospital . . .

Some instinct made him look back the way he had come. He saw very briefly, trembling on the brink of escaping sense, two nuns side by side, walking through the hall he had just left. He was able to see without being seen at this moment, because he was at right angles to them as they approached the hall and he saw them through the glass partition that separated the hall itself from a secondary passage which he had not noticed in passing. He did not know whether they had seen him but thought not, as neither made any sign. However, they had turned right into the hall: which meant, if they continued through it, that they would be emerging in a matter of moments on the corridor where he was at present standing. And then they would certainly see him. He had therefore a very short time in which to decide on a course of action. If he stayed where he was, the sisters would come upon him. They would see at once he was not a patient. Probably ignorant of the presence of Mooncranker, let alone attendant strong boys, they would think him an intruder. He would no doubt be able to reassure them but the thought of their initial impression, their first view of him as a loitering shirt-sleeved marauder, was intolerable to him, as if no subsequent explanation could ever efface it, and he decided, in that split second, on evasive action. The nearest door to him had number one hundred and twenty-five on it. Farnaby turned the knob gently, opened the door and slipped in, closing it behind him.

The room was in darkness. After a moment or two he was able to detect the deep regular breathing of a sleeper. Rather stertorous. Impossible to tell from it gender or number. He waited there with his back to the door, hardly daring to breathe for fear of arousing the occupant of the room. Even in these few moments he thought it strange, the knowledge thus effected of another human being, lying there in the darkness, perhaps gravely ill, oblivious of his presence. He waited for two or three minutes then a sort of rising panic obliged him to re-enter the corridor. He opened the door very slightly, looked up and down. The creature on the bed behind him stirred, murmured. Perhaps it was the light the open door admitted. Nobody in the corridor. Soundlessly Farnaby slipped out. He resumed his way along the corridor. No sign of the nuns now. No sound of any sort, except the scuffle of his own feet on the floor. Turning right at the next junction he entered a corridor that seemed familiar. The numbers on the doors were in two figures. Forty-three, forty-four ... That red fire hydrant on the wall, surely I remember that. He walked about two-thirds of the way along this corridor, stopped, stared at the number, the white door, as if trying by some effort of the will to impose attributes that would make it indubitably Mooncranker's. Then he took a deep breath, opened the door slightly and looked in. It was not Mooncranker's room. There was only one bed in it and a man was sitting on a chair beside the bed. This man did not look up immediately and Farnaby was on the point of withdrawing, had in fact begun to turn into the corridor again when he saw another door opening further down and realized that at any moment someone – some member of the hospital staff probably – would be emerging on to the corridor and would see him loitering at this door where he had no business to be. He was paralysed for the moment, with indecision, and in that moment the man on the chair looked over his shoulder and saw him. He said nothing, but Farnaby could see from his expression and the posture of his body that he was not startled or hostile. As if in a dream he closed the door and advanced towards the bed. And when he looked down at the man's thin, quite ordinary face, he thought that face showed a dreamlike quality too. In the bed was a youth of perhaps nineteen with a flushed face. His eyes were closed. Farnaby knew at once that this youth was very ill. The man at the bedside caught his gaze and nodded. His face was calm and stricken. *'C'est mon fils,'* he said.

Farnaby in this moment ceased to feel an intruder because he could see that this man was so filled with grief that nothing mattered, there was no room in his mind for questions of identity. 'I am sorry,' he said, apologizing for his presence there uninvited but also, more importantly, for the gravity of the boy's condition.

'He is dying,' the man said. He looked down at the smooth, flushed face. 'In some hours now, he will be dead.'

'Are you sure?' Farnaby said. The youth seemed sleeping merely. But there was no perceptible breath.

The man nodded and a livelier expression appeared on his face. The need to establish a fact caused him to lose some of that tranced grief. 'Yes,' he said. 'The appendix is burst.'

'Burst,' Farnaby repeated.

'He seemed to recover from the operation, but since this morning he is sinking. The doctor told me there is no hope, none at all. He will die, perhaps before the morning.'

'I am very sorry,' Farnaby said again.

'I cannot understand it,' the man said. He lifted the bed-clothes a little, and showed Farnaby the boy's strong neck, broad shoulders. 'He is not yet twenty years old,' he said, and his face in saying this had again returned to the dream, where strong young men decline and die and others in shirt sleeves enter rooms not their own in the middle of the night. 'He wants the nurse who changes the dressings. This is all he asks for. But she is not on duty now. She is the day nurse. An hour ago he opened his eyes and asked for her. Not his mother, not his sister. Only the nurse who was changing the dressings every time, in the days we all thought he was going to get well. She will not be here before the morning.'

'Any nurse would do,' Farnaby said. 'He would not notice the difference now, I think.'

'Oh, yes. I think he would. There has been a relationship between them. She is young, you see, the same age as my son.'

'Yes, I see,' Farnaby said.

'They get an idea into their heads, you see.'

'Yes. Well, if you will excuse me –' He looked down for the last time at the young man's face, which was turned aside on the pillow. There was no mark of pain or suffering on it, only a deep flush round the cheek bones. The eyes were closed, the rather short lashes quite motionless. Farnaby wondered what colour the boy's eyes were. He smiled a little at the seated man, trying in the smile to convey his sympathy. He began to move away from the bed.

'*Une seconde,*' the man said, and he got up from his seat. 'I will go and see if I can find out when that nurse comes on duty tomorrow. Perhaps I can make him live through the night if I can promise him the nurse in the morning. Perhaps they can get her to come early.'

'Perhaps.'

'Will you stay with him for a few minutes until I return?'

The man's face had become eager momentarily at the prospect of action. '*Si vous n'êtes pas pressé,*' he said.

'Of course.'

Almost as soon as the man had left the room, the boy's eyes opened and he began to speak. '*Doucement, Mathilde,*' he said. 'Mathilde, be careful.' His eyes, blue and wondering, looked at something beyond the bed. He swallowed thickly. His strong white throat worked painfully. '*Qu'est-ce que tu fais?*' he said. 'What are you doing?' His breath caught suddenly and noisily, then was released in a gasping pant. '*Oui, comme ça,*' he said more loudly. 'Yes, yes, like that. Aah ...' he sighed, on a long note of easement and relief, and Farnaby realized that in his delirium the youth was re-enacting the changing of his dress-

108

ing by the nurse Mathilde, the painful removal of the plaster probably, and something else, some other ritual solace that had accompanied the change of dressing, something else Mathilde did for him ... With a sudden compassionate insight, Farnaby saw through to the core of the dying boy's delirium, and understood. He took out a handkerchief and wiped the dew of fever from the boy's brow. His own eyes filled suddenly with tears as he did so, and it was through tears that he saw the boy's father return.

'They have asked for her,' the man said. 'She is coming in one hour.' He turned to the bed and his face lost expression.

Farnaby muttered something, made his escape. Outside, in the corridor, his problem was waiting to be resumed. After brief consideration he decided that he should perhaps have taken the other direction, turned left instead of right at the last intersection of corridors. Accordingly he retraced his steps, past the fire hydrant again, along the other side. He did not know, so confused had he become, which side of the corridor Mooncranker's room was likely to be, so he adopted a different technique, opening doors only very slightly, a mere crack, and peering in. Several doors he opened in this way upon darkness, one a large ward with rows of beds on either side, a dim night light at the far end. It could not be this corridor at all then. Try another one just to make sure. He chose an unnumbered door, opened it very very slightly, taking care to avoid the slightest noise. When the crack was wide enough, he applied his eye to it. As he did so he thought he heard, from some distant part of the hospital, the sound of a human shriek. He listened, but the sound was not repeated. There was, however, a sort of regularly repeated gasping or low grunting sound from the room into which he was peering, and it was this that caused him to linger there, though he knew at once it was not Mooncranker's room, but obviously an office of some kind. The light was too dim to make out things in any detail. Most of the space he could see was occupied by what looked like a large filing cabinet. He inched the door open wider, enlarged his field of vision, and saw two human figures apparently naked, rhythmically copulating in the dimness on a low article of furniture, presumably a table. The gasping sound was coming from one of them. He could not distinguish male from female, but one narrowbacked creature was kneeling between the legs of the other and moving back and forth with a sort of insensate regularity. The other was lying back on the table, face raised towards the ceiling, open-mouthed.

No way of telling whether it was doctors or nurses or patients thus whiling away the night. The face of the supine one bore a general resemblance in configuration to that of the lady doctor who had examined Mooncranker...

Suddenly Farnaby thought he heard steps behind him along the corridor, and the faint rattle of a trolley. He closed the door with immense care on the labouring back and open-mouthed face, then made off quickly along the corridor, coming after some moments to swing-doors he felt sure he remembered, and through them into a square hall where against the wall, hunched forward in solitary meditation, sat the sandy-haired man in the overcoat, who looked up at his entrance and amicably grimaced.

'Excuse me,' Farnaby said, in his light, diffident voice. 'Are you English by any chance?'

'No' exactly,' the man said. 'I'm frae Aberdeen.'

Farnaby exclaimed, 'Oh a Scot!' with sudden exuberance, as though he were applauding a boundary. He was delighted to find this reliable person in such a place. That accent stood for common sense and a decent reticence the world over; and the appearance of the man before him, sandy hair, high colour, keen blue eyes – though bloodshot now, he noticed, and rather strangely lingering in regard – all proclaimed the practical no-nonsense person, both feet planted squarely on the ground, attributes deeply reassuring, after his recent experiences, to Farnaby, who now announced his name.

'Andrew McSpavine,' the other returned promptly. 'Will ye no hae a seat, laddie?'

'Thanks.' Farnaby sat down. 'I'm afraid I'm a bit lost,' he said, attempting a rueful smile.

'Ay, that happens frequently, frequently,' McSpavine said.

Farnaby, after waiting a moment in the hope of some help, said, 'I think I know the way now, actually.'

There was silence between them for a few moments, then

McSpavine sniffed loudly, clearing his nostrils of some blockage. 'I hae sailed the seven seas, laddie,' he said.

'Oh really,' Farnaby said. He was somewhat bothered by the fixity of McSpavine's regard. Nothing shifty about this chap, he told himself, by way of reassurance. There was a strange, sweetish odour about him too. 'Are you waiting for someone?' he asked, curious to know why McSpavine was sitting here in the middle of the night.

The Scot sat forward, looking at Farnaby intently. 'My Flora has just passed away,' he said. He groped under his coat and brought out a silver-plated pocket watch, to which he briefly referred. 'Thirty-seven minutes ago,' he said. 'I'm just sitting here trying to think it all out. The pree-cise significance.'

'I am terribly sorry to hear that,' said Farnaby, who had been taken completely by surprise. He looked away in embarrassment.

'Ay,' McSpavine said. He had taken out a yellow oilskin tobacco pouch and a short cherry-wood pipe. 'I hae sailed the seven seas,' he said, shaking his head slowly. He began filling the pipe. 'It was me that got things going,' he said. 'Trying to keep the old tub going. Nothing but the wee scoundrelly lascars to rely on. Mulattoes an' quadroons. Persons o' doubtful loyalty.'

'You are a ship's engineer then?' Farnaby said, uneasy at this loquacity, and the abrupt change of subject after the reference to Flora's death.

'*Was*,' McSpavine said. He sniffed again.

Farnaby watched the fingers, which were not as blunt and capable as he would have wished, were in fact thin and distinctly tremulous, stuffing dark shreds into the cherry wood. Good strong sailor's shag, no doubt. McSpavine had a myriad little lines at the corners of his strangely unblinking eyes. Laughter lines, Farnby told himself. A genial seafaring man. His uneasiness was growing.

'Was, laddie,' McSpavine said. 'I gave it up when I married Flora. Started up a newsagent's business, in Welwyn Garden City.'

'Welwyn Garden City,' Farnaby repeated politely.

'It was my Flora's native habitat.' McSpavine looked gravely at Farnaby. 'I sit here,' he said, 'trying to work it out. I should never hae brought my Flora out to foreign parts. We had a nice wee house in Welwyn Garden City. Terrace house. But she grew restless, it wasn't enough for her. We had no children, d'ye see, and as she grew older she felt that life was passing her by. She listened to my stories of the seagoing days. She was always on at me to take her for a trip and in the end I did.'

There was a pause while McSpavine finished filling his pipe and put it in his mouth. Farnaby immediately grew alarmed in case McSpavine intended actually to smoke the pipe on hospital premises.

'I took her wi' me,' McSpavine said, muttering indistinctly round the stem of his pipe. 'Marseilles, Venice, Izmir. She loved it all, laddie, every minute of it, it was more multifarious than she was accustomed to. The life, the teeming life. The piquant contrasts, rich and poor, the grand boulevards with wee beggar men hoppin' about on their stumps, donkeys in the streets, oranges on the trees. Then we got to this city, and she died.' He consulted his pocket watch again. 'Fifty-two minutes ago.'

Farnaby said, 'You shouldn't blame yourself, it would have happened anyway.'

'Ay,' McSpavine said, 'but maybe she'd have had longer if I had left her there in Welwyn Garden City, leadin' her peaceful existence. The piquant contrasts and all the picturesqueness she was exclaiming about might have stimulated the growth of the disease. That is a thought that is heavy to me.'

'I shouldn't think so,' Farnaby said. He was growing concerned about leaving Mooncranker for so long unattended.

'She lay for eight days gettin' weaker. Smilin', smilin' all the time. The very faintest o' smiles. So there was no difference, d'ye see, between life and death, no difference whatsoever. I was watching her face, and I didna know myself exactly the moment that she died. She looked the same before and after.' McSpavine's voice had changed: it had become slower, taken on a droning, obsessive note. The Scottish accent too seemed to be less in evidence. His eyes had narrowed, as though he found difficulty in focusing, and this brought out the innumerable wrinkles, the network of lines round them – lines of laughter in the salt spray and horizon-scanning, Farnaby tried to remind himself, in an attempt to preserve his earlier feeling of the Scot's reliability and hearty good sense. This, however, he realized, was now almost all dissipated, dissolved as it were in McSpavine's loquacity.

'She made no sudden movement,' McSpavine said, gesturing with his pipe and peering at Farnaby. 'She went right on smilin', but the doctor said "*rigor mortis*", and I knew from the cut of his jib that Flora had gone where the weary are at rest.'

Farnaby, who could not quite believe that his companion had uttered these words, looked for a moment blankly before him then said, 'It must have been a great shock to you.'

'Weel,' McSpavine said cautiously, 'it isna sae much the shock of Flora's going, though that might be taken as originatin'...'

He said no more for some time. Farnaby stood up, seeking in his mind phrases consoling and valedictory. Before he could speak, however, the other said, 'The moment of death was not detectable. If I could have had a sign, maybe I would never have gone back.'

He looked round the room, as if to interrogate it on this issue. The glazed white walls reflected light evenly. Everything in the room was equally distinct. The vertical lines where the corridor began, set at an angle from them, were white and cruelly sharp. Farnaby was aware as he stood there of the life of the hospital all round him, as a great seething hush in which pain was being suppressed by white-robed attendants, continually denied its proper screeching expression.

'That's what I did, I went back,' McSpavine said, speaking as it seemed not now to Farnaby but to the stark white room. 'To fix the time of death,' he said. 'Since she hadna made any sign herself. I thought it only fitting to know the time, by the clock, the hospital time, of *rigor mortis*. I didna trust my ain.' He looked up at Farnaby. 'There must be a dividing line, laddie,' he said. 'There must be a line drawn between the living and the dead. So I went back. Not to Flora's room. There wasn't any clock in Flora's room, but there is a big round clock in all the public wards. I went in the one nearest, just in the doorway to see the clock. It was dark in there, just one light at a table at the far end, the nurse's table, but I could see the clock on the wall, it was eight minutes past three, laddie. I was checking it against my own, standing there in the door. Everyone was sleeping. Then this young woman, her bed was just under the clock, she sat up and looked at me. Young wi' long hair. She sat up in bed in the middle of the night and she saw me standin' there. And she smiled at me, laddie. Such a smile. It is that I've been pondering over, in conjunction with my Flora's passing. Trying to get the pree-cise significance. Because my Flora was smiling too, d'ye see?'

McSpavine smiled himself at this point, or at least the left side of his mouth slipped suddenly downward. Farnaby not knowing whether it was a real smile or merely the semblance of one, compromised in his response by nodding his head. His initial sense of the other's sturdy probity had now quite gone. McSpavine's very appearance seemed different. The face that looked up at him now was pale, peering, loose-mouthed.

'I must be getting along,' Farnaby said.

'Twas a smile only inceedentally levelled at me,' McSpavine said, with an increase of urgency, perhaps evoked by Farnaby's move to depart. 'I realize that. But it aroused a wish, an unco' powerful desire, for carnal knowledge of the wee lassie.' He took the pipe out of his mouth and gestured with it towards the ceiling. 'I wanted to creep into the bed with her,' he said. He looked at Farnaby and an expression of extreme gravity came over his face. 'Not a minute after,' he said. 'Less than fifty seconds after my Flora had been pronounced *rigor mortis*.'

Farnaby, to whom this confession of inveterate lechery came as a culminating stroke of disillusionment, at once began to move away towards the entrance to the corridor.

'Shock of grief,' he mumbled. 'Demoralized, quite under-standable, very natural in fact.'

Without waiting for more, and without looking behind, he passed through the swing-doors and began to walk away, rapidly at first, then more slowly as he realized that he was coming to Mooncranker's corridor. He turned left and tried to remember how far down it should be. About one-third of the way, he thought. Number seventy-nine was the one he selected finally as being most likely. Inch by inch, gripping the door-knob tight, he opened the door, approaching his face to the widening crack, tense for any enormity. Light, an empty bed, beyond it another, and Mooncranker's calm profile, open-eyed. The apparatus of sustenance still in place. With a great surge of relief and homecoming, Farnaby opened the door wide and walked in. Mooncranker did not turn his head. Farnaby stretched out on the bed again.

'The most extraordinary things have been happening to me,' he said.

6

Mooncranker, who had been awake for the last twenty minutes or so, heard this entry and this preliminary remark without any sense that they affected him, as if he were listening to a distant barking or crowing across a desolate landscape in some inconceivably bleak dawn. He no longer felt sleepy but his sense of externals was muted, his body extended under the sheets did not seem responsive to his will and impulse. It was as if by looking at things he distanced himself from them, made them unreal: the slightly tremulous concentricity of the light reflected on the ceiling above him; the looming con-traption of bottles and tubes beyond the bed. Interiorly, how-ever, with a sort of desperate patience, he was attempting to recreate, complete in every detail, the last occasion on which he had seen and talked to Miranda, the time immediately before her departure. Patience was needed because other memories, largely irrelevant, persisted in obtruding, mingling, obscur-ing the girl's image. Perhaps it would help to frame it into words.

'We had breakfast,' he said, in a remote voice. 'Yoghurt and honey, toast. No, not Turkish coffee, please. She doesn't like Turkish coffee at breakfast time. She likes *café au lait*. She always likes abundant things, plentiful things. Can't you get an

115

English breakfast at this hotel? She's very young, you know. An excellent shorthand typist, however. Not much good, I said, asking for an English breakfast in a Moslem country. Bacon figures largely in an English breakfast, don't forget that. Well, she hadn't forgotten of course, but she is rather wilful at times.

'I went out to buy a paper. *New York Herald Tribune* of the day before. After that I decided for some reason or other to have a bath. I think it was while I was in the bath that she made up her mind, instead of going shopping to the Covered Bazaar as she had intended, to go off altogether for a while. I don't think she intends to leave me for good.'

'I'm sure she doesn't,' Farnaby said, with a vague attempt at consolation.

Mooncranker turned his head on the pillow very slowly, until he was looking directly at Farnaby.

'That is why I believe she has gone to this thermal pool. She knew it was the place I would think of first. I had been talking to her about it rather a lot.'

For some moments, hazily, he tried to understand the nature of his obsession, the almost numbing hold on his imagination the hot pool had taken right from the first, from his first reading of it.

'Did you find out anything about that groom?' he said.

Farnaby, who was beginning to feel drowsy, could not at first think what Mooncranker was talking about. Then he remembered.

'It seems,' he said, 'that the man had nothing to do with grooms or anything of that sort, and it was quite by accident that he turned up when he did.'

'Accident?' Mooncranker said. 'Nonsense. He came for me.'

'There is no groom,' Farnaby said patiently.

Looking sideways at Farnaby's long, pale, earnest face on the pillow, Mooncranker felt a return of the suspicion that this lying fellow was in league with the hotel staff against him, and perhaps also impersonating Farnaby in order to entrap or entangle him in some way. He was attacked by a sense of his utter folly in putting such a person on the scent of Miranda, actually asking him to go after her. In the chagrin of having been so hoodwinked he could not speak, could merely stare silently at the other's face on the pillow.

'He came to fumigate the room,' Farnaby said, in the same patient voice. 'That was what he was really after. The particular insect foe I could not determine. They didn't know the word in English. Bugs, I suppose. Though the Armenian person reacted most strongly to termites.'

'Armenian person? Termites?' Mooncranker repeated in a surprised and offended voice. 'Do you really expect me to believe that? It was the *groom*.'

'Well, that is what they told me at the desk. He had come to spray the place in order to combat an insect pest. He was an exterminator, sir, not a groom, and that explains his clothing and equipment. I suppose he thought our room was unoccupied. He was probably as startled to see us as we were to see him.'

Farnaby saw that Mooncranker had commenced smiling to himself as if he knew better. He closed his eyes. He felt very sleepy now. He was aware that Mooncranker was talking again, something about bicycles, but he made no attempt to follow. After a while, he slept.

'To deal with my correspondence,' Mooncranker said. 'Three days a week at first. There was a basket sort of thing at the front which invariably contained an apple, a Penguin book and a torch. Brand new, shiny bicycle . . .'

He stopped talking for a moment, absorbed in the radiant image of Miranda that autumn, cycling down the street towards his house, pedalling up and down, up and down, her handlebars gleaming, her face uplifted, glowing with health. Mondays, Wednesdays and Fridays.

'After that, I took her on full time,' he said. Glancing sideways he was annoyed to find that Farnaby had fallen asleep. Insensitive lout.

She was real to me before that, long before that. On the tennis-court I saw her first, she was wearing a white headband and a sleeveless dress with pleated skirt. Honey-coloured hair and a richness of colouring not usual in English girls, not at all usual. Tanned arms and legs. She was then fifteen or so, a charming young person. This lout on the next bed, completely

117

supernumerary now. Insolently sleeping there. He was somewhat younger than Miranda. Oh, yes, I remember. Don't imagine that I have forgotten anything, Farnaby. I remember that summer in every detail, summer of my umpiring. You and she played together often. You suited each other's style. You were complementary and every game cemented that relationship between you, while I watched the bright arms, the bared teeth against the glare, the arching and angling of the lithe body, play of the pleated skirts, gleams of white pants beneath. I suffered, to see how they helped each other on the court, retrieved the fortunes of the game by some *coup*. Yes, they played so well together, everybody agreed. And in the final of the tournament, when they were up against George's boys, bigger and older, how I was torn. I wanted Miranda to triumph but not in that company. Once or twice, in umpiring, I gave the points against them that should have been theirs. Several times. But it was of no avail. They won. She kissed him, full on the lips. They went off together, into the shrubbery or so it seemed. I remained for some minutes, though my umpiring now was over. Jane brought a tray with glasses and ice, a great jug of lemonade. Kind anxious face, Jane, something of stoicism in the gentleness of the mouth, out of place completely in that loud hirsute set of males. She stood there with the tray, asking where the others were. And she called, I remember her calling out 'James, Miranda', and no answer coming. The winners had disappeared...

When Farnaby awoke faint light was coming through the curtains. Someone had been in and switched off the lamp near Mooncranker's bed. He turned his head and looked across but could make out nothing but a vague bulk under sheets, a dark shape on the pillow. The suspended bottles on either side of Mooncranker gleamed dully, he could see no darkness of liquid in them. Inside and outside the hospital everything was completely silent. Farnaby began to reconstruct the shopping expedition that must have preceded the gift to him of the sausage-meat Christ. Bright summer morning, down the broad high street with its old-fashioned cobbled verges, its market cross in the centre. The green-painted bus-stops. Mooncranker in a spotted bow-tie, wearing an alpaca jacket somewhat sagging as to pockets, the negligent academic, carrying a stick. Up the high street past the warm pharmaceutical smells wafting from Boots, the odours of last night's slopped beer from the 'Red Lion', past the ice-cream parlour and the foyers of both Odeon and Gaumont to the row of shops opposite the Metropole Hotel. Smell of sawdust and wet slabs and freshly minced meat. Mooncranker smiling vaguely in the doorway, waiting perhaps for some lady to buy chops. How much sausage-meat would be needed, not more than four ounces, surely. But can you go into a butcher's shop and after the usual salutations ask for only a quarter of a pound of sausage-meat? Surely not. Perhaps you incorporated it with other things. Perhaps it was simply an item on your list, slipped in between best steak and neck of mutton. He would think you needed it for seasoning or stuffing, which in a sense of course you did. Then home again, home again. But that is what distresses me, even now, makes my heart beat more violently and my cheeks go hot here on the pillow, that it must have been premeditated, the whole thing. No mere random impulse of malignity, no casual or incidental damage, no. It was thought out, planned in advance. What shall I do to young Farnaby? It involved an expedition probably and certainly you must have taken trouble to get the consistency just right, did you mix it with bread crumbs? That is what it is, sir, the sustained unfaltering cruelty of it, which makes me think I was specially singled out. Children do not realize, sir, that harm done to them is a stray individual matter, they think it is the cosmos. The whole cosmos in your person handed me that object ...

Mooncranker stirred and groaned. The light was appreciably stronger now. Farnaby could see that the professor's eyes were still closed. After a moment or two, however, he groaned again.

'Are you awake, sir?' Farnaby said, in low tones.

'I fear so.' Mooncranker had awakened to physical pain and vague anguish of spirit. The inside of his mouth hurt him considerably and his head ached. In spite of his sleep he felt exhausted. He gazed up at the bleak ceiling, grey in the dawn.

'Listen, Farnaby,' he said. 'Are you listening? I must have

her back.' He moved his tongue slowly over the sore roof of his mouth. 'I would go myself,' he said, 'but I don't feel quite up to it.'

A silence followed. Mooncranker grew frightened. 'I will pay all expenses, of course,' he said. 'Plus a sum for the inconvenience. Whatever you think reasonable.' He did not know why it had become so important that Farnaby should go. No one else, of course, that he could ask; but there was another reason for insisting, both vaguer and more imperative; an obscure yet urgent sense of fitness.

'Just tell me one thing,' Farnaby said, but before he could proceed, Mooncranker started speaking again, in haste to forestall the question that he felt to be coming.

'It is not far from the ancient city of Laodicea. The pool, I mean. It is itself on the site of the city of Hierapolis, about which less is known, though I myself believe it is of even more venerable date. I talked to her a lot about it. About the pool, I mean. Water constantly at about blood heat, reputed to have miraculous healing properties . . .'

'No, but tell me one thing,' Farnaby said. He was lying on his back, staring up at the ceiling. 'Why did you give me that little effigy of Christ on the Cross, made of sausage-meat and all wrapped up in white bandage? Your giving that to a thirteen-year-old boy I cannot understand. I mean the motive behind it.'

His heart was beating with excitement, now that he had at last put the question so fully and clearly.

After a moment or two Mooncranker said, 'Your parents wrote that you were going through a religious phase.'

Then there was a prolonged silence, through which Farnaby waited patiently, thinking that something more must be added.

Finally, however, he said, 'Are you saying that they suggested it to you?'

He had not spoken of it to them, nor indeed to anyone; returning after that summer holiday to the same house but now his mother only, to pursuits and preoccupations in which Christ figured scarcely at all, except as a sort of repugnance, a memory to make him wince. Shame had prevented any explanations. That and the sense that there was no solace anywhere for it, since the adult world itself had dealt him this blow. And, perhaps most of all, the peculiar horror of the circumstances...

It came to him again now in a heavy wave of recollection, how summer had conspired to shut out the world, thickening the clumps at the base of the lime trees, weaving grass among the shrubs, hanging everything with flowers. Scents too hemmed him in. The space inside the branches almost swooningly private and screened. The white crucified figure above him on the seamed trunk as he knelt. But kneeling was ambiguous, accompanied by anticipation of pleasure that quickened his heart, not at all the calm resolve of confession with which one knelt in prayer. It was this, this impure excitement, that grew stronger as his solitude and impunity came home to him, affirmed as always by the white flowers, that rank sweetness, the helmeted and softly aureoled figure on his cross on the tree; corrupted by the former occasions on which in this enclosed space he had extracted from his flesh lonely pangs, always before, however, or at least so he thought, always with some reluctance, some residual sense of offending Christ, until this day when an ingenuity rose in him, element in his excitement, a sort of cruelty directed at the suffering figure on the tree. Kneeling still, steadily braving the image, only in the last moments, in the very throes of his ecstasy ceasing to gaze at it, raising his face to the remote formations of cirrus in the sky above him ... For a moment he was tempted to say something of all this to Mooncranker, in an effort to make him understand. How he had afterwards approached the effigy, to see a stirring amidst the strands of white bandage, an activity that might have been caused by a breeze, though there was none; and as if this perception had sharpened his other senses, he had smelt for the first time the putrid odour, no longer a strand merely in the complicated rope of summer, but sharp and single, odour of Christ's decay, and had seen, while nausea climbed in his throat, the folds of the bandage stirred by peeping white maggots, from which he could not – culminating horror – immediately escape, his stumbling retreat to light and air cut off by gasping track-suited Uncle George pounding round the lawn...

Mooncranker said, 'The hot springs rise on the hillside among the ruins of the city and they are channelled southwards, gather into pools farther down. I have read a good deal about it, everything I could find. There are fallen columns and fragments of antique masonry in the pool itself, you can see them through the clear water, marvellous sight. The pool is deep enough to swim in. The temperature of course is constant, in all seasons, and there is a sort of – '

'I'm afraid I can't accept that,' Farnaby interrupted, but gently, looking again with a feeling of wonder at Mooncranker's exhausted, bird-like profile.

'I assure you it is all quite true,' Mooncranker said.

'No, I don't mean about the pool, I mean what you said before, about my parents. I don't believe they had anything to do with it. I wish you would think back to those days, sir. There must have been some reason behind it.'

Resigning himself with a sort of obedience, in response at any rate to Farnaby's evident eagerness, Mooncranker sought in his mind for a steady view of those summer days, but Miranda took up all the foreground, the peach tan of her arms and legs, her darkly blushing face, the faint grass stains on the white skirt of her tennis dress, her eagerness, listening to him. Farnaby's hand he thought he remembered again, the scratched, long-fingered, thin-wristed hand. No doubt, no denying that the thing had been given to the boy, and by him. But to find the feeling again after these years and especially now, deserted and frightened as he was ... Desire he could remember, and jealousy too: things related to possession; but the malignity that had inspired the gift, the distant spurt of malevolence, impossible now to rediscover. Into his groping mind there came the memory of heat and stillness, boy and girl crawled laughing out of the glassy laurels, while he stood there above them. The laughing children faded, themselves merging into that white opaque stillness, which was all around him now, he was alone in it, nothing remained, memory and senses were sealed off, there was no possible answer to Farnaby's question. Gradually, into this glazed stillness where his being lay, there crept a desire that his life could end, here and now, or soon.

Farnaby said, in self-deprecating tones, 'I thought my actions had been responsible for it, for Christ decaying.'

'I don't understand,' Mooncranker said.

'Did Uncle George know about it?'

'I'm sorry dear boy, I can't talk about it now, I simply can't. Will you go?'

'No,' Farnaby said. He paused. Anger against Mooncranker rose in him, anger at this selfishness, as he thought it, this refusal to explain. 'No, I won't go,' he said.

Desperately, Mooncranker sought in his mind for an acceptable formula. The ability to find formulas had been one of his greatest assets as a chairman of discussion groups.

'It was a theory of outrage,' he said. 'In those days I believed in moral progress. Just as material progress depends on checks and obstacles in order to breed ingenuity as it were, so I believed that outrage, the violation of traditional pieties, could extend man's moral range, give him energy to embrace contradictions, *apparent* contradictions...'

He fell silent, exhausted by this effort. All he wanted now, was to be rid of Farnaby.

'Do you mean you foresaw it?' Farnaby said, in wondering tones. 'You foresaw what would happen and the shock it would give me?'

'I wanted you to reconcile the divinity and the decay,' Mooncranker said. 'Will you go?'

'She may not have gone there at all. And in any case, how should I recognize her?'

'Recognize her?' Mooncranker turned his head slowly to regard him. 'Recognize her? But you know her, dear boy. It is Miranda, the girl you used to play tennis with.'

For a moment Farnaby thought Mooncranker must be lying. Then immediately he knew it was the truth. And he knew in that moment that he would go. Automatically he glanced at his watch: almost six o'clock. Soon they would be bringing breakfast...

'Very well,' he said. He closed his eyes, waiting for the day.

Part Three

1

Getting out of the taxi, extruding and finally extricating his
long-legged angular body, in his not completely coordinated
way, hasty and wavering and somehow graceful too; counting
out into the driver's palm Turkish coins of small denomina-
tion, several of which were dropped in the process; bidding the
driver farewell – 'depart rejoicing' as the Turks say: all the
while he was aware of an unsought, unwished for enlargement,
he had a sense of space and distance, the sky immense above
him, the breeze smelling of snow. He had not looked out much
on his way up from the town. Rehearsing his lines of inquiry,
for one thing; and then the taxi itself had not afforded much
of a view, being of ancient American manufacture with very
narrow windows like gun embrasures. So he had not noticed
how high they were getting. Now, deposited before tall gates
on a level circular forecourt, he felt the breeze at his ankles,
raised reluctant eyes to distant, snow-capped peaks.

'God be with you,' the taxi-driver said, smiling broadly, and
once again as politeness demanded he told the driver to depart
rejoicing, noticing that in fact the broad smile was persisting as
the man drove away. A genial soul, or perhaps he overcharged
me. Mooncranker's money anyway.

Tall gates of wrought iron standing open, flanked by high
brick walls. Nothing inscribed or emblazoned upon them either
in admonition or blandishment. Some yards of tarmac drive-
way then a building with swing-doors. Swing-doors the world
over admit you to where the action is and sure enough he saw
on his left a counter and a man behind it of large build and
behind the man a row of keys hanging. He knew himself then
to be in the region of order, due form and procedure, things
were beginning to turn out a little as he had envisaged, this was
a reception area to which new arrivals addressed themselves,

with a person on duty trained to answer inquiries courteously.

He approached this person now, with his own blend of diffidence and hauteur, slightly splay-footed, suggesting a sort of crippled grace as he hestitated at the counter. The man did not smile or even change expression, which was disconcerting. Farnaby said, 'Good morning,' setting down his suitcase, remembering with some further loss of confidence that it was in fact mid-afternoon, but in any case there was no reply.

'Can you tell me,' he said, 'if there is a Miss Bolsover staying here? Miss Miranda Bolsover. *Buda kaliormi?*'

The name sounded improbable in these surroundings, tentatively proffered to this sombre Turk, and Farnaby himself could not quite believe in it: it seemed like a code or password that the other by some unfortunate chance had not been informed about when coming on duty. '*Ingiliz kiz, ismin Bolsover,*' he added, rather hopelessly. The man behind the counter raised his hand as if enjoining patience, then turned abruptly and disappeared into some recess beyond.

Minutes passed. There was a silence over the place. Perhaps they were all taking their siestas, he thought. Looking inwards, beyond the counter, he saw a sunlit section of terrace, a table and chairs painted pale blue, part of a red beach umbrella, paraphernalia remote and bright and empty like someone else's private idea or dream of leisure. Wisps of vapour rose from beyond the paving of the terrace and he surmised the pool lay there, though some sort of superstition prevented him for the moment from actually going to see. He still felt slightly uneasy at being so high above sea level, having assumed that hot springs would be a phenomenon of the plains, nearer earth's burning core; these glimpses of intestinal steam were oddly disquieting.

At the side of the counter there was a glass-fronted structure, presumably a show-case of some kind. Empty now, however, completely bare of everything except for one large and living moth, a beautifully marked black and yellow moth which must somehow have managed to get itself imprisoned there. Farnaby watched the creature crawl slowly across the glass, something it had doubtless done quite often. Its wings were frayed and ragged: freedom now, even if it could be achieved, would

125

come too late. Nevertheless he cast his eyes over the front of the case for possible means of freeing the creature. He was relieved not to find any. Better off where it was, with its wings now useless, under the glass where it was warm. Or one last heroic effort to fly and the cold air quickly killing it? Crucial choice.

He picked up a travel folder that was lying on the counter and finding it was in English began to read it. He was disappointed to find it was not about the pool, but some resort he had never heard of, in the far south of Turkey.

All comers will find something here to their taste, with green hills rolling down to bathe in the warm sea and the promenades lined with majestical dishevelled palm trees.

What other attractions there were he never discovered. Looking up vaguely, mind at grips with sportive hills and palms like duchesses in disarray, he saw before him a man of short stature with a brilliant smile.

'Good day sir. How do you do? I am the manager,' this man said.

'I was just asking the clerk –' Farnaby began.

'Excuse me. That is not a clerk. That is a gatekeeper. *Kapici*, yes. It is a husband of a cleaner woman. I place him sometimes here when I am called away.' The manager's smile flickered for a few moments, as if someone were tampering with the source of power. 'To avoid an appearance of emptiness,' he said. 'You would like a room perhaps?'

'Yes, please,' Farnaby said. I ought to have known that, of course, book a room first. Then afterwards you can make casual inquiries. 'You have rooms vacant I suppose?' he said.

'Ho, yes. Now is the beginning of the dead season. Moreover, there are vacant rooms, yes.' He smiled with full brilliance at Farnaby. 'I will give you the room number twelve,' he said, with what seemed a burst of enthusiasm or generosity, and Farnaby, who had been taught always to respond to manifestations of good will, uttered his thanks.

'That's a good room, is it?' he said.

'All the rooms are the same,' the manager replied.

After a short pause, Farnaby said, 'I think you may have an acquaintance of mine staying here.'

'Yes? You wish for a room near his?'

'It is a woman, a girl rather.'

'So much the better.'

'Her name,' Farnaby said austerely, 'is Miss Miranda Bolsover. Perhaps you could check whether she is here or not.'

'But there are a number of girls here. You will see her, if you stay.'

'Yes,' Farnaby said. 'That is so of course. But she may not be here.'

The manager made no reply to this and there was now a silence between them protracted to a point surprising to Farnaby. Looking more closely at the manager's face he realized by the remoteness of its expression that the man was not thinking about this problem. In fact he appeared to have suspended thought entirely until the need for it should be over.

Farnaby glanced again at the section of terrace, the red parasol, the faint swirls of vapour beyond. 'Don't you keep a register?' he said. He had been sure that a register would be kept, even in this remote part of Turkey, even a thermal pool reputed to possess healing properties. Keeping a register was the proper thing to do. 'After all,' he said, in his light, rather bleating voice, 'you do offer accommodation, don't you?'

'Register?' The manager was flickering again.

'A list. Don't you keep a list of guests, don't you enter their names in a book?'

'*Maalesef.*' The manager shrugged, repudiating blame without attaching it elsewhere. 'Moreover in the dead season we relax formalities,' he said. 'If you could describe your friend ...'

'No,' Farnaby said. 'I will wait and see for myself.'

'As you wish. Will you see the room now?'

'Very well.' This man obviously never kept registers, either of the quick or the dead. Miranda might have given a false name anyway, he told himself. Still, he felt a certain sense of outrage.

The manager snapped his fingers with astonishing loudness, and the gatekeeper appeared, expressionless as ever. There was an exchange of Turkish between them and then the gatekeeper picked up Farnaby's case and went off with it. Farnaby and the manager followed.

Emerging at last on to the terrace he felt exposed, vulnerable. It was as if he had left some dark sheltering place to be bombarded and pierced with sensations of light. Sunlight, in the windless enclosure of the pool, was reflected in dazzling coruscations from white and blue tiling, moved on the water itself in rippling gleams, patterned with shifting infusions the wreaths of steam lying above the surface. Farnaby was constitutionally timid, with a developed sense of traps and hazards, and this assault of the light reduced his confidence, reviving certain fears of radiance or brightness, recurrent since his childhood, fears of being gutted by an intensity of light as by fire. There was thus from the start an impression of danger and brightness which both sharpened and distorted everything he saw and hindered him from making cool appraisals; a disability not fully apparent to him until much later, though it affected him now as he walked along the terrace, not permitting more than a confused sense of persons here and there in the pool, immersed to their chests and motionless, as if the water had thickened, and trapped them there. The pool was much larger than he had thought, shaped like an irregular figure of eight, with a white footbridge spanning the narrowest part and white wooden cabins on three sides, joined each to each, numbers painted on them in blue paint. All this he took in with quivering eyelids, head lowered to the suddenly voluble manager, to whose dapper steps he tried to accommodate his own. They passed together over the narrow bridge.

'And this place is known to the ancients,' the manager said, 'from long before. It is very very interesting from the historical side as well as the waters do good to your health. See, the ancient columns and marbles that are lying there two thousand years, maybe more.' He pointed downward over the side of the bridge.

'Yes, I see them,' Farnaby said. Sections of column, fluted marble drums, shining faintly in the depths, traced with lines of tiny radiant bubbles. He averted his eyes, not wishing to add the weight of the past to his other burdens.

Number twelve turned out to be a little to the right of the bridge, more or less in the middle of the row facing directly across the pool towards the entrance. The door was not locked. The gatekeeper deposited his case, the manager gave him a beaming smile.

'Senemoğlu,' he said. 'My name is Senemoğlu. Anything you want, you ask me. Yes?'

'Yes,' Farnaby said. 'Thank you.' And he was finally alone, in the welcome dimness of the cabin. Calm came to him and a certain stealthiness of feeling at the narrow confines of the cabin. It seemed to him like a cell. A small square window was set into the rear wall, very high up, so that it afforded to normal view merely a section of blue sky, faintly curdled now, he noticed, with cloud. There was a duckboard at the door, a narrow bed with an iron frame, a washbasin, a small table with a paraffin lamp on it, a single hard-backed chair, and a large oil stove. The simplicity of the furnishing and the fact that all the cabins were identical – the manager had said this, hadn't he? – reinforced Farnaby's sense of inhabiting a cell, monastic or penal he couldn't decide which, but it seemed to him unmistakably a place in which people had lived briefly and in some sort of heightened consciousness. Some must have larger beds or at least two such beds or more, for families and so on, but perhaps they are all split up by the manager, by Senemoğlu, into unicellular creatures. To avoid an appearance of emptiness. No, surely not, devoted couples would refuse . . .

This thinking about beds led him to wonder in which hut the lady he was looking for, provided she was there at all, was at present reclining. Miss Miranda Bolsover. She would have just a single bed too. Perhaps she was lying on it at this very moment, alone and lightly clad. Farnaby lay down on his bed and placed his hands behind his head, the better to think of this. Glowing limbs wantonly displayed, breasts of a striking fullness, thrust into prominence by the position of the body, a smile both dreamy and provocative. He sat up suddenly, with feelings of guilt and self-abhorrence. He had stores of guilt, returning from almost any reverie with handfuls of it like mud from an ocean bed, to daub himself with. Now he realized suddenly he had been associating Miranda with the strippers in

129

the photographs he had seen on the way to Mooncranker's hotel. It was not in any case seemly for him to think of her like this, as if she were somehow plastic and he could shape her lineaments to his desire. She existed, already formed. And he was fixed in his relation to her by Mooncranker's having sent him to fetch her. Mooncranker's runaway secretary mistress. If she was Galatea then Mooncranker it was who had breathed on her, Mooncranker who had smoothed the flanks. Dear boy, you must get her back for me. I need her, you see. Majestical dishevelled Mooncranker. In the white hospital room, under his sheets, sustenance from the bottles passing along the tube into the veins of his arm. Aquiline nose directed at the ceiling while he intravenously fed. Glucose and water and vitamin B. Dear boy. There is a thermal pool in Anatolia reputed to possess medicinal properties. I have reason to think. In my present condition. I have dehydrated myself through drinking, paradoxical, yes. In an effort to forget Miranda. The sisters rustling down the corridor, the fan whirring high up on the wall, time always the same time in that white room, his deep-toned voice following circular courses. I will be eternally grateful to you. Eternally, yes. To dally throughout eternity with Miss Miranda Bolsover...

He sat on the edge of the bed and took out his wallet. From it he extracted the photograph, the only one of Miranda Mooncranker had had in his possession. Farnaby had insisted on having this, not being at all sure that he would recognize Miranda after all these years. But he did not think it would be much use. For one thing it had been taken several years previously when Miranda was still at school – not much later perhaps than the time when he had known her; and for another it was not of Miranda alone but was a school group photograph, a double row of girls in white blouses and gym slips. Mooncranker had borrowed Farnaby's fountain pen and with trembling fingers had inscribed on the shiny sky above Miranda's head a windswept asterisk. 'That is she,' he had said. But it was a bad photograph. All the girls looked much the same, fairish, plumpish, gymslips to the knee. Smiling a poignant group smile. Looking at the photograph was like looking at twenty-one Mirandas. The exact repetition of their

costume and smile made him think of their perhaps more varying private parts, a double row of silky pubic mounds; a sense
of multiplicity recalling the boundless sexual ambitions of
adolescence. Feelings of lubricity invaded him at the thought of
getting it away with the whole of a compliant fifth form. It
was the stern inclusiveness of it that was so exciting . . .

In order to get rid of these thoughts which had nothing after
all to do with his mission, he stood up again and setting the
chair below the window, climbed on to it and looked out. The
view from his window was impressive but bewildering too because nothing much of what he saw could be identified with
any certainty. The ground rose steadily away from him in
green enfolded ranks of hills, the nearer ones smoothly terraced, green and soft and scattered everywhere to the horizon
with evidences of ancient habitation, ruined basilicas, higher up
the fan shape of an ancient theatre, crumbling walls and heaps
of masonry. There were flocks of sheep among the hills and he
could hear the faint manifold tinkling of sheep bells, a sound
persistent, obtrusive yet remote, like the frailty and sorrow of
great age made audible. *Timor mortis conturbat me.* Within
the range of his vision there was no sign of this ruined landscape coming to an end. Over to his left, which he thought of
vaguely as westward, on a level below the first hills, was a long
double line of stone, box-like structures. They continued till the
angle of the window shut off his view. Sarcophagi he guessed
after a moment, marking a funeral way for dead dignitaries.
Mooncranker had said nothing of necropolises, and for a
moment Farnaby felt aggrieved, as if the other had concealed
this deliberately.

No sign of human beings in this extensive vista, where were
the shepherds? Only the blank sky and the hills, softly, sepul-
chrally rounded, with the softness of barrow and tumulus,
speckled with ancient pale granite and marble, sheep seeming
at this distance to swarm, or pullulate rather, like maggots in a
green fleece, and everywhere the rubble and low stone walls
that followed the curves of the hills for a few dozen or a few
hundred yards before tilting abruptly into the ground. High in
the sky three large whitish birds, wheeling slowly.

Oppressed, Farnaby got down from the chair and lay on the

bed again. What place was this he had come to? He turned on his side, face to the wall, attempting to shut off thoughts of the rubble-strewn hills, the glittering specious pool. And after some minutes, one delicate big-knuckled hand holding for comfort and consolation his subdued testicles, Farnaby fell asleep.

2

He slept deeply. It was twenty minutes past five when he awoke. He washed at the basin and changed his travelled-in, slept-in shirt for a clean one. Then he went out on to the terrace. There was nobody in the water now. One youngish man was sitting at the first of the tables on the opposite side. The sun was low in the sky, directly behind this man, and the walls of the building beyond the terrace, and the beach umbrellas along the terrace itself cast long shadows over the gleaming, fuming water.

He went across the bridge, intending to find himself a table farther along, but as he passed the man said good evening to him in English and smiled up and Farnaby said, 'Do you mind if I join you?' thinking that perhaps he had found a compatriot, but 'Not at all,' the other said in accents unmistakably American. Farnaby seated himself at the table and returned the smile, which was a nervous, rabbity one, distinctly incongruous with what seemed to Farnaby his leisurely confident manner of speech, although this impression of confidence was one that the speech of Americans always gave him. He was younger than he had seemed at a distance, hardly more than twenty or so. He had a long narrow face with a pale, prematurely wrinkled forehead and prominent white teeth. His complexion was marred by several inflamed-looking pimples concentrated on the right side of his face. Beside him on the table was a small transistor radio.

'You're new here, aren't you?' he said, and Farnaby was at once carried back to school days, when there had always been someone to ask that question, not the strongest, but not the least dangerous either. Asking you to declare yourself. It seemed to be as complex a question now as if the intervening years had never happened and surely, he thought, a question normally encountered only in places with inmates, fellow sufferers, places to which one had been consigned. Confronting the narrow salesman's smile on this immature face, Farnaby was visited by an eerie sense of *déjà vu*, of something threateningly familiar behind the apparent novelty of his surroundings. Nevertheless he answered as he had always answered, coolly, as literally as possible: 'Yes. I arrived this afternoon.'

'Thought so,' the other said. 'Thought I hadn't seen you around.' He placed both elbows on the table, leaning forward, as if prepared even at this early stage to be frank and confidential. 'Would you like to listen to the radio?' he said.

'I don't mind,' Farnaby said.

The other pressed a button on top of the set and a man's voice was heard, very faintly singing. 'Can't turn it up too loud,' he said. 'There've been complaints. My name is Lusk. Eugene Lusk. I been here four days.' He contrived to make this last remark sound like a sort of claim to seniority.

'James Farnaby.'

'Glad to know you. You're British, aren't you?'

'Yes.'

'This is coming to you from the American base in Izmir,' Lusk said, looking at the radio. 'It is specially put out for the military.' He turned up the sound and it was now in fact military music, a brass band playing a march. After a moment Farnaby recognized it for the triumphal march in 'Aïda'.

As if summoned by these strains, a portly man emerged from one of the cabins in the row facing them and walked with a curious smooth rolling gait along the side of the pool. He was smartly dressed in a cream-coloured suit.

'Who is that, do you know?' Farnaby said.

'He is a Levantine,' Lusk said. 'Name of Spumantini. Runs an agency in Izmir. Electrical equipment. He is after an English lady staying here, named Mrs Pritchett.' He smiled wrinkling his forehead. 'She doesn't give him much encouragement,' he said.

'How do you know all this?' Farnaby asked.

'You got to keep your ear to the ground,' Lusk said. 'In a place like this you got to watch points. You can't tell what might be important.'

Farnaby watched the infatuated Levantine with considerable interest. The man's body was shaped like a barrel, with legs in the cream slacks rather short. A heavy, handsome, fleshy face; a pronounced thrusting motion of the thick thighs as he walked, graceful and rather repellent, as though the man were in a not quite human element, subject to some slightly more resistant substance than air. He seated himself at one of the tables farther down from them.

'They come out here for a drink, you see,' Lusk said. 'You will see them coming out.'

There was a short silence between them, filled with the continuing strains of 'Aïda'. Then Lusk said, 'Yes, they'll be out.' He spoke with a certain satisfaction, as if glad at thus being able to reduce the complex humanity at the pool to this single predictable shape. 'Afternoons resting mainly,' he said. 'Then a drink or two here on the terrace, then the pool, dinner, pool again. They stay in the water half the night, some of them.'

'Is that so?' Farnaby said. He was beginning to hope now, after what the other had said, that if he sat on here and waited Miranda would sooner or later appear, to take part in these ritual preliminaries to immersion.

'I am in the Peace Corps,' Lusk said. 'That is the basic reason for me being here.'

'Are you looking to the peace of the pool?' Farnaby said smilingly.

'No, no, I mean here in Turkey. I am based in Izmir right now. No, this is just a kind of vacation.' He advanced towards Farnaby a face narrow, pale-lashed, serious, smelling of lemon-scented cologne. 'I heard a lot about this place,' he said. 'In Izmir, I mean. You know, the guys there, they were always singing its praises. You go there, they said, you can get yourself a good time.'

The band had changed over now to 'Speed Bonny Boat' which they were playing very fast as if it were a light infantry march. A short and enormously fat woman with a tiny permed head, dressed in a lilac-coloured towelling beach-dress, emerged on to the terrace from one of the cabins in the row on their left, followed by a bald man in a dark blazer who seemed skimpy by comparison. They walked along the terrace one behind the other, towards the tables, he with head slightly inclined, she setting moccasined feet with dainty care, calves quivering at every step.

'Who are *they*?' Farnaby asked.

'Krauts,' Lusk said. 'Herr and Frau. A lot of overweight people come here, the manager told me that. The water is supposed to be good for the glands.'

He said no more for the moment and Farnaby watched with fascination the progress of this couple until they too had seated themselves. A man in a white jacket approached them and stood at their table in a deferential manner. They appeared to be ordering drinks.

'I'm from Atlantic City myself,' Lusk said. 'Where are you from?'

'Reading.'

'Oh, is that in England?'

The waiter moved away from the Germans' table and Farnaby saw from the brilliance of the smile that it was in fact Senemoğlu, the manager. Apparently he combined the two functions, at least in the dead season.

'They told me a lot about this place,' Lusk said. 'There's girls here on their own.' He looked anxiously at Farnaby for a moment, then said, 'Crying out for it.'

'Crying out for it, eh?' Farnaby said. Two more men had appeared on the terrace, though he had not seen them emerge from any of the cabins. One was a tall, sharp-featured, rather saturnine-looking man, the other tubby and wearing a straw hat with a black band. They were arm in arm.

'Homosexuals,' Lusk said, anticipating his question. '*Practising*,' he added, with a sort of respectfulness, as if it were of merit that they had not lapsed.

'Are they English?'

'The tall one is a Greek. I don't know about the other. They talk to each other in English. Shall we have a drink?'

'That is a good idea,' Farnaby said. Lusk clapped his hands together and peered, wrinkling his brows anxiously. After a moment he relaxed and Farnaby guessed that Senemoğlu had acknowledged the signal.

'Crying out for it,' Lusk said, reverting to the former topic. 'Didn't you know that?'

'I suppose they come for a variety of reasons,' Farnaby said rather coldly – he had not liked the imputation of inexperience.

'They come for a good lay,' Lusk said. 'In the great majority of cases.' The eyes, pale and beseeching, were at odds with the confident pronouncement. They seemed to Farnaby eyes which had not been able to take much for granted in life, except perhaps the condition of being alone: friends that advised him to come, not offered to accompany him.

'And you have come here ...?' Farnaby said.

Lusk drew back and looked away across the pool. 'Just a look,' he said. 'Sizing things up.'

Senemoğlu now approached and stood before them smiling widely. 'Good evening, gentlemen.'

'What will you have?' Lusk said.

'I think I'll have a vermouth. With ice, please.'

'I'll have a gin and Fruko,' Lusk said. 'You know, like I usually have. Don't put the Fruko in, just bring the bottle separately. They put too much in,' he said to Farnaby.

Senemoğlu said, 'Very good, sirs,' but did not move away at once. Beyond him on the terrace, Farnaby saw three slender, brightly-dressed Negroes, two men and a woman.

'What is it?' Lusk said, looking up at Senemoğlu.

'Herr and Frau Gruenther find themselves incommoded by the radio. They ask if you will adjust it to a lower volume.'

'My God,' Lusk said bitterly, reaching out an arm at once, however, to the radio. 'Just hold me tight in your arms tonight', a woman's voice was singing. 'And this blue tango –' Moodily Lusk switched it off altogether.

'Thank you,' Senemoğlu said, withdrawing.

'See what I mean?' Lusk said to Farnaby.

'Who are those blacks, do you know?'

'They are new arrivals,' Lusk said. 'Probably G.I.s, from the base at Izmir. Do you live in Izmir?'

'No,' Farnaby said. 'Istanbul. I'm doing research there. Tell me,' he added, making a strong effort to appear casual, 'do you know of anyone staying here by the name of Miss Miranda Bolsover?'

'No,' Lusk said, after a moment or two of apparent reflection. 'Can't say I do. I might know her by sight of course. Is she a friend of yours?'

'Yes, an old friend.'

'They are crying out for it. That's what the boys in Izmir said. This pool is known for it throughout the length and breadth of the land.' His eyes bolted nervously round the pool. 'They told me that,' he said.

'I thought people came here for health reasons mainly,' Farnaby said.

'A good lay is a health reason,' Lusk said.

Senemoğlu came with the drinks, beamed, bowed, retreated.

'I have every reason to trust those boys,' Lusk said defiantly, as if Farnaby had impugned their testimony about the sexual opportunities the pool afforded.

'Cheers,' Farnaby said. 'May the cries not fall on deaf ears.'

'My trouble is, I'm a romantic,' Lusk said. 'I always look for an affinity, that's my trouble.'

Farnaby looked away across the pool and then along the terrace. The sun had sunk below the horizon now, sunlight no longer lay on the water. The wreaths and swirls of vapour had thickened over the surface and coalesced into a thin pall, like mist. Darkness was in the air as a sort of graining and a scent of night. Most of the tables were now occupied and a confused sound of conversation carried to him. At the table nearest theirs was a couple he had not seen arrive, a youngish, thickset man with a large blunt head, and an expressionless, rather unkempt-looking blonde girl. They sat silently, not looking at each other but out towards the pool. Surely that could not be Miranda?

'That has been my error, up to now,' Lusk said. 'We should be able to pluck a woman as we pluck a rose, don't you think so?' He leaned forward again.

'I suppose we do tend to complicate things,' Farnaby said. He felt the urgent heat of Lusk's breath on his face, and drew back slightly.

'Simplify it further,' Lusk said, looking again in a hunted way about the pool. 'Reduce it to gestures.'

Farnaby said, 'I don't understand you, quite.' He was regretting now having sat next to this person. He looked along the terrace again and picked out the Levantine, at a nearer table now, talking to a middle-aged woman with short dark hair, who he thought might be Mrs Pritchett. Beyond them was a woman sitting alone, whose age was impossible to determine because her face was disfigured by the flaky encrustations of some skin disease. She seemed to be looking directly at him, and he glanced hastily away. This at least could not be Miranda.

'I mean, like, will you or won't you? Simple as that,' Lusk said. 'That's all you need to know. Failing that, find a topic.'

'Topic?'

'Something to talk about.'

Farnaby looked again, unwillingly, at the lady with the diseased skin. Light was failing from moment to moment, the discoloration of the face was not now so apparent, what marked it out still, in the deepening dusk, as afflicted?

'Yep,' Lusk said. 'There was a guy I knew in Atlantic City and he wasn't even an American, he was a Pole, he had a Polish name. We all called him Buddy Basil.'

It is the impassivity of the face that denotes disease. Blight does not cause writhing but a stricken stillness rather.

'He was over thirty years of age,' Lusk said, 'but he had this great topic, he used to ask the girls if they had a bad time with their periods. Doesn't sound very promising, you'll say, but it was the way he did it, the way he looked at them.' Lusk leaned forward, mouth a little open, breathing ardently. ' "Do you have a bad time with your periods?" he used to say, and I am not kidding, it was like a snake with a chicken.'

'That was a good ploy of Buddy Basil's,' Farnaby said. 'What's your topic?'

Lusk drew back and looked away. 'Of course,' he said, after a moment, 'it's no good going bang smack into the topic, let's say it is periods, no good rushing in, you got to sort of steer the conversation, but he was an artist at it, Buddy Basil was. He had this foreign accent that sounded kind of sympathetic or concerned maybe ...'

Farnaby nodded and glanced again to his left, along the terrace. The faces above the tables had a sort of depthless quality, perspectives seemed obliterated, as if everything were on one plane: effect of the dusk and the perpetual slight haze which hung in the air, and the reflected light from the water, quite uniform now that the sun had gone down. It struck him suddenly as a loss, as a missed opportunity that he had slept through this declension of the light, through the draining of the afternoon sky; as if by so doing he had forfeited some essential clue.

'If I tell you my topic,' Lusk said, 'will you promise not to use it?'

Farnaby looked at him for a moment in surprise. 'Of course,' he said. 'But you needn't tell me at all if you'd rather not.'

'I think I got a good one,' Lusk said. The prominent, jagged-looking Adam's apple leapt suddenly in his throat. 'I ask them what towns they've been in,' he said.

'Yes?'

'Then I kind of say what are the men like, can a girl go out on her own. Then I take some city, Athens is the one I am using at present, and I say that in Athens it is their proud boast that a girl can walk around the city any hour day or night without being molested, then I just wait to see how they react to this and nine times out of ten they come up with some sort of personal experience in some town or other and I listen to this, and they are talking to me, they are presenting me with a slice of their lives and it's on a sexual topic, broadly speaking a sexual topic, so there we are talking on this intimate level and they are associating me with it, by transference.' Lusk paused, gulping excitedly, staring at Farnaby.

'By transference, I see,' Farnaby said.

'My theory is that something is bound to emerge. All you have to do is stay with it.'

'It sounds very promising,' Farnaby said.

Darkening vapour hung above the pool, rising towards the tables along the terrace, the people seated there seemed to be resting on it or emerging from it. There were two figures in white jackets now, he noticed, moving about among the tables.

Perhaps Senemoğlu had been joined by the husband of the cleaning woman. A row of lights, spaced at intervals along the side of the pool nearer the entrance, suddenly came on. Set into the wall and paned with thick glass they gave out a soft diffused light, each one with a separate fuzz of radiance round it, forming a row of milky blobs along the poolside. Light streamed softly from them across the water and upwards over the terrace, and faces from time to time in the course of the several conversations seemed to dip into the light as though refuelling. Among others he caught sight of the aureoled moon face of the German woman, eyes shadowed, permed hair bright, a tiny glistening mouth moving in speech; and the heavy smiling face of the Levantine talking to a severe profile which did not respond.

'I think I'll go and get ready for the pool,' he said.

'I tried it out a few times,' Lusk said. 'I didn't actually come up with anything, I mean nothing concrete emerged, but I am perfecting it.'

'Keep at it,' Farnaby said. He stood up. 'Maybe I'll see you in the pool later on?'

'You bet,' Lusk said. 'Do you really think it is a good topic?'

'Certainly I do.' Farnaby smiled down at Lusk, then moved away. He walked towards the bridge. Before crossing it he stood still for a minute or so, looking over the pool. Then, with a sense of foreboding, he made his way along to his cabin.

3

Farnaby stood quite still at the edge of the pool, immersed to the top of his breast-bone. Vague forms moved before and around him ruffling the water, sending it lapping very softly against him, eddying against his breast in a way that seemed at first like a series of signals, attempts to communicate; an impression curiously reinforced by the fugitive patterns of light that glanced across the surface, various enough to be a code, sudden running glitters and dilations, coils, bobbins, tremulous moons that sidled and broke. He experienced during these first moments in the pool, a painful sense of expectancy, almost of

140

dread, which he did not at first understand, though later he supposed it due to the movements of all the bodies in the water, movements more or less continuous, setting up a kind of prolonged, soft rustling, in its gentleness strangely difficult to endure, as if constantly presaging some greater violence which never in fact arrived.

It was characteristic of Farnaby to seek to allay uneasiness at unaccustomed sensations or indeed to dilute any too vivid experience by some sort of moralizing or descriptive process. He indulged in this out of self-defence and at the same time discounted it in advance so that he was held in a slight tension, a sort of controlled retreat from the senses. Now he began, in an experimental way, to question the randomness of all this movement and these changing effects of the light.

He stood for some time, looking about him. He was in a rather deep part of the pool – it got deeper, he had discovered, in both directions as the loops widened. The narrow part, the waist of the pool, was the shallowest, and consequently the most crowded.

Farnaby moved his arms in a sort of experimental swimming motion, cleaving the water below the surface and close to his sides, without moving any other part of his body, glancing at the same time up at the sky which was thickly scattered with stars. The night air was cold and he felt pleasure at this contrast, air of the spacious night on his face, body sealed and private in the warm water. The smell of the water rose to him, faintly sweet and brackish, not unpleasant. Like the distant smell of decomposing grass. Piled grass, rotting from within, from the warm damp core, in summer ... A sort of generalized excitement stirred in Farnaby, for the moment without an object or discernible source. He took a deep breath and crouched farther down in the water lowering his head vertically and with care. The water rose over his chin and tightly closed mouth. When it was lapping over the bridge of his nose he saw fifteen-year-old Miranda in her white tennis dress glimmering on the water, hair falling round a face full of suppressed laughter, her long legs refracted and dangling as if they were below the surface. He held this vision until his heart hammered against his ribs and roaring filled his ears. He came up gasping for air. Miranda vanished, fragmented, white dress and pale limbs scattered into the stars.

'Sounds like somebody drowning over there.' A husky, lazy female American voice. This was his first intimation of how sounds carried in the pool. Someone he could not see had heard his gasping. He thought it might be the black girl he had seen with the two men on the terrace earlier. A man answered her now: 'Yeah, remember Smithy, when he went out that time in the middle of the pool, he got in too deep and he went under and he came up and he says, Help! but so quiet and polite nobody took him seriously, him being the little old quiet-spoken coloured man. " 'Scuse me ma'am, I'm kinda drowning." You know Smithy, he couldn't swim, he never grew up near no water. He damn near drowned that day and twenty people watching.'

'Smithy, yeah.'

Farnaby took some steps along the side of the pool to where the water was rather shallower, waist high. Here, closer to the bridge, you could see better. The mist was suffused with light and immediately around him the water showed a milky phosphorescence. He moved one arm slowly upwards through the water and saw just before it broke the surface the tiny gleaming bubbles trapped in his arm hairs. He was aware of other forms standing or moving not far away and he continued to hear splashes and voices, though there was something odd, as he was beginning to realize, about the acoustics of the place, making it virtually impossible from the sounds alone to determine distance or even, with much accuracy, direction. Voices and laughter, and the water sounds too, though amazingly distinct and vibrant, were liable to tail off, or be severed abruptly, apparently through chance shifts in speaker's or hearer's position.

'– more civilized than here,' Farnaby heard a voice say. Again American. Male, confident-sounding, slightly nasal. It was Lusk's voice. 'It is their proud boast in Athens that young women can walk out alone, even after nightfall, they don't –' The rest of this speech was lost but after a moment or two he heard a girl's voice, hurried, rather breathless, giving an effect of suppressed excitement: 'I don't know about here, but if it is anything like Sicily, wow! Not even in the day time –'

Farnaby stood listening, with a tension of anxiety, seeking to discover some recognizable quality in this voice. Might it be Miranda?

'That is their proud boast in Sicily,' the girl said, and they laughed, Lusk's laughter sounding insincere and placatory, showing too clearly a desire for happy intimacy; the girl's briefer, more neutral. At this point they must have moved away because the laughter was cut off abruptly and Farnaby heard or thought he heard, in this dream-like moment of transition, a harsh whisper in what sounded like German, coming from a different direction altogether. He peered through the mist. The voices of Lusk and the girl had seemed to proceed from the darkness beyond the bridge, but this was an unlikely source surely. Nevertheless, eager to see the girl's face, he moved along the wall a few tentative steps in this direction, only to find himself confronting a white-skinned stocky man whom he recognized after a moment as one of the people he had seen earlier on the terrace. A yard or two behind this person he made out the fair-haired young woman who had been with him then. Proximity made some sort of salutation unavoidable, but for several moments Farnaby and the other man, whose thin hair was plastered sleekly over a blunt seal-like head, looked silently at each other. Then the man inclined his head in a punctilious, Teutonic way, and uttered a gobbling plosive syllable that sounded like *Plopl*.

'I beg your pardon,' Farnaby said, thinking he had not heard aright. The man uttered the sound again, in exactly the same manner. *Plopl*.

There followed some moments of numbed silence while Farnaby tried to make sense of this sound. Once again it was as if some signal or password were expected, some response he had not been schooled in. The world fell away steeply on all sides leaving himself and this unintelligible person on a desolate height together.

'Yes,' Farnaby said, unable to endure the silence any longer, and smiled through the dimness. Was it simply a watery sound, a sort of playful onomatopoeia?

'Adrian Plopl,' the man said, with yet another slight bow.

'Er, Farnaby. James Farnaby.'

'Are you interested in photography?' A foreign voice, guttural and slow, laboriously over-inflected, giving an effect of kindness and simplicity of heart, like a connoisseur of bird song or an Alpine toymaker.

'Yes,' Farnaby said. The man moved closer and Farnaby found himself being regarded intently by small, widely spaced eyes. 'That is,' he added, 'I am interested in a general way.'

'Not as a practitioner?'

'No.'

At this moment Farnaby became aware of someone standing not very far away, just outside his direct line of vision. He turned his head, saw in what seemed a sudden local burst of light, glints of dark hair hanging heavy about an oval face, a long-necked, slightly drooping form, facing inwards across the pool, standing quite still. There was an immediately poignant impression of loneliness about this figure which Farnaby never afterwards forgot, and something else, something wilful, a sort of imperviousness. He had no sense of recognition; indeed this apparent listlessness conflicted with the images he had retained through the years, images of certainty and gaiety, of clear moods flowing into robust physical expression; nevertheless he felt sure that this was Miranda.

'Everything is in the selection,' Plopl was saying, 'You have to have the vision of the child, the *innocent* vision. If you do not have that, I advise you to give away all thoughts of becoming a photographer.'

'But I have no ambition to be a photographer,' Farnaby said.

Perhaps aware of being watched, the girl turned her head and looked towards him. The long, heavy-seeming hair swayed across her face. In the faint light a smile or at least the sense of a smile was exchanged between them, a willingness to be aware of the other's existence. Or am I imagining this? Perhaps it is accident, coincidence, that she should continue to look this way, perhaps she doesn't see me at all. Perhaps it is too dark for her to see, though light enough for me. He felt a sudden exalted subjectivity of sensation. The girl raised a white arm, the fingers of her left hand moved across her forehead, lifting aside the dark fringe of hair, a gesture clearly habitual, left to right, the back of her hand for a second obscured her face, a hand innocent of rings. She looked away, and at once Farnaby experienced a sense of loss.

'Very interesting,' he said to Plopl, seeking some graceful way of extricating himself from this conversation, so that he could approach the girl.

'I beg your pardon,' Plopl said.

'What you say is very interesting.'

An earnest male voice, somewhere behind Farnaby, said suddenly: 'I know a person in Izmir who can't resist tearing up books and paper.'

'You must seize the moment,' Plopl said. He did not know why it had become important to impress this aloof-looking Englishman. 'Make that moment eternal,' he said. He squeezed water out of his hair, blinking at the thin form before him. 'Are you interested in Zen?' he asked anxiously.

'He is a teacher, as a matter of fact,' said the man behind Farnaby. 'So he has a lot of temptation in his daily life.'

'Zen?' Farnaby said. 'Not really, no.'

The girl began to move away. Peering after her, Farnaby made out another, he thought female, form; an impression confirmed, a few seconds later, by the burst of upper-class contralto laughter that came from it. 'My dear,' he heard this person say, 'I belong to the older generation myself, for that matter.' More laughter. Then the girl's voice, clear, without special accent, saying, 'Oh I don't include you in that, Mrs Pritchett.' This was Mrs Pritchett, then, the beloved of the Levantine. The two women moved farther off and he heard nothing more.

'That's what photography is,' Plopl said. 'Arresting the flux of time.'

'He says these outbreaks are always followed by a sort of post-coital sadness.'

'If you have no eye for the significant moment, you are never going to be a photographer, not ever.'

'I have no wish to be a photographer,' Farnaby repeated. Plopl did not seem to register what one said to him, as though equipped only for transmitting. He seems to have got it into his head that I aspire to be a photographer. Had he not delayed me I might have been able to ascertain whether the girl was

145

indeed Miranda, before that Pritchett woman carried her off. Nevertheless, he was unwilling, even now, to offend. 'Are you a photographer yourself?' he asked, with some deference.

'Freelance,' Plopl said. He continued to regard Farnaby intently. His hair, of a Central European fineness and straightness, fell in a wet fringe over his narrow simian brows, and troubled his vision. Still fixing Farnaby with his obscured regard he stepped back, reaching behind him to where he knew Pamela would be – he had stationed her there ten or fifteen minutes before, and she rarely changed position on her own initiative. Plopl felt the soft flesh of her upper arm and dug his fingers into it with habitual severity, drawing her forward at the same time to his side.

'This is my mod-el,' he said, retaining his grip, sounding more than ever kind and simple in his tastes.

'And library books,' said the man behind Farnaby. 'He sometimes tears up library books.'

From his remarks about arresting the flux, Plopl had not sounded the sort of photographer who used models. Farnaby had an impression of a broad expressionless face, framed by tangled, hay-coloured hair; square shoulders; enormous breasts, contained by patterned nylon, appearing to float on the surface independently like beach balls.

Farnaby said, 'How do you do?'

The girl made no reply, but she drew an inward breath rather hissingly, and it became obvious to Farnaby that the grip on her arm was hurting her.

'You have to use the material to hand,' Plopl said, a remark, it seemed, aimed in derogation at his model. He released the girl's arm and she stood there quietly beside him. Vapour from the surface of the water rose up around the torsos of both.

Farnaby looked across to where the dark-haired girl had been, but there was no sign now of either her or Mrs Pritchett. He experienced a sense of desolation he could not account for. It was as though his will were for the moment suspended, in abeyance. He looked blankly before him at the glazed, misty surface, the milky, elongated ovals of light shed by the lamps. The air felt chill on his shoulders. He crouched at the knees, lowering himself into the warm, sealing water until it rose to his chin. A little water entered his mouth. It tasted bitter.

'I will show you some of my photographs,' Plopl said. 'Maybe tomorrow. Are you planning to stay long?'

'Oh, several days,' Farnaby said. He began to move off, released by this assurance of a future meeting.

'Very well.' Plopl was gratified by the effect he felt he had made. Right from the start, with superstitious certainty, he had known that this was a person whom it was important to impress. His heart warmed with tenderness and camaraderie. He said, 'We will have a drink, yes?'

Farnaby nodded his assent and with an intensification of purpose turned away and began to move off across the pool in the direction the girl had taken.

As he drew nearer the middle he became aware of a certain unevenness in the depth, slight variations, and he began to move more cautiously, remembering the slabs of antique masonry he had seen earlier, in the brilliant afternoon, from the footbridge. Though they, surely, had been in the area immediately adjoining the bridge itself. He tried to remember where exactly he had seen them, pale fluted drums beneath the glittering surface, but the afternoon seemed already too remote for such exactness of recall.

It was much darker out here, in the middle of the pool. Someone, another man, passed in front of him, very close, causing him to slow down his own rate of progress even further, in fact to stand still for a moment or two until the other should have passed. This other did not turn his head but proceeded slowly across Farnaby's bows with a lordly rolling gait of his barrel-shaped body that Farnaby recognized suddenly – it was Spumantini, the Levantine commercial agent. He was holding his right arm, the one farthest away, rather daintily out of the water, but Farnaby could not see if there was anything in his hand. Light fell for a few moments on his calm, fleshy, senatorial profile. Then he was past, receding into the darkness. Farnaby glanced after him in an attempt to see the reason for such a purposeful sort of proceeding but the bulky form was lost after two or three yards. Perhaps, Farnaby thought, he had passed behind an angle or bend in the containing wall. He proceeded after a moment or two on his way, looking from side to side in an effort to pick up the traces of the dark-haired girl again. His feelings of excitement at this prospect intensified and they were not, he recognized, at all appropriate to a sense of mission, but rather concerned with moving through this fostering element towards a possibly willing quarry. He tried, experimentally, to remind himself that it was not a hunt he was engaged on but the performance of a solemn duty, enjoined upon him by Mooncranker, who had lain there with his speaking mouth, helpless under the sheets in the strong white light, strapped to his source of sustenance; but the reminder did nothing to lessen his excitement. It was in a predatory spirit that he had accepted the mission in the first place. Besides, this might not be Miranda. She had looked about the right age, and with shorter hair and a more upright posture could have been the girl marked on the photograph. Or any one of half a dozen others on that fifth form row...

Suddenly he saw them again, straight before him, not two yards away, the girl and the woman standing close together in silence. Perhaps they had broken off at his approach. It was too dark to see their faces clearly. Farnaby stood still, vainly peering. They were aware, however, of his presence there. Both at the same time turned faintly luminous faces towards him. He began to move cautiously round them in a half circle until he reached the wall again, some yards beyond. He settled himself low in the water, only a mist-wreathed head showing, to listen to what he could of the conversation...

Spumantini, who had come upon them only a few moments before, but more circumspectly, was now stationed more or less equidistantly, against the wall on the other side. He was short sighted – hence the softness and solicitude which appeared to be the permanent expression of his brown eyes. He had left Mrs Pritchett, as he thought securely, in a corner, while he went to fetch cigarettes and lighter from the pocket of his beach robe on the terrace. Returning, he had lost his bearings somewhat and casting round in the dimness had made out a form roughly the right height, though rather in the wrong direction. Nevertheless, he had launched himself immediately through the water, feeling beneath the broad soft pads of his

148

feet the slightly slippery marble fluting of columns, only to find when almost upon the figure that it was too tall, it had shoulders too angular, moreover, and clinchingly, it began to speak in a man's voice, saying in light diffident tones, 'I have no wish to be a photographer.'

Spumantini stood still. A certain brutality, born of his frustration, stirred in him. He would have liked to take the thin form before him in a certain wrestling grip he knew of, which if successful did damage to the spine. He reminded himself that he admired their institutions, thought briefly but with gratitude of his British passport. The Englishman was built like a plank, shoulders and waist seemed not much different in width. How different from his Mrs Pritchett, with her sloping shoulders and globular buttocks, her fullness which was however not gross. He thought of Mrs Pritchett's cleavage and the various convexities of her person. All were delectable. But what made Mrs Pritchett special was not merely this controlled abundance, which after all any *Pavyon* girl might be expected to possess. No, it was her accent which fascinated him, her British lady's accent, upper-crust as he designated it, the throat-formed, strangulated sounds that came from her. She was the real thing.

Spumantini looked into the obscurity beyond Farnaby, turning his head slowly, narrowing his short-sighted eyes. Perhaps it had been there, that other corner, where he had left her. He recommenced his wading, diagonally across the pool, keeping his cigarettes and lighter clear of the water. As he drew level with the Englishman someone in a guttural and deliberate voice said, 'We will have a drink, yes?' and the Englishman turned away and began to move outwards across the pool. Spumantini quickened his own pace, passing quite close to Farnaby but without glancing at him. Almost immediately he heard Mrs Pritchett's voice again, over on his left, saying 'Call me Belinda,' something which she had never said to him. She must have struck up a conversation with somebody. He moved softly towards the voice, making no sound through the water, turning his head slowly from side to side. After a moment or two he again stopped, with his broad soft back against the tiled wall. He was content for the moment to wait here. He listened.

149

He thought of taking Mrs Pritchett to his villa in Karsheaka, which overlooked the great blue sweep of the bay. White walls. Foam of bougainvillea. Showing her the cacti on the terrace, the blue jasmine and the white, the sharp-leaved lemon trees. The gin and the tonic in correct proportions. Afterwards, in the shaded bedroom, from which all flies should previously have been driven, he would undress Mrs Pritchett amid odours of Cologne and attar of roses. In his ears her contralto ecstasies . . .

'What do you know about the older generation anyway?' Mrs Pritchett said. She took care to keep her voice amused and conversational.

'Quite a bit, one way and the other,' the girl said. She had not yet reciprocated in the matter of first names.

'It's sexual, it's basically sexual,' said an earnest male voice somewhere beyond them.

And a woman replied, 'But it must cost him a bit, replacing all those books, it must take a fair slice out of his salary.'

'The acoustics are odd in this pool, aren't they?' Mrs Pritchett said, in lowered tones. The girl's face was close to her own, an almost perfect oval, and very fragile-looking, framed by the heavy, burdensome-seeming hair. 'There are parents, of course,' she added.

'Oh, I don't mean parents,' the girl said. 'I stopped telling my parents things quite early on. They never seemed able to handle it somehow. I mean they turned everything into something else. So I stopped telling them things. Then they said I was secretive. Which I am, I suppose. I don't really know why I am telling you all this now, as a matter of fact.'

'Something in the water,' suggested Mrs Pritchett, raising her head slightly and giving the girl a full smile. They were standing very close together and in the small movements and adjustments that both of their bodies were constantly making in the water, Mrs Pritchett's knee brushed against the girl's thigh.

'Besides,' Mrs Pritchett said, 'the darkness confers a sort of protection on us, doesn't it?' As soon as she had said this she regretted it. She did not need the girl's uncertain laugh to tell her it was the wrong note. This terseness, this premature attempt to establish complicity, had damaged her prospects before. 'Or perhaps that is the wrong word,' she said quickly.

'In Athens,' a confident nasal voice said. 'Any time, day or night. That is their proud boast. You can't say that about Istanbul.'

The girl laughed again, more purely in amusement now. 'He's still going on about that,' she said softly.

'Who?'

'I don't know his name, just the voice. He was having this identical conversation with someone else about an hour ago.' She laughed again and Mrs Pritchett laughed too, a full-throated, rather barking laugh. 'That must be his gambit,' she said. 'Are you on your own here?'

'Yes,' the girl said, in a changed voice. 'I'm having a sort of holiday on my own.'

'A very good idea,' Mrs Pritchett said fervently. She moved her knee through the water again but met nothing. 'It's nice, isn't it?' she said. 'At night I mean. In the pool.'

'Oh, yes,' the girl responded slowly, as if in doubt. Then with a sudden eagerness she said, 'I don't know about protected, really, it isn't as if –' She turned her head restlessly, and the heavy hair swung across her face.

Some men were speaking in Turkish quite loudly. Mrs Pritchett looked over her shoulder, saw a number of dark forms surmounted by hats at one of the tables on the terrace. Presumably they had come up from the village to drink and watch the crazy foreign bathers. There did not seem to be any Turks actually staying here.

'I don't mean that we are in danger, of course,' she said. 'Except in so far as one always is.'

Suddenly, from some unidentifiable corner of the pool, they heard a whispering voice, that could have been a man or woman, saying, *'Findest Du ich habe abgenommen?'*

'Good heavens,' Mrs Pritchett said. She looked at the girl's face but could discern no particular expression on it. 'Do you think that is the voice of the spirit of the place?'

'I don't know,' the girl said. 'It was German wasn't it?'

I must be careful, Mrs Pritchett told herself. I must not be too bold. The young are more hypocritical than we are.

'I see what you mean,' the girl said. 'About the pool. You don't need to put on any sort of show, do you, and people can't get at you much, can they?'

'You cease to be a target,' Mrs Pritchett said. She was surprised, and in some vague way alarmed, by this consonance with her own feelings, expressed however differently. 'Yes,' she said. 'I know exactly what you mean. How strange that we should both have felt this. In any case,' she added, 'you mustn't be reluctant to speak freely to me – confession is good for the spirit.' As she uttered these words the desire to confide in this girl, to secure her interest and sympathy by speaking of intimate things, rose strongly in her.

'Yes, it does you good, I suppose,' the girl said, vaguely and carelessly, looking away across the pool.

Mrs Pritchett said, 'I think so too.' She paused, conscious for a delicious moment of being forbearing, having this child at the power of the confidences she was shortly to make her.

'I was meaning confession in a general sense,' she said, her voice fastening harshly but with a certain gratitude on this depersonalized view of things.

'I don't think it will do in any sense,' the girl said, in her clear, rather lazy voice. 'Not for me at least. I feel the one sinned against, not sinning. I mean it may be all wrong spiritually, but that is how I feel.'

'You must have had a bad time,' Mrs Pritchett said, infusing her tone with sympathy.

'I got involved with an older man,' the girl said.

Mrs Pritchett waited, but no further details came. After a moment or two, the girl said, 'Your husband is not here with you then?'

'My husband and I were divorced several years ago,' Mrs Pritchett said. The urge to present this girl with something of her life was now too insistent to be any longer denied. 'As a matter of fact,' she said slowly, 'I was to have married again, but I backed out at the last minute.'

She paused on this for several moments. Then, as the girl said nothing more she began again, in slow deliberate tones, almost as though reciting: 'Mark, his name was. He was a widower himself. A partner in a firm of solicitors in Penrith.

He played cricket sometimes for the Penrith second eleven.'
She always began like that, even when she was only telling the
story to herself. It was important to get these preliminary details right, establish poor Mark as a living man. 'But his main
interests,' she said, 'were going to bed with me and trout-
fishing. I put them in that order though I don't know where
the true emphasis lay, I mean I don't know which came upper-
most in Mark's mind. Actually, he liked to combine the two
things. Not simultaneously, but over the weekend, you know...'

The attentive oval of the girl's face was turned towards her.
Her voice quickened, lost its first diffidence. 'He used to take
me to this cottage,' she said, 'which belonged as a matter of
fact to a friend of his, a doctor by profession, also of Penrith.
He used to take me there in his green M.G. Mark, that is. I
walked out on him a month, less than a month, before the
wedding day, left him standing in midstream, literally and
figuratively, he was actually standing in the river fishing when
I decided to go. He ate his aphrodisiacal buttered trout alone
that night...' Her tone had become harsher, more vibrant, as
at some residual pain, though still of impeccable modulation.
'He was a good man,' she said. 'I just couldn't stand him.'

At this moment, moving outwards a little and turning her
body in the water, Mrs Pritchett caught sight of Spumantini,
crouching not three yards off, presumably listening to their
conversation. Rage rose in her at the sight. Was she to be
dogged for ever by this hideous lecherous Levantine? Checking her first impulse, which was to assault him with her nails,
she said quietly to the girl, 'Shall we move on a little, into the
deeper part? I am getting chilly round the shoulders.' The girl
assented and side by side they waded out, feeling the water rise
gradually higher over breast and shoulders. When she judged
they had gone far enough, Mrs Pritchett said quickly, 'Let's
just cut across to the other side, shall we?' and she took the
girl's arm with gentle urgency. That will have thrown him off
the scent, she assured herself. Myopic beast.

Farnaby, who had contrived to hear a good deal of this
conversation, failed however to notice their withdrawal because he allowed himself to be distracted at this crucial point
by two male voices in altercation, voices which had been

153

getting steadily more obtrusive, one precise and mincing, the other definitely foreign with a displeasing abrasiveness about it, and very harsh aspirations.

'Discharge,' this latter voice was saying, 'in art as in life. That is my theory Henry. More than a theory. It is an article of faith with me.'

'Like most of your ideas,' the other man said, 'it manages to be sentimental and brutal at the same time.'

Farnaby was able now to see the forms of the two men, who had approached to within two or three yards of him: the one addressed as Henry thin and somewhat taller than average, with what seemed a sort of superstructure on his head raising his height still further; the other bulky, bald, with thick drooping moustaches. He recognized them for the couple that Lusk had described, with an effect of grudging praise, as *practising*.

'No, no, no,' the man called Henry said, spacing the monosyllables pedantically. 'It is glorified *mallachia*. It is a masturbatory theory, Alexis.' He looked at Farnaby while saying this, presumably in the wish to include him. With something of a shock Farnaby saw that the superstructure on his head was a plastic mob-cap, doubtless intended to keep his hair dry. The bald man nodded to him.

'We are having a discussion,' the bald man said. 'This is Henry Samson and I am Alexis Petsalis.'

'How do you do?' Farnaby said. 'My name is James Farnaby.'

'Mr Samson is a painter,' Petsalis said and would have continued if Farnaby, grown more adroit since being cornered earlier by Plopl the photographer, had not excused himself on the grounds that a friend was waiting for him. In order to make this convincing he was obliged to move away. He took several steps outward towards the centre of the pool, then moved in again at an angle of about ninety degrees, calculating that this would bring him once again within hearing distance. To his dismay, however, he saw that Mrs Pritchett and the girl were no longer there. He went right up to the wall, but there was no sign of them. Suddenly he saw Spumantini again, but the Levantine turned at once and began moving away along the poolside. Farnaby stood still and the former irresolution

154

returned to him. He looked across the pool in an effort to make out individual faces and forms. Snatches of conversation came to him without his registering them as sense.

A man loomed suddenly out of the mist wading steadily chest high in the direction of the bridge. When he drew level Farnaby saw with irrepressible aversion that he had a large goitre at the side of his neck, a livid bulge like a fungus. The man passed without turning his head, and Farnaby looked after him, in the grip of a sort of dread, as if there had been something relevant to himself, some threat or warning, in the sudden appearance of this unfortunate, bemonstered man, who now rapidly receded into the mist. Peering after him, Farnaby made out two forms, standing close together, one tall one short, whom he took to be Samson and Petsalis, still engaged presumably in their discussion about the nature of art; and beyond them he thought he saw a white glimmering spherical object like a ball or a bathing cap. Then Petsalis extended an arm and light struck through the vapour and elicited from his raised hand glitters and splinters of brightness, not the soft gleam of wet flesh that his eyes had grown accustomed to since entering the pool – it was as though the man's hand had been endowed with magical properties. Farnaby thought that all the people in the pool must be looking towards this radiance and wondering about it. Miranda too would be watching. Then Petsalis took his other hand to it, eclipsing its light, and by some characteristic series of gestures it became all at once evident to Farnaby that it was simply after all a cigarette case: the Greek was offering his friend a cigarette. This restoration of the commonplace reassured him, quickened his purpose. I must find Miranda without delay, he told himself. He began to move slowly and cautiously along the side of the pool, keeping a watchful eye ahead.

'Well, their proud boast is unfounded,' the girl said, in cold rather sarcastic tones, 'but completely, because I have a friend who has actually lived in Athens and she told me that the things they get up to in those Athens trolleybuses in the rush hour have to be seen to be believed.'

'Is that a fact?' Lusk said, disconcerted by the unfaltering speech of the girl, the clear current of scorn in her voice, above all the absence of laughter, even of smiling – he could not see her face very clearly because they were in a dark part of the pool, but it was completely serious as far as he could make out, a heart-shaped, level-browed face. It was the third time that evening he had tried out his topic. The other two had been laughing and friendly but had somehow drifted away. Third time lucky, he told himself.

'Well,' he said, 'I had it on good authority –'

'Yes,' the girl said, 'they jam them in so tightly in those trolleybuses, there is no limit to the number of people standing, I suppose you know that, you can't move, you don't even know who is groping you.'

'My God, is that a fact?' Lusk said.

'It's not only hands, either,' the girl said. 'My friend had a new summer dress completely ruined. No, it's the same in Athens as anywhere else, all men are the same, all they want to do is get into your knickers. I expect you're the same too, aren't you?'

'I guess so,' Lusk said, laughing nervously. He could hardly believe it, she was as good as inviting him. The boys back in Izmir had been absolutely right. He tried to feel jubilant but could not. The girl's frankness intimidated him. He would have preferred some dissimulation. He had an odd feeling that the girl was using the topic on *him*.

The pause was threatening to become ignominious. Lusk sensed the beginnings of a new disdain in the girl. He splashed his arms a little, bending his legs in order to lower his slightly chilly upper half into the water. From this position he spoke. 'You'd think,' he said, 'it would get cold after a while. Kind of like being in a hot bath. But it never does.'

'It can't, you see,' the girl said, in the same clear, unfaltering tone. 'It is constantly replenished. You didn't think it was the same water all the time, did you?'

'No, I didn't, as a matter of fact.'

'I believe that is what you did think.'

'It certainly is not.'

'It comes from under the earth. It comes from a subterranean spring. Didn't you know that?'

156

'Yes, I knew it,' Lusk said. He was disturbed by the hostility in the girl's voice. Perhaps she was annoyed with him for not rising to the occasion promptly. Never had he felt less like rising, in any sense of the term. It struck him as unfair, terribly unfair, that he, who spent so much of his time in lustful fantasy, bursting out of his trousers when there was no one around, should feel so cold and shrunken now when his topic had borne fruit, when at last there was a prospect, more than a prospect by God, this girl was crying out for it. He mustn't let the occasion slip. Tonight's the night, he told himself. Perhaps a drink would be a good idea.

'How about a drink?' he said.

'*Raki,*' the girl said.

'Okay.' Lusk raised wet hands out of the water and clapped for Senemoğlu. God let him not ignore my clapping, he prayed.

'What I couldn't stand about him,' Mrs Pritchett said, 'what in the end proved impossible to suffer, in the sense of live with, come to terms with, was just this complete inability of his to admit experience...'

By a process gradual, insensible and at the same time partly willed, they had moved along the side of the pool, away from the lights and the voices, into an area where the water was quite deep – rising now to the base of Mrs Pritchett's collarbone and the tip of the girl's chin.

'How can I explain it to you?' Mrs Pritchett said. 'He was afraid of being swamped.'

The other listened, occasionally moving her burdened head from side to side as if in restlessness or the stress of not completely understanding.

'When did you say this happened?' she asked.

'Oh, not so very long ago.' Mrs Pritchett's strong white teeth were revealed in a momentary smile. 'I wasn't a girl, by any means. But I have come to regard it as the central event of my life. Walking out on Mark, I mean. Much more so than anything to do with my marriage. For the first time in I don't know how many years I found myself free. Free to travel, to come to wonderful historical places like this. Free above all to be myself.' She moved forward a little, and her instep brushed against the front of the girl's leg.

'Mark was good to me, in his way,' she said, after a moment. 'He just wasn't right.' She thought briefly of that kindness, distant now, like the weather in a country one will never revisit. 'He had a strong character,' she said. 'Perhaps I am boring you with all this.'

'Oh no,' the girl said. 'Not at all.'

Though strength, Mrs Pritchett thought, is perhaps not the right word, a soft enveloping obstinacy more like it, he enveloped my clumsiness and violence, my voice too loud, too excitable. Regarding my oddities as outrages on him, slight of course, and salutary, so long as he could contain them.

'It was as though he needed to be outraged,' she said. 'So that he could sort of billow out and keep on containing me. Do you understand what I mean?'

'I think so, yes,' the girl said.

'Goodness,' Mrs Pritchett said gaily, 'we *are* having a heart to heart, aren't we?'

The girl said, 'I think it is very interesting.'

'Do you really?' Mrs Pritchett felt a strong impulse to raise her hand and touch the girl's face. 'How marvellous it is,' she said, 'to find a sympathetic listener. And how rare. Anyway that's what I hated most, that sort of indulgence and containment going on. He went on struggling to fit me into his scheme of things. In the end I was doing or saying anything, you know, anything that came into my head, to break out of it. Deliberately eccentric things. But he had to go on trying to keep it all in place. As I look back on it now, the only thing to do was walk out.' As stifling, this helpless, obstinate accommodation of Mark's to her vagaries, as the physical weight of him in the narrow bed at the doctor's cottage.

'It was a failure, really, from the start,' she said. 'I remember the evening when I left him. I suppose all this had been on my mind, but at the time it seemed like an impulse, there was no planning in it. I just walked away from him along the river bank. It was about eight o'clock, an evening in June. Masses of buttercups everywhere and one of the fields by the river had been planted with beans and they were in flower. Tremen-

158

dously fragrant, you know. Mark was standing in the middle of the river facing downstream. You have to, you know. The water was silver, flowing past him, and he looked dark against it. He wasn't moving and the water was, and it struck me at the time as a symbol somehow. He never saw me go and I have never seen him since, though we did exchange letters.'

'You didn't think, did you,' the girl said, 'that they brought you the *raki* in *glasses*?'

She seemed to be implying that such ignorance indicated a deeper inexpertise or disability on Lusk's part.

'You seem to know what gives round here,' Lusk said.

'I keep my eyes open.'

'Do you mean you have never been here before?'

'I don't mean anything of the sort.' She refilled her glass with *raki* from the carafe on the edge of the terrace behind them.

In the pause that now fell Lusk heard a voice saying 'Listen Henry, what I am saying can be applied to sexual intercourse. If you love a person your whole being is concentrated on that person, you want to spend yourself on that person, you want to discharge on that person. It is the same when writing a poem or painting a picture.'

Then the speaker must have changed position for Lusk heard nothing further. He wondered if the girl had heard it too. She gave no sign of having done so.

'The guys in Izmir told me this was a great place,' Lusk said. 'They told me to come here. They told me you could meet people here. And I met you, so they were dead right.'

'Who were, for Christ's sake?'

'The guys in Izmir, these friends of mine.'

The girl drained her glass, set it down on the terrace behind her. She stood very erect, looking at Lusk. 'Why don't you stop beating about the bloody bush?' she said. Lusk stared at her.

'Going on about those turds in Izmir,' she said. Her shoulders rose in a swift shrug. 'You're after the same thing they're all after,' she said, with no abatement of that clear confident tone. 'All right,' she said, as if yielding at last to a long course

159

of importuning. 'Shall we go to your cabin or to mine? God, men are such animals.'

Lusk regarded her dumbly. His shoulders felt chilly.

'For Christ's sake,' the girl said.

Lusk swallowed some slight blockage in his throat, advanced a stumbling pace and put his arms round the girl. Her back was slippery with wet. She pushed herself against him and he felt her abdomen leap like a fish.

Mrs Pritchett had the feeling that every word she was saying was a dart, a projectile, as though she were not so much speaking in sequence of words to the girl's mind as tattooing her tale in a pattern with needles on to the stretched and quivering sensibility. Never, she felt, had she been so listened to. The pale, glimmering oval of the girl's face seemed to float above the surface detached from the body. And on this patient oval she inflicted her tale. So much was she absorbed in it, and so much did she feel the subjection of her companion, that it came as a shock, almost a violation, when the other in a tone no different from that in which she had with mild queries abetted the story, excused herself and smiling moved away. 'I'll be back in a minute,' she promised, and Mrs Pritchett surmised she was going to the loo – there were four rather rudimentary brick-built ones in a line at the side farthest from the entrance and another alongside the reception desk, but there was in any case no possibility of seeing in which direction the girl had gone, because in a matter of seconds she had vanished into the milky vapour. Mrs Pritchett followed her mentally, however, visualizing that slender form moving through the water, the taut thighs set one before the other, bearing steady above them the navelled, nippled stalk of the body...

'Aha, Mrs Pritchett,' said the thick respectful voice of Vittorio Spumantini from close behind her. 'So here you are?' This was a disingenuous speech on his part because he had known her whereabouts for quite some time. 'I was wondering, will you have supper with me,' he said. 'Are you feeling peckish?'

Mrs Pritchett looked through the dimness at the pale expanse of Spumantini's face, on a level with her own, imagining the expression there would be in his brown, spaniel eyes. Some of the former rage returned, mingled now with resignation – she would not, she knew, find it easy to shake him off the scent again. Noting her hesitation, Spumantini entered into more detail, a habit of his which she particularly disliked. 'We go in,' he said, 'we have something to eat, maybe a drink or so. Yes?'

'I know what the word supper implies, Mr Spumantini,' Mrs Pritchett said. Spumantini underwent an erotic throb at the severity of the words and the contempt implicit in the absolute correctness of the elocution, the ineffable drawl on the second syllable of 'supper', the obstinacy with which she pronounced the first part of his name 'spew' – doubly contemptuous this, as he had attempted to correct her once.

'It is a genuine offer,' he said.

Mrs Pritchett considered. She did not want to mix Spumantini up with the girl. It would be embarrassing and might put the girl off – she might feel she was intruding, that she was *de trop*, especially if this creature allowed his admiration to express itself too crudely. And there would, after all, be further opportunities for getting to know the girl better...

'Very well,' she said coldly. 'I'll go and get changed now. I'll meet you in the dining-room in about twenty minutes.'

'I always looked for affinities before,' Lusk said uneasily. 'That has been my trouble.'

The girl lay on her back under the sheet, with her eyes closed, white-faced and breathing heavily. She was like a patient under anaesthetic. Not so much of a girl either, as Lusk could not help noticing. She must be twenty-six or seven, he told himself, with feelings of awe. The oil lamp at the bed side had been already lit when they entered. She had turned it low but there was enough light in the room for him to see her frail-looking, delicate-boned face, the frictive shine of her eyelids. The mouth was thin, slightly open to emit the noisy breath. Reclining on one elbow Lusk took an alarmed inventory of her features. 'I guess I'm a romantic, at heart,' he said.

'For Christ's sake,' she said, without opening her eyes. *'Get on with it.'*

Despite this urging, because of it rather, he hesitated still. Things had happened so quickly: emerging from the pool, going along the chilly terrace into her cabin, slipping out of his trunks and into the bed. He had had no time to recover from the dread suddenness of the invitation, no time to generate desire. The woman too had seemed to his bemused senses to move with the speed of light, stripping off her bathing suit, rubbing herself down with a powder-blue towel and slipping between the sheets all in a blur almost. She had not smiled or touched him or made any gesture of kindness or tenderness. Now she lay there on her back as if about to undergo an operation. It was not thus that Lusk, dreaming in his lonely room in Izmir, listening on the fringes of others' conversations, hearing talk of lissom, eager girls, not thus he had envisaged things.

He shifted a little in the bed and squinting down below the sheet, saw a taut throat, a well-muscled shoulder, sallow vertical creases at the left, the nearest armpit, the arm itself pressed virginally close to the flank; beyond this the left breast, or most of it, softly heaped, as if the flesh had drifted, duned randomly, like snow. Surmounted by a rather chewed-looking nipple –

'What are you waiting for?'

Looking up, Lusk met blue eyes, furiously hostile. He felt himself beginning to blush. Partly in order to conceal his blushes he ducked his head down and took the nipple in his mouth. The nipple and the flesh round it tasted peculiarly bitter. A world away he heard her voice saying. 'Beastly little opportunist,' apparently in reference to him. 'Degrading myself,' he heard her say. Of course it was simply the pool taste, he decided, the bosom tasted of the pool. He continued to mumble and suck at it, listening to the remote voice somewhere above him, a dull, droning voice, consistent with a prosy sort of fever, saying, 'If they could see me now.' It dropped to an indistinguishable mumble for some moments, then rose again:

'After everything they did for me. All the money my father spent on my education. He was a vicar, you bloody twerp, and would have turned his mind away from anything repulsive.

162

Instinctively. I was given piano lessons, you untutored oaf, what are you doing down there? I had a pony of my own. My godfather too, a commissioner of oaths and affidavits ...'

'It can't be like this,' Lusk told himself. Sucking a bitter breast, while a voice referred to him as twerp and turd. *It can't be like this*, he insisted to himself in a small blind frenzy of revolt, not ceasing, however to roll the nipple round under his tongue.

The girl turned towards him, uttering a sort of groan. 'You filthy beast,' she said loudly. 'I belong in the gutter with this filthy beast.'

All this groaning and abuse was clearly audible to Herr and Frau Gruenther who, after a frugal supper, were standing in the pool just outside the girl's cabin.

'Disgusting,' Herr Gruenther said. 'Is it not, my dear?' *'Ich werd mich bei den Verantwortlichen beklagen,'* he said loudly, glaring angrily at the closed door of the cabin.

'You horrible *parvenu*, you cockroach,' said the girl in the cabin, gulping and snapping.

'Mmaagh' said Lusk for all reply. His mouth was still full of bosom, which he did not dare as yet relinquish, being terrified of the girl's spasming and the fury of her eyes.

'Let us walk farther off,' Herr Gruenther said. 'They have no shame. Words of love are not for public ears.'

They walked a little way along the pool. 'There is also the music of the young American,' Herr Gruenther said. 'I will include that eternal transistor in my complaint of the morning. The manager must take action. Are we to have the fruits of a shallow civilization always in our ears?' He snorted with indignation.

'Feel me here, darling. No here,' Frau Gruenther said. She guided his hand to the inside of her thigh. *'Kannst Du einen Unterschied sehen?'*

'A great difference,' her husband said loyally. 'A kilo at least has gone.'

Frau Gruenther's head, encased in its white rubber bathing cap, was almost completely spherical. She was short in stature, had been known in her youth as *petite* in fact; now the ramifications of her chin rested on the water, whereas he was only immersed to his chest. In the folds and accretions of her face, eyes, nose and mouth were tiny, curiously rudimentary, features dabbed in without regard to scale.

'It is all a question of the massage,' she said. 'All the time I am in the water I am rubbing myself, according to the instructions. That is the secret of it.'

Herr Gruenther tried now to extricate his hand, but his wife had brought her thighs close together in the meanwhile, and he found himself trapped, his hand enveloped in warm spongy flesh.

'I think we should stay here some days longer,' she said. She must have forgotten it was there. This indifference to his own flesh recalled with a pang to Herr Gruenther nights of their early marriage when he had stalked her slim form across wide snowy sheets. He lowered himself in the water and looked up at the starry sky, sensing from his wife's movements that she had recommenced her massage. Without doubt she had forgotten completely that his hand was there. Could it be that such contacts, because of her bulk, the distance between centre and periphery, were only intermittently signalled to Hilde? He entertained for some moments with a sort of bemused pity, this notion of Hilde's flesh progressively losing touch with her brain. Or perhaps things would come through finally, but grotesquely delayed, so that Hilde would be continuously responding at inappropriate moments to vanished stimuli. Supposing for example hours or days from now, talking to someone, having tea, or at the hairdresser's, she were suddenly to become aware of someone's hand high up between her thighs ...

'You beastly fucking little bastard. You beastly fucking little shit,' intoned the girl loudly. 'Oh you snotty twerp and pisspot.' She uttered a hollow joyless groan.

Into Lusk's mind, as he lay there, still feebly licking the nipple, came a total sense of the girl's strangeness, the contempt with which she had treated him right from the beginning, and her eagerness for it, avid, she was avid, squirming even now to get under him, all this struck him suddenly as *sick*, and a question occurred to him, one that would show her he was no novice, not a person to be taken lightly. A man of the world in fact.

He raised his head and said, 'Excuse me but are you a nympho?'

'What did you say?' Her body was suddenly still.

He saw the white face and large-irised blue eyes some six inches from his own. They narrowed as he looked, and the mouth drew together in a thin line.

'Are you –' he was beginning again, laboriously and with a sense of foreboding, when the girl's face drew back sharply and her right arm, which had been under the sheet, rose into the air and came swiftly across her body in a kind of looping, chopping blow. Her clenched fist, wielded sideways, not in a punch but a sort of hammer blow, caught Lusk squarely on his right eye, causing him for some moments intense pain. He placed a hand over his injured eye and sat up in bed. The girl pushed him violently in the chest.

'Get out of my cabin,' she said loudly. 'Take your beastly person out of my cabin.'

'I asked you a civil question,' Lusk said, still holding his hand over his blinded eye.

The girl sat up, frantically with one hand clawing at her hair, with the other heaving the sheet up to her chin. 'I'll report you,' she said. 'For indecent assault. Get out of here.' Her whole head was trembling and she gulped several times as if she had swallowed something inadvertently.

'Okay,' Lusk said. 'I'm going.'

'You'll hear more of this,' the girl said. 'You beastly coward, you deserve to be horsewhipped.'

Lusk got into his cold wet trunks and blundered to the door.

'Rotten stinker,' the girl shouted after him.

He walked along the terrace, dazed with the enormity of what had happened to him, a wounded creature between water and sky. In his cabin he bathed the eye in cold water. Then he sat down on the edge of his bed and wept for some minutes.

Farnaby spent a long time wandering about in the water, trying to pick up the traces of the girl he thought was Miranda. When hunger finally obliged him to quit the pool, he found the dining-room almost deserted. Plopl and his girl were sitting at the far end of it with their backs to him. They appeared to have finished their meal, and were sitting silently side by side. They did not see him come in, and he had no wish to draw their attention to his presence. Mrs Pritchett, accompanied by the Levantine Spumantini, passed him on their way out. So Miranda, if it were indeed Miranda, had not dined with her. The only other persons in the dining-room were a girl in a wheel chair, with high deformed shoulders, and opposite her a middle-aged, square-faced woman whom Farnaby thought might be a nurse. They too appeared to have finished eating. Senemoğlu appeared in his white jacket, the brilliance of his smile in no way impaired by the news he brought Farnaby that owing to the lateness of the hour there was nothing to be had but fish soup. The hours for the evening meal, he told Farnaby, information in fact already posted up on the back of each cabin door, perhaps monsieur had omitted to look, the hours were seven to ten. It was now almost eleven. Farnaby apologized, accepted the fish soup, which turned out to be quite delicious. Senemoğlu did not reappear and none of the other people in the room paid him any attention. They were still there, sitting in the same positions when he got up and left. However, standing in hesitation just beyond the door, he noticed after a moment or two a white-coated figure hovering at his side. He looked up and caught a smile, brilliant even in the half dark: Senemoğlu.

'Did you find her?' the manager asked. 'The young lady you were looking for.'

'Oh,' Farnaby said. 'No, not yet.'

'You will,' Senemoğlu said confidently. 'I am sure that you will find her or some other.' He was beginning to withdraw.

'Is it too late for me to get a drink,' Farnaby said.

'No, not at all. What would you like?'

'Vermouth, please. A sweet vermouth. With ice.'

'Very well, sir.'

'I'll have it on the terrace,' Farnaby said. He began to walk slowly along the terrace towards the nearest table, seeing almost with surprise the soft gleam of water below him – he had been forgetting the nearness of water, and yet it was the reason, was it not, for the presence of all of them there. Or was it? He was troubled by a sense of other reasons, vague but compelling like evidence he had chosen to disregard. He glanced up from the still water to a sky that itself looked liquid, with stars melting in it, softened and enlarged.

Senemoğlu was there with the drink almost immediately. He placed it on the table and receded bowing into the darkness. Farnaby sipped the vermouth slowly. The night air was cold, but he felt warm enough in the heavy worsted trousers and thick pullover he had put on after emerging from the pool.

Across the vaporous surface of the pool light fell unevenly, erratically. The heads of the creatures inhabiting the pool were darker grains or clots in the mist. Glimpses of pale shoulders, arms, faces turning. Occasionally the grains moved, described arcs or lines, sometimes at speed enough to score a brief, glittering wake. Cast a net down here, you could make quite a catch. Squirming conglomerate mass struggling in the meshes. Perhaps Miranda among them. Delicately, carefully, extricate her slender limbs. Difficult to distinguish, though, as they gulped and threshed together. No characteristic marking, all the same kind of fish really.

He looked with a sudden impatience that was almost disgust away from the pool and its denizens, over the cabins and the invisible hills beyond, at the night sky. Nothing we could come here seeking, he thought, that has not been sought and found before. He thought of the view from the window of his cabin, the ruins scattered over the hillsides. Old, he informed himself sagely. He was beginning to feel drowsy. Immeasurably old ...

Suddenly, quite close to him he heard a throat being cleared with a harsh abrasive sound. Then a chairleg scraped on the floor as if someone were shifting position. Peering forward Farnaby made out at the next table a seated figure which he had not noticed before because of the deep shadow cast by the parasol shade – it was apparently the policy of the management to leave these permanently in position. Farnaby had the impression that this person was regarding him, had in fact turned in his chair for this purpose.

'*Merhaba,*' he said. '*Iyi Aksamlar.*'

There was no reply to this, but after a short while the person hawked again, then said, 'Hae ye a match, laddie?' As if in a dream, Farnaby found this accent familiar.

'Yes, I think so,' he said wonderingly. He got up and walked to the next table with his box of matches in his hand. 'Here you are,' he said. He looked down at the meagre form, the thin face. He said, 'It's Mr McSpavine isn't it?'

'Ay, that's right.'

'What a fantastic coincidence,' Farnaby said. He sat down opposite McSpavine and leaned forward, elbows on the table. McSpavine started lighting his pipe. The flame of the match dipped into the bowl with his breath, sprang up again briefly, casting light over the sharp-jawed face.

'Why, who are *you*?' he said at last, rather mumblingly, the stem between his teeth.

'Don't you remember me? Farnaby, James Farnaby. We had a covnersation in the French Hospital in Istanbul. When was it now, not long ago ...' He paused. Time before the pool seemed to have become undifferentiated.

'Oh, ay,' McSpavine said after a moment. 'I remember you, laddie. We talked about my Flora.'

'That's right.'

'I hae sailed the seven seas,' McSpavine said.

'Yes,' Farnaby said. 'I remember your saying that you had been a ship's engineer.'

McSpavine turned his head aside and spat delicately into the darkness. 'Wee fanatical skipper,' he said. 'Mutinous crew. Scoundrel lascars. Give her every ounce you've got McSpavine. Aye, aye, sir. No coal left, choppin' up the bulkheads. Hotter'n hell in these engine rooms, sir.'

He fell silent for a while, puffing at his pipe. After a few moments a long fluttering sigh escaped from him. 'I'm becalmed now, myself,' he said. 'In the shallows and miasmas.'

Farnaby again noted that the Scottish accent seemed to come and go like some sort of recurrent impediment in speech.

'I sit here,' McSpavine said. 'Tryin' to work it all out.'

'But what made you think of coming here?'

'By different roads we came to the same place,' McSpavine said.

168

'No, but I mean, it is rather an unusual place to come to . . . in the circumstances.'

'You mean with my Flora dying? Ay, weel, I was guided.'

'How do you mean?'

'I heard a feller talking of it, in the hospital,' McSpavine said. ' 'Twas after my Flora breathed her last. I went in to see the clock. We must know the difference between the living and the dead, laddie. The pree-cise moment must be marked. If we canna tell by the face, I mean. My Flora looked the same before and after, the same smile. There was no way of tellin' she had crossed the great divide.'

McSpavine relapsed into silence again. After a few moments Farnaby said diffidently, 'So you went back to look at the clock.'

The figure opposite him made a sudden movement, as if startled. Then the voice resumed:

'I saw the lassie in the bed, sitting up. Not more than twenty. She smiled at me. At least,' McSpavine added cautiously, 'I got in the way of her smile. And Flora went out of my mind, after forty years of matrimony. And her not cold yet, still smiling. I could think of nothing but climbing into the bed with the wee lassie . . . I went into a sort of hall and I sat down for a bit. I talked to a young fellow there –'

'That must have been me,' Farnaby said.

'Oh, ay,' McSpavine said, rather doubtfully. 'I stayed for a while,' he said, 'thinking things out, then I started leaving. But half way down the corridor I felt giddy, I thought I was going to fall, so I leaned against one of the doors, holding on to the handle to keep myself up. And while I was standing there I heard a man talking through the door. A beautiful slow voice. His voice came at me from the cracks in the door and he spoke to me about this pool. I listened, laddie, and I didn't feel giddy any more, the words he was saying cleared my mind. He was telling me to come here.'

'But good heavens!' Farnaby said. 'That must have been Mr Mooncranker that you heard.'

'Oh, ay?' McSpavine said, indifferently.

'Yes,' Farnaby said. He was surprised at McSpavine not showing more interest in the identity of the person who had directed him here. 'It is an amazing coincidence,' he said, 'because Mr Mooncranker was talking to me at the time, and you must have been overtaken by giddiness just at that very moment...'

McSpavine made no reply. It seemed to Farnaby that if they could not talk about this they could not talk about anything. He looked across the pool. He could not see anybody in the water now, but he thought he could still hear wading sounds from the remoter recesses. He looked at his watch: it was twenty minutes to one. 'Well,' he said, 'I think I'll turn in now.' McSpavine muttered something indistinct round the stem of his pipe.

'Good night then,' Farnaby said. He made his way along the terrace, treading soundlessly. Past cabin number nine where slept Mehmet, the Gruenthers' Turkish driver. Past the cabin of the Gruenthers themselves in which they lay lost in the two separate mounds of their existence, her dreams too trivial to cause any commotion in her bulk, he between sleep and waking in the lee of her back groping in memory for the scene of childhood holidays, distant fields, a fuming of marguerites, white horses in sunshine. Past, though he did not know it, the cabin of Miranda, whose mind was full of her new friend and the confidences that friend had made her. Flushed and excited, quite disinclined for sleep, she lay on her back in the darkness. She could see through her window a square of night sky casually presented to her. She gazed wide-eyed, unblinking at the distant spaces. Her body was burning under the sheet. Her mind touched inadvertently on certain points of similarity between Mooncranker and Mrs Pritchett, lingered rather alarmedly on these, sheered away. The whole of her life up to now seemed unsubstantial and somehow *preliminary*, everything that had happened to her. Her being, as she moved restlessly in the bed, responded to some moan of anguish and excitement being sounded outside in the night, some deep chord of feeling. She wondered if she had a temperature.

Past the cabin of Mrs Pritchett who, as her habit was, read a chapter before composing herself to sleep. Always a factual sort of book and usually something relevant to her immediate situation or experience. She sat propped up against the pillow, face composed, even severe, lips compressed. Poplin pyjamas buttoned to the neck. She read:

Cybele, the chief deity in the religion of the Phrygians and other pre-Greek peoples in Asia Minor. She was an all-powerful goddess, the supreme feminine being, the embodiment of Mother Earth. The god of heaven (*Papas* or father) was subservient to her, and so were the demi-gods Attis, her lover, and a band of demonic beings known as the Corybantes ...

She looked up from her book. Presumably the Corybantes would be women. She saw them with prepared nails waiting on the orders of their mistress. Marvellous days those, for a woman of character. The only men in close attendance appeared to be the Galli, the eunuch priests of Cybele. Or was Galli just another name for Corybantes? The book did not make this clear. It would have been in such places as this that her cult was established. Perhaps on some level space among these very hills behind them, Attis was yearly mourned. What was the Corybantes' real purpose? Were they emissaries, devotees, divine accessories of some sort, or simply servants of the Great Mother? The book did not say. Brow slightly furrowed, she read on:

Whatever form the original cult of Cybele took, in historical times it had become a religion of orgiastic rites. There were masked assemblies and processions of the Corybantes and ecstatic dancing accompanied by wild music on flutes and various percussion instruments ... The participants scourged themselves until they drew blood and aspirants to the priesthood marked the culmination of their frenzy by emasculating themselves in imitation of Attis ...

Farnaby went past all these people and so to bed.

4

He slept fitfully, and dreamed about that riverside scene related by Mrs Pritchett to the girl he thought of now as Miranda. In this dream he had several identities. He was Mark the fisherman, and a person who watched from the bank, and the fish. Mark stood in midstream, bulky and elemental, absolutely motionless, darkly outlined against a silver sky, and the luminous water flowed quickly past him, around him and between his firmly planted legs, and it was Farnaby's hand, incongruously delicate, holding the rod, managing the ratchet, Farnaby too who waited downstream, facing the current, looking up to the filmy surface where the light broke, looking against the sliding light for dark flecks of food, the barbed fleck that meant death, Farnaby's hand dashed the fish's head on a stone and the round eyes flew out, eyes with which seconds before he had seen bubbles and colours, his eyes, his hands, and he watched it all from the bank where the air was heavy with sweet odours...

He awoke in half light, wide-eyed. He looked at his watch: it was exactly five o'clock. He lay for a while longer, looking up at the ceiling on which he could make out an extensive design of cracks and fissures like a map, with land masses and seas and strings of islands. He sensed the silence hanging over the pool. It seemed to him that he could hear a very faint tinkle of sheep bells and also the sound of human voices very far away; though these sounds had the curious property of eluding conscious listening, of being heard only when attentiveness lapsed. This dawn, in its immediate stillness and its distant intimations of sound, was like a distillation of all the wakeful dawns of his life to Farnaby, and his body, fully extended in the bed, grew tense as if waiting to be disposed of.

After some more minutes he got up and put on his swimming shorts which were still rather uncomfortably damp. Over them he put on his thick camel-hair dressing-gown, which somewhat resembled a monk's habit, and stepped out barefooted on to the chilly terrace. It was still not light enough for him to see far across the pool, though light was increasing from moment to moment. The water below him was palest blue, almost grey, hung with vapour which did not now in this faint daylight seem to swaddle the surface so much, merely took away direct reflections, absorbed the light so that the mist itself had a luminosity that should have belonged to the water. He stood gazing, feet cold, body still heavy with sleep. Hanging ethereal in the sky to the west towards the sea, there was what seemed the crest of a great mountain, though morning haze contended with cloud and snow to render its outlines indistinct. The cabins with closed doors slept all around the enclosure.

He took off his dressing-gown and dropped it on the terrace beside him. At once the cold air swooped on to his thin and shrinking body. Hastily he sat at the edge of the pool and from this sitting position slipped down into the water which was deliciously warm and welcoming. He began swimming a cautious breast stroke towards the bridge, looking down as he swam at the antique masonry glimmering below the surface. The marble sections of columns shone white, gleamed through the refracting water as did the immaculate pebbles on which they lay – centuries of immersion in this mineral-laden water had given them no faintest crust or scurf or patina; they were as free of deposit as bleached bones. Not so the brick, he noted, still peering down; there were fragments of brick here and there, parts of a terracotta pavement by the looks of it, and these were coated with a pale greenish substance, like pale moss, though almost certainly chemical. He duck-dived to the bottom to touch some. It was slippery, like wet moss.

He rose to the surface, spluttering slightly, aware of the faint sweetish reek of the water. The water ran into his eyes and stung a little. He pressed the lids of his eyes with his fingertips as if to press out the water and when he opened his eyes he saw across the pool the girl of the night before, whom he had failed to find again the night before. She was standing in the shallower part, up to her waist in the water, wearing a dark red bathing costume, and she was looking towards him. She must have entered the pool while he was swimming.

This meeting, or rather it was not that quite yet, but this fact of their being both together in the otherwise deserted pool, providential as it seemed to him, had an intimidating effect, and he looked diffidently away, in immediate misery that this one failure of nerve might damage all his future prospects with the girl, just as, if it were really Miranda, he had spoilt things somehow, by some obscurer weakness, in the past. After moments of anguished irresolution he looked at her again. Their eyes met and both of them smiled with an amusement

173

that seemed amazingly pure to Farnaby, somehow pristine like the morning, mutually perceived amusement at their own awkwardness, clumsiness, or so Farnaby felt at least, and to him this smile, prolonged as it was beyond the normal time for such signals, marked some special quality of acknowledgement on the girl's part, recognized something conspiratorial in their situation. Though whether this was their conspiracy coming to fruition, or somebody else's, he could not determine for the moment. Nor, for the moment, did it matter. Across these few feet of luminous water, with the strange vapour faintly swirling around them, the snows of the mountain beyond, their two bodies stood still in the warm, sealing liquid, blood quickened, confronting each other with this bold smile.

'I couldn't sleep,' he said at last, moving a little towards her. The details of her face were still not quite distinct.

'Neither could I,' she said, her voice rising in a surprised, rather excited way. And the smile left her face completely, as if this coincidence were a very solemn thing.

'Isn't it marvellous,' he said, 'early in the morning like this, when nobody else is around?' He did not know, in saying this, whether he meant the pool or the fact of their isolation. She assented, still solemnly, her head declined a little, her brows partially obscured by the sweeps of honey-coloured hair.

'No one to stare,' Farnaby said, speaking with what felt to him a dreamlike ease as if his lips and larynx had not to labour at all but words formed weightless on his breath. 'No one chattering around you. No voices. I mean I think it is a great place in itself but for me it is spoilt to some extent by all these voices, disembodied voices.'

'Yes,' she said, 'you never hear the end of anything, do you? You either want to know nothing at all about people, or more than that.'

'Quite,' Farnaby said fervently. Her head was slightly turned away from him and he looked at her steadily, taking advantage of this averted gaze, not unwilling either that she should be aware of his scrutiny. Which she could have ended any time by looking at him, meeting his eyes. But did not. He observed her with a sort of detached, potentially loving closeness of regard, as one might look at a flower: a curiosity at the life form, warmed with admiration. Her face was narrower than he remembered the childhood Miranda's, less instinct with laughter, though there was still that sun-flushed depth, almost a duskiness, in the complexion, and the eyes too he thought he remembered, though graver now, dark eyes slanting upwards very slightly.

'Yes,' he said, taking in all this in a series of visual raids on her. There was no single feature that established her beyond doubt in his mind as Miranda, there was only his general sense of familiarity, of recognition and also a more superstitious feeling of necessity. He knew he should ask her now if that was her name, announce himself, say why he was there. But he delayed doing this, from instinct rather than any deliberation, feeling obscurely the need to exist independently in her view, to form something between them first, so as not to be set down as an adjunct merely, an emissary of Mooncranker's. He had not after all come to reclaim Mooncranker's secretary, but had at the last moment agreed to come because it was Miranda. She was the reason, and he would have to make her understand this somehow – but the way was not by blurting out that Mooncranker had sent him.

He said, 'I wish it were all mine. The pool I mean. Instead of the property of the Turkish state. Then there'd only be my own voice in it. And yours of course. I would invite you. You would be my permanent guest.'

She looked at him now and smiled again, but a different, more secretive smile. 'Wouldn't it be wonderful,' she said, 'to have it for one's own?' This smile, slow and secretive, just catching the corners of her mouth, transformed her face, gave it a sort of ancient irony and knowingness, which lasted only a few moments, after which it broadened, lost its sybilline character, became more openly joyous, almost gleeful. This was how that particular smile began and ended and Farnaby at once formed the ambition to provoke it as frequently as possible. 'We could have who we liked here,' she said. 'Just the people we wanted.'

Farnaby made no reply for the moment. He had suddenly felt himself assailed once again by a sense of the girl's physical existence, the wonder of it, and by a sort of gratitude for it.

The desire stirred in him to reciprocate, demonstrate his own reality, a reality which had nothing to do with the words he had been uttering. He realized that it was his identity he wanted to present her with, to lay before her, so that she could then reassure him about her own. Still however, perhaps out of fear that he might after all be wrong, he delayed.

'What made you choose Turkey?' he asked. 'Not many girls come as far as this on their own.'

'I suppose not,' she said. 'I didn't come on my own actually.'

'Here to the pool do you mean?'

'To Turkey. I just came to this place on an impulse really. Because I was fed up. Anyway, going back to what you said, I think a lot of girls would be scared of coming to Turkey, you know, they think of the people as very primitive.'

'Rapists one and all.'

'Well, more or less.'

'I think a lot of that feeling is unfounded,' Farnaby said. 'They may be primitive, but they are decent people. Obviously you must be careful. I mean I think it's unreasonable for a girl to go round half naked and then raise loud complaints when a Turkish peasant, who rarely sees a woman's ankle, gets carried away. No, I put it down to the philhellenism prevalent in England – Greece the cradle of civilization. Well that is true I suppose, but the English turn everything into a moral issue. They set against Pericles some bloodthirsty Sultan. Greece is the light side, Turkey the dark, so this myth gets built up, wicked barbarous extortionate Turks occupying beautiful Greece for four hundred years, grinding down the ideals of Hellenism with their greed and sloth and essentially uncreative...' In the midst of this speech, which he felt quite strongly about, he noticed that she had a tiny scar, circular in shape, high up on her cheek bone towards the right temple – the one turned towards him. This sight and the attentiveness to her which it renewed in him, caused him to falter in his argument. She was listening, or appeared to be, with concentration, face turned in profile away.

'Whereas the fact is,' Farnaby said, looking at her, 'the fact is that fifteenth-century Greece was a backwater, Athens no more than a village, and Turkey took it over as part of the

Balkan job lot. They were more cultivated than any people in Europe at that time. The Turks I mean...'

He wondered suddenly if he was boring her. Impossible to know what she was thinking. 'Anyway,' he added, rather lamely, 'it seems difficult for people who like Greeks to like Turks too.'

'I think it is so stupid for people to take sides like that,' she said.

'I think so too.'

'What part of England are you from?'

'I was born in Berkshire,' he said. Then he added slowly and carefully, 'I had an uncle and aunt who lived at Sinningford, in Surrey. I spent a summer holiday there once.'

'That is where my parents' home was.'

'I know,' Farnaby said. His heart was beating rapidly. 'I know who you are,' he said. 'You are Miranda, aren't you? Miranda Bolsover.'

'Yes.'

'Do you remember a boy called Farnaby, James Farnaby?' She looked at him a moment and her eyes widened. 'I knew I had seen you somewhere before,' she said. 'Of course I remember. What an extraordinary thing. What are you doing here, are you on holiday?'

'No,' he said, 'I live in Istanbul.'

'Isn't it an extraordinary coincidence?' she said. 'You have grown tall. But I remember you were tall for your age.'

He said, 'It is not really all that much of a coincidence. Let's have breakfast together, and I'll explain things.'

'Can we get breakfast yet? It must be still pretty early.'

'Oh yes,' he said. 'I expect we can get something. And we can talk before anyone else arrives.'

'Good idea,' she said. They smiled at each other again with the same amusement, the same complicity – accomplices now in extorting what they could out of this meeting...

Senemoğlu was already up and about, dressed in his white jacket. The smile with which he greeted their entrance was a complex blend of congratulation for Farnaby and distress at their earliness. The bread had not arrived yet, he explained – it came up from the village every day. So madam could not have

177

the toasted cheese-sandwiches she had immediately asked for. There was yoghurt, however, and honey and fresh fruit. They said that would be fine. Miranda asked for *café au lait*. 'I can't bear Turkish coffee in the mornings,' she said happily and with a certain intimate assumption of his involvement in her tastes and preferences which excited him but at the same time recalled Mooncranker lying swathed in the hospital – had not Mooncranker remarked on her dislike for Turkish coffee?

He ordered a large orange juice and they both watched with pleasure as the fresh oranges were sliced into halves and crushed in the fruit press, which occupied a central place on the counter. Heaps of fruit and vegetables lay alongside it, piled in wire-mesh baskets, carrots, tomatoes, apples, lemons.

'That is one of the things I like best about this country,' Farnaby said, 'the way there is always a big fruit press like this, and you can get fruit and vegetable juice any time you want.' The piled fruit glowed in the baskets, Farnaby's orange juice came frothing out into the tall glass, at a sink behind the counter a tap was turned on and the gushing sound of water filled the room for a few moments.

'It must be very healthy,' she said.

He watched the frank enthusiasm with which she stirred pale gold honey into her yoghurt. She had a full underlip, rather childish, slightly puffy-looking as if she had been stung on it and the swelling had not quite gone down. She was wearing a grey dress and a dark blue woollen jacket. She had tied her hair back. He took in these details with wonder at her separateness, which he had not felt before, in the tension of establishing who she was, who they both were.

'It is amazing,' she said, 'that we should both be sitting here like this. I never thought we would meet again, did you? I didn't even know you were in Turkey at all.'

He said, 'No, I didn't think I'd ever see you again. I'm glad it has happened.' He began to tell her what he was doing in Istanbul. He would have liked to protract this moment, make it stretch out indefinitely, this charmed moment in the quiet room with the potential of this meeting still vibrant between them, her face before him, not the face he had remembered, both more and less beautiful, listening, responding; to protract the conversation, remarks uttered without particular emphasis, casually, almost it might have seemed indifferently, but word by word reconstituting the past, reaffirming the time they had spent together, shared, the fact that they were together again now, all this as precisely in a way as if a mosaic were being filled in, even the pauses between them supplied something necessary, and the glances they exchanged. Or so at least Farnaby felt, offering cigarettes, speaking, smiling, while he glimpsed through the open door early sunshine powdered with mist lying across terrace and pool.

'Do you remember that time,' he said, 'we were playing that game of pretending to be stalking animals and we went into the bushes, do you remember?'

Her face was full of laughter. 'Yes,' she said, 'of course I remember, and we couldn't get out because of the gardener, what was his name...?'

'Matthews.'

'That's right, Matthews, he was watering the garden.'

'So we crawled through the bushes all the way across the garden and –' Suddenly, much too late, he saw where this would lead them.

'Yes and when we came out –'

They looked at each other, and the laughter faded from her face. 'It was Mooncranker I came to Turkey with,' she said.

'I know that,' Farnaby said.

'What did you mean when you said it wasn't such a coincidence? Did Mooncranker send you?'

'Would you like some more coffee?' Farnaby said.

'No,' she said. 'Thank you, no.' She leaned forward, setting her elbows on the marble-topped table. 'I think you'd better tell me,' she said.

He told her then, the whole story, beginning with Uncle George's letter. Told her with the desolate conviction that she would immediately be overcome by pity for Mooncranker and guilt for deserting him and that these two emotions in conjunction would quench completely and for ever any interest she might have been feeling in himself.

'Which hospital did you say?'

'The French hospital at Harbiye. I thought that would be the best one. They are more used to foreigners there.'

She nodded. She did not, to his surprise and hope, seem particularly shaken by the news. 'I suppose it's all my fault,' she said.

'I don't see how you can be held responsible –'

'I saw it coming, you see. It isn't the first time you know. I can always tell when there is a bout coming on. There's a sort of, I don't know, a sort of physical obtrusiveness about him then. He always seems to be just in front of you, sort of hovering or wavering about. It is terribly oppressive.'

Farnaby looked at her in silence. It was intensely disagreeable to him, this knowledge of hers that could only have been gained through intimacy, the proximity of their bodies. He had not so far allowed his imagination to dwell with any particularity on her relations with Mooncranker, absorbed as he had been by his vision of her in the past, as if she were still in some way encapsulated in that distant summer.

'Not the first time, then,' he said at last, on a note of rather gloomy interrogation.

'Heavens, no. And this time he had actually started drinking. I couldn't bear it. The thought of going through all that again. I just had to get away.'

'But you intended to go back again.'

'I suppose so, yes.'

'Or at least,' Farnaby said, 'you made sure he knew where you had gone. So that he could come after you.'

She looked at him for a few moments without replying, frowning slightly as if in doubt, yet somehow watchful too, and he suddenly saw how her face had changed from his recollection of it, how all faces change probably: it had become tentative, used to responding to the expectations of others, used to dissembling too. All that vivid autonomy of childhood had gone from it. In the faint lines, that would deepen with age, there was an aquiescence full of sadness, and Farnaby felt a constriction of the heart at this discrepancy, this failure of the memory to tally, a failure in which, however, he obscurely sensed a source of tenderness between them, as if both views of her would in the end be mutually reinforcing, the sorrows of her face now lending poignancy to the independent flame and vehemence of her life then, that summer.

'I really don't know,' she said, 'what I intended to do. I suppose I didn't really mean to break with him completely. I wasn't going *to* anything, you see. I mean, it was all related to him.'

'Well,' Farnaby said, with conscious duplicity, 'when you love somebody...' He continued to look away from her, out across the pool.

'I don't think it's that so much. One gets involved. I admired him. I was only nineteen when he took me on as his secretary, and he was something of a celebrity. A lot of people had heard of him, you know, and they said, Oh are you his secretary, that kind of thing. It seemed glamorous at the time. Apart from that he always seemed to care what I thought. Even before that, when I was still at school, well, that summer when you came, you remember, he used to talk to me a lot, and he always listened to what I said. He took me seriously.'

Farnaby turned to look at her again and saw that her air of perplexity had deepened. She was moving her head very slightly from side to side, as if seeking a more satisfactory explanation of her involvement with Mooncranker.

'But surely,' he said, 'that was only because he found you attractive. I mean, any man, in those circumstances...' He had spoken gently, but with a stirring of excitement not far removed from violence, a quickening of the heart at the thought that he was now at last going into action, assuming the offensive, subverting Mooncranker's position, and that this had been his intention all along.

'No,' she said, 'that's not it. It's partly true of course. No, he had a sort of reality about him. It is difficult to explain. He was capable of taking you into that reality, gathering you up into his life, somehow, and I needed that.'

'But do you always want to be ... absorbed in other people's lives like that?'

'I don't know,' she said. There was a longish pause between them, then she said, 'He got me on his side, you see. And then, when they sacked him –'

'I didn't know he had been sacked.'

'Well, his contract was not renewed, it amounts to the same

thing. Of course, he was often slightly drunk, but it began to get worse, people began to notice it. Viewers wrote in to complain.'

'I see.'

'That's really why we're on this lecture tour. He's been going around talking about his experiences in radio and television. It's the same lecture he gives everywhere.'

'Yes,' Farnaby said. 'I've heard bits of it.'

'I sometimes think he's just a pretext,' she said, rather obscurely.

Farnaby nodded sympathetically. He had, however, been listening with divided attention, lost in the strangeness of her speaking face and the insidious thoughts of Mooncranker making free with the body he divined under her clothes. Imagination is not kind enough to do justice to the loves of others; remembering those frequent references to vitamin B, Farnaby thought of the girl as nurse, or masseuse, someone providing Mooncranker with an essential nutrient or service rather than as a partner in a mutually pleasurable act.

'I think you are dramatizing things,' he said, and with these words he felt excitement again, a renewal of the impulse to damage Mooncranker, oust him. 'You don't leave any vital tissues in his grasp,' he said.

He saw in her face an expression difficult to define, almost complacent, or placated at least, as if she were glad to be under discussion. Not only that, but as if she were responding to his words with gratitude or relief. Simultaneously with this perception there came to him the sweeping, almost mystical certitude of power that he had first begun to feel when advising Mooncranker to prepare himself for hospital, but this time far less cautious and reluctant, based as it now was, not only on Mooncranker's helplessness, but on what he sensed in the girl as an extreme, almost neurotic suggestibility.

'That is,' he said, 'if you really want to get away. I don't know much about it, of course, and perhaps it is presumptuous of me . . .'

'No,' she said. 'No, I don't mind.'

'Well, quite frankly, I think the whole thing is unsuitable. It is too sordid for someone like you to be mixed up in.'

As soon as he had said this he sensed that it had been a mistake, too forthright.

'Yes,' she said, 'I suppose it must seem like that to you.' She smiled again, the mouth thinning and curving upward into that almost helplessly joyous expression that he thought now he remembered, an expression quite involuntary, accidental, because she had been hurt by his words. He suddenly felt a hot indignation at Mooncranker's rhetorical profile, his debilitated form under the sheets, his cunning exploitation of the girl's self-esteem as well as her generosity. Drip – drip – drip, he had fed on her. Well, he would feed no more.

She said, 'When I walked out on him this time, I felt I was destroying him.'

He could not tell if she was exaggerating, dramatizing things, seeking to rebut his accusation of sordidness, or speaking the plain truth.

'Don't you believe it,' he said. 'Mooncranker is a survivor.' But she was not yet ready to hear this. She even looked slightly offended, and in his compunction at this he allowed too great a silence to develop between them. Helplessly he watched the small signs of preparation she was making, straightening herself on the chair, pushing the coffee cup forward some inches.

'Well,' she said at last, looking rather oddly at him. 'I'd better be thinking of packing, I suppose.'

'Please,' Farnaby said, as one breaking from a spell. 'Don't go yet. A few hours isn't going to make any difference. Mooncranker is installed there in the hospital. He's not coming to any harm is he? He won't expect us back yet. Let's spend today together. Look, it's a sunny morning.'

She looked, obedient to his gesture.

'There won't be many more days like this,' Farnaby said, basing his arguments with instinctive cunning on the weather, rather than his own desires.

There was a weakness in her face that he had not noticed before and perhaps only noticed now or only designated now as weakness because he knew how she had allowed herself to be prevailed upon by Mooncranker, was possibly going to allow herself to be prevailed upon by him. The face lost balance at the chin which though well-formed was too small;

and this, together with the rather long and burdened-seeming neck, gave her an appearance of fragility and a vulnerability half dreamy, half anguished. All of which conflicted strangely with his memories of her robust, confident girlhood, as though something had been tapped and taken from her. He watched with a wildly beating heart while she contemplated the weather, the promise of the morning.

'We couldn't spend the whole day together,' she said. 'I have promised to go for a walk with Mrs Pritchett this morning. I mean, if I stayed, I would have to do that.'

'Well, after that,' he said. 'The rest of the day.'

After a further pause, which seemed endless to Farnaby, she said quietly, 'All right, yes,' and turned to him an unsmiling face. He knew then, with triumph and misgivings, that this decision was for more than an outing.

He was walking slowly along the terrace back to his cabin, thinking about Miranda, when one of the nearer cabin doors opened and Lusk took a step out and stood somewhat irresolutely for a moment there. Seeing Farnaby he hesitated, then beckoned in a slack-armed way.

He stood aside for Farnaby to enter. The room smelled strongly of hair oil and bourbon and it was very hot – Lusk must have turned his oil stove up.

'How's it going?' Lusk said. He was wearing a white T-shirt with a rather babyish round neck. He sat on the bed, where he had obviously been lying. Somewhere out of sight the transistor was playing faintly. Farnaby took the little hardbacked chair. 'Not so badly,' he said, noncommittally. He had noticed at once that the left side of Lusk's face was bruised along the cheek bone and that the area round the eye was darkly discoloured.

'Have you had an accident?' he said.

Lusk's Adam's apple jumped at this question, and he began to glance in a nervous bolting way round the room. 'Accident?' he said. 'Jesus.' He began speaking rapidly to Farnaby who however missed the first part of what was said because he had begun thinking about Miranda again, with an almost incredulous wonder at her physical existence, the shape of her

184

shoulders, the composure of her face, the terrifying and exciting malleability he sensed in her...

'...didn't need the Topic at all.' He became aware once again of Lusk's pale beseeching regard. 'We would have got there without it. She was crying out for it. We went to her cabin.' He fell silent for some moments. Then he said, 'Have some bourbon. I'm having some.'

'No thanks,' Farnaby said. 'I've just had breakfast. What happened then?'

Lusk drank and grimaced in a way he had perhaps seen tough guys do. Much of his behaviour had this derivative quality, as if Lusk had carefully watched other people and remembered their gestures and expressions.

'She abused me,' he said, looking with sudden intensity at Farnaby. 'She called me all the names she could think of.' In what was perhaps an effort at self-protection, in the event of Farnaby's finding all this comical, Lusk now contrived the appearance of a debonair smile. 'She just lay there,' he said, 'calling me every low-down thing she could think of. All in this British voice.'

'What kind of things did she call you?'

'Twerp, turd, sewer-rat,' Lusk said, still valiantly smiling. 'Stuff like that.' He took a drink of bourbon. 'She said her uncle would personally horsewhip me,' he said. 'Oh, I was going to ask you. She told me her uncle had been in the Black Watch. Am I right in thinking that is some kind of secret society?'

'No, it's the name of an infantry regiment,' Farnaby said. 'What happened then?'

'Well, I wouldn't tell this to just anybody,' Lusk said, 'and I'd sure appreciate it if you will keep it *sub rosa,* but I was immobilized.'

'Immobilized?'

'I just could not proceed.' Seeing that Farnaby had remained grave, Lusk now abandoned the attempt to keep up his smile. 'My attitude to sex,' he said, 'has always been basically a romantic one.' He rose and went towards the bottle of bourbon. 'When this girl spoke to me like that,' he said, 'I just could not

185

manage to maintain my erection. And I am not ashamed to admit it, because in my opinion only an extremely insensitive human being *could* have maintained his erection in the face of abuse like that.'

'Quite so,' Farnaby said.

'Could you have maintained yours?' demanded Lusk.

'I very much doubt it,' Farnaby said.

'It began to seem very strange to me. The whole thing. I mean, she really was wanting it to start with, and then all this, you know, calling names, it didn't add up. There was something, you know, *abnormal* about it. Something *sick*. Now if there's one thing I can't stand,' Lusk said virtuously, 'it is anything sick like that. Anything kinky. A sound mind in a sound body has always been my motto. Well, it came into my mind that she might be a nympho. I read about this kind of woman but I never actually met one. So I asked her. You know, like with perfect courtesy. I can be very urbane. "Get on with it, nosepicker," she was saying, real crude abuse like that, and she was sort of groaning, so I raised myself up on my elbows and I said, "Excuse me lady, but are you by any chance a little old nymphomaniac?"'

Lusk uttered this question in a Southern drawl, attempting at the same time, though without much success, to assume a sort of dandified head-wobble. 'You got to admit,' he said, 'that it was a good question.'

'Yes,' Farnaby said. 'But did you ask it in a spirit of inquiry or merely out of pique?'

'Both. To be quite frank with you, both.'

'Well,' Farnaby said. 'Did she admit to being one?'

The look of old-world urbanity vanished from Lusk's face. 'She never answered my question. She evaded it,' he said. He drank some more from his glass. It seemed to Farnaby that the whisky was beginning to take effect on him. He had lost his bolting nervousness, was more deliberate in manner, yet seemed in some way bewildered.

'She punched me in the eye,' he said. In slow, dreamlike motion, he imitated the hammer blow. 'Then she told me to get out or she would report me.'

'Well,' Farnaby said, attempting some sort of consolation.

186

'She would not have reacted with such ferocity if your question had not come near the mark.'

Lusk, who had been touching his face tenderly, appeared to brighten a little. 'Right,' he said. 'That's right. I got her on a raw spot there. Good job I got quick reflexes. I was always known for my quick reflexes. If it hadn't been for that, she would have got me with the other hand too. It is not very disfiguring, is it?'

'No, hardly noticeable at all,' Farnaby said.

'You got to keep on,' Lusk said. He seemed to be cheering up considerably now. 'I saw a very pretty girl this morning,' he said. 'Early. Before breakfast. She had been in the pool. I watched her walk along the terrace to her cabin. Very good figure.'

'What number cabin?' Farnaby asked.

'Number twenty-three.'

'Was she wearing a dark red bathing-suit?'

'That's right. Do you know her?'

'Well,' Farnaby said cautiously, 'I know who you mean. She has made friends with an older woman here, who looks a bit of a dragon. I should watch out for her, if I were you.'

'I can take care of myself,' Lusk said, moving his shoulders in an uneasy swagger. As if to prove this, he turned up the transistor, and a euphoric man's voice filled the room singing, 'Love is everywhere, in the magic mystery of moonlight, in the haunted splendour of a June night.'

When, some moments later, Farnaby left, Lusk was swaying to the music, helping himself to more whisky. Farnaby went back to his own cabin and lay down on the bed, the better to think about Miranda. He thought about her in the dark red bathing-dress, standing in the water. How tenderly, with what a gentle pressure at every point the water, the warm, bitter, mineral-thick water, had held her, borne her body up in tender, molecular chains. The water, more palpable than air and therefore perhaps more sentient, more *knowing*, aroused his envy. He remembered, with a clarity almost hallucinatory, how drops of water had adhered to her, bold droplets in the hollows of her body; from this loving lodgement he surmised more intimate invasions of her person by the ubiquitous water,

labyrinths of her ears, pale pink of ducts, subaqueous frondage
of more hidden places, pores, follicles, the minutiae of tissue ...
He thought with a sort of romantic yearning how marvellous it
would be to take Miranda to some place, some kingdom for
ever secure from invasion. Some lines of poetry came into his
mind, deeply familiar and evocative:

> At the mid hour of night when stars are weeping, I fly
> To the lone vale we loved when life shone warm in
>   thine eye ...

Suddenly, he heard a light tapping at the door. He sat up
and swung his legs down to the floor. 'Come in,' he called
running a hand through his hair. He had for some moments
the wild hope that it might be Miranda, changing her mind
about the walk, or perhaps simply with some remark to add to
their earlier conversation. But the head that peered round his
door was surmounted by a Tyrolean-style hat fashioned in
thick, green, rather fibrous-looking material with a jaunty jay-
blue feather in the band and the face beneath, pale, broad,
flabby, without detectable bone, was that of Plopl, the photographer. He had not remembered to start smiling before entering, so his face when Farnaby first saw it was glum and also, it
seemed, rather uneasy; however, he smiled broadly on seeing
Farnaby's look of inquiry, and said in his soft, painstaking,
incredibly good-natured voice, 'Ah my good fellow, you are
here after all. I do not disturb you, do I?'

'No, not at all,' Farnaby said.

Plopl pulled from an inside pocket a fairly large manilla
envelope, but did not for the moment do anything more with
it, merely held it in his hand while he looked round the
room.

'Your room is just the same,' he said.

'The same?' Farnaby echoed, thinking for a moment that he
meant things in the room had not changed.

'The same as all the others.'

'Oh, yes. They are all built on the same pattern, I believe.'

'I like that,' Plopl said. 'It is proper, it is correct, that they
should all be the same exactly.' He had put his hat on in a
hurry, Farnaby thought: bits of his pale brown hair had

188

escaped confinement, hung out below the band in rather unsightly wisps.

'I believe,' Plopl said, 'that in our civilization many things should be standard that are at present...'

'Diverse?' suggested Farnaby.

'Exactly.' Plopl smiled, obviously thinking that Farnaby's readiness in supplying the word indicated complete assent. 'Not for reasons of equality or getting rid of the privilege,' he said. 'But for the aesthetic.'

'Oh, yes,' Farnaby said, rather blankly. He looked at the envelope in Plopl's hand.

'When I walk down the street, it is the same,' Plopl said, waving the envelope gently back and forth. 'Unless the houses have all the same appearance I do not feel comfortable. Things that are fixed, the background of life, should be all the same. Movable things, paintings, decorative objects, above all photographs, these things must be ... diverse. I have got something here that might interest you.'

He drew some postcard-size photographs from the envelope.

Before Farnaby saw them he had a sudden piercing intimation of the sort of thing it was going to be. He looked for a stunned moment at the nude recumbent model, attempting a dreamy gaze while her body strained upwards with unnatural tension, throwing her large breasts into prominence. In the next one she was bending, legs close together, presenting the substantial portals of her buttocks.

'It is so difficult,' Plopl said softly, 'for a true artist to make a living these days.' He watched Farnaby's face 'Ars longa, vita brevis,' he said. 'A true artist has to be unscrupulous ...'

'Ars rotunda, you mean,' Farnaby said, with a nervous laugh, unable even in the midst of his embarrassment to resist the joke. But Plopl did not seem to register it. A sort of calm had descended on him. The Tyrolean hat was set squarely on his head, and the face beneath it, pale, plump-jowled, thin-lipped, meticulously shaven, regarded Farnaby with confidence.

'You will not see tits like that again,' he said, with quiet authority.

'I don't expect I shall,' Farnaby said, proffering back the

photographs. 'They are very good,' he added, nodding and smiling to show that as a man of the world he was in a position to make such comparisons or at least endorse them. 'Superb,' he said. He had been speaking as a connoisseur, not as a customer, and was therefore startled to hear Plopl's next words:

'I can let you have them for, well, how much shall we say? Gentleman's agreement, eh?'

'No, no,' Farnaby said quickly. 'I don't really –'

'One pound fifty,' Plopl said. 'Four classic poses. A special price, just for you.'

'No, I don't want to buy them,' Farnaby said, and there was a driven note in his voice, a note almost of distress at the misunderstanding, which Plopl must have heard and understood, because his manner changed.

'I have others,' he said, more loudly and somehow defensively. 'In my cabin. More artistic. You wait here, I will go and get them.'

'Not just now if you don't mind,' Farnaby said. 'I have to go out now,' he added, with an impulse of kindness, seeking to reduce as far as possible Plopl's discomfiture at being rebuffed in this way.

'The artist,' Plopl said, falling back on what was obviously a well-tried formula, 'has to be unscrupulous. He must not permit himself to be involved in *petit-bourgeois* codes. He has to send forth his grandmother to clean up houses in her declining years if it will further his art.'

You'd be more likely to get granny to strip, Farnaby thought, but he said nothing, merely nodded sagely. Plopl's brows and lashes, he noticed, were so fair as to be almost colourless. His eyes were glossy brown. The brow beneath the brim of his hat was visibly moist. He seemed in his squatness, his feathered hat and benevolently foreign voice, a creature curiously abject and yet with a definite assertiveness of his own, an ultimate intransigence. He also displayed a mannerism, now that he had lost his salesman's suavity, which Farnaby had not been able to see the previous evening, a habit, no doubt quite unconscious, of working his features very slightly, stretching his mouth and wrinkling up his nose a little before speaking, rather as if speech were an activity needing to be fuelled or powered in this preliminary way.

'She's no good, that's the trouble,' Plopl said morosely. 'She has no sensitivity.'

Farnaby guessed he was talking about his model. 'Perhaps posing for photographs doesn't really interest her,' he said.

'Nothing interests her,' Plopl said, 'except one thing, and that is masturbating with an electric toothbrush. She has no hobbies, no intellectual pursuits. She never reads anything. I think she is educationally sub-normal.'

'Good heavens,' Farnaby said, startled by Plopl's unseemly frankness in the matter of the toothbrush.

'Begging,' Plopl said. 'That is what she was doing. She was begging in the streets. "*Ein lira,*" she said to me, she took me for a German. Istiklal Caddesi, this was. Do you know Istanbul at all?'

'Yes, a little,' Farnaby said. Plopl appeared dashed by this, and fell silent.

'Do go on,' Farnaby said.

'She was filthy. She was in a terrible state. I took her home with me, back to my apartment. The first thing I did was make her take a bath. She was verminous. I fed her,' Plopl said, 'I bought clothes for her. Well, that was six, seven weeks ago and she has been at my side ever since.' Plopl's features worked in that combination of effects that was becoming familiar to Farnaby. 'She is devoted to me,' he said. 'You know, like a dog.' He stood looking at Farnaby a moment or two longer as if gauging some possibility. Then he gave a stiff little bow and went quickly out through the door.

Farnaby waited some minutes, in order to give Plopl plenty of time to disappear. Then he emerged on to the terrace. It was his intention to take a walk in the hills behind the pool. Perhaps, he thought, with a quickening of excitement, perhaps I shall catch a glimpse or two of her, of Miranda. Farther down the terrace he saw the Levantine, tapping with respectful knuckles at Mrs Pritchett's door. He tapped then listened, head inclined, then tapped again. Then he softly called, 'Mrs Pritchett,' and leaned forward, ear not far from her door. Farnaby saw him try the door and ascertain that it was locked, but he lingered still.

'I think Mrs Pritchett has gone for a walk,' Farnaby called along the terrace.

The Levantine turned with a smooth yet ponderous sway of the body. He looked at Farnaby remotely and sternly. Farnaby smiled in a conciliatory manner. 'I believe Mrs Pritchett has gone off for a walk,' he called again.

The Levantine looked at him a moment or two longer, then said slowly, 'Do you know in which direction she has gone?'

'Up into these hills, I think,' Farnaby said. 'Exploring the ruins.'

The Levantine looked rather blankly in the direction Farnaby had indicated. Then he nodded briefly and walked away along the terrace with his strangely distinctive gait that somehow resembled wading.

Part Four

1

The desire to end his life which Mooncranker had started to experience in the hospital in the early hours of the morning, while he groped for pretexts acceptable to Farnaby, did not disappear shortly afterwards, as it had always done before. Its intensity fluctuated but it remained with him, proving a source of strength in a way, providing much needed resolution in dealing with the lady doctor, who was angry with him for leaving the hospital so soon; even surviving the torpors and discomforts of the journey to the pool. It was so far not an intention to do any outrage on himself, but simply a languorous wish to achieve the state of being dead, the most immediate effect of which was a sort of deliberate dwelling on things. He described everything to himself as if he were writing a memorial, the sunlit terrace, the vaporous surface of the pool, the rows of numbered cabins, the manager's deference and flickering smile.

It was the middle of the morning when he arrived. There were a number of people in the water, but not Miranda and not Farnaby, and he immediately assumed that they were together somewhere. This was no more than he had expected but it gave him pain.

He seated himself at one of the tables and ordered coffee. He looked over the row of cabins facing him, at the ranks of sage and granite hills beyond. For a moment or two he seemed to make out figures moving about on them, then the figures disappeared. Perhaps Farnaby and Miranda were up there. One thing is certain, Mooncranker told himself, that oaf will not be endeavouring to advance my cause. But isn't that why you sent him here? At this question he experienced some return of that numbness and helplessness he had felt under Farnaby's questioning, and he looked down at the water, slowly, almost languorously, noting the fluting of the columns. Corinthian, in all probability.

An enormously fat woman in a white costume and a white bathing-cap came out of one of the cabins. Mooncranker watched wonderingly her quaking mass descend some steps into the water. Near the bridge two Negroes flicked drops at each other, raising mirthful, half-blind faces. A tall, sharp-featured man, in what looked like a plastic mob-cap, conversed with a shorter, plumper, moustached companion. No words of their converstaion came to Mooncranker.

He had finished his coffee and was wondering if he felt strong enough to go exploring in the hills a little, when a thin, sandy-haired person in a hairy, British-looking sports jacket went past his table.

'Excuse me,' Mooncranker said, speaking on an impulse, 'but do you know anyone staying here called Farnaby, James Farnaby?'

The man did not reply immediately, merely stood there peering, and Mooncranker thought perhaps he had been mistaken in the tweed. He was about to speak again when the other said,

' 'Twas you that spoke to me in the hospital.'

'I do not recall –' Mooncranker began, courteously, but with a certain reserve.

'There couldna be two voices so like,' the other said, shaking his rather shrunken-looking head. 'I hae sailed the seven seas,' he added.

'Really?' Mooncranker thought the man might perhaps be drunk, or wandering in his mind. There was, however, the disturbing reference to the hospital.

'I'm afraid I do not remember our conversation,' he said.

'It was all intended,' the other said, and nodded his head slowly. 'The laddie you are looking for is up there in the hills.'

'In that case,' Mooncranker said, rising, 'I think I'll be getting along. See you later perhaps.'

The other man said nothing. Mooncranker smiled briefly at him and then began to make his way along the terrace towards the exit.

2

From here you can get a better idea of things, Farnaby told himself dutifully. He had been clambering about for some time and now found himself high up in the hills, among the ruins of the ancient city. At this angle the water of the pool could not be seen, only the neat rectangle of buildings surrounding it; far below lay the valley of the Meander, where the fabulously devious river squirmed towards the sea, its course marked out by the bright russet of the platans lining the banks. Beyond rose the mountains, dominated by the snow-capped peak of Buba Dagh – Senemoğlu had told him this was the name. Majestic Summit, Farnaby informed himself. About 1,500 feet up here, I should say.

Feeling himself alone and immune he gestured widely at the firm-edged world of morning. There was no blur or stain on anything. Distant mountain, near rock, the trees in the valley, all had the same clarity, without distorting radiance or gloss. Because of this even light the landscape seemed immutable – Farnaby felt himself and the hillside and everything around fixed in their spatial relations, like pieces in a mosaic or gemmed surface. My whirling atoms come finally to rest. The level terrace immediately below – one hundred, two hundred feet? – was presumably the main avenue of the city. Somewhere hereabouts Miranda and Mrs Pritchett are walking and talking. Miranda serious and attentive. She will have fallen into the role of disciple, for the morning at least, as she would probably adopt any role she felt unambiguously as somebody's need. Dear malleable Miranda. Excitement at her persuadability invaded him once again. Her narrow feet not far away, bearing her body about these mounds and thickets in sensible shoes – she will have dressed the part for Mrs Pritchett. Stepping about, hitching her skirt up to get over obstacles. Mrs Pritchett voluble, stressing the facts. Seen them once, or thought I did, in the distance, Miranda in a headscarf, Mrs Pritchett in a flame-coloured garment ... He cast his eyes around in the hope of catching sight of them, but nothing. Might be anywhere amidst these slopes and hollows, ruined walls, soft heaps of grass-grown rubble. What he did see, higher up and away to the right, were two figures, male and female, the male with something over his shoulder like a rifle. Rifle? No, it thickened at the end into a box-like excrescence. A camera on a tripod. Plopl and Pamela off to do a bit of shooting on location.

He made out numbers of crumbling sarcophagi at the far end of the terrace. The whole area nothing but one vast cemetery. Under this turf, bones, acres and acres of bones, and objects that people are interred with. Other monuments, of course, there must have been: he glanced at the mounds and hummocks all around him. Agora? Temple? Baths? He had not the sort of imagination that could invest these remains with a function. What struck him now was their oppressive extensiveness as a whole. An obscure feeling of disrespect rose in him, and deepened almost to brutality, a violent repudiation of this ancient rubble and any claim it might make on human piety. He did not understand this feeling very well, but knew that it had somehow sprung from thoughts of Miranda...

'Do not go so fast,' Plopl said. 'I am not a mountain goat.' Breathing heavily, he set down his tripod against a rock. He took out a large green handkerchief and mopped his brow and neck. He looked up with resentment at Pamela, standing indifferently, sideways to him a little higher up. 'No sense in climbing always higher and higher up, you fool,' he said. 'What we must look for is some little level area which is not overlooked.' He had been out of temper since his failure to sell Farnaby the photographs, a failure very damaging to his self-esteem and also to that sense of the male *camaraderie* existing between Farnaby and himself which he had experienced right from the first, the evening before in the pool. For Farnaby to have bought the photographs would have constituted a bond between them, a basis for friendship. Now, Plopl felt, he had offered himself and been rejected. Moreover, there was the question of money. One hundred and fifty pence was not a large amount, certainly, but it would have helped. They had not enough between them at the moment to pay the bill ... Plopl's brow contracted. Feelings of misery and disappointed

196

hopes invaded his being. His face felt prickly with heat. He looked up once again at the motionless form above him in the pink cotton dress. Cow.

'You will keep a look out if you please,' he said savagely, 'for a place where we can take the photographs. And *you* will carry the tripod and camera.'

Mrs Pritchett and Miranda stopped near the theatre and Mrs Pritchett began reading aloud from her book:

A Phrygian city, altitude twelve hundred feet, on the right bank of the Churuk Su (Lycus) about eight miles above its junction with the Menderes (Meander) situated on a broad terrace six hundred feet above the valley and six miles north of Laodicea. On the terrace are springs that have deposited calcareous material in their neighbourhood. To these, and to the 'Plutonium' – a probable fissure in the limestone rocks – the place owed its celebrity and sanctity ...

'I wonder why they say "probable",' she said, frowning. 'Either there was a fissure in the limestone rocks or there wasn't, one would think.'

'Maybe they didn't know exactly where it was,' Miranda said softly, pushing back the hair from her brows and looking upward to where the marble benches of the theatre hung above them.

'Oh, they must have known, surely.' Mrs Pritchett spoke sharply, sharpness being the only response she could find to the other's baffling vagueness, assumed from the outset this morning. The girl seemed wrapped up in herself, impervious. She was like a different person. Mrs Pritchett, who had been hoping for a good deal from the walk, was irritated and distressed, and these feelings caused her to become harsher in manner, over-positive.

'If the place owed its celebrity and sanctity to it, they must have known where it was,' she said. *'Surely.'*

'Oh, I didn't mean them,' Miranda said, and then paused, with a casualness that seemed to Mrs Pritchett to border on the perverse.

'What did you mean then?'

'I meant the people who wrote the guidebook,' Miranda said. 'Not the devotees themselves. Or maybe it was never in any particular place at all, maybe it was a sort of legend put out by the priests you know, to make themselves seem powerful.'

'I doubt it,' Mrs Pritchett said. 'No, I think it must really have existed. There is another reference to it, a bit farther on . . .' She began to turn over the pages of the guidebook.

'Who is that down there?' Miranda said suddenly. She was looking down the hillside the way they had come.

'Where?' Mrs Pritchett turned to look. In the distance she saw a male figure moving towards them. After a second or two it disappeared from sight, presumably lost in some fold of the ground.

'It looked rather like the American boy,' Miranda said.

Mrs Pritchett shrugged slightly and then looked into Miranda's face, the beautiful, oddly set eyes, the slightly swollen-looking mouth with at the moment a very slight tendency downward at the corners, as at some residual deprecation. No inventory of the girl's features could explain the sort of interior flinching Mrs Pritchett now experienced at the soft heedlessness of the girl's expression. It was as though she were obliged to tense or stiffen the walls of her heart against some threat of flooding . . .

Farnaby had seen Lusk too, moving with a purposeful air across the lower slopes. Once or twice he seemed to stumble and once he flung out his arms as if to maintain balance. Then he disappeared into a narrow scrub-covered declivity which led up between two rocky spurs of hill and Farnaby guessed that he was working his way upwards towards the level shelf of ground immediately below the theatre. He wondered about this for some moments, because it seemed an odd route for Lusk to have chosen, then he dismissed it from his mind.

He looked down again at the neat rectangle of buildings surrounding the invisible water of the pool. A self-contained world when you were within that enclosure, but from here merely a small and incongruously regular shape among the hills. He began to walk diagonally across the face of the slope.

His feet caught in low shrub and protruding rock. Still a good way above him, the tiered ranks of the theatre. Dating from Roman times. Excellent state of preservation. To me however it bears an irresistible resemblance to the *mons venus*. Definitely, with that vertical fissure of a central aisle, vulvar. Of or pertaining to. In an excellent state of preservation. Lying up there in an age-long position of readiness, waiting for a phallus of the right dimensions. A randy Titan. Epic theme. Now towards those doubtless Byzantine walls. Just within them on a prominent hilltop the substantial remains of an octagonal church. Perhaps this was the church of St Philip. What said Mooncranker on his sick bed? Drip, drip, the vitalizing fluid into those thirsty veins. *I am in danger of becoming dehydrated.* Flawless plaster of the ceiling, wings of shadow, tremulous, calm profile, slow voice. *The apostle Philip was martyred in this city in the year A.D. 80.* Perhaps this was the church they led him forth from. Something sexy about martyrs. Perhaps the ravishment of it all. Oh, those cunning folds of the loin cloth, the blood-bedewed dreamy-eyed saints. Who was that tender-fleshed one stuck all over with arrows? That wasn't Philip. The real thing must have been beastly, of course. Brutal in the extreme. They probably took him out and crushed his skull with a stone. No pretext for ecstasy in a crushed and mangled corpse. That is why crucifixion is so effective, it preserved the human dignity ... Bandaged Christ amid the glint of flies' wings ... Suddenly Farnaby stopped dead, looking down at the ground before him. Did she know? Did Miranda know what Mooncranker was going to give him? She had avoided him afterwards as if in her mind at least some momentous event had taken place. And how could Mooncranker have known of his interest in Christ at that time? What had Miranda said? *He got me on his side.*

I must get the truth from her. A tearing impatience, resembling the ardour of love, possessed Farnaby. In an hour perhaps, two hours at the most, he would see her again...

Keep right on to the end of the road, Lusk told himself. This elusive hare, experience. He had fallen twice since entering the gully and beginning his ascent, the second time heavily, so that he had lain some moments dazedly looking up at the sky. Now he was on his feet again and the going was a bit easier – he was through the thick of the scrub. The bourbon he had consumed, however, was impairing his vision, making it difficult for him to gauge distance with any confidence. After Farnaby's departure he had stayed on in his room, brooding over the débâcle of the night before. He had thought also, with increasing fixity, of the girl in the red bathing-suit whom he had seen walking along the terrace like a vision of rosy-fingered dawn. He felt sure she would respond to the Topic if he could get to her. Then, by the merest chance, as he was opening his door on his way to the john, they passed him, obviously setting out for a walk; the girl, and the woman Farnaby had described as dragonish. Hell with that, Lusk mumbled. I can take care of myself. He had watched the way they went, gone back and with injudicious haste finished the bottle, then started after them. Now, passing a tongue over dry lips, he gazed upward into the sun. Somewhere higher up they awaited him, crying out for it. He stumbled again and almost fell, saving himself only at the cost of grazed knuckles. Take it easy. Lusk paused to get his breath, straining his eyes to catch a glimpse of the two women somewhere up there against the bright sky.

'Higher up,' Plopl said savagely. 'Get higher up on your shanks pony. I want to see the arse rising clear.'

Naked, flushed with exertion, her fair tangled hair tumbling about her face, Pamela pushed her body upward, supporting herself on elbows and heels. Her face, held back stiffly between raised shoulders, regarded Plopl sullenly.

'Keep those bloody legs parted,' Plopl muttered, more to himself than the girl. He sank to his knees and raised the camera. He had it now: between the narrowing cleft of the legs, which were raised aggressively at the spectator, in a position of prominence rarely encountered – the dark wound of the vagina. Beyond this the pubic bush rose almost vertical, foresting the belly. The long plane of the torso and then – most cunning touch of all and one which Plopl had envisaged when he first thought of the pose – the gully formed by the raised legs reduplicated on a smaller scale by the breasts, between which, tilted forward, outlined against the sky, could finally be seen Pamela's inexpressive face. Most of the main erotic zones caught in a single concentration. The whole relieved from 'Health and Efficiency' banality by the strain and effort evident in the pose. And by the face, of course: it was the face that gave distinction to the picture, sullenly enduring what the body was forced to do. No swimming-pool nude this, but a real cry of the flesh, an affliction. Sweat ran down the side of Plopl's face. The camera clicked. He took several pictures from different angles. Then he told Pamela she could relax for a while.

His own excitement subsided rapidly, the blend of repugnance and desire he always felt on these occasions. He had not even so much as got an erection during this one, and the familiar worry descended on him again: it happened less and less frequently during these photographic sessions that he got one. That had been one reason for coming here – he had been told in Istanbul that the water had aphrodisiacal properties, something to do with the alum contained in it. The other reason had been the prospect of selling pictures.

Plopl sighed heavily, remembering the time in the weeks immediately after meeting Pamela when simply posing her successfully and getting the picture had been so exciting to him that he had been ready to mount her immediately. He looked round him. They had found a good place for it, anyway, a rough clearing in the scrub extending well into the hillside so that it was screened on three sides by the hill itself and though overlooked on the fourth, the open side, which was very steep and rocky, no one could have seen them from any point higher up because of the thick overhanging vegetation at the start of the incline. They were as free from observation here, he thought, as they would have been in his apartment in Istanbul ...

Pamela was sitting on the rock, with a folded towel under her. She scratched briefly at her arm below the elbow. Her body was relaxed now, round-shouldered. Her feet turned inward slightly. She looked up at Plopl without expression, shaking the heavy fringe clear of her eyes. He looked at her, forgetting for a moment or two his nagging fear of impotence, the loneliness of the artist, the rage her very existence increasingly

201

roused in him, forgetting everything in the self-congratulation, the pleasure at his own acumen, that the sight of her afforded him. He had seen it from the very beginning, from that first moment in the street, looking at the girl's buxom figure, her young, blank, infinitely violable face; seen what first-rate material she would make. Her sullenness was proof against all grotesqueness or contortion imposed on her body. Such lack of cooperation made every picture seem almost like a rape. All this he had seen from the start. What he could not have foreseen was her stupidity, her inarticulateness, an ignorance that made her credulous, pathetically easy to dupe. He had told her he would report her to the police for begging if she tried to leave him; he had told her begging was an offence punishable with prison if you did not have a licence. All this she had believed, or so it seemed. At any rate she had not tried to run away. To make absolutely sure he kept her passport under lock and key. As he did the electric toothbrush he had taught her to masturbate with, which he let her have from time to time as a special treat...

Plopl mopped his face and neck again. He felt the stickiness of his shirt against his back. This physical discomfort recalled the humiliation of his failure with Farnaby earlier in the morning. The Englishman had not been impressed, not at all. Plopl felt a return of his doubt and self-mistrust. Nude poses were not enough. What was needed were some pictures of actual sexual intercourse. 'Listen,' he said to Pamela, 'we shall now try something slightly different...'

Mooncranker moved out through a gap in the walls, only to find further scatterings of ruined masonry. Looking back through this gap it seemed to him that he saw the distant figures of Miranda and another lady in a bright shirt or blouse. They disappeared again almost immediately, leaving him wondering whether he had in fact seen them at all – the whole landscape was pitted with granite outcrop, clotted with shrub, gashed everywhere with gullies and hollows; an army could move across it without being more than intermittently glimpsed. And the very clarity of the light seemed hallucinatory to him now, more apt to breed illusive images than any mist or haze. Moreover he was confused by the sound of water that was suddenly all around him, the trickle, gurgle, rush of running water. He had emerged, it seemed, into an area where the myriad streams rose to the surface. Soft sounds, but curiously thick and implosive, perhaps because of the charge of minerals the water bore. Here and there on the slopes round about he could detect the presence of water; make out, by the stray gleams they emitted and the vapour that hung about them in the still air, the courses of descending streams. The whole area was combed, riddled with channels of moving water. He remembered his own slow voice pronouncing. *The ancient city was fed by underground springs which made her baths among the most famous in antiquity ...*

Suddenly he saw the man he had talked to at the poolside, not very far below him, moving along a narrow path, little more than a sheep-track, that ran round the hillside. 'Hallo!' he shouted. The other looked up briefly, then proceeded on his way without any further sign of recognition. After a few moments he disappeared round the side of the hill. Mooncranker speculated about this person for a while – he had come after their conversation to the conclusion that the Scot was more or less crazy, or at any rate that he lived for a lot of the time in a private world of his own. Where could he be going to now, with such apparent air of purpose? He soon forgot all about him, however, in a continuing wonder at the sounds of the water which pervaded the hillside. Some of these streams no doubt fed the pool below. The composure, the apparent autonomy of the buildings, the sense one had within them of inhabiting a self-contained world, all this was an illusion, among manifold illusions. The water possessed all in common, hills, ruins, pool. Cities of the past and any to be built there ... He saw Miranda and the other lady again – there was no mistaking the latter's orange-coloured blouse. They were standing together presumably in colloquy, but now in quite a different spot, beyond the theatre, near a ruined basilica. Some hundreds of feet below them he thought he glimpsed another figure moving upwards, though it was difficult to be sure about this because of the darkness of the background vegetation. Far away, on the horizon, a line of persons, dark against the sky, walking very slowly in immemorial procession. He felt sure for some reason that these people were local, inhabitants of the hills...

McSpavine hurried round the hillside, aware of behaving with less than customary courtesy, quite unrepentant, his thoughts absorbed in the paradox of Flora's last hours. So luxuriant he had imagined the growth, in the final stages, behind the wall of Flora's face, so intricate with tendrils, that it must progressively muffle all expression on the face itself, which had not happened, of course – Flora's face had been right up to the end more mobile and expressive than he had ever known it, passing from luminous acquiescence to wild alarm and thence to a sort of excessive shrewdness of appraisal, as if she were re-enacting key scenes from her life. The performance had brought out a fine dew of sweat on Flora's brow, as she moved restlessly on the bed, repeatedly moistening her lips with water, like a person needing refreshment after such strenuous efforts. An artistic debility, not illness. And when all this talent and demonstration was over, when the brain was finally choked, what was left was this smile. A smile not peaceful exactly, but *healed.* This smile persisted on Flora's face through the hurried interchange between doctor and nurse. '*Rigor mortis*' the doctor had said, words clearly not applicable to Flora. It persisted, he was sure, while they drew the screen round, excluding him from whatever ministrations to the body were to follow. And when he went back to see what time precisely Flora had passed away. And when the young woman had smiled at him, and he had stood there in the desolation of his lust, Flora too had been still smiling, the smiles of the dead woman and the living one commingling...

Before him the ground inclined steeply down to a sort of rocky gully, then rose again more gradually in enfolded ranks of hills. Beyond, right up on the skyline, McSpavine made out a number of human figures walking slowly along in irregularly spaced procession. The sun was painful to his eyes, he was compelled to look down, and it was at this moment, dazzled, bewildered by the line of walkers, that he heard a hissing sound which seemed to be coming from higher up on his right. Turning his head he saw a child, a girl of about thirteen, standing against the wall. She was dressed in the voluminous, brightly patterned clothes of a peasant woman, with a white headcloth. He stared wordlessly up at the girl, who kept her thin, dark face turned directly towards him. Clutched against her breast she had a cloth tied up in a bundle.

'*Merhaba,*' McSpavine said at last. 'What is it you want, lassie?'

The girl gestured to him to draw nearer, a gesture as if the thin fingers were digging or scrabbling. She squatted down against the wall and began to untie the knot of her bundle. McSpavine moved up the slope towards her.

There you are, Lusk mumbled to himself. I got you. Not a hundred feet above him they stood together looking at a book. Climb as high as you like, baby, you will not outclimb Lusk. He stood still for some time to recover his breath, holding on to a piece of jutting rock. To the ends of the earth, he told himself drunkenly. I'll follow you. All my life through. Da-dum-di-dum. He looked down rather giddily at the steep and tangled route by which he had come. He was aware of having cut and scratched himself in a number of places without feeling any localized pain. He looked up again at the two women, standing with their backs to him. More slowly, with an effort at circum-spection, he began to move up towards them, rehearsing his opening lines as he went.

'Now then,' Plopl said hoarsely. 'Are you ready?' He was quite naked. Pamela was lying, also naked, spreadeagled on a rock some five yards away, in a position of sexual readiness. Plopl checked his camera. The sun was hot on his back and buttocks. Peering through his coupled rangefinder he saw there was still a slight duality of image, two naked girls overlapping each other, forming a three-breasted figure. He adjusted the focus until they merged. A faint fugitive sound of sheep bells came to him while he was engaged in this. Once again he checked the aperture and shutter settings: all was in readiness.

His idea was to take a delayed action photograph of himself

205

and Pamela having sexual intercourse – with himself just beginning to penetrate Pamela, so that the prospective customer should see, not just two bodies in congress, but the actual member, half in – half out.

'Get ready,' he repeated. He was about to depress the delayed action setting lever when he realized that in the tension of these last-minute adjustments to the camera he had lost the rather inspiring erection he had had to begin with, he was now sticking out more or less horizontally. 'Just a minute,' he said. 'Hold it a minute.' Pamela gave no sign of having heard him. She lay on the grey slab of rock, knees slightly raised, eyes closed against the sun. Her body gleamed whitely.

Plopl gritted his teeth and began playing with himself, in an effort to restore his now distinctly sullen penis to that former readiness and rigidity. For quite a long time nothing very much happened. 'Oh God,' Plopl groaned inwardly, raising a sweating face to the pale immense sky, stroking himself with terrible impatience. At last, reluctantly, there was a stiffening under his hands, a rearing up. Not to the previous peak, which he thought must have been caused in the first place by the artistry of the idea, but sufficient for performance.

'I am on my way now,' he called out threateningly to Pamela, and he pressed down the lever. Almost immediately afterwards, in haste not to lose what he had thus painfully recovered, he pressed the release and began lumbering across the clearing towards the recumbent Pamela, caressing himself feverishly, hurting his soft feet on the rocky earth, hearing behind him the whirring of the delayed-action mechanism, which stopped however, terminated in an ominous click, before he could get there, while he was still half crouching over Pamela's body.

'*Merde!*' Plopl shrieked. '*Verdammt nochmals!*'

He thought for a moment of hitting Pamela with the flat of his hand, then decided against it. He knew what had happened, what must have happened. In his haste he had not pressed the release all the way down. Instead of getting twelve seconds he had only had about five. Pamela had turned her head. She was looking down, in bemused inquiry, at Plopl's limp and shrunken adjunct.

206

'Right,' Plopl said, his lower jaw rigid with fury. 'Right, we are going to try again.'

'Did you hear that?' Mrs Pritchett said. 'That sort of shrieking noise? It came from down there somewhere.' They both looked down over the sheer side of the hill they were standing on, where the ground plunged down in a series of steep rocky folds to a tangle of arbutus and thorn. 'I think it was a human voice, don't you?'

'It certainly sounded like it,' Miranda said. 'Though sounds get distorted, I suppose,' she added vaguely, 'over these distances.'

'Yes, dear, I am sure they do,' Mrs Pritchett said, conscious of being tactful. It had occurred to her that she was wrong to assert so frequently her own order of perceptiveness over the girl's, perhaps it was this that was causing the provoking vagueness on the other's part that seemed so like recalcitrance to Mrs Pritchett's essentially authoritarian mind. She did not, however, really believe that this could account for it. With every moment that passed the distressing conviction was growing on her, that the girl had something – almost certainly some man – on her mind.

'You see,' she said, reverting to the Plutonium, 'it says here that it was fenced off in the first century because it was regarded as dangerous to animals and men.'

They had stopped on a sort of narrow platform, with the ground falling away fairly steeply on both sides. In front of them was a level area roughly rectangular in shape, on which could be made out the ground plan of a temple, grass-grown bosses marking portals and colonnades, and the remains of slender pillars scattered here and there.

'The sun has been catching you,' Mrs Pritchett said suddenly. 'You are quite burnt. You will start peeling if you are not careful.'

'I don't usually,' Miranda said.

'I have some stuff that I could let you have. Splendid stuff. Sun-tan oil, you know, but a special preparation. I'll bring it for you, when we get down.' With an effort she withdrew her eyes from her companion's face and looked down at her guidebook. 'This was the temple to Apollo,' she said. 'Same period as the theatre, second century AD. Or rather, no, it was extensively *rebuilt* in the second century.'

At this moment they heard a plangent nasal American voice behind them, saying, 'Excuse me, ladies.' Both Mrs Pritchett and Miranda turned inwards to see where this totally unexpected voice was coming from. They were in time to see a young man with short hair and a white T-shirt clamber up on to the level and begin walking rather unsteadily towards them. He was smiling broadly.

'Excuse me, ladies,' Lusk said again, then paused, daunted by this sudden eminence, the nearness of the two ladies, and the difference in their faces, both however curiously at variance with his expectations, the older one severe, the younger solicitous or perhaps alarmed. He kept up his smile, his mind a blank, breathing spirituous breaths towards them.

'There was something I wanted to ask you,' he said. Mrs Pritchett caught the odour of whisky. She regarded him a moment or two longer, the wide meaningless smile, the bruised, discoloured face. Something in her own face changed.

'Kindly go away,' she said, with impeccable modulation.

'Now wait a minute,' Lusk said. 'You ladies are British aren't you? Do you know London?'

'No, not very well,' Miranda said.

'Not very well?' Lusk repeated, in surprised tones.

'Ignore him,' Mrs Pritchett said. She turned her back on Lusk and regarded once more the temple of Apollo. After hesitating a moment Miranda did the same.

'Can a girl walk out, you know, alone, in the streets of London after dark?' Lusk said, addressing their backs. 'That is what I wanted to ask you. Because in Athens –'

'So it is presumably much older than that,' Mrs Pritchett said in clear tones. 'The theatre, I mean. It was probably damaged in the earthquake.'

'Earthquake?' Lusk said. 'They can in Athens. Hey I'm talking to you.'

'They would have been able to see everything,' Miranda said, in a voice not quite her own. 'The audience. Sitting up there in the theatre they would have been able to see their homes, wouldn't they? Everything they cared about.'

'They would not be molested,' Lusk said, 'on the darkest of nights. What do you think of that? I'm asking you a question.'

He leaned forward and tapped Miranda on the shoulder. Mrs Pritchett saw the girl flinch. At once she turned on her heel intending to administer a blistering reproof but the sight of his face enraged her suddenly, with its inane smile, stretching now with a sort of complacency because she had turned to him. This drunken, immature face became in that moment expressive of all hateful male attributes, vain, vulgarly predatory, the reason too for Miranda's disappointing vagueness and unresponsiveness, caused she felt sure by some man not much different from this. No words could be wounding enough. She paused for a choked moment, then drove her clenched fist with all the force and fury at her disposal into the young man's face, feeling her gemmed knuckles strike and jar on the cheekbone. The power behind this blow was considerable. The tremendous joy and release of its delivery was something she was destined never to forget.

Lusk took two steps backward, which brought him near the edge of the level on which they were standing. The smile was still on his face, though terribly shrunken. Some words he uttered, of remonstrance presumably, but they were incomprehensible to Mrs Pritchett who was in any case beyond the reach of words, her mind full of the desire to inflict further damage on the young man – that first blow had by no means satisfied her, though it had been a revelation in its way. Steadying herself and planting her feet more firmly she struck again, with the same fist – her left hand keeping the place in the guidebook – and yet again, misjudging the distance this time and almost overbalancing, uttering several harsh sobbing sounds, aware that Miranda was talking on her right in frightened tones but unable to make any words out, the young man stumbling backwards in retreat and not smiling now but making, possibly because he could not fully believe what was happening, no real attempt to protect himself, certainly none to retaliate. Nor any sort of sound.

With horror and glee Mrs Pritchett observed that the young man's upper lip was split and that blood from this wound was spread all round his mouth as though he had been eating something messy. Higher up on the cheekbone too he was cut. Her breath came in gasps, mixed with vituperative expressions which she had not known her vocabulary contained. Her fury was dying now, but with the persistence of personages in a nightmare the young man's messy mouth again formed a smile, reassuring perhaps in intention, and he took a step forward, raising his arms as if to take Mrs Pritchett in some kind of restraining grip. At this, with a muffled screaming note strangely sustained, like mourning, she launched herself upon him and with her nails scored parallel gashes down the side of his face. For a moment the bloody face was turned upward, the mouth open as though for some vociferous appeal, then he had stumbled away, out of reach, off the platform of grass, and gone plunging and leaping downward over the shrub-covered slope, careering at breakneck speed over piles of rubble, spurs of rock, clumps of thorn, to vanish from sight behind the ruined walls of the Roman baths, though the crashes of his violent career could still be heard.

The two women stood side by side not looking at each other, while the silence settled round Lusk's flight. Mrs Pritchett was quivering internally, though whether in distress or exhilaration she didn't know. The guidebook was still in her left hand, her finger painfully nipped inside it, marking the place. The discomfort to this finger recalled her slowly to their purpose on the hillside. She glanced at Miranda whose face was lowered, concealed by the sweeps of hair that had swung forward over her brows, and then at the sky, surprised suddenly by its remoteness, the distant formations of cloud. Surely the sky had been quite clear when they had set out. There was a change, a hush over everything.

'The cheek of it,' Mrs Pritchett said. 'Did you ever see such cheek? I think it jolly well served him right, don't you?'

Miranda looked up. 'He didn't mean any harm,' she said. 'He got himself into a situation.' Her face was white, and she avoided looking at Mrs Pritchett, who now saw that their expedition was irretrievably ruined.

'We'd better go down,' she said, remembering for solace her promise to give Miranda the sun-tan lotion. They began in silence to retrace their steps.

Feeling himself bemonstered, aware of blood running on his face, the taste of blood in his mouth, Lusk went headlong and at phenomenally accelerating speed down the steep and treacherously uneven slope, his legs following frantically a body that fought for balance. Horror at what had happened to him mingled with his fear of injury. Sobs built up in his throat without his panting breath being able to utter them. He rushed down the hillside, arms working wildly, panic increasing with his speed, leaping boulders, plunging through thorn, making darting last-minute detours round hollows and holes, startling birds and sheep in his frenzied passage. He did not feel cuts, bruises, lacerations. His whole being was centred on staying upright. Blind to everything but this he went crashing downwards.

'Now then,' Plopl said loudly. He looked across the sunlit clearing at Pamela's white body supine on the rock. It seemed remote, unattainable, like some dream of impossible felicity. A sense of being trapped in this self-imposed series of actions settled heavily on him. 'Get ready,' he called. His left hand hovered over the delayed-action lever. With the other he applied distasteful last-minute friction to himself. 'Go!' he shouted, to alert Pamela. He pressed the setting lever and release catch and set off with lumbering speed across the clearing, still stroking himself clumsily as he went. He heard the mechanism whirring behind him. Pamela's white legs loomed before him. He was almost there, reaching forward. 'Legs apart!' he shouted. Suddenly, from the undergrowth immediately beyond the rock, he heard a series of crashing sounds and a moment later a figure horrifically bloody came bounding through the bushes, seemed to fly across the intervening space with arms extended like wings, narrowly avoided the rock on which Pamela was lying, stumbled, recovered, caught Plopl a glancing blow which, in his awkward half-crouching position, threw him off balance, so that he fell heavily and painfully, winding himself.

Plopl lay for some moments on his side, face contorted, struggling to recover his breath. He was aware of a sharp pain along his left side, where he had grazed his tender flank on the rock. The camera had stopped whirring. There was absolute silence in the clearing. After a few moments Plopl sat up, looked dazedly around him. There was nobody in the clearing at all. Pamela too had risen to a sitting position. Across the intervening space they regarded each other in silence. Then Pamela's face broke slowly into a smile.

How difficult, Mooncranker thought, toilsome and perplexing, to discover the source of all this water, to trace it back, through the fantastic diversity of its routes, the ditches, channels, spreading pools, the grooves and runnels it had worn for itself in the rock, a whole interlocking mesh of water-courses, follow it to the point where it first seethed up, discharged from some age-old heartburn of the earth. Perhaps impossible. Difficult now to distinguish the natural from the artificial among these streams. Whatever peoples had lived here – Seljuk, Roman, Lydian, Phrygian, Greek – had made attempts to contain the water, conduct it in definite channels, probably to feed their baths. There was evidence, here and there, of earthenware pipes and gutters. Most of these now were dry – the water had taken different paths, fashioned its own contrivances.

He negotiated an area soft and yielding underfoot, where the water had seeped and spread, saturating the ground. Circling this area, which he felt to be rather fearsome, he followed the line of the wall for some distance, disturbed by this anarchic behaviour of the water, multifarious, untrammelled, ungirdled, this chaotic squirming of living and dead watercourses, with their continuous unlocalizable sounds of trickle and gush, nowhere any form or pattern, nothing for the mind to grasp.

He stopped again after some minutes and stood looking down at a deep channel some two feet in width, with vertical banks between which the water flowed dark green and slow. Possibly because it ran slower or had been above ground longer, this water was cooler apparently, emitted at least no steam – he could see the surface clearly, dark green in colour, but this would be due to the green bed of the ditch no doubt; and opaque, strangely cold-looking. He knelt and immersed his hand to the wrist: the water was tepid. He remained thus for some time, staring down. Nothing at all growing, he suddenly realized, at the sides of the ditch or on the banks or anywhere around. Not even weeds. Nothing but a sort of thin, light green moss on the stones, and that was probably chemical, some sort of deposit. Over the whole hillside nothing much growing. Was it this that was troubling me, this incongruity? Water everywhere, the hillside running with it, clamorous and steamy with it, feverish veins of water, and yet no trees, no bushes of any size, nothing but sage-green shrub.

He rose to his feet. With a feeling of surprise he saw larks high in the sky and became aware of their song. The line of figures was still there, moving slowly across the horizon. He registered these impressions with a curious intensity, an overmastering sense of time and patience and blight. Something was seeking to enter his mind, invade his being, something as pervasive and incessant as the water sounds or the song of the birds, taking him over, absorbing his heart beat, the pulse of his life, into a wider, older continuity, which no apparent contradictions could give pause to. For a very brief time Mooncranker heard nothing, saw nothing. Then he was himself again, separate, intensely alone. Miranda's face came into his mind as it had been the morning she had left him, and he experienced a complex blend of vindictiveness and desire. He began to descend.

3

'No, no, no,' exclaimed Mrs Pritchett in her well-bred, strangled contralto, holding up one hand in humorous protest; a capable hand, broad-palmed, fingers slightly spatulate; the knuckles somewhat scraped-looking after her fracas earlier that morning, though she had in the interim rubbed them with her special handcream. She always took care of her hands. Hands show our age like almost nothing else, she was fond of saying, hands and throat. In her other one now was a bottle of glinting liquid, amber in the light, ripe fig colour in the shelter of her creamed, creased palm.

'No, no,' she said, 'I insist.' Full of business on the threshold of Miranda's cabin, this kindly bustle disguising a certain languorous disturbance within, experienced since the brilliant idea had come to her, of not simply lending the bottle to Miranda as she had promised, but volunteering her own fingers to rub it well in with. 'You don't know, you don't know, how positively lethal this sun can be.' Inside the room now, like her own in every outward respect, yet what a change was effected by an alien hairbrush, for example. Odours of talcum powder and lemon balm. Miranda – backing somewhat awkwardly in the narrow confines of the cabin, obliged for the moment to play hostess. Mrs Pritchett took her in with a series of smiling glances: hair carelessly pinned up, exposing the soft, rather long neck; full underlip curving in a faint embarrassed smile; the belted waist of her cream and brown cotton dress.

'Take the word of an old campaigner,' Mrs Pritchett said playfully, holding up in deprecation of any further protest the bottle of sun-tan oil ruddy and glinting in the light that shafted down on to it from the high square window. '*Ambre Solaire*,' she said, in an archly exaggerated accent. She controlled her breathing, concealed her interior disarray from her young friend, turning and closing the cabin door slowly and carefully. When she looked round again Miranda was standing against the bed, still awkwardly smiling.

'You shouldn't have bothered,' she said.

'No bother at all, my dear,' Mrs Pritchett said, with a sort of domineering jocularity, and she nodded her head at Miranda. 'This will do the trick.'

'Well, thank you very much. Are you in a hurry for it?'

'What *can* you mean?'

'Well, I thought, if you were, I could bring it back as soon as I've finished with it.'

'Oh, no, no, *no*,' Mrs Pritchett said firmly. 'You need someone to rub it well in. You can't reach your own back, now can you?' She paused for a moment. 'It is medicinal too,' she said, 'you see. It tones you up. But it must be rubbed in well, that is essential. It must get into the pores.'

Roguishly, finger and thumb poised delicately over the bottle, she paused, smiling at Miranda. Then with the same playful delicacy she nipped the white cone-shaped top and

214

tried to turn it, but it wouldn't turn and it still wouldn't when she tried harder. Meanwhile, Miranda, realizing that Mrs Pritchett intended to do this service for her, wondered if her bra was very grubby and watched with some concern the other's increasingly violent efforts to remove the bottle top. Smile gone, a pallor of exertion at the temples, Mrs Pritchett was holding the bottle in a convulsive grip against her tummy, and twisting.

'The blasted top won't come off,' she muttered.

'Shall I have a try?' offered Miranda, but Mrs Pritchett yanked the blouse out of her skirt to help her get a grip and with a great effort managed to unscrew the top at last.

'*Finalmente*,' she said, panting. 'The threads had got crossed somehow.' She summoned a smile. 'These things are sent to try us,' she said. But to Miranda, this open-mouthed, audibly breathing woman, blouse hanging unheeded, savagely out of skirt band, was alarming, bringing back to her mind the whirl-wind attacker on the hilltop, those breathless vituperations, that upturned bleeding face. She realized that she was afraid of Mrs Pritchett ...

'Just unbutton your dress and slip it over your shoulders,' Mrs Pritchett said, advancing on Miranda, holding the bottle as if it were a syringe. 'I think that would be the best way. Oh, I see, there's a zip there, is there, well in that case dear I should just take it off altogether, yes, that's right. My goodness, just look at you, you would certainly have had blisters. You are like a lobster on your shoulders and back. Didn't you feel it at the time?'

'Not really.' Miranda was sitting on the bed in her bra and pants with her back to Mrs Pritchett. She shivered involun-tarily at the first touch of the cool oil along her shoulders and Mrs Pritchett's velvety yet imperious fingertips stroking firmly from the tops of the shoulder-blades outwards.

'No, it's the water,' Mrs Pritchett said. 'You don't notice at the time how hot the sun is. Even as late in the year as this.' She raised the bottle, tilted it, and poured a drop or two of the thick fluid into the downy declivity between Miranda's shoulder-blades, immediately below the girl's nape. Both hands flat, fingers slightly splayed, she moved her palms with a firm pressure outwards over the squarish, unexpectedly compact and athletic shoulders – the girl was much more robust than she seemed when clothed; perhaps it was her posture that was deceptive, or the burdened-seeming neck – rested a moment there, then down, with oily adhesiveness, down the outsides of the forearms to the elbows.

'It has to be rubbed well in,' Mrs Pritchett said, rather thickly.

Miranda felt a warm tingling sensation across her back where Mrs Pritchett's fingers were plying. It was a healing-burning sort of feeling, by no means unpleasant. However, sitting there so awkwardly, her back chastely towards the other lady, her legs over the side of the bed, hands in her lap, she had only her own vertical posture to resist the pressure of Mrs Pritchett's palms, nothing at all to hold on to. Consequently, after the first few passes, she was hard put to it to maintain herself upright. This was partly because, as it seemed to her, Mrs Pritchett was increasing the pressure from moment to moment. Miranda sensed an urgency in those hands and set it down to Mrs Pritchett's healing fervour, though with less than complete conviction. In any case, whatever it was, it was now pushing her forward each time, driving her to perform an apparent obeisance towards the window, the source of light. Up she felt the slippery soft hands go, slowly outwards to the shoulder, nudging her forward to her periodic reverence, slipping down the arms, bringing her upright again.

'It would be better, dear, if you lay down, I think. On your tummy.'

'But haven't you finished yet?' Miranda said, in a sort of rebellion, half turning towards her solicitous masseuse. She was flushed and her voice sounded sleepy or dazed, as if she were divided by veils from full consciousness.

'Finished? Oh dear, no.' There was the slightest of snaps in Mrs Pritchett's voice, denoting hurt perhaps at this attempt to curtail her ministrations. 'It has to penetrate to the subcutaneous fat,' she explained, after a moment. She patted the bed. 'Just you lie here and relax,' she said. 'Leave the rest to me.'

Miranda, divided between reluctance and compliance, looked for some seconds at Mrs Pritchett's face. It was deeply

216

flushed, brilliant-eyed, slightly smiling. 'Come on now,' Mrs Pritchett said, holding up hands shiny with oil. 'We mustn't keep nurse waiting, must we?'

She had adopted by some instinct or insight exactly the right tone for lulling Miranda, breaking down the girl's residual resistance; playful, basically threatening, transporting her to school sickrooms, not so very far behind, when illness was regarded as weakness in the moral fibre somehow, perhaps even something to be ashamed of, and the way to reinstatement was unswerving, uncomplaining cooperation in all the details of treatment ... Obediently, and without another word, Miranda stretched herself downward on the bed. She felt after a moment Mrs Pritchett's hands stroking the thin tissue that sheathed her shoulder-blades. A strange smell had begun to expand in the cabin, like the exudation of some mammalian gland, attractive or rebuttive: the odour of the sun-tan oil. Miranda heard the other's voice above her talking in richly elegiac tones about Mark, her former fiancé and how she had walked away from Mark along the darkening river bank, past scented fields where cattle grazed ...

Without pausing in her massage or her speech, Mrs Pritchett looked down at the girl's body. She could now with impunity dwell on the rounded, polished shoulders, the blunt sprouting of shoulder-blades, sheathed buttons of the spine. The skin was not really red as she had told Miranda except just along the shoulders, but reddish gold, like dark wheat – the girl had a depth, almost a duskiness in the skin which would always prevent that lobster redness. She was not yet completely relaxed, Mrs Pritchett noted: the arms were tensed, still held close to her sides and there was a slight, periodic clenching of the buttocks beneath the thin white cotton knickers. She continued her massaging movement, catching each time the thin fold of flesh which rippled into her hand, escaped again at the shoulder. And while she worked, with an obscure, slowly mounting excitement, on Miranda's flesh, feeling the girl's body more relaxed every moment, she continued the saga of Mark.

To Miranda the voice of Mrs Pritchett and the gentle yet remorseless pressure of her hands were becoming meshed, like a soft harness or a net. She was entering the territory that lies between sleep and waking, though sleep seemed dangerous at first, like a sudden descent into a dark place, or like some sort of submergence, and she resisted it, though sinking further and further into sleep and a sort of warmly sensuous desolation. She did not drown, the voice and the hands kept her from drowning, she was moving still, not gliding now, but flowing along a dark river, the voice leading her, the hands conducting, the river was bearing her. There were black cows on the banks, completely black, and she heard the breaths of the cows, the plashing of their feet in the black water, soft tearing of grass as they grazed along the banks...

'Your bra is rather in the way dear,' Mrs Pritchett said, and with oily fingers undid the two little hooks from their eyes. Then she dexterously slipped the shoulder straps down to the girl's elbows. She now had the whole of Miranda's naked back to work on, divided into two zones of darker and paler gold by the thin white line where the bra strap had been, the whole expanse gleaming and lustrous with oil. She could follow with her hands the long curve inward of the torso to the waist, and even below this to the compensatory initial convexities of the nates, before the thin band of the knickers stayed her. Miranda, in relaxing her arms, had moved them out some few inches from her sides, enabling Mrs Pritchett to see the launching outer curves of each breast. She ventured her hands along the exposed flanks, beginning at the armpit, rubbing lightly with the tips of her fingers along the outer curve of the breasts. This, since there was no flinching, no abatement of the girl's deep, slumbrous inertia, she incorporated into the massaging movement, which was now a great cunning sweep, beginning at the hollowed base of the spine, proceeding outwards to the shoulders, returning via the flanks to the tops of the knickers in which each time her fingers caught and tugged a little.

Thus circumspectly she extended her range. And when she realized, from the girl's heaviness under her hands, and from the complete relaxation, indeed abandonment, of her body – that virginal clench of the bottom quite gone – that she was tranced, resistless, Mrs Pritchett pressed her own hot thighs together and, while not pausing even for a moment in the massaging and caressing of Miranda, encouraged her own increasingly lively feelings by setting up a frictive movement there.

'We must get into the subcutaneous fat, we absolutely must,' gabbled Mrs Pritchett, forgetting Mark as she experienced the approach of sensations never connected with him, but knowing by a sort of instinct that she must at all costs go on talking to Miranda so as not to break the spell. 'That is the secret of it.' She raced on, dry-mouthed, rubbing her robust thighs together. 'Oh!' she cried, with a preliminary pang of pleasure. 'Oh, dear, yes, we absolutely must get below the surface, that is where the healing soothing balm is fully and to best advantage – ah!' A further slight ejaculation, a sort of buzzing sound escaped her. She edged the elastic band of the knickers down slightly, revealing the initial cleft of the buttocks. More than this was not possible for the moment because of the weight of the girl's body. Nevertheless she persevered, with each sweeping massage plucking a little at the band.

Miranda lay face down in fathomless indolence, her body tingling, yet heavy and inert, drugged by the monologue and by the repeated massaging movement, words and hands holding her as in a net, drawing her netted through dark water very slowly, more slowly than the flow of water; banks and fields were moving slowly too, nothing was still but the fisherman, Mark, standing there in midstream, black, immovable. Not swimming, not floating, but *towed*, she moved towards him, outdistanced continuously by the water but drawing nearer, and passing saw it was James Farnaby; the river changed, silvered over, there was a wreckage of birds' nests on the bank and she felt a sleepy tenderness for the boy's serious face, left behind now; the silver water flowed past and around her, endlessly inventive and circumventive, waylaid at the edges, trapped in eddies and swirls and pointless scummy sidings but never ultimately blocked in its career to the sea, minutely to sweeten that salt immensity. The hands massaging her duplicated that ceaseless current, caught however, briefly cluttered, like water in a blocked channel, over and over again, in the elastic of her knickers, tugging down slightly, freeing themselves, caught again, a reiterated intolerable blockage. Breathing deeply, a slight impatience troubling her as at some temporary obstacle in a dream, Miranda arched her rump clear of the bed, remaining thus, under the dream-like duress, long enough for Mrs Pritchett to reach round and pull the knickers down at the front, down to the girl's knees.

Sighing, Miranda settled down again, feeling the long flow of the hands from her nape to the backs of her legs without let or hindrance. She heard a brief buzzing sound above her. At that moment there was a brisk knock on the cabin door and a man's voice shouted, 'Anyone at home?' Miranda recognized it at once for Farnaby's, and it brought her full awake. She sat up quickly, reaching for her wrap, which lay across the foot of the bed.

'Don't answer,' said Mrs Pritchett, but Miranda answered almost immediately, in a voice full of gaiety and alertness. 'Yes, is it you James? I shan't be a minute.' She went towards the door.

Mrs Pritchett sat helpless, a prey to violent emotion, and saw the door being opened. Then she rose. She heard Miranda utter some bright form of greeting, heard the pleasure in the girl's voice, saw with hatred a tall gangling male form, its arms occupied with foodstuffs. 'I thought we might have a picnic,' she heard this creature say and saw the look of delight on the equine face as he looked down at Miranda in her pretty flowered wrap. She saw Miranda hesitating, out of politeness to her presumably, she obviously wanted to go – this was the fellow, almost certainly, who had been occupying her thoughts all morning. Mrs Pritchett moved towards the door. 'I'll leave the oil with you,' she said. She gave Farnaby a queenly glance, effectively concealing the turmoil within. He made way for her awkwardly, banging his shoulder against the door.

Mrs Pritchett walked slowly away along the terrace, towards her own cabin, that cabin she had stepped out of earlier with such high hopes, clutching the bottle of sun-tan oil. The noonday sun lay on the pool, cutting athwart the vapour in glittering swathes. She noticed several persons standing silently in the bright water, among them a high-shouldered, rather distinguished-looking man she had not seen before. A young Negro in scarlet swimming trunks came out of a cabin opposite and stood at the edge of the pool, chewing something, looking down. The sound of music, rather dirge-like, presumably from a radio somewhere, came to her. She felt terrible.

A man who had been sitting on the terrace in the shade of a beach umbrella, now emerged from under it and stood in her way. It was Vittorio. He stood there before her, brawny and servile, in a white towelling shirt and beige slacks. He smiled and she saw the flash of gold teeth. Vittorio's wiry black chesthairs curled up out of the vee of his shirt, extended to the base of his throat. The customary revulsion with which she noticed these things was complicated on this occasion, blended with feelings quite other. She stopped. 'Hello,' she said. 'How are you today? Why aren't you in the pool?' She uttered these questions with customary severity and contempt.

Vittorio stood regarding her, allowing the impeccable elegantly throttled contralto tones to reverberate in his mind. The heedless authority of it, and the contempt, acted as always on him like a sexual stimulant, making him feel abject and brutal. He smirked at her, raised a beringed hand to smooth the hair above his right ear. 'I was wondering,' he said, 'if you will have a drink with me?' He made a gesture towards the table.

'No, thank you.' Never was a drink refused with such finality.

'It is a genuine offer,' Vittorio said.

'I am going to my cabin,' Mrs Pritchett said coldly. She began to move past Vittorio. He stood aside to let her pass and some happy intuition, some subtle transmission from his good angel, or some fortuitous access of insolence caused him to murmur as she passed, 'Perhaps I could accompany you there?'

There are times when, drawing a bow at a venture without much hope of success, we see by certain preliminary signs, almost incredulously, that what was nothing more than a visionary gleam may be after all within our encompassing. It was so now with Vittorio. He had hoped, at best, for some crushing reply, which would have afforded him fresh examples of what had first attracted him, the delicious half-gobbled vowels, authoritatively trailed diphthongs, the plosive and the palatal commingled in ultimate derogation of all he stood for. Instead, she gave him in passing a single glance difficult to read and said, 'If you like.'

For a moment or two he gazed after her, hardly believing it. Then, 'I go now to get Scotch whisky,' he called, 'from my cabin, Johnny Walker.' And he hastened to do this, not wishing to give Mrs Pritchett time for second thoughts.

They began the whisky with Vittorio sitting on the chair and Mrs Pritchett on the edge of the bed. But after a little while Vittorio moved on to the bed too, and they sat side by side. Mrs Pritchett drank too quickly. She began to tell Vittorio about her experiences during the war as a major in the W.R.A.C., training telephonists. Her voice became slurred and she frequently lost track of what she was saying. Vittorio listened gravely, drinking almost nothing, watching the decline of Mrs Pritchett with soft, solicitous-seeming eyes.

When the bottle was just over half empty Vittorio kissed Mrs Pritchett on the throat and the side of the neck and behind the ears. He was not rebuffed nor even reproved. He therefore put a large paw against Mrs Pritchett's chest and gently pushed. Mrs Pritchett slowly and statuesquely fell back on to the bed and lay there in a supine position. She frowned up at Vittorio, who was commencing without haste to undress her. She lay frowning and speechless until all her clothes were off. Her body was plump, very white-skinned, marked with thin red weals where her brassière and girdle had been. Vittorio peered down at it in his short-sighted way. He could even now hardly believe that he had this upper-crust English lady naked on her back. He removed his own clothes and knelt above Mrs Pritchett, drawing apart her nerveless thighs as if they were tongs. She looked up dizzily to see that his burnished, wiry pubic hair grew right over his abdomen and continued in a dark band to join the more coppery pelt on his chest. Vittorio had thick hair from groin to throat, which made him unique in her experience. He also had a very highly developed sexual organ, now at its meridian – the view of it afforded by her recumbency was formidable.

'Good heavens!' Mrs Pritchett said.

Vittorio kneeling above her, felt a great surge of power and triumph. 'Say something,' he urged her, eager to hear once more the divine accent.

'I don't know if I can accommodate *that*,' Mrs Pritchett said. A sort of ripple passed over her face, like a rapid grimace, and the next moment her eyes filled with tears, thick tears which welled out and ran down her cheeks. 'It's all wrong,' she said. 'We've all gone wrong somewhere or other –'

Vittorio gritted his teeth with savagery and vengeance, and rammed himself into her with one great thrust.

'I thought you might like to go for a picnic,' repeated Farnaby, looking closely at the girl's flushed, still rather sleepy face. There was in these first moments of seeing her again a sort of delighted incredulity, she had slipped a little from his previous image of her, had to be refocused as it were, and his delight lay in the fact that this slight redefinition enhanced her. He wondered how often this process had to be repeated, before all blur was eliminated, total familiarity achieved. Perhaps it never was...

'What a super idea,' the girl said. She raised a hand to her hair, which was not, Farnaby noted, in pigtails, as it had been in the pool, but pinned up on her head rather carelessly. He noticed when she raised her hand how the sleeve of her wrap fell away to the elbow, revealing a rounded forearm, pale along the inside.

'Perhaps you could put the things down on the bed for the time being,' the girl suggested. 'While I get ready.'

Obediently he moved forward, but the commotion of his feelings plus the unusual nature of his burden and his sense of being in an unfamiliar place, affected his powers of coordination, always weak, and he began to dither slightly, caught his foot against one of the legs of the bed, opened his arms to save his balance and so let fall his parcels. They all landed on the bed except for the bag of apples which fell on to the floor and burst, sending apples all over the place.

'Oh dear,' he said. 'I am so sorry.' He was distressed by the thought that she might find him inept.

Miranda heard the contrition in his voice, took instinctive

credit for the disturbance in him and felt pleasure at it. 'Never mind,' she said. 'We can easily pick them up again.'

Together, on their knees, they hunted about – the apples had gone rolling about the floor. Several times, while engaged on this hunt, laughing and exclaiming, their bodies collided slightly and these collisions generated a sort of rivalry between them, as to who could recover the most apples. Both together made a dive for the last one, which had rolled down towards the foot of the bed, fastened on it more or less at the same time and briefly wrestled over it, Farnaby holding the apple firmly while the girl sought to prise it out of his grasp, without success at first, while he looked laughingly at her. Suddenly he was visited by a vivid sense of the children they had been together, and immediately after this noticed that the front of her wrap had parted a little in the struggle, being held together only by a belt at the waist, he glimpsed the upper part of her breasts and realized that she was naked under the wrap, and at this his hold on the apple weakened and she recovered it. Sitting back on her heels in triumph she held the apple up, then saw the stricken look on his face and immediately her own face changed, the smile disappeared. She drew the front of the wrap together. For some moments they regarded each other seriously. Then she said gently, 'You'd better wait outside while I get ready.'

I see them go, Mooncranker informed himself. I see them go, clutching foodstuffs. They stop outside the cabin to cram these comestibles into a bag of traditional Turkish design. I recognize with a pang this bag. She bought it in my company, in a street in Istanbul. The question, as I remember, was to choose something typical, avoiding at the same time any hint of the touristic. A geometrical motif was thought best for this. Black and white with black cord. Into it now go the things they will eat together. Sitting in some lonely place they will dip into this bag, which I once for some minutes scrutinized carefully, eager that she should not make a choice she would regret. Strange how often it is through the memory of trivia we experience desolation. I am standing here in the pool, seeking neither to advertise nor to conceal my presence. Simply standing in my bath, a slight breathlessness besetting me after some half hour of immersion. They do not look my way. They do not look towards the pool at all. They look only at each other, eyes for nothing, no one else. Did I expect this? Across these yards of steamy water, said to be healing, I watch them, she who was my darling in a lime-green dress for scrambling in the hills. I recognize that dress. He, the treacherous Farnaby, my emissary. How oddly he walks, as if not sure the terrace is solid. Should I announce my presence? No, not yet. It is clear that lout is busy betraying me, but was it not for this that I really sent him here, did I not relinquish my life-line the moment I asked him to reclaim Miranda? Still they do not look my way. Round the pool, over the bridge. Into the restaurant, presumably to buy further items. They do not appear again, have left presumably by an outer door ...

I raise my thin arm, the mineral drops cling briefly, slip over the loose folds. Most of me is gristle now, not flesh ... The mind's gristle is impotent imagination, accretions of a life-time's largely unfulfilled desires. I should write that down. Desires that outlived all possibilities of performance, that were never acted upon, but persisted, caught like insects in the gummy secretions of the time and place, like beetles, trapped beetles stuck on their backs, still able to wave their legs at the random stimulus of memory, or the fear of death. All my little iridescent beetles waving their legs in valediction, since I may not survive this night's darkness.

The water drops from my arm, which has a glazed unhealthy appearance. The underlying blood vessels stand out in prominent fashion. I raise my eyes from them to see a fair-haired girl approaching me, wading slowly, water up to her midriff, she appears to be floating towards me on her buoyant breasts.

'Good afternoon,' I say to her, when she has drawn near enough, and she says 'Hi,' a flat, noncommittal monosyllable. I can detect no particular expression in her small blue eyes. Her hair, voluminous and tangled, has not been tended properly. An attempt has been made to tie it behind with a piece of pink ribbon, but quantities of hair have escaped and hang in dampish blond tendrils about her face. A broad, flat-nosed face, with a curious stillness on it. She is looking at me directly.

'It is very pleasant here, isn't it?' I remark. 'Amid these historic surroundings to take one's ease, converse with one's fellows.'

'Yes,' she says.

She glances over her shoulder at the row of cabins behind her. She moistens her lips.

'How long have you been here?' I ask her, to keep things going.

'Three days. No, it's four. Are you a lawyer?'

'Good heavens, no. Why, do I look like one?'

She regards me in silence for several moments, with a mute expectancy I am already beginning to find oppressive.

'I bet you know about the law,' she says at last.

'I know something about it.'

She draws a little nearer to me in the water. 'Can you be sent to prison for begging?'

'I believe so. If you haven't a licence, that is.'

'I don't mean caught in the act. Just reported.'

'I'm afraid I don't understand you, quite,' I say, and then, mumbling and breathing quickly – this quick breath her only mark of agitation – she tells me a story of a man, a photographer, who is threatening to report her for begging.

'But when was this?' I ask at last, still in some bewilderment.

' 'Bout six weeks ago now.'

'But good heavens ... What's your name?'

'Pamela.'

'But my dear Pamela, he can't do anything about it now. Have you been living with him since then?'

'We been together, yes.'

'Well, he has condoned it, hasn't he?'

Stare from Pamela.

'He can't do anything about it now.'

The girl's tongue protrudes, a clean pink, and licks quickly round the full mouth.

'How old are you?' I ask her, on an impulse.

'Seventeen.'

226

For a moment, looking into the blank, anaesthetized-looking face, I am tempted to get out of the water and go to my cabin for a card with my address on it. Then I remember who I am, why I am here. 'He has given up all right to prosecute you,' I tell her, and leave it at that.

'He can't do nothing to me?'

'Not a thing.' I look at her with awe almost. One hears of subnormal intelligence but rarely converses with one. A girl like this could be persuaded to do almost anything...

'Well,' she says. 'I better be getting back. He will have finished the developing by now. Thanks mister. You helped me a lot, really you did.'

'Not at all.' As she climbs out of the pool, I gaze at her beautiful round high buttocks and her sturdy but well-shaped thighs and calves. She walks away along the terrace, cautiously re-enters one of the cabins. Almost immediately I dismiss her from my mind, return to my own situation, which is grievous.

Drops of water from my arm glitter in the sun, rejoin the bright surface. Looking down I see my limbs refracted, my poor shanks foreshortened. In such stasis, sealed off from time, time refracts itself too; it is again late afternoon of the day Miranda became my mistress, slipped blindly from her typist's stool, gave herself to me on the carpet and afterwards cycled home again changed, while I lay in my celebratory hot bath. Soaking out the Adam whose seed was spent already. In a trance, dazed in every pore, I heard the beat of my heart, as I hear it now, transmitted via the ear-drums. I remember my heart's drum-beat that night in the hot bath, how many years ago now, I lay amidst the shining white enamel, thinking of Miranda cycling home through the dusk, bats and moths for company. On a bicycle, she was on a bicycle, that first day she came to work for me. An April day, in red. I was standing at the window. She smiled and waved. Her face glowed with youth and health, her teeth were white, the handlebars of her bicycle glittered in the sun. That day the beginning ́of my death, that angel on the shining bicycle the angel of death who as is well known can assume any form. Slow drum-beat of my heart then as now funereal. In lime-green she clambers about the hills, to what end? I visualize them with a peculiar sorrow,

227

not for myself only. She is so easily led, and he – did I not sense his destructiveness, right from the beginning, ill as I was? He stood there gleaming under the chandelier. There because of a gift I made him, which had gone on festering in his mind. Because of that too I sent him for her, relying on his vengeance. Things conspire to our death, it seems, just as they do to our love...

'Pardon me, sir.' A nasal, American voice from the terrace behind me. It seems I am not to be left alone this afternoon. Turning I behold a young man with short hair and a bruised and scratched-looking face. He is standing on the edge of the terrace, bending down towards me. 'Do you have any kind of ointment I could borrow?'

'Ointment?'

'I heard you talking English, a while back, to that girl. I thought, maybe he has some kind of skin cream I could borrow.'

'I'm afraid I have nothing of that sort. Have you had an accident of some kind?'

'Accident?' He utters a scornful *huh*. 'Nothing accidental about it. Case of assault.'

'Really? I am sorry to hear that.'

'Assault and battery. And it was a woman too.'

'You astonish me.'

'The women are worse than the men,' the young man says, with an assumption of worldly acumen that consorts ill with his raw and battered appearance.

'The female of the species, eh?' I notice that the young man has a nervous, rabbity face, with light-coloured eyes that seem almost constantly in movement. He emanates a smell too, a compound of sweat and sour whisky.

'Up there,' he says and jerks his head towards the hills that rise in ranks beyond us.

'Did you come across a Maenad?' I ask him.

'Who?' he says. 'I don't know her first name. Her surname is Pritchett. She is one of those upper-class English ladies. You know, kind of handing out the tea and saying do you take sugah, that kind of thing.'

'I know the type you mean. Hair off the forehead, pearls at

228

the neck. But they do not usually attack young men among the hills.'

· 'Well she was with this other girl. Pretty girl. Good fuselage too, know what I mean?'

He assembles his features once more into that worldly knowingness that is so at odds with discoloured eye, cut lip, scratched cheeks.

'It was this chick,' he says, 'that I was interested in really, but I talked to them both, I didn't leave the old girl out, I know my manners. Christ! Since we were all up there together, three people with a language in common, for God's sake, I believe in human contact. I believe in holding out the helping hand. Above all, I believe in *communication*. We have got to get through to people. The peace of the world –'

Suddenly his face changes. 'That's her now,' he says. 'The Pritchett woman. I don't want to meet her. I might lose my temper. You haven't got any ointment then?'

'Try the manager. He seems an obliging sort.'

'Maybe I'll do that,' he says, already retreating. It seems I am destined not to hear the end of this story. I watch for some moments the person he has designated as the Pritchett woman. She looks ill to me. Face a chalky white. Being supported by a stout foreign-looking man with a fleshy profile and two-tone shoes, who does not seem her sort at all. They move rather slowly along the terrace and seat themselves at one of the tables.

Time, I think now, to get out of this pool, dress myself. I shall sit at one of those same tables and wait for them, for Miranda and Farnaby, to come back . . .

4

They did not talk much, each conscious of the other's nearness as something which made the rest of the world more remote. As they climbed higher, clambering among the detritus of centuries, of millennia, all that each was afforded of the other was a series of glimpses, fleeting impressions, overlaid almost at once, as their relative positions shifted, now Farnaby ahead, now Miranda; so that their physical sense of each other was attended by feelings of strangeness, almost unbelief at first, they each felt isolated in their own actions.

'Have you got any place in mind?' she said suddenly. 'For the picnic I mean.'

He stopped and stood there, a yard or two higher than she was, looking down at her. 'No, not really,' he said. He made a vague gesture. The sunlight had softened and hazed in the course of the morning, the containing bands of hill and mountain had loosened, lost their firm edges, there was a graining or powdering of mist in the air, slightly fluffing the outlines of things. The girl looked up at him in silence and by some grace of intuition or sympathy he felt her loneliness and half-hostility, and knew that she was giving herself to something, going out of herself and her accustomed self-regard, for his sake and the sake of the occasion. He smiled and said, 'Let's go higher, shall we?'

They went on again in silence, reaching after some minutes a place where the hills divided, forming a cleft between them not more than four or five yards wide, with a brighter seam of greenery, a foliage more vivid running through it, as if the grey scrub were a skin that had cracked and fissured here, to show flesh. They followed this track, obliged for much of the time to walk in single file. Miranda went first and he watched the way she set her feet, the slight flexing of the muscles in her legs. She walked with a natural grace, the sway of her figure strong and controlled. On either side of them rose myrtle and hollyoak, and higher up on the slope he saw slender trees with long, tremulous, yellowing leaves.

The strip of green broadened, extending high up the slope on their right. Quite suddenly the path narrowed again, the bushes rose high on either side, arching overhead, almost meeting, darkening the air, obliging them to walk one behind the other. A smell of coolness, dankness, came to them from the vegetation. Farnaby was aware of a feeling of irrevocability, as if the path they were taking now, this narrow fertile seam, committed them both absolutely. Impossible to see anything except the narrow defile of the path before them, curving gradually away through the bushes. Sunlight fell on the topmost leaves, lying heavy and still on them. There was no breath of wind, yet there was a sound, a rustling in the air. Aware of this, they both from time to time looked up, into the leaves above their heads, as if to detect some stirring or agitation, but could see none.

'Stop a minute,' Farnaby said.

She stopped and turned to face him. Farnaby took some steps towards her.

'I did not suggest coming up here because of *him*,' he said. The loneliness of the place, and the proximity of the girl filled him with weakness. He put his hands on her shoulders, almost as if seeking support. She was tall, not needing to raise her eyes much to look into his, as she did now, but with a curious absence of expectation, which pained him obscurely.

'I could have asked you at once who you were, couldn't I?' he said, 'and told you who I was and why I had come. Why do you think I didn't?'

She looked at him steadily. He could feel the warmth of her shoulders under his hands.

'I suppose you didn't want me to think you were simply on an errand for Mooncranker,' she said. She paused, lips parted slightly, and his heart felt an impact, a blow at her beauty, which was not hers only but that which he had bestowed on her over the years, treasuring her face, he and others, of course – he suddenly in this moment saw her as shaped by a necessity in the minds of others, himself, Mooncranker, who else? – the complex and variegated pressures of memory and desire, like shaping hands. Galatea. 'He involves people in errands, yes,' he said slowly. 'You've been involved in one yourself, in my opinion, a long one. I don't know whether he thinks I came here on an errand for him – it is difficult to know what he thinks, in any case he is not in a fit state, at the moment. But if he does think that he is quite wrong. I came here for my own sake.'

Suddenly, from somewhere beyond the bushes, up on the hillside, a bird sang briefly, paused, sang again : a slow song, trickling down to them, both secretive and deliberate-sounding like the very voice of this green clandestine passage they had stumbled upon in the midst of the bare hills.

The bird did not sing again, and in listening for it they became once more aware of the hushed sound that was everywhere around them like a sigh.

They walked some yards farther. The bushes thinned, revealing the slope beyond them, tangled with vegetation. Miranda stopped and stood looking down.

'That's where it's coming from,' she said, pointing at the bankside, but quite low down on the hill. 'It's all these leaves rustling.'

'But there is no wind at all,' he said. 'Not a breath.'

The leaves at the base of the bushes, and the stems of the grasses, were moving, trembling, continuously, with a very faint but incessant motion, as if fanned from a long way above. Glancing higher he saw a wide arc of the hillside in similar motion. It was like the breath of a god.

He squatted and looked more intently down. His eyes caught fugitive gleams from below the leaves on the undersides of them or caught in the fine hairs of grass stems; tiny globes trembled there, balancing their brightness against disintegration. The touch of a hair; the shiver of a leaf; perils. His eyes were involved in stretching and contracting webs of light in this world below the lowest leaves.

'It's water,' he said. 'The bank is running with water.'

She got down too and their shoulders touched, moved apart, touched again. 'It's the water that is making the sound as well as the leaves and things,' she said. She turned to him a face alight with the interest of the discovery. 'I mean, it's all these thousands and millions of little drops weighting the leaves and bending them and then dropping off, releasing them, and then it is the sound the water itself is making, sliding and slipping down over things.'

'Yes,' he said, smiling at her enthusiasm.

'Where's it coming from, do you think?'

'Somewhere underground,' he said vaguely, 'there's no shortage of water hereabouts after all.'

'Yes,' she said, in the same tone of excitement, 'but this is different. This is fresh water.'

'Of course,' he said, remembering the vegetation all around

232

them. He pushed spread fingertips under the leaves, against the slippery stone. 'It's cold,' he said. 'Cold as ice.'

They smiled at each other then, like children with a secret, and got up and went on together, again in silence but not now uneasy at it. Soon the path broadened, and they debouched on to a level area scattered with the ruins of an ancient temple, around which on all sides the hills rose again. They paused here, sensing the deep seclusion of the place, the religious emotions of people long dead. A few thin pillars still stood, forming an arbitrary pattern; others lay in fragments over the grass. Such places convey a sense of order and meaning, no matter what the interval of time, the dilapidation. In the basin formed by the hills it stood there, pavements and steps and broken columns bathed in misty sunlight.

Hand in hand they crossed the grass-embossed markings of colonnade and tholos. A hot, very sweet smell came to them, and they heard a distant reverential sound of buzzing. Grass grew up through the cracked pavement, and delphiniums and grape hyacinths. They reached a low stone wall and saw immediately beyond it the source of both scent and sound: an area here about the size of a tennis-court was flooded and in the still water great masses of staring white flowers with yellow centres grew, their roots it seemed in the water itself; and tumbling about on them and in them a multitude of fawn-coloured bees buzzing liturgically while they looted. The flowers, incessantly stirred by the bees, gave off that ravishing, that almost swooning scent.

Together they climbed up on the low wall, stepping carefully along its crumbling, irregular top, which was overgrown with creepers and clumps of moss and grass. They began walking along the wall in order to encompass the flooded area. It was impossible now to determine whether the land had subsided here or whether some sort of pit had been originally contrived. The sound of the bees filled their ears and their progress was marked by the slither of lizards quitting the wall as they approached. These sounds and the excessive sweetness of the flowers began to affect Farnaby as in some way almost menacing. It seemed to him that he might quite easily go down feet first and be swallowed up in a lizard-ridden wall or go plunging

233

into the flowers without disturbing a single bee. Echoes of old stories came to him, stories of mergings and metamorphoses, evidence of the perilous plasticity of human beings. He began to have difficulty with his balance on the wall, became increasingly agitated at the problem of how to set his feet. Knowing from experience that his coordination would deteriorate further and not wishing to cut a poor figure before Miranda, he jumped down, hearing the slithering again, that swift retreat into the undergrowth.

'Somewhere about here,' he said, 'would be a good place for the picnic.' He took several deep breaths.

She jumped lightly down from the wall and he caught her, resting his hands for a short while at the sides of her waist. Sun-flushed, bright-eyed, steady-nerved, she seemed for the moment so superior to him that he experienced a sort of awe. And something of this must have showed in his eyes because her own gaze after a moment wavered and fell and she moved sideways, releasing herself.

They made their way to a grassy, slightly sloping bit of ground some yards from the wall, and sat down for their picnic.

'There wouldn't have been a temple here at all, I suppose,' Miranda said, 'if there hadn't been water, fresh water.'

'No, I suppose not. I wonder who the temple was dedicated to.' He smiled at her. 'Aphrodite perhaps.'

'That's an elm tree, isn't it?' She pointed.

Farnaby looked across. 'Yes,' he said. 'I think so, yes. There's a Maltese plum tree over there too.'

'Its leaves are quite yellow, aren't they? The elm, I mean.'

'Well, it is October,' Farnaby said. 'I don't suppose there are many elms in these hills. It's the water, of course. And being so sheltered too, I suppose.'

'Can I make you a sandwich, or will you just have a piece of bread with salami on top?'

'Yes, don't bother to make a sandwich.'

'A ghastly thing happened this morning,' she said. She began to tell him about the behaviour of the young American, and Mrs Pritchett's dreadful assault on him. 'I shall never forget his face, all covered with blood,' she said.

'Good heavens,' he said. 'What a terrible experience. He's a fool, but did he really deserve to be treated like that?'

'Well, that was what was so frightening about it, I mean, her reaction.'

'Were you frightened?'

'Yes, I was, for a while.'

He looked at her fixedly for a few moments. 'In those days,' he said, 'you know, when I first met you, you were only young then of course, but you never seemed frightened of anything.'

'I don't believe I ever was, then.'

'Have some wine,' Farnaby said. 'It's *Kavaklidere*, I hope it's all right.'

'Delicious.'

'Perhaps being frightened is something you learn later,' Farnaby said. 'Like being prudent or well-balanced, all the things applauded by our elders.'

'No, I don't think so,' she said. 'We could never learn it so well.'

'Do you remember,' he said suddenly and rather loudly, 'do you remember the present Mooncranker gave me that summer?'

The question had come without premeditation, emerging through the force of its own gravity, as though it could hang no longer on the weakening stalk of his reticence. 'You know the one I mean, don't you?' he added. 'That little effigy of Christ on the cross?' His heart was beating almost painfully.

She turned to him a face in which the full interest and vividness of the day and the scene contended with what seemed to him a certain wariness or reserve. This stilling of the face was very brief. The next moment she smiled a little and said, 'Yes, I remember.'

'But you never saw it,' he said, unwilling to believe she had fallen so casually into the trap.

'You must have talked to me about it,' she said.

'Perhaps that was it.' He knew, however, that he had talked of it to no one. Certainly not to her, whom he had not seen again after Mooncranker's little presentation ceremony. It came to him now with the force of a conviction that she had

235

deliberately avoided seeing him. If this were so, it could only be a mark of her complicity.

'There was meat in it,' he said.

'Meat?'

'It was made of sausage-meat. Under its wrappings. You remember, perhaps, that it was wrapped round with white bandage.'

'Oh, yes, I think so.'

'Well, underneath there was sausage-meat. Mooncranker, or somebody, went out and bought sausage-meat, then he moulded it into a little figure, arms outstretched you know, wrapped it up in white bandage, tied the whole thing to a little wooden cross and gave it to me.'

Miranda said nothing to this. He offered her more wine, which she refused, then poured a little into his own glass. 'It rotted,' he said. 'Of course. You know, when I hung it up on that tree, I showed you, didn't I? Well, it rotted there. Mooncranker must have foreseen that.'

He had spoken with a deliberate lack of emphasis, not wishing her to think that he was dramatizing things; but there was such a charge of horror and outrage still in that distant episode that his voice deepened with emotion as he spoke of it. She was looking at him steadily, lips slightly compressed, eyes clear, depthless.

'Any idea why,' she said, 'why he should have done that?' But this was too guileless, and at the same time struck him as challenging somehow. He looked for a moment longer at her serious, mild-eyed face and suspected in that moment that she, she, had fashioned the Christ, moulded the meat into shape with her own fingers, no doubt at Mooncranker's behest, but she had done it. Whence this idea came he did not know, but knew once it had entered his mind that it would always be there. It was the role Mooncranker would have required from his accomplice: her simple knowledge of what was to happen would not have been enough, not corruptive enough; he had made her an instrument, to her own damage and the damage of that distant boy who had been left alone to see and smell the corruption.

'I have often wondered why,' he said, looking away from

her. 'I think there are a number of reasons. He is a destructive man and he wanted to ... devastate this sort of private area where I had these feelings about Christ. Well, he certainly succeeded there. But he wouldn't call it that, he would probably describe it as a salutary experience, get rid of cant and religiosity, that kind of thing, some sort of philosophical gloss to disguise the fact that he is simply one of those worms that settle on fresh green leaves. The bits they don't eat, they smear.' His voice which had risen with anger at Mooncranker, now became quieter. It would not do, he sensed, to belittle Mooncranker too much to her. He said, 'It gave me an awful shock you know.'

'Yes,' she said, 'it must have done.'

'He used to talk to you quite a bit about such things, didn't he, during that summer?'

'He took me into his confidence,' she said, with a certain dignity.

And that, Farnaby thought, had been the cleverest stroke of all. How had she described him, that day when they had walked down the river together? A *humanist*, that was it. He could hear her fifteen-year-old voice now, earnest and proud, saying, 'He doesn't trust institutions at all.'

'I've never been able to forget it,' he said. 'You weren't around then, were you? When it happened I mean, when I discovered it.'

'No,' she said. 'I think I had gone back to school, probably.'

'Yes, that was probably it. How did he know I was interested in such things, do you think?'

'What do you mean?'

'Interested in Christ and so on.'

'Well, I may have told him that.'

'Oh, I see,' Farnaby said slowly. 'You talked about me sometimes, did you?' It had occurred to him that if Miranda were really as implicated as he suspected, she could only be concealing her part in it out of guilt or else fear of antagonizing him. Either way it seemed to him to mean that she cared enough to want to preserve the relationship between them, not to damage it, perhaps beyond repair, by injudicious or premature admissions. And he sensed obscurely that to drive her into confessing would be a tactical error at this stage – better, he thought, to work on her feelings of guilt and remorse...

'Do you think Uncle George knew anything about it?' he said.

'I shouldn't think so.'

'No, I don't think so either. At the time you know, I thought everyone was in it. That was why it shocked me so much. I thought it was the whole of the adult world. There was no one for me to turn to. You had gone away. My parents were in the midst of a divorce. Uncle George was hardly the sort...'

Miranda stood up without haste. 'Pity to waste all these crumbs,' she said. 'I'll go over and put them in the water and see if any fish come up for them.'

'Good idea,' he said, with a certain surprise at being interrupted and a sense too of releasing her from a difficult situation.

She hesitated a moment, then walked slowly towards the clamorous, scented water, through thin shadows cast by the columns, over the grass-grown pavement, into an area of broken mist and sunshine, the glowing yellow tree beyond her. She held the paper-bag with the bread-crumbs away from her, waist high.

Painstakingly, with a sort of self-violating exactness, he began to reconstruct the events immediately before Mooncranker had handed him the gift. Mooncranker had spoken to someone unseen, giving instructions, presumably. Then the white-clad figure glimpsed briefly on the landing, seen again immediately, almost, at the back door, slipping out. Hidden first by Mooncranker's form and then by the wall of the house itself. Taller than Mooncranker? Impossible to tell, I did not see their two forms together. Henry and Frederick, who were also dressed in white, were on the tennis-court at the time. I remember their voices. It could not have been either of them. I decided that, moreover, long ago. Aunt Jane? Something, some element in the situation, that puts Aunt Jane out of the count, apart from the inherent improbability of Aunt Jane leaguing herself with Mooncranker. The figure at the landing, then at the door. Almost the same moment. There must have been an interval. Perhaps the two images fuse like this in my mind because the interval was so brief. Is this why I have always discounted adults, because only a young person, someone like Miranda, would have raced down the stairs so quickly? Impossible to be sure now. But what would either of them be doing in that house? It was not her house, nor Mooncranker's, they were guests like myself. Somebody else, in whose room the Christ was kept in readiness? Mooncranker saw his chance, saw me standing there, passed the word on to that swift white-clad person who went racing up to get it, from some hiding-place on the upper floor, Uncle George's room perhaps, or Aunt Jane's...

A nightmarish sort of general suspiciousness descended on Farnaby. He felt for some moments now as he had felt at the time, that all the figures peopling that summer had been in the plot against him, all had known what was going to happen, all of them had had some prearranged part to play. The sickening universal sense of duplicity and treachery returned to him, and he thought of the blind, helmeted head of the Christ high up on the tree, the sliding light and the glint of flies' wings, the heavy odour of flowers and his own final, piercingly horrible *perception* – for he had been vouchsafed something then, been afforded a glimpse into a pit, and with Uncle George's gasping face before him had fainted on the edge of it, and had risen changed – so far it was Mooncranker's victory...

'Oh, nothing is happening,' she called to him over her shoulder. He watched her intently, noticed the diffidence of her movements, the way she seemed to hold the paper packet almost with apprehension, as if it might change its texture or shape in her hands. This gentleness was not part of his memory of her at all, perhaps it had been assumed with the years and sorrows, the long course of ministering to Mooncranker.

Weakness there, all the same, he thought, watching her lean over the wall, and scatter the crumbs carefully into the water. Mooncranker had seen that from the start.

'They don't seem to be hungry,' she called in soft, almost plaintive tones. She stood with her burdened look in full sunlight. The mist-fluffed sunshine lay on her like pollen.

'Perhaps it isn't their lunchtime,' he said. He felt sure all this was merely a diversion. She is weak, he told himself. She allowed herself to be prevailed upon, and used. Mooncranker must have seen in her the victim predestined. To find two such persons under his hand as Miranda and myself! And so young. More than he could have hoped for. Strange that my own experience of her that summer was of glowing strength and certainty, no hint of such weakness. Mooncranker saw it.

She came back to him, stepping among the antique rubble, golden slender legs. She was smiling.

'Well,' she said, 'they weren't interested.'

Farnaby smiled back at her. The horror of the gift and his suspicion was receding but he was conscious now for the first time of a rather helpless feeling of distance from Miranda, a sort of obligatory detachment.

'They are probably feasting underneath the surface,' he said.

They walked together round the outside edge of the site, to a point behind the flooded area, and stopped again just outside the zone of shade cast by the elm. Miranda with frank enthusiasm was demolishing an apple in a series of large bites, each one of which sounded clean and final like wood snapping. Mist lay among the branches of the elm, thickening the mass of the tree. The rays of sunshine struck through the foliage, not so much penetrating the mist as infusing it with tints of pale blue and rose. From the upper branches they heard a clatter of wings and a number of pigeons rose into the sunshine and wheeled in a body, the sun eliciting flashes from their breasts.

'It happened accidentally, really,' she said, with a certain inconsequence, which he recognized or remembered as her habit. 'Things like that often do, don't they? I mean, courses of action you set yourself on, or just a train of events that happens to you and becomes part of your life.' She was not good at explaining things, needing, as he again thought he remembered, someone else's more positive assertions to set her going.

'Oh come,' he said, helping her, 'we choose our own way, surely.'

'Not really,' she said. 'I didn't with Mooncranker, anyway. I mean, of course there was a time when I could have drawn back from a physical action, from actually sleeping with him, or anyway I could have got out of it afterwards, not gone on with it. But that isn't the important thing, is it?'

'Well, I don't know.' Farnaby, with the ardour of his twenty-three years, peered doubtfully through the lower branches of the yellow elm at the white columnar flowers of the Malta plum tree slightly below and to his left. There were three fig trees in a group beyond this. It did not seem to him that it would ever be possible to take sleeping with Miranda as a matter of course. He counted five tortoiseshell butterflies on the flowers.

'Actions you can refrain from,' Miranda said, and he was suddenly aware of a change of mood in her, an increasing sadness. 'But things you get into aren't actions. It is a sort of permission you give to your will.'

A leaf drifted down from the elm, fell into the dark green heart of the Malta plum tree. Farnaby heard the remote incessant sound of the bees, the scrape of the dry leaf. He looked down at the back of his palm, at the faint blond hairs incandescent in the sunlight. The changing leaves, the massing of the trees caused by the mist, the stillness and doomed warmth of the place, all reminded him of autumns at home in England. Elsewhere, among the bare hills and sulphurous streams, he had not been aware of the seasons, the landscape seemed changeless, but here one felt the extended summer, there was something precious in these middle hours of the day, something precariously achieved, full of sadness. He felt the sun resting on his hands, with a sort of loving particularity, as it rested on water and marble and flowers and leaves.

With an effort he summoned resistance to the sadness of the place, the feeling it conveyed of inevitable decline.

'By action you can break out,' he said. 'A relationship between people isn't something self-perpetuating.'

'Once you undertake a role ...' she said.

'I don't believe that.' He looked at her. 'Unless it is something that satisfies mutual *needs*. Permanent invalid, permanent nurse,' he said, deliberately. 'How did it happen, how did you get into it all?'

Miranda made a vague gesture. 'I don't know, it wasn't a series of steps,' she said. 'He made an impression on me from the start. I mean, you know, that summer. He used to talk to me a lot, as if he thought I was intelligent. About being a humanist, and people coming to terms with reality.'

'I was held out to you as a boy full of damaging illusions, I suppose,' Farnaby said.

'You were, I suppose, yes. He sort of made fun of you, in a gentle way.'

'I can imagine.' Farnaby felt a fresh spasm of hatred for Mooncranker. My turn will come, he promised himself. He felt a sort of cautious exhilaration that she had accepted without demur his definition of her relation with Mooncranker.

'I don't know,' she went on slowly, her face turned away from him. 'There was a feeling ... It seemed to me that he knew so much. He lived, he seemed to live in a different area, where life was more serious somehow.'

'Serious,' Farnaby echoed. 'Serious?' He heard a faint thudding noise not too far away, as of something falling into piled leaves. Chestnut perhaps. Figs long ago departed probably. Or something larger, a quince. But would quinces be growing wild here? He pictured the yellowing quince on the tree, heavy with ripeness, burdening the stalk, the mist and sun eroding the stalk and then in the secrecy of the mist the fruit falls, crashes into the debris of summer below. 'He has a gift for enlisting accomplices,' he said bitterly.

'And then, he became a well-known person too. I might have forgotten all about him. He went away at the end of that summer, did you know? He went to London and he didn't come back much. I didn't actually see him again, not for, oh, five years, but people mentioned his name you know. Your uncle met me one day in the street and talked to me about him, how well he was doing, and then I saw him on television, interviewing people and being the chairman in discussion groups. He became a well-known figure.'

'Yes,' Farnaby said. 'I can imagine that. I mean, I can imagine Uncle George giving you all the details. I bet he got it all right, didn't he?'

'How do you mean?'

'All the details. I bet he got them all right, didn't he?'

'Yes, I suppose he did.'

'He always got things like that right, you know,' Farnaby said, remembering Uncle George and his maps and timetables.

'He changed, after your aunt died. Have you seen him lately?'

'No,' Farnaby said. 'I haven't seen him for years. Do you mean he deteriorated?'

'You'll find a big change in him.'

He did not pursue this, wishing to hear more about Mooncranker. In the pause that followed he heard another soft rustling thud like a fruit or chestnut falling.

'Then I went to secretarial college,' she said. 'I was still living at home and I needed a spare-time job, to help out, you know, to be a little independent. Your uncle wrote to me, and said Mr Mooncranker had been asking about me, would I like a job looking after his correspondence.'

Uncle George again, Farnaby thought. Further evidence of Mooncranker's genius for enlisting accomplices. Mooncranker of the long, tenacious memory, the nursed desire. He had kept his sense intact for five years of Miranda's malleability, preserved the memory of the impression he had made on her. Farnaby felt a surge of hatred for Mooncranker again, combined now with misery at his own deprivations. For a moment Mooncranker was a compound of all those with quicker speech, readier wits, more assurance, and Farnaby in imagination dashed him to the ground.

'He had been married,' she said, 'in the interval, but he was living apart from his wife. I used to go to his house on a bicycle. He came back to live there after his mother died, you know.'

They moved slowly away from the trees, on to the grassy rectangular area of the temple itself.

'I remember the road well,' she said.

Out here in the open, sunshine had achieved a conquest of the mist but in the hollows of the hills around there was a smoky haze, like a lining.

'I was only nineteen,' she said, as if offering this fact to Farnaby in mitigation.

Farnaby looked at her without speaking. It seemed to him there was an amazing purity about her face, a purity which depended somehow on the cooperation of the air around it, as though neck and cheek and brow had shaped the arcs of air that lay adjacent, or as though the air itself, warmed and somehow intensified by the contiguity, had melted, moulded round her, like a sort of bright immaterial armour, an effect similar to the edge of air round flame or round a bright leaf on a day of brilliant sunshine; so that for the moment she took on for him the quality of the place itself and the season, achieved, tranquil, heedless of the time and decay which besieged it.

She was conscious of his gaze but did not return it; and this close unresisted scrutiny gave Farnaby a strong sense of impunity and supremacy, he began to feel sexually aroused by what seemed her submissiveness; and now at last the possible import of her tone came to him, the fact that she seemed almost to be excusing herself for her relations with Mooncranker, as if seeking to soften his judgement of her, which could only mean, he thought exultantly, that he had already established a claim in her life . . .

'I was unhappy,' she said. 'Or thought I was. Cycling towards a sort of refuge if you know what I mean. He used to recommend books for me to read, poetry and so on. He has written a book himself, you know.'

'No, I didn't know,' Farnaby said. 'What about, humanism?'

'No, about Henry the Navigator. He gave me a signed copy.'

She paused, and Farnaby saw how much she must have been pleased by that gift. More than by gems, probably . . . He found that he was clenching his teeth.

'Then one day,' she said, 'he spoke to me kindly, I don't even remember what he said. I was feeling miserable. I can't explain why. I often felt very unhappy during that time in my life, well, before that really, I think that summer you and I met I was already having bouts of it, crying for no reason, but then other girls did that too, no, it was later, when I was about eighteen, I began to be, you know, consciously unhappy. I wasn't badly treated at home or anything. Neither of my parents was very interested in me. They were only interested in each other, or rather, as I look back on it now, my mother was interested only in herself and my father only in her, anyway they didn't have much time for me, they didn't care how I got on at school or anything like that. They didn't really listen when I talked to them.'

'Good grief,' Farnaby said. He was shocked to hear of this indifference of her parents. Nothing in his memory of her suggested any such secret unhappiness. Perhaps again perspicacious Mooncranker had seen it. More probably she would have confided it to him. In any case Farnaby could see now how potent and heady for her it must have been to have someone near enough her father's age taking her seriously like that, discussing ideas with her, broaching the subject of the sausage-meat Christ ... 'Good grief,' he said again.

'That happens quite a lot, I think,' Miranda said. 'Just as much as the other way, shutting out the husband or wife because of loving the child too much. My mother is very beautiful. You never met her, did you?'

'No, but she would be, she would be beautiful.'

'I don't know –'

'Well,' he said, '*you* are beautiful.' He found that his heart was beating heavily with the daring of this speech.

'Do you think so?' she said. She smiled a little, rather shyly he thought, and he was about to reaffirm his words when she began to speak of Mooncranker again.

'It was something quite ordinary he said, I mean. Something like, "You shouldn't be unhappy, an attractive girl like you." Something like that. Anyway I started crying, like a fool, and he got down on his knees beside me and gave me a handkerchief. I was sitting at the typewriter. I couldn't see and I couldn't speak and I couldn't stop crying and I really didn't know what he was doing, I didn't feel anything much at all, but there we were, both of us on the floor, I remember feeling very surprised when I heard him sort of cry out and saw his face without his glasses on. Well,' she added swiftly, seeing something stricken in his face, 'you asked me how it happened.'

Farnaby said, 'I'll bet he's got that written down in his notebook.'

'What?'

'In her moments of acute distress, press home.'

'Oh no, I probably wanted something like that to happen. I didn't foresee the rest of course.'

'What do you mean?'

'Well, everything it got me into. I didn't know about the drinking at first, then I thought, you know, I could influence him to stop, but of course that was silly of me. Nothing could stop him.'

'What he needed you for was to mop up afterwards,' Farnaby said bitterly. He was still suffering from the thought of Mooncranker having his way with weeping Miranda. It was this that had caused him to speak so directly and even perhaps insultingly to her.

'No,' she said, 'you mustn't simplify things like that.' But she spoke gently, sensing the hurt in him. 'There was much more to it than that,' she said. 'Sex wasn't a great part of it, though.'

Farnaby said nothing, looked steadily at her. She met his eyes at last, with a sort of luminous candour. 'He hasn't wanted very much in that way for two years or more,' she said. Then, as he still said nothing, she sighed and moved her shoulders like someone awakening. 'Well,' she said, 'I suppose we'd better be going down.'

These last words with their suggestion of resumed duties and commitments, galvanized Farnaby. He gave a sweeping look over the whole area, glimpsed or sensed as it were in one wheeling composite impression, water and staring flowers and slithering wall and mist and yellow sunshine, marble column and glassy leaf, all caught in this startled moment, arrested in their sadness and decline.

'No,' he said loudly. 'We are behaving as if we were doomed. As if it were clear where our duty lies, and so on.'

'What do you mean?'

'Autumn,' he said. 'A deserted place like this, just breathing resignation. It is half rotten already, everything we're looking at. That is the beauty of it. Ripeness, acquiescence, they are indistinguishable from decay.'

She looked at him with a sort of wondering doubt on her face. He said, more quietly, 'So we are supposed just sort of sadly to say good-bye, are we? Why should the loss be ours, mine at least? He just lies there and lets the season work for him.'

'There is no reason to say good-bye,' she said. 'But you can't suddenly pretend that other people don't exist.'

'Don't you see?' he said. 'We fall into assumptions about duty and obligation and so on. Without any reason. There is no *reason* for it. Only what is expected somehow by people already corrupted. The authorities, those who exact sacrifices from us, are *corrupt*. All my life I have been doing it. Falling in with what was expected, with what they call the logic of the situation. Situations have no logic. This bloody Ottoman fiscal policy, for example.'

'Aren't you interested in it?' she said.

He paused, breathing deeply. He looked at her, then looked away, half losing the thread of his argument.

'Listen,' he said, 'will you stay a bit longer here? You promised me one day, didn't you? Well, will you stay longer than that, another day? I have some claim, after everything that has happened. Besides, Mooncranker is safe there in the hospital.'

Seeing the doubt in her face, he went on quickly, striving to forestall an immediate negative, give her time for second thoughts. 'He is well looked after there,' he said. 'He has to stay there several days, in any case. Five days at least,' he lied. 'Please will you stay a bit longer?'

'Why are you asking me to do this?' she said.

'Because it is natural and right to do it,' Farnaby said with sudden passion. 'Because I feel there is something between us and I don't want it to be lost by a false sense of obligation. Once before it was lost like that. It's not going to happen again, if I can help it.'

He had spoken vehemently, and saw now both wonder and fear in Miranda's face. 'If I had not come here,' he said, 'you would probably have stayed several days, wouldn't you?'

'Perhaps, yes. I don't know. I don't know.' Miranda looked suddenly worried and unhappy.

'Please stay,' he said, aware that he was irreparably tampering with her life, appalled and delighted at the sense of power that came surging up in him at the sight of her troubled face.

'He will be lying there worrying,' she said.

'I can send him a telegram if it would make you feel better.'

Now that they were discussing practical details, he felt the battle was more than half won. Still, she had not agreed to stay. They had begun to retrace their steps, leaving behind them this doomed enclave among the hills, following the green track downwards. As they went, he continued his attempts to persuade her and she listened, appeared to assent, but made no promises. Then, when they were almost down again, standing together on what was actually the last or lowest crest, point of vantage, before the hill took its final tilt to the level of the pool, standing there together in silence at last, looking down over the vaporous water, the whole expanse of which was clearly visible now, they saw a grey-haired man sitting in the sunshine at the poolside talking to Plopl the photographer, and both recognized him almost at once, though Miranda was fractionally quicker to do so. 'That is Mooncranker, there,' she said, quietly but with extreme surprise.

Farnaby felt every vestige of colour leave his face. He turned and took Miranda by the arm.

'Promise me one thing,' he said, in a voice he could hardly recognize as his own. 'Promise you won't simply go off with him.'

She looked at him now, all irresolution gone from her face, which was suddenly the face of the young girl he remembered, strong, reliable, honouring a childhood pact, a friend in a tight corner. 'No,' she said. 'I wouldn't do that.'

5

It was round about four o'clock when Mooncranker got out of the pool. In the business of showering and dressing his feelings lightened somewhat, for this brief interval of time it was like numerous other occasions in his life when he had been preparing himself for some definite event, perhaps even something pleasurable. There was a purpose in it, some sort of social requirement.

This more optimistic feeling persisted as he strolled round the poolside choosing a table, and while he was ordering his lemon tea. But as soon as he felt again his isolation, as soon as he began to look steadily down at the water below him, that slow, meticulous, memorial habit descended on him again, aided this time by the deep, almost slumbrous relaxation of his body after the long immersion, and he began once more to record things – his precise position half-way down the terrace, full in the sunshine; the slightly shivered or refracted look of cornice, capital, fluted drums of the drowned marble pillars below the surface, the marble fresh and gleaming still, no dimming of it by the chemical water, no slightest loss of lustre, and that is amazing, after centuries of immersion, though the ceramic tiling alongside has a deposit on it, a sort of calcareous crust. As if marble were the privileged inmate, less noble substances undergoing gradual befouling...

A very badly crippled man, walking with the aid of two crutches, appears from somewhere on my right, from a cabin, or perhaps the entrance area, I do not see which, and makes his way towards me, swinging his trunk, nearer and nearer by painful degrees. He bows his invalid's head, which is covered with soft brown hair, and smiles the white smile of those acquainted with pain, and *gunaydin*, he says, *gunaydin effendim* and I reply in kind, watching with a sort of obscure anguish as he manoeuvres himself into a chair farther down from me, watching the collapse of his body into the chair. The movements of a cripple are unpredictable, like those of insects, though there is sometimes a sort of beauty in them. There was a slightly crippled grace in young Farnaby's movements as he walked along the terrace...

'Excuse me, sir, have you a moment to spare?' This voice comes from my left, taking me completely by surprise. An afternoon full of encounters. I should perhaps have done better to wait in my cabin. Turning, I see before me a plump serious face, of unhealthy complexion, brows slightly knitted as if from studious habits, hair brushed forward in a thin fringe, small, shiny eyes.

'Yes, what is it?'

His features work briefly, as if rehearsing speech. 'I am a photographer,' he says. 'I have some pictures here that I think might interest you, as I can see that you are an educated gentleman.'

A foreign voice, vaguely Teutonic, instinct with a sort of blurred kindness. 'Plopl,' he says now. 'My name is Plopl.'

'Mooncranker. Won't you sit down.' I utter this invitation somewhat coldly as I have suddenly remembered blank-faced Pamela. This must be the very man. He is evidently delighted however, even by this qualified welcome. His face breaks into a smile.

'Thank you, thank you,' he says, and sits. He is holding now in stubby fingers a package or perhaps envelope, yes envelope, which he must have drawn from his person while actually in the process of sitting down. 'These are some of my photographs,' he says. His nails are black-rimmed.

'Let me see them.' With resignation I extend my hand.

Still he retains the envelope. 'I thought,' he says, 'that a gentleman like you, a cultivated man, would not ... It would not be the obvious appeal. I take photographs of many sorts, you understand, and for different purposes. The artist has difficulty to maintain his integrity in the world of today, as you probably know, sir.'

'Yes, yes.'

His face works. In his earnestness he has come out in a slight sweat along the cheeks. 'I have to cater sometimes for the depraved taste,' he says. 'We must live, after all, is it not?'

'I see no necessity for that, but I should like to see the photographs.'

'I will be frank and above boards with you. In certain aspects of my work I can take no real pleasure, no satisfaction. It is for the multitudes. To you I am showing my serious work, my studies in the oneness of all physical existence, the basis of pain in every phenomenon.'

He hands over the envelope. I am about to extract the pictures when Mr Senemoğlu, the manager, returns with a second glass of tea that I suppose I must have ordered. I offer the photographer tea, but he declines.

'How is it passing?' Mr Senemoğlu asks, setting down the glass. I do not for the moment understand what he means. I become intensely conscious of the hands of all of us, my own nerveless hands holding the envelope; the photographer's hands, stubby, hairy-backed, seeming as if they might scuttle away at any moment, as if they belonged among foliage; the manager's thin, instrumental hands. The life in all these hands is horrifying and the manager's question seems somehow relevant to this horror.

'It is passing,' I reply, in a noncommittal tone, and Mr Senemoğlu smiles, a brilliant smile, but with no warmth or particularity in it.

'There is not a lot of world here now,' the manager says, it seems with an apologetic intention. 'It is not so gay.'

'I prefer that.' I think shudderingly of the pool in seasons other than this dead one, pullulating with bodies like fry or spawn.

Mr Senemoğlu inclines his head, as if deferring to this preference. He withdraws at a dignified pace. I think of Miranda and Farnaby together, getting better acquainted among the hills. I take the pictures out of the envelope, conscious that the photographer is scanning my features.

There are eight altogether, postcard-size. All of them showing in close-up a face I recognize as the girl Pamela's, in a series of expressions, sullen, grimacing, contorted. After some moments I seem to discern a pattern, a development, and as if in a dream I arrange them on the table before me, the face in the first one vaguely troubled as if by something teasing the memory or making some claim on the understanding, eyes wide open, staring straight ahead, lips compressed. The mouth opens a little as if in dawning wonder, an intimation that the truth is about to be perceived, the distant experience recalled. Then pain, the face grapples with pain as if that truth or experience is too harsh to be managed, as if the girl is fighting to control or contain it, fighting with closed eyes and clenched jaw not to let herself be flooded, overborne; then the fifth picture, the face smoothed again, sorrowing, then again violently contorted, raised blindly in an agony of supplication, straining for the release to be found in a cry or scream, and indeed the penultimate picture shows Pamela with mouth stretched open in a silent scream. Last of all I place a Pamela restored to blankness, sullenness.

Thus I arrange the pictures on the table. Then looking up meet the shiny eager gaze of the photograper.

'Ah,' he says. 'So you arrange them in that order?'

'I think so, yes.'

'Interesting, that you should place the expressionless face, the face blank and stupid, right at the very end. It is as if you are saying, life returns to this, this is the phase we are aspiring to, blankness, insensibility, the vegetal life. I myself would place that particular one here, at the beginning. It is the un-awakened face.'

'You may be right.' I look at the pictures again. 'All the same, I prefer it at the end.'

'My own vision is more dramatic, she utters right at the end the scream.'

Plopl nods his head in self-approval. Despite myself I am drawn into this discussion: 'The photographs depict a crisis of some sort, do they not, Mr Plopl? A conflict. She appears to be struggling to retain control. I prefer to think of conflict as followed by resolution. If the resolution has a bestial oblivion in it, I cannot help that. No, I prefer it at the end.'

I grow impatient with myself, my slow, pedantic voice. 'They are marvellous photographs, Mr Plopl,' I say. 'I don't know how you managed to extract these expressions from your model. She must be an actress of considerable ability.'

'She can't act for toffees. No, she is just the plastic, malleable human material. I see that you have put the grieving face' – he points with grubby forefinger across the table – 'this one, you have put it between faces of conflict and stress. Now why have you done that, sir?'

'It seemed the natural place for it.' Again I am obliged to defend my choice. 'She seems to be seeking for some outside help. Her attitude in short is somewhat *prayerful*. Now it seems natural to me to place this in the midst of agony. The sudden perception of a possible refuge.' I look down again at the blind, brutal face of Pamela.

'Interesting, jolly interesting,' the photographer now says, after some preliminary movements of the features. 'There are many possible variations, permutations in the order of these pictures, which I can let you have for just seven hundred and fifty new pence. I have known people to put that particular one second from last, just before the spasms, yes, the way a person arranges these pictures indicates his world view, we can say...' His round face, rather heavily jowled for one still comparatively young, glistens with sweat, glows with interest and enthusiasm. In the warmth of my admiration for the pictures, his nature is blossoming into confidences. 'After all,' he says, 'if we did not know the story in advance, how would we arrange the Stations of the Cross?'

'How indeed?' A telling point. 'What do the pictures actually depict?' I ask him.

'What do you think?' He looks almost coy.

'They could be many things,' I say slowly. 'Hysteria. The stress of some ordeal. A person attempting to endure pain without total loss of dignity. Perhaps, having taken some drug she is fighting for reasons of her own the onset of the symptoms.'

'Pain being the dominant note,' he says.

'Oh, certainly. What is it actually?'

He leans back in his chair. He utters a sort of triumphant titter. 'It is the process of a clitoral orgasm,' he says. 'Self-induced, of course.'

I shuffle the pictures together and place them beside his elbow on the table in a neat stack.

'Yours,' he says, 'for seven pounds. Try it on your guests. Reveal your character, justify your choice. Cheap at the price. A unique series of photographs.'

'Seven pounds seems rather a lot.'

'Six and a half then, that is my final offer.'

I hesitate. There is no doubt that the pictures have a certain quality. On the other hand ... Suddenly the absolute point-lessness of haggling comes home to me. Strange that a reluctance to be overcharged should accompany me in what may be my last hours. They may not be, of course. Then I shall have need of money tomorrow ...

It is at this moment, while the photographer is still regarding me with eager expectancy, that the two of them, Miranda and

Farnaby, emerge on to the terrace from the entrance area and begin to walk towards me. 'Later,' I say swiftly to the photographer. 'We'll discuss it later.' The photographs disappear into his jacket pocket. We stand up to greet the approaching couple, both of whom are smiling slightly. Some words are exchanged of greeting and salutation. It is my impression that Miranda is rather flushed, Farnaby rather pale. In the momentary confusion of my thoughts I do not make out more than this. The photographer retires from the scene. I suggest that the three of us sit down and have some tea. Miranda says that would be lovely. The ready acceptance of offers of food and drink was always one of her most endearing traits. Farnaby, after a distinct and no doubt painful hesitation, says, no, he has one or two things to do, he will see us later. He still hesitates, hovers, but at last, with a smile for Miranda, takes himself off along the terrace, with that odd, slightly lunging walk of his – he has summoned, albeit with a struggle, the tact to leave us alone.

Wasted of course, for what can I say to her? I know why she left me. Know too from the small wary signs she makes that she is conscious of needing to be careful in what she says, what she admits, and this can only mean she feels obligation elsewhere. This being so, she will seek a pretext for anger with me ...

'Why did you come chasing after me?' she says now, and there is anger in her voice. 'As if I were a schoolgirl running away from home.'

I look at her face. There is a tightness in my chest and throat. All my assurances and protestations are used up, I have squandered them over the years, besides it was not love for Miranda that brought me here, not the simple desire to have her back again ...

'I came because I had to.'

She looks at me steadily, with an expression I do not remember seeing on her face before, troubled, perhaps affectionate, but clear and appraising.

'You should not have come,' she says. I see that she is still, very naturally of course, regarding herself as central to the matter.

At the door of his cabin Farnaby hesitated a long moment, resisting the temptation to turn round and go back to them again. He stared in misery at the white-painted number on his door, thinking of persuasive Mooncranker, intimacy and habit also pleading for him, Miranda's listening face, her terrible malleability. Again there came over him in a sickening wave the sense of those two conspiring against him, as they had done to such effect that distant summer ... With a great effort of resolution he opened the door and went in. Once inside unhappiness swept through him like a physical pain. He stood still for some moments, then lay down on his bed, and pulled the top blanket over him as if in fact seeking relief from physical suffering. He lay on his back, staring up at the ceiling, in whose intricate pattern of cracks he seemed to discern heraldic birds and beasts. He did not fully understand the nature of his pain, the feeling of loss and dereliction that had made him creep into bed like a sick creature. It was somehow antecedent to the present situation, as though he had behaved with tragic recklessness long before, in the clouded past ...

Gradually, as warmth spread through his body, this feeling lessened. By slight adjustments, he made of the heron on the ceiling a kneeling noseless child, then a peninsula, then a lagoon with spidery vegetation, knuckled promontories, skeletal floating creatures, all lost for ever as he pressed back his head, reassembled into a web or net, a mesh of great complexity with jagged holes where creatures formerly imprisoned had found egress ... His eyes closed on this interpretation and after some time he slept.

It was after six when he awoke, to a sense of crisis which persisted, indeed grew stronger, while he washed and got ready to go out. Neither Mooncranker nor Miranda were anywhere to be seen on the terrace, and the only people in the pool were the two black men laughing together in the shallower water at the far end, and the Greek, who smiled and beckoned him into the water. Farnaby mimed politely that he would be coming in later. A very badly crippled man got up from a table opposite and began making his way along the terrace, puny body slung between crutches. Farnaby went to Miranda's cabin and tapped on the door, but there was no answer. A terrible suspicion entered his mind, but he dismissed it almost at once, remembering the pact that Miranda had made – she would never have gone off without saying anything.

He walked back round the terrace, crossed over the bridge and went into the dining-room, taking in rather confusedly the fact that several of the tables were occupied. He saw Mooncranker and Miranda almost at once, sitting together at a table in the far corner, and made his way towards them, noting as he drew near that there was none of that animated air of reunion between them that he had been dreading. They were sitting in staid silence, eating.

'Do you mind if I join you?' he said, diffidently, but already pulling out a chair. Miranda looked up and smiled at him, a smile of such transfixing radiance that it caused a check in his breathing. Mooncranker, who had observed this smile, made a gesture of welcome. 'We thought we'd dine early,' he said. 'I hope you don't mind?'

'Not at all.'

'I can recommend the soup,' Mooncranker said. 'But the *Imam Beyilde* is not so good, unfortunately.'

'The *moussaka* isn't bad,' Miranda said.

Farnaby, who still felt rather breathless, forbore looking at her face again so soon, anticipating already the slight shock of pleasure and awe he would experience when he did so. He felt faint surprise that she should be capable of such calm comment about the food, but this passed after a moment into a sense of her mystery, the opaqueness that her whole personality still possessed for him.

'I don't think they soaked the aubergines enough,' Mooncranker said. 'Or perhaps at all.' With his great curving nose and statesmanlike sweep of hair he looked incongruous, out of place, in the primitively appointed dining-room. Farnaby noticed now for the first time how dark and elderly his lips were. 'I'm not hungry, really,' he said. 'An omelette will do for me.'

'Oh come now,' Mooncranker said.

'No, really.'

'Have some wine, while you're thinking it over,' Mooncranker said. He himself did not seem to be drinking anything. '*Baska bir bardak*,' he said to Mr Senemoğlu's back as it was retreating towards the kitchen.

Farnaby and Miranda exchanged a glance, then he looked away, at the other people eating there. It was still too early to be very full. The Levantine, in a mauve shirt with a pattern of flowers on it, sat alone. Farnaby watched him spearing slices of tomato with accurate motions of his fork. The German couple had almost finished their meal, she held a bright red apple in one swollen hand – Farnaby noticed that the hand itself was small, small-boned, the distension of flesh on this delicate framework looking like a symptom of disease. The same was true of her features, on which the flesh had billowed, self-generating, protoplasmic. Her husband, whose neck was encased in a navy-blue cravat, looked abstracted and at the same time harassed, as though lost in a not very reassuring dream. One or two others were there, whom he did not remember having seen before.

Farnaby was suddenly possessed by a sort of childlike wonder at the existence in this place, at this moment of time, of such persons, with himself among them, himself and Miranda and Mooncranker seated here together at what was undoubtedly a crucial point in all their lives; and though he had resolved beforehand to be impersonal in his talk, to avoid all suggestion that their situation was abnormal, he now looked impulsively towards Mooncranker sitting straight and high-shouldered opposite him, and said. 'What do you suppose we are doing here, all of us? Really, I mean.'

'Well, there are as many reasons as there are people, I suppose,' Mooncranker said, with an immediacy of response, even a glibness, that was slightly surprising – it was quite as if this question had been put to him before, or as if at any rate he had had reason to ponder it in the past. He paused now, however, as though considering. 'In one sense,' he said, after a moment or two, 'the pool is a place that people come to because people must congregate somewhere. Mustn't they? It is like asking why starlings foregather on one roof rather than another.'

'Surely not,' Farnaby said, embarrassed now at having spoken thus boldly. 'Roofs are all pretty much the same, aren't they?'

'They are to *us*,' Mooncranker said, more sharply. This contradiction had annoyed him. Regarding Farnaby's long, good-looking, though rather equine face, he was assailed suddenly by that ancient venom felt first when he had seen them together on the tennis-court and though there was no way now open to him of harming Farnaby, moreover he too wished to speak mildly, avoid any note of stridency or drama, anything that might provoke them into declaring themselves, despite all this, there was a harsh, sarcastic note in his voice when he spoke again.

'I suppose you want to pronounce for starlings too,' he said.

'It was you that brought starlings into it,' Farnaby said. The two men looked each other in the face for several moments without speaking and Mooncranker all at once perceived that a great change had taken place in the other since their conversations in hotel and hospital. Farnaby was no longer tractable, he had shed completely that former deference, was capable now, if pressed, of pugnacity, and all this because of Miranda, there could be no other explanation, these were attributes of courtship. Mooncranker thought of the smiles and glances that the two of them had exchanged since the young man's arrival, foundations of the edifice they were building. His malignancy towards Farnaby flickered out and all warmth went with it.

'There is the presence of water, of course,' he said slowly. 'You will have noticed how people flock to water, lakes, pools, streams. They will get into it, if that is practicable, if not they will sit around it. Water that is contained, I mean, bounded by the land. At holiday times they litter all available banks and shores.'

'Yes, I suppose that is true,' Farnaby said. It was not what he had meant, of course. He could not find again the sense of wonder that had led him to the question in the first place. Besides, Mooncranker's manner, this slow, rhetorical mode of address, had begun to trouble him rather, reminding him of that first evening at the hotel. 'And then of course,' Moon-

258

cranker said, 'think of the attraction of a pool like this, up here among the hills.' He smiled a little and looked around him, feeling a return of that languor and that helpless closeness of observation that descended on him when he thought of his death and that it might be imminent.

Lights in the dining-room had not been put on yet, though it would soon be necessary. The room faced on to the pool itself, light entered through the long, plate-glass windows, a curiously shifting, fluid light, that seemed to exercise its own selectivity, dwelling with intensity on some things, leaving much indistinct. This effect must be due to the reflected light from the pool, Mooncranker thought, this incessant faint flexing of light, moving in ripples or spirals over white walls, white table-cloths. Because of it nothing seemed entirely static in the room, everything was in gentle, diffused flux, and this suggestion of impermanence extended to the people in the room, and the implements they were using. He wondered if there were people bathing in the pool at this moment. Perhaps they were swimming, disturbing the surface, sending out rings of ripples that would conflict with others, each seeking to preserve its own doomed concentric system – his mind lost itself among the complexities of such an activity, the endlessly competing ripples, none lasting more than a matter of seconds ...

'I beg your pardon?' he said, under the impression that Farnaby had spoken to him. 'Yes, very attractive, you know, this little pool, enclosed by the cabins, terraced, *managed* – it is irresistible. And if it can be considered therapeutic in any way, so much the better.'

'Do you think it is?' Farnaby asked.

'People *think* it is,' Miranda said suddenly, 'and that comes to the same thing, doesn't it?'

Miranda and Farnaby smiled at each other, a lingering smile.

'Therapeutic?' Mooncranker said. 'Oh, yes, I think so. For some people. Sexually stimulating too, of course – the possibilities for erotic encounters must be greater by far than ... I don't know what the figures are. Yes, licence has always flourished, has it not, in baths and so on – there is a distinct connection. Are you up in that aspect of history at all?' he said to Farnaby.

'Not really,' Farnaby said. 'In Greek and Roman times the baths seem to have been an adjunct to –'

'No, of course,' Mooncranker said. 'Your subject is Ottoman fiscal policy, as I remember.' He was finding it increasingly difficult to sustain this conversation. A strong desire for alcohol came over him but he resisted it, knowing that drink would plunge him into life again. 'All truly sensuous peoples have discovered the usefulness of warm water,' he began, then saw that Farnaby and Miranda were involved in conversation with each other, exchanging remarks about the chocolate caramel that Miranda was just beginning to eat. He fell silent. I should have stayed in the hospital. Then I should have been safe. She eats her caramel in small deft spoonfuls. The sultans were flattering their imperial persons in alabaster bathtubs while our great Elizabeth sat stinking in her jewels. She is ignoring me, deliberately ignoring my presence. I did not think her capable of such cruelty. No, not true, I always knew she was capable of anything.

'Which are you then?' Farnaby turns towards me and smiles. Treacherous oaf.

'What do you mean, dear boy?'

'Which are you, hypochondriac or sybarite?'

'As one gets older the two merge into one.'

At this moment I become aware of a figure hovering just behind my right shoulder. 'Can you spare me a minute of your valuable time?' Scottish tones, voice uneven in texture as if this person could not hear himself very well. Farnaby looks up, smiles, says 'Good evening' – someone he knows then, someone he has already met. Suddenly the overhead lights are switched on, and a radio too, somewhere, a palm-court orchestra from some sad European tea-time. Turning slightly in my chair I see a thin rather untrustworthy face peppered with little bursts of blood vessels under the skin. Farnaby is effecting introductions. 'Of course,' I say cordially. 'Of course, Mr McSpavine, won't you join us? We have met already, as a matter of fact.'

'No,' he says, 'I'll not do that.' He is holding something,

260

some object, wrapped in what looks like part of a brown corduroy trouserleg. He begins to unwrap it. 'I want your advice on this wee head,' he says. For a horrific moment I think Mr McSpavine is about to uncover a human head, hacked as a trophy from some person he has encountered on the hillside. But the object that emerges is no bigger than a fist and made of marble. A woman's head. He turns it in his hands, holds it up for my inspection. A level-browed, matronly face, conventional enough in feature, but *smiling*. Eyes vague to the point of blindness, beneath the brows of a patrician lady, and finely sculpted lips curving upward in a smile full of life, full of joy, as at something perceived or apprehended.

'Did ye ever see a smile like that on the face of a lassie?' McSpavine inquires.

'No,' I am compelled to admit, 'no, I don't think I ever did. It is a marvellous head. Where did you get it?'

'Up there.' He jerks his head to indicate the hills, in a way that reminds me for a moment of the wounded American. He narrows his blue, bloodshot eyes and advances his face. There is an odour about him of stale hashish. 'I thought I recognized your voice,' he says. 'You are the one I heard talking in the hospital, the night my Flora passed away.'

'What do you mean?' I am again beginning to think he is demented.

'Never mind, never mind, 'tis of no significance now. Tell me, d'ye think it is genuine?'

I take the head and look at it closely. The marble is cold, smooth to the touch. The eyes are blind, being unprovided with iris or pupil, mere rounded stones under the lids, and this adds to the ecstasy of the smile. It is not what she sees, the smile is somehow antecedent to her existence and the reason for it, as though the carver started with the smile as a premise.

'I see no reason to doubt its authenticity. You'll have to get expert advice on it, of course.'

'No, but your own opinion,' he says. ' 'Tis that I'm asking ye for.'

'I think it's genuine enough. It's extremely unlikely to be a fake if you bought it from some local person here.'

'Aye, I bought it from a gypsy lassie up there in the hills.'

'Hellenistic probably. No, the only thing that troubles me is the smile.'

'The smile,' he repeats. 'Now why should the smile trouble you?'

'Well,' I begin, 'you realize no doubt why the city up there was so large and important?'

Mr McSpavine, who unnoticed by me has placed a pipe in his mouth, now removes it as if about to say something. At this moment, however, I hear Farnaby say to Miranda, 'Very extraordinary the way we met. It was in Istanbul, at the French hospital, the same night...' She is listening intently, leaning forward as if afraid of missing a single syllable. 'His wife had just died...'

McSpavine nods his head repeatedly as if in agreement with what Farnaby is saying. 'It is the same smile,' he says now, addressing all of us. 'The smile my Flora had on her face when she died and the smile of the other lassie sitting up in bed. One dead and the other living, the same smile. It seems simple enough now, but I had to come all this way to see it. There's no contradiction, d'ye see?'

'I don't quite follow you,' Farnaby says, glancing at Miranda.

'This was a great necropolis,' I observe, trying to finish my explanation. 'That head will almost certainly have come from some sarcophagus or tomb, some funereal monument. That being so, it should express a noble resignation, it should not be smiling. That is what I cannot understand.'

McSpavine begins to wrap up the head again. 'I'll be going tomorrow,' he says. 'No point in staying here now.'

Glancing sideways, I see the blankness of night outside the windows: darkness has fallen while we have been discussing the Scotsman's *trouvaille*. At once I feel a strong impulse to get out of this lighted room, into the obscurity of the pool.

'No need,' McSpavine says, 'to bother about clocks, or defineetions of death, somatic, cellular, onset of putrefaction, laddie, flaccidity of the eyeballs, no need at all. There's no distinction useful to make, between the living and the dead. I had to come here to find it out.'

He gathers up his bundle and moves off slowly.

'I think he must be mad, a little dotty,' Farnaby says, and 'Yes,' Miranda says, looking at him in agreement, 'he certainly does seem very peculiar. He must have been devoted to his wife.'

'Extraordinary thing, though,' Farnaby says, 'extraordinary coincidence, that he should have been passing your door at that very moment...'

Something here I do not fully understand. But I feel the presence of night outside like an urgent invitation. I am filled with impatience to be involved in it. I see Farnaby and Miranda smile once more, full upon each other.

'You can tell me about it in the pool,' I say. 'Shall we go into the pool now?'

7

Farnaby had made whispered arrangements with Miranda to meet him in the pool, beyond the bridge. In this way he hoped to find her again without any loss of time, prevent any other predator in the pool from forestalling him. However, on emerging from his cabin, dressed only in swimming-trunks, he was delayed by Plopl the photographer, who was in a state of great agitation, so much so that for a while Farnaby could not make out what he was saying.

'Who, what?' Farnaby said, peering at the other's face, which was in obscurity, as he was standing with his back to the poolside lights.

'My model, have you seen my model?' Plopl said in hasty trembling tones.

'Not since this morning,' Farnaby said, taking some steps along the terrace. 'Why?'

'She has gone,' Plopl said, moving along beside him. 'She has cleared out.' He laid his hands on Farnaby's arm. 'While I was sleeping,' he said, and choked a little on the word, as if this innocent sleep made Pamela's perfidy the more monstrous. 'She broke into my drawers,' he said. 'Now she will be miles away.'

'Can you not follow her?' Farnaby said, knowing this would

be difficult. He felt a distinct feeling of delight at this flight of Pamela's.

'How can I know where she has gone?' Plopl demanded tearfully. 'She will have taken the first *dolmus* out of the village.'

'Well, I am sorry to hear it,' Farnaby said. The chill air was striking on his unprotected body. He felt a renewal of his desire to be with Miranda again.

'Bitch and cow,' Plopl said. *'Dieses gemeine Weibsbild*. She has stolen her passport from me and money. She has taken also an electric toothbrush.'

'You have your camera still,' Farnaby said. He paused and then with deliberate malice said, 'The artist is never at a loss so long as he has his means of expression. You will be able to go on snatching the moment from the flux.'

'True, true,' Plopl said. 'But I cannot pay my bill here, unless I receive help. You are a man of the world –'

'Yes,' Farnaby said, 'but I'd better be getting into the water now, it is rather cold out here.' He moved away, began to descend the steps into the pool, leaving Plopl muttering incoherently in the dimness.

He went directly to the place where he had arranged to meet Miranda. She was not there however. He stationed himself with his back against the wall to wait. Almost immediately he heard a voice, a soft, leisurely male voice that he recognized after a moment as that of the Negro whom he had heard speaking in the pool the evening before. It was strange, but he was still talking about his friend Smithy, the one who, out of a reluctance to draw attention to himself, had almost drowned. 'Yeah, Smithy,' the voice said. 'Can't figure him out. Gets himself treated after the seventh, did you know that? They have seven children.'

'Seven children!' A female voice this. Farnaby tried to remember the faces of any of the Negro party, but could not.

'Gets himself treated, now he can't have no more. You never see such a change in a guy, he stopped smoking, he stopped drinking. He only drinks Seven-Up, now.'

'He used to drink a lot.'

'He never stops eating now. Don't never go with him to the movies, I am warning you, he is rustling with paper-bags the whole time, bags of candy, bags of nuts, Jesus. Popcorn. He can't stop.'

Farnaby peered through the gloom. It was very dark here, the poolside lights did not penetrate much beyond the bridge, which cast a deep shadow over the area immediately adjoining the wall, though the central part, immediately out from where he was standing, was more brightly lit. The water was quite deep here, rising to his shoulders. He could see nothing of the Negroes, whose voices seemed to be coming from somewhere over on his right. Suddenly he saw Mooncranker's tall, high-shouldered figure walking along the terrace, presumably on his way to enter the pool. Instinctively, though he knew he could not be visible to the other, Farnaby shrank back against the wall. After another moment he heard someone moving through the water, then he saw Miranda silhouetted with the lights behind her a little way out from the side. 'Over here,' he whispered, and at once she moved towards him. 'I thought you had got lost,' he said softly, when she was standing beside him against the wall.

'I had to get back out again,' she said, in the same low tone. 'To throw Mrs Pritchett off the scent. She saw me get in and came up and started talking to me, so I said I was just getting out for a minute. Then I got in at a different place.'

'Do you think she saw you?' Farnaby felt a rush of exhilaration and triumph at the thought of Mrs Pritchett circumvented for his sake.

'I don't think so. Anyway I don't think it matters, because I saw that man, you know, the one who follows her around, I saw him, just now, going towards where I left her ... I expect he will have found her by now.'

'Mooncranker is in the pool, somewhere,' Farnaby said. 'I expect he will be looking for us.'

'Yes, I expect so.'

'Speak quietly,' Farnaby said. 'Sounds carry in this pool.' He paused and then, against all his sense of seemliness – for it was, after all, her business, and for her to volunteer information about it – he asked her the question that had been causing him anguish all this time: 'Did he try to persuade you to go back with him?'

He could make out in the dimness only the pale oval of her face, framed by the darker hair. The water, which rose to the tops of his shoulders, covered everything of her but this.

'No, he didn't,' she said slowly. 'He didn't say any of the things I was expecting him to say. He seems to have changed, somehow.'

'How do you mean?'

'Well, I don't feel it's because of me that he came here, not basically.'

'Not because of you? He comes rushing down here, when he should still be in hospital –'

'We are just a pretext, somehow. He worries me.'

'I shouldn't worry about him.' Farnaby wished he could take up some marvellous eraser and wipe Mooncranker clean away from her thoughts. 'Mooncranker is a survivor,' he said.

'You don't know him at all,' she said. 'You can't think of anything but the injury he did you.'

He fell silent, warned by the reproof in her voice. Mooncranker was not to be dislodged so easily. In the silence that fell between them, the Negro's voice was again clearly audible:

'... church on Sundays, we both Baptists, Smithy goes with all the seven of them, not her though, not Rachel ...'

'She gets a rest.'

'Yeah. Well, when the preacher says about the pure in heart staying for communion and them who wishes to leave may do so, ole Smithy gathers up his flock and zooms for the door, he don't never stay for communion since he got himself treated ...'

'He don't smoke, he don't drink, he don't chase after women, what's a guy like that doing, running for the exit when they hollers communion?'

'Shall we move along a bit?' Farnaby said. They edged a little along the wall, but found they could not go very far because the water got steadily deeper.

'Shall we cross to the other side?' Miranda said.

'No, let's not do that. Somebody might see us. No, we're all right here.' Their slight change in position had put the Negroes out of earshot. They stood together for some moments in silence. Then Farnaby said, 'It is strange to think that I owe all this to Uncle George.'

'All what?'

'Well, being here with you. If he hadn't written to tell me that Mooncranker was in Istanbul, I should probably never have found you again. I never liked him, you know, but I am grateful to him for that.' Farnaby was beginning to experience the slight breathlessness attendant upon immersion in the pool. He thought for a moment of Uncle George's gasping mouth, sucking and expelling air, his lips collapsing with each exhalation, breathing in and out rankly sweet breaths of cow-parsley and elderflower and of how his own breath had failed and he had swooned and lain unnoticed, afterwards rising cold and changed ... 'We do not correspond regularly,' he said.

'You did not see him much, did you, after that summer? He changed you know, as he got older. Particularly after she died. One rather awful thing happened. Well, it was funny too, in a way. I don't know if I should tell you, since he is your uncle –'

'That's all right,' Farnaby said.

'Well, I went to see him once. With another girl. It was her idea. She was very religious. She believed in practical Christianity, going and talking to people, especially the elderly, and people on their own. Your uncle was quite alone at this time, both the boys had married and left home. So she persuaded me to go with her and just sort of sit with him for a bit, that was the idea, she wanted him to feel that people cared...'

Confused by the glaze and shift of light along the vaporous surface and by the sense of myriad furtive life in the pool, the prolonged and somehow stealthy rustling of the water, Mooncranker stood still near the steps by which he had entered, up to his waist only, his upper half tense in resistance to the cold. He had lost the sense of urgency which had possessed him earlier, the desire for immersion in the warm water and darkness, feeling now merely rather sick, and frightened.

Find them. Find Farnaby and Miranda. He held to this idea, constituting as it did a sort of plan. He began to move outwards across the pool, looking as he did so to left and right. He saw no sign of them but caught glimpses of other faces, other forms, some of whom he thought he recognized. Reaching the other side, he paused again, peering about him. He began to move along the side of the pool into deeper water. After a few steps he saw before him two figures, one short and stocky, the other taller, with a kind of mob-cap on its head, such as girls wear in the bath.

'I have a mission,' this person said suddenly to his companion, in a lisping voice. 'It is to bring painting back to its former virile state by restoring the supremacy of the male nude.'

Mooncranker made a detour round this couple, returning to the wall some yards beyond them. The water now was chest high. He felt a faint heat from the surface strike against his face. Across the pool he saw the windows of the dining-room still lit up. Light from this source fell across a section of terrace and water. Mrs Pritchett and the Levantine were standing close together in this brightly lit area. While Mooncranker watched the Levantine raised a hand and placed it on the nape of Mrs Pritchett's neck. She did not move, remained gazing blankly across the pool.

'Oh come now, Mr Henry,' a voice said behind him. Suddenly he saw Plopl the photographer standing at one of the cabin doors. Looking at the number on the door he saw with a disagreeable shock of surprise that it was his own, number three. Plopl appeared to be listening, had presumably just knocked. He wants to sell me those pictures.

A strong desire to remain undetected by Plopl came to Mooncranker. He began to move cautiously away from the light towards the bridge. He passed under the bridge, not stopping until he was in the deep shadow beyond it. A small group of people who had been talking here, now turned to regard him, he saw only the whites of their eyes and the vague shapes of their faces, realized after a moment that they were black. He moved again, outwards now towards the centre of the pool. He stumbled a little, fell forward, his face was for a second immersed in the water. He straightened himself, compressing his lips with a sort of prudery against the faintest taste of it. Water

268

on his eyelids and lashes beaded his vision with a fringe of bright drops. He advanced one pace then stopped dead, hearing Miranda's voice, very low but quite distinct, saying, 'He didn't seem to know why we had come.'

Mooncranker sank lower in the water, listening.

'My friend kept trying to talk to him, you know, about how life would open out for him if he thought of others, and how we are never alone because people care, things like that. She was preachy and earnest, a bit bossy too, probably, I mean I think she took herself too seriously, she was thinking of herself bringing light and hope into your Uncle George's life, at least that's how I see it now. At the time I thought she was noble. She was quite good-looking too, though she wasn't, you know, frivolous about it. There again, she probably took more trouble over her appearance than I suspected at the time. She wore glasses. Anyway, he didn't seem to know what she was getting at. It was rather awful really. He kept getting up and fetching silver cups, trophies he had amassed from various sports. He kept putting them into our hands. His head had developed a sort of tremble, did you know? Very slight, but continuous. He kept handing us these shining cups. You are never alone, remember that, she'd say, and he would get up close with one of these cups and we both had to keep sort of edging away. Then he started showing us photographs of cricket teams with himself in them, sort of young and smiling in a blazer. He kept pointing himself out to us. Well, this went on for some time, then my friend, she was sitting next to him on the sofa, she jumped up as if she had been stung and she dropped the photographs all over the floor. I remember them on the floor. He had put his hand right up her skirt, you know. It was rather awful. He bent down and gathered up all his photographs and when he got up I saw tears in his eyes ...'

Hearing this story had a totally unexpected effect on Mooncranker. He found great difficulty in believing it at first, so much was it at variance with all the assumptions he had been accustomed to make about George Wilson, salt of the earth, sportsman, parent, purveyor of hospitality. Then he realized that of course it was true, it was not even surprising. George Wilson was a man who would react to his own palsy by thrusting a hand up a girl's skirt ... The fact that Miranda had never told him of this incident which she was now telling to Farnaby showed the intimate stage they had reached. But it was not this that took away his will, withered his intention of advancing upon them: it was the nature of the story itself, the useless evidences of prowess, photographs of blazered youth, the desperate little spurt of lasciviousness which Miranda had pitied, probably, at the time – the pity was in her voice still, but for him too now, he was lumped together with Uncle George, spent lechers both. She was pronouncing on him too. *It was rather awful really.* That is the very tone of epitaphs. Impossible, impossible to speak to them now. As if a corpse should quibble at a funeral oration. And he had not wanted, he suddenly realized, with a pang in which were the beginnings of final peace, he had not wanted to speak to them. It was not for that he had come into the pool ...

He turned and walked away from them, moving softly, making no noise, farther into the darkness. He found himself now out of range of the lights, in a place where the walls formed a shallow recess. Here he stopped and stood in the darkness, open-mouthed, slightly breathless, up to his chin in the lapping water, his body held balanced and sealed in the warmth. He thought longingly of his drowned body, beyond pain, an object suspended in water, containing water, no distinction between within and without. The sweetish, brackish smell rose to his nostrils. He closed his eyes, allowed the weariness and loneliness to weight his head. Experimentally he lowered his face into the water, opened his lips for the water to lap over, though keeping his teeth clenched shut for the moment ...

'Why do you think he hasn't tried to find us?' Miranda said.

'Perhaps he is trying now.'

She shook her head. 'I wonder if he has started drinking again.'

Farnaby looked up at the night, which was deep, starless – he surmised banks of cloud drawn across the sky, eclipsing the stars that last night had been so numerous. Mooncranker's whereabouts, so long as he was absent, had become a matter of supreme indifference to him now. He did not however wish Miranda herself to perceive this indifference lest she should judge him callous.

'Don't worry about him,' he said. He put his hands on her shoulders, and she at once moved closer to him, set herself within his embrace. He put his arms about her, felt her body in the water, taut against his. Fire ran through him, desire for her mingled with a sort of strategic cruelty, a need to press his advantage while she seemed submissive. 'You knew about it, didn't you?' he said, in a harsh and vehement whisper. 'You knew he was going to give me that ... thing made of sausage-meat, didn't you?'

'It doesn't matter now,' she said. 'It happened a long time ago.'

'Doesn't matter?' he echoed, in wonder. What could she mean?

'Did he ever give any reason,' he said, 'any definite reason for doing it?'

Miranda hesitated a long moment. 'He said it wasn't healthy,' she said at last. 'You know, for a boy of your age to be so –'

'Healthy,' Farnaby repeated. *'Healthy?'* He raised his face to the sky again. Suddenly a laugh broke from him, paining his tightened throat. The ludicrous word revolved in his mind. 'Who *is* healthy?' he said. 'Do you know anyone who is?'

Miranda lowered her face, rested her forehead against his chest. He drew her closer to him. Their bodies pressed together in the water. Confusedly there came to Farnaby the knowledge that she was his victim now: there had been a shift, but she was still the victim, she was still where she had been; and he felt an unwilling pity, a sense that something had been done to her, somewhere, remotely, she had been tampered with, damaged. To him, too, something similar had been done, unlocalizable, antecedent to anything he could remember. It was not Mooncranker who had done this, he was an opportunist merely, perhaps an involuntary one at that, profiting from what he found in that summer garden: the girl's readiness for flattery, for conspiring in evil, the boy's corruption. All this had been accomplished already, before Mooncranker appeared on the scene, long before...

He sought for the sense of a time when they might both have been free and whole, presenting no opportunity to the despoiler. But there was no such time.

'I'll take care of you,' he said. It sounded oddly like a threat, and Miranda raised her head to look at him, but it was too dark to see the expression on his face.